CHAPTER 1

SHORTCUT TO POWER

A lot had happened in such a short amount of time that it was unbelievable for Gary, and there were still countless questions going through his head. What would he do at the next full moon? What was this strange system? And so on. On top of all that, Gary was still a normal teenage boy who was attending high school.

In his class there was one student who hadn't moved at all from her seat, and that was Xin. She had kept her head down, which was still pounding from lack of sleep. After everything she had experienced that night, the most frightening thing was waiting for her when she got home, because she had been forced to confront her father.

Because he was the mayor, it was impossible for her to keep something of that magnitude hidden from him, especially since the bodyguard assigned to her had been killed on active duty, leaving her no other choice but to tell him the truth. Xin had confessed to everything, though she claimed that she had wanted to celebrate with some of her friends because of the rugby match, before they had been attacked by an Altered.

The news report later revealed this fact, and because of that and the police report, her father believed her. Unlike what she had expected, he had hugged her tightly and had just been thankful that it appeared to have been a random attack rather than someone trying to go after her.

Of course, that hadn't been the end of it. That morning, having thought things over during the night, he had told Xin about the changes that would happen to avoid such a situation. The increase in the number of bodyguards was the least of her troubles.

The worst part is, I can't even complain about him changing the rules of this deal. Still, he could at least have allowed me to go home by myself. How am I supposed to make any friends if I have to drive to and from school? I guess the only freedom I have left is when I'm in school. Xin sulked as she heard giggling behind her.

The high-pitched laugh had become annoying, and it was giving her a bigger headache than usual.

How great would school be if Tiffany weren't around . . . She has yet to actually do anything since our talk, but I can't shake this feeling that she is plotting something big.

However, right now Xin was simply too tired to care whatever that banshee was preparing. Her last thought before she fell asleep at her desk was where Gary had actually disappeared to yesterday.

When he returned to class, Gary spent some time talking with his best friend, Tom. During the breaks they were trying to come up with ways to prevent what had happened the first time, and on top of that, Tom was trying to figure out ways to deal with the other omega wolf.

"The only weakness we know of is chocolate. Even that is something we can't be too sure of. In the worst-case scenario it might be unique to you, but even in the best case, it's not like we can get rid of him by throwing a chocolate cake in his face. Say, do you think if I smother myself in chocolate, it might act as a repellent, so he won't eat me?" Tom asked.

"That is the strangest suggestion I have ever heard," Gary replied; he couldn't believe what he was hearing. "Do you want me to wear gauntlets and smear them with chocolate to deal poison damage to him or something?"

"If it works, why not? Although it might be a bad idea for you to be the one to use them. Double-edged sword and everything. Who cares if it sounds stupid? You have to remember that our freaking lives are on the line here! And for some reason that werewolf seemed to have taken a particular liking to Innu," Tom whispered.

Over to their right, Innu was snoring lightly. Gary had a feeling that he already knew why the other werewolf was after him.

"I don't think something like chocolate is going to do much. At best it might make him vomit Innu out if he tries to eat him, but it won't really stop him from killing him. Eating human flesh seems to empower a werewolf. I can only assume it provides either an increase in stats or more stat points to assign, or maybe a direct increase like for hunting down a target. As long as one can actually live like that, the pros seem to outweigh the cons. It really seems to be the easiest and fastest way to get a power boost."

Later in the afternoon, it was time for club classes again, and when Gary and Blake met they looked at each other and exchanged nods. It seemed that their little talk had improved their relationship.

Instead of their regular training, Mr. Root talked about the game: what went well and what went wrong, but in the end, how it was ultimately not their fault that they didn't win. Eton High had used an even dirtier method than usual, so not losing was already a huge achievement. Most surprisingly, he actually thanked all the nonregular players for taking up their role, calling them out by name instead of just referring to them as "the benchwarmers."

All of the regular players gave them a big round of applause, and Gary was starting to think that Mr. Root actually was one of the better adults he had seen in his life. Practice continued as normal after that, but Gary noticed one thing: a certain student hadn't arrived.

His mark is too faint, so he can't be in school. Just what is he up to? He seemed fine yesterday . . . Maybe he isn't over Barry's death yet?

Apparently, Gary wasn't the only one who had noticed Gil's disappearance; he overheard some of the students talking about it.

5

"Hey, have you noticed that Gil isn't here?" a student asked. "I heard that he went to Principal Young this morning to drop out."

"Seriously? Are you sure he didn't just plan to transfer to another school? You know, he and Barry were inseparable. Maybe he just wants to be elsewhere to not be reminded of his friend."

"I thought the same, but someone told me that Gil had actually joined a gang. I doubt he needs to go to school if one of the big gangs accepts him."

As the students continued talking about Gil, Gary could think of only one gang that he probably had joined: the gray color gang, which was related to the Gray Elephants.

Tomorrow I have that fight with Innu, so we were supposed to do some training today, but if we run into Billy again, there isn't much chance I can beat him. If I meet Gil again, I wonder if that quest will activate again. I wouldn't mind farming him for some Exp. At that moment he exchanged a glance with Blake, remembering that there were others out there.

It should be okay. As long as I don't transform, I'm just a normal high schooler. I can't avoid taking risks. If I just sit around, my friends and family could all be in danger. I need to get stronger.

As he considered his last remaining hunting target, Gary thought back to the last time he had seen Gil with the color gang, how he had almost killed a defenseless old man. That had just been a test after joining the gang. Now that he had proven that he didn't shy away from dirty work, he might actually be given worse things to do . . .

Billy has eaten multiple people already; that's why he was so much stronger than me. If I did the same thing, I might gain the power to rival him. I can't bring myself to end innocent lives like Billy does, and Barry was just an accident.

But some people don't deserve to live in this world anymore, and if I have to kill, if I have to get stronger to protect the people I care about, then I would rather they die instead of my friends.

As he thought about this, saliva was dripping out of Gary's mouth, without his realizing it.

CHAPTER 2

AN IMPORTANT
BOND

After training was over, Innu came to Gary to tell him that there would be no practice today. Although Innu had just joined the school, Kai had advised him to join the rugby club, and when he had arrived the other day, he was not surprised to see Gary there. Kai clearly loved to pull strings and act as the puppet master behind everything.

As for Innu's reasons for canceling practice, for one, he was still mentally tired from what had occurred the day before; he didn't want to stay out. His other reason was that he considered it important to rest before an important match, like the one they would have tomorrow.

Too much training was just as bad as no training, and whoever they would face in their match tomorrow, he was confident that they could deal with it. Before leaving, he told Gary that he would update him on anything to do with Billy, but since Innu would be staying home today, it was unlikely anything would happen.

It seemed that Innu hadn't put together that Billy and the werewolf were the same person, but Gary couldn't blame him. Were it not for his Werewolf System, even he would find it impossible.

The fact that training was canceled was great news for Gary, who quickly hit the gym on his way back. There was no need for him to consume extra meat; he already had his fill thanks to the generous donation of a certain Altered superstar.

105/628 Exp

I know that my stats have gone up, but training is starting to seem pointless with how long it takes me to increase any of my stats naturally. With a measly 5 Exp per session, it will take me ages to level up even once.

If I want to get stronger, I need a faster way to earn Exp, and for that I'm going to have to take risks. By now, the color gangs should have calmed down, so perhaps I can incite another turf war. I can't just sit around and allow Billy to get stronger on his own. But first, I need to do something else.

When he got home, Gary pushed the door open and was surprised to see his mother in her work clothes. She wore a plain blue top and a badge with her name on it. He figured that today might have been one of her very rare free days, or perhaps her shift had been moved to later.

"What are you doing here, Mom? Did they call you for a late shift again?" Gary asked as he popped his head into his room, hoping to find his sister, yet she was nowhere to be found.

"Yeah, they have me on the late shift again," his mother replied while she was texting someone on her phone, with a smile on her face. This worried Gary; she was either talking to one of her friends or talking with a man, and Gary dreaded the thought of meeting another person from Slough.

That and he didn't like the idea of a new person being introduced into his family; *he* was the one who would help them out of their situation, not a stranger who didn't know the struggles they had gone through.

His mother worked as a cashier at a twenty-four-hour supermarket. They called her in for extra work at all sorts of times, and she always accepted. And because they knew she always said yes, they always asked her first.

But Gary hated it; the later the shift, the more likely there would be trouble. The only saving grace was that the supermarket was in the Underdogs' territory, so no one touched it. If they did, they would be facing the biggest gang in Slough.

Still, that didn't stop some gangs—or strays—from trying to cause trouble once in a while.

"If you're looking for Amy, she's staying over at Stacy's tonight," his mother shouted, noticing that her son was looking in every room and even knocked on the bathroom door.

"She went out? Well, as long as she stays indoors, I guess they're safe, but I really wanted to do something today." Gary was a little bummed because he had been planning to create a Bond Mark with her.

Although it was unlikely that Billy would go after his sister, it wasn't impossible, and eventually the Underdogs might unearth his real identity and the people around him. After what Tom had said about protecting him as a full werewolf, Gary was confident that Billy wouldn't harm them.

Well, I guess I will just have to leave it for next time, then.

There was still one other person he could mark, though. He pulled out a chair and sat down opposite his mother. She carefully turned her phone over, which made Gary even more suspicious that she was talking to a man. However, seeing this gave him an idea.

"Mom . . . I don't mind you talking to other people, but . . . I get kinda jealous sometimes. I know looking after me and Amy can be hard sometimes. It's just that I get worried that sometimes . . . you might leave us." Gary had his face down and was putting on an Oscar-worthy performance.

His mother immediately gave him a big hug.

"Gary, you and Amy are the most important people in my life, and that won't change. You even saved up all that money for me. I hate to admit it, but you can't even imagine how much it has helped our situation. I wouldn't give you two up for anything in the world! I will never leave you!"

"You promise?" Gary asked, holding out his pinky.

"I promise!" his mother replied as her own pinky touched her son's.

And at that moment, a notification from the system appeared.

A spoken deal has been made.
Would you like to mark "Maya Dem"?
Yes
3/5 Marks have been assigned

Gary was pleased that the system was pulling through for him for once, but then he received another message he never expected.

You have successfully bonded with another person!
The system has decided to reward you for your hard work. Keep going!
At the end of each day, you will receive 10 Exp for every active Bond Mark.
Protect those promises, and the people you trust.
Loyalty is the number one priority for every upright werewolf!

Huh, is the system sick today or is this supposed to be a type of reward for surviving the full moon? Either way, it's finally giving me some good things for once! With this, I can easily get 30 Exp every day with the Daily Quests!

That's not all, I still have two free marks . . . Hey, system, what do I have to do to increase the number of marks?

CHAPTER 3

THE ALTERED ROOKIE

Just when Gary thought the system might have turned over a new leaf, it returned to being as unresponsive as ever. Even though he had leveled up, he realized that either he would have to unlock a way to increase the number of marks, or the system would decide to drop him some tips.

Nevertheless, Gary needed to be careful about the promises he made. According to his system, if the other party broke a promise, then his Bond Mark would automatically turn into a Broken Mark, making the person into a hunting target. While that might not be bad in his daily life, it would lead to disastrous consequences during a full moon. So he wanted to avoid that at all costs.

Fortunately, when he saw his mother on the phone, he came up with a perfect plan. He made her promise that she would never leave him. Gary was convinced that she would never do such a thing. If she had wanted to, she could have left him and his sister ages ago. So her promise created an unbreakable Bond Mark.

"Thanks, Mom." Gary smiled, elated that he would be able to protect his mother whenever she was in danger. Like Tom's, the mark that appeared was green, although its smell was different. He would have to try his best to use his nose rather than his eyes more.

Now I just need to think of a promise that I'll be able to keep with Amy. It would be best if it could be something as foolproof as Mom's. Right now, nothing comes to mind, at least nothing that she is guaranteed to keep.

A little while later, his mother received a call, and it was time for her to go to work. Gary knew her shifts were long ones, so when he left the house later that night, he would not need to worry about sneaking out.

While he waited for the sun to set, he noticed something odd about Gil's mark. For some reason it was becoming clearer, leading him to believe that Gil was moving toward him.

What is he doing? The guys at school said that he dropped out to join a gang, but the gray color gang's territory isn't anywhere near here. Could he have some sort of personal business in this area?

When it was finally dark, Gary headed out. He wore his trusty hood to cover his hair, and he had made sure to wear something black. At first glance, he looked like just another member of the black color gang.

Curious about Gil's mark, which had become slightly paler but still seemed to be in the area, Gary followed it. However, even before he saw Gil, he could hear the sound of conflict from a mile away.

Sneaking through some trees and past the roads, he found the source. Underneath a bridge, members of the red color gang and the gray color gang were fighting members of the black color gang.

Initially, Gary thought it was a three-way fight, but after he watched for a while it became clear that the other two gangs had banded together to attack the black color gang.

What is going on? Did the Gray Elephants take over the gang behind the red color gang? No, could it be that the two of them entered an alliance? Shit, if that's really the case, this could endanger everyone in Slough!

Then Gary realized he could hear even more fighting going on. This wasn't just a small scuffle between two gangs; there was a war going on. The other two color gangs had clearly invaded the black color gang's territory.

Crap, why did it have to happen today of all days? If they're pushing the black color gang this much, it will force the Underdogs to act! Gary started to panic, looking around to see if he could still escape if things went south.

However, another thought crossed his mind.

Wait, there's chaos; too much for the police to handle. In the past, they would let the gangs take each other out, only coming at the end to arrest the losing side. If that's the case, can't I take advantage of all of this? As long as I avoid the members of the real gangs and just go after the color gangs, this might be my one chance to earn big-time!

Just as he had expected, things were about to change. Some distance away, Kirk was walking confidently through the streets. Instead of his iconic red suit from whenever he appeared on TV, he wore a black suit with a yellow-spotted tie, representing the Underdogs' Cheetah Squad.

Following him were five menacing-looking men. They had received reports from the black color gang members who had called for backup, and they had arrived just outside what looked like a pub.

"Didn't your superiors warn you to only go so far? We don't usually involve ourselves with the affairs of color gangs, but you guys have pushed it too far this time. You do know that this pub belongs to the Underdogs, right?" Kirk asked with a smile.

Several injured black color gang members were rolling on the ground in front of him, while members of the gray and red color gangs seemed to have suffered minimal casualties. There were still more than a dozen of them on each side, with the total around thirty. Immediately, the one closest to Kirk ran forward with his baseball bat and swung it with all his strength over his head.

Not wasting any time, Kirk took a stance and threw out his fist. The second the bat and his fist collided, the piece of wood snapped in half.

"What the . . ." The gray color gang member looked at his bat in disbelief. "Is he a robot or something?"

"You idiot, that's Kirk Summerfield! He's an Altered who recently won that rookie tournament!" one of the red color gang members shouted. Kirk was a well-known public figure, yet not many knew that he was also a member of the Underdogs.

The gangs were quick to run away. Alas, they didn't get far. Kirk had transformed the bottom part of his legs to run past them all and block off the juveniles' path of escape. He would have been even faster if he hadn't taken off his expensive shoes beforehand.

"Since you guys are already here, I'll have you answer a few questions. You didn't think I would let you go this easily after what you did, right? First, who are you working for? Second, why do your bosses believe that they could just barge into our area and take over? And lastly . . . have you seen a kid about this height, around sixteen years old, with green hair?"

CHAPTER 4

THE SISTER OF THE DEM FAMILY

Amy Dem and Stacy Turnhell had been inseparable since kindergarten. They had known each other since forever, and they had been lucky enough to be able to always attend the same school.

Unlike Gary, Amy had always received good grades and had even passed the 11 plus, a test students took at age eleven to determine whether they could enter a grammar school.

The grammar schools were state funded and were exclusive for the best of the best, those who the state believed had the most potential. This came as a blessing to the Dem household, as it meant everything would be paid for. Their mother was very happy when she found out that she would not have to worry about school supplies or any other things Amy might need for any club she might choose to join.

Gary hadn't even come close to passing his test, but Amy and Stacy had both managed to place relatively high, allowing them both to choose which school to attend. Although not the most prestigious one, Amy had chosen to go to Slough's only all-girls grammar school, so her family wouldn't have to worry about her.

Now that she was in grammar school, she and Stacy were the only ones from her old school who had passed the test, making the two friends naturally grow closer to each other.

When Amy had come over, Stacy had told her that they would be doing something very special today. After putting on the black dresses Stacy had prepared for them, they left the house.

"I really don't feel comfortable in this. Are you sure this makes me look slimmer?" Amy complained as she walked. The dress felt far too tight, something she just wasn't used to. Originally, Stacy had also prepared some high heels, but this was as far as Amy would go. She had tried to slip them on and felt like her toes were being squeezed to death. She didn't understand why other girls put themselves through such torture.

"Come on, it's just for today!" Stacy encouraged her, pulling out some red lipstick and a mirror as she masterfully applied a thick coat on her lips, making them seem bigger than they already were.

Stacy was not a natural blonde. In the past she was quite shy, but ever since she entered high school she had become far more outgoing. Amy didn't know what had caused this seemingly sudden change; her best guess was that Stacy just wanted to create a completely new image in a new school.

At least when it was just the two of them alone, Stacy still acted like always, so Amy hadn't addressed the change. For all she knew people changed as they got older. Her brother and his green hair were a perfect example of that.

However, lately Stacy had become far more interested in fashion and makeup, and it showed. She had applied her makeup well, as if she had spent hours watching video tutorials to learn it. It was scary how Amy's best friend could turn a few years older with a couple of steps.

Both of them were merely fifteen years old; Amy was just one year younger than her brother, and usually parents didn't let girls so young go out, but for some reason, Stacy's parents didn't seem to care as long as her grades weren't affected. As for Amy's mother, with how busy she was with work, it had been ages since she had last seen Stacy, probably still thinking of her as the shy little mouse she used to be.

"Here, let me help you out a bit," Stacy offered as she came over. With surprising expertise she applied some of her makeup and lipstick on her best friend. At first Amy had wanted to reject this, but she found it hard to say no when looking at her happy friend. She didn't want to ruin the mood between the two of them.

"Done. You look amazing. You really should start wearing this more. Just say the word. I got Mom to buy me new makeup after I aced that last test, so I will be happy to share my old stuff. It really brings out your looks."

Stacy held out the mirror, and Amy barely recognized herself. The person who looked back at her appeared to be a young and very pretty university student. It was definitely something she could get used to . . . though she would still rather wait a few years for such a change to occur naturally.

The two girls hailed a taxi, something Amy was thankful for. Walking the streets, especially at this late hour and dressed up like they were, seemed to be a guaranteed recipe for trouble.

"Why do we have to dress up, anyway? I thought we were just going to karaoke?" Amy asked.

"Yeah, but we're meeting someone today. Shoot, did I forget to tell you? Oh, I'm so sorry, I was so excited that I thought I told you already. My boyfriend's going to be there and he also invited some of his friends. Who knows, maybe one of them has green hair like your brother," Stacy said teasingly.

Amy wasn't feeling so great, and it wasn't just because of what Stacy had insinuated. She had thought it was just going to be the two of them, like it always had. Stacy had mentioned her "boyfriend" a few times recently, but Amy had believed that she had just made him up to look better compared to the girls of their class.

At their age, their only chance of meeting boys was through school, yet at an all-girls school that was impossible. Most of their male teachers were up there in years, but even the youngest one was easily more than double their age. She hadn't seen Stacy hang out with anyone around school, so just where had she met him?

"I mean . . . at least we'll be in a public place, so I guess it's going to be okay," Amy mumbled, still a little worried.

Eventually, the taxi pulled up on the main street of Slough. It looked different at night with all the lights, but it was considered a relatively safe area. The general public believed this was due to the mayor, who had promised that the town center was the one place where he would guarantee their safety.

This was another reason why Amy thought it was okay to be here, until she got out of the taxi with Stacy. Immediately Stacy ran up and hugged someone who was more than a head taller than her. The "boy" wore a gray beanie with his hair sticking through slightly. He also had both ears and his bottom lip pierced.

He wasn't alone either; he had brought along two friends, one of whom was currently smoking. Alarm bells were screaming in Amy's head at the sight, but mainly because Stacy's boyfriend was clearly older than them. The three of them had to be either in their last year of high school, repeaters, or most likely university students . . . unless they worked somewhere else, of course.

"I've been sooo looking forward to this! I'm glad that we finally get to meet!" Stacy told him.

Hearing this, Amy just wanted to slap her forehead. The two of them hadn't even met?

Stacy, please don't tell me you actually met him on Binder or some other app! Oh, who am I kidding? Given the age difference, where else could they have met? I bet she lied about her actual age and that's why she was so adamant about putting on that makeup. Amy believed she had seen through the situation.

The next second, the two of them were holding hands, and Stacy turned around.

"Come on, Amy, you're a great singer! You're always hogging the mic when it's just the two of us, so let's show them what we got!"

Every bone in Amy's body was advising her not to go inside, yet she couldn't leave Stacy alone with those strangers. If she made up some excuse like her stomach hurt, then who knows what might happen to her best friend. Three young adults with one naive little girl . . .

What if they do something to her? . . . No, I can't leave her alone. She must have known that it would be dangerous alone; I'll just have to try to convince her to go home early.

Who knows, maybe it's all just in my head. There's always a chance that they might be decent guys . . . but if not, I'll just have to tell them that I got a sudden stomachache or something. She shouldn't mind too much if this is their first meeting.

Amy thought about what to do in this situation. The police would be too slow to respond; they had too much to deal with in Slough. Who knows how fast they would react even if it became an emergency.

Just in case, she typed out a text, noting her current location. She didn't send it out to anyone yet, but it would only require a tap to send it to the one person she trusted most.

CHAPTER 5

WHITE POWDER

An opportunity was exactly what Gary needed. Billy was far stronger than him, and if Gary wasn't willing to eat people like Billy was, then there was almost no way for him to catch up, so much so that he had even thought a number of times about just exactly what he might do to Gil.

However, the system was a strange thing, and, noticing that a gang war had arrived, the system had answered him once more.

New Quest received
When Two Fight, The Third One Takes The Prize
As an outsider you have been chucked into the midst of a (color) gang war.
Are you following trouble or is trouble following you?
Either way, show them the strength of an omega wolf that follows no one!
Quest reward: 50 Exp per defeated person

The system was still telling him to get his hands dirty but not too dirty. Seeing the fights on the bridge out in front of him, along with the system screen, he couldn't help himself.

Gil, you will just have to wait a little longer.

When they entered the karaoke club, the boys rented out the room and were even nice enough to pay for it on their own. At first everything seemed fine, apart from the fact that Amy found herself on the couch, sipping juice, between two guys she had never seen before.

Meanwhile, Stacy was busy brushing her body against her boyfriend, who had introduced himself as "Hawk," of all things. Amy was convinced that that couldn't be his real name; no parent would ever subject their kid to that.

The fellow to Amy's right, whose name was apparently Pierre, was slightly larger on the bottom half, making him look like a pear. The one on her left, who had told her to call him Ben, was in complete contrast to his friend, seemingly nothing but bones. Given their outer appearances, she easily remembered their names.

The room was quite large, with a bench around the back and two microphones. At the moment, Stacy and Hawk were doing a duet.

"So, Amy, I guess you don't have a boyfriend since you're here on your own tonight?" Ben asked carefully.

"Unfortunately, I haven't found the right one yet. It would have to be someone my brother approves of," Amy replied truthfully. Just like Gary, she also had a hard time lying to others, but she hoped mentioning him might perhaps make them back off somehow.

"A brother . . ." Pierre murmured. "Who does he wor—I mean, is he still in school? Could he be someone we know, perhaps?"

Pierre seemed to have wanted to ask something else at first, but he had quickly corrected himself. Amy had no clue why, though, as she had almost instantly replied, "He goes to Westbridge." The next moment she regretted it. Now that she thought about it, it would have been far better to have named a university, to make it seem that Gary was older.

Unfortunately, her answer seemed to have calmed them, and they continued their questioning, but thankfully it looked like Stacy and Hawk had just ended their duet.

"Finally, me next!" Amy quickly jumped up from her seat and almost snatched the microphone out of Stacy's hand, as she chose a longer song and began to sing straightaway. This was her only saving grace from the other two.

It felt like forever but according to the clock, we've only been here for half an hour. I haven't even had time to speak to Stacy. Why didn't she pick up on me telling her that I needed to go to the bathroom? Amy was trying to figure out a better excuse, but by the time the song had ended she hadn't come up with anything better, and she decided to sing the next one as well.

When Amy was singing, she was in her element; it really was something she truly enjoyed doing. She closed her eyes as she hit a high note, but suddenly there was no background music, and the large screen that showed the lyrics had been turned off.

"Hey, everyone, I think that's enough singing for now, let's do something more fun!" Hawk suggested. It was clear he was the one who had pulled the plug, and he swiftly pulled out a deck of cards, which he laid down on the table.

Looking toward Stacy, Amy didn't even try to hide her annoyance. The guy could have at least waited for her to finish her song, and Stacy could only form the word *Sorry* on her lips, her eyes pleading with Amy to not make a big deal out of this.

Sitting at the table, Hawk dealt out cards while Ben lit up another cigarette. This only further annoyed Amy, as they were all in the same room together. Although smoking was allowed, he could have at least asked them before forcing them to enjoy his secondhand smoke.

A short while later, a waiter entered the room and placed some more drinks on the table, which Ben seemed to have ordered earlier when he had left the room. Judging by the foam, it was clear to the high school girls that they had just been served alcohol.

If they can order alcohol, just how old are these guys? They have to be at least eighteen . . . This is worse than I thought. Come on, Stacy, even you should see that this is going to end badly! Amy cried internally, but her best friend was too busy flirting with Hawk.

The guys began to drink without any hesitation, and Stacy joined them after her boyfriend talked her into it. Amy had a bottle in front of her, which she just picked up occasionally and pretended to drink from. The smell alone was strong enough to keep her from trying it, and she was definitely not going to start drinking around strangers whom she'd known for less than an hour.

After playing cards for a while, though, Amy was slowly lowering her guard. The guys had talked a bit about themselves and had even managed to make her giggle by telling some jokes.

Maybe I was just being too cautious, judging them based on their appearance too quickly. Living here for too long does that.

Alas, Amy soon discovered that she had been right all along. As the round finished and it was her turn to shuffle cards, Hawk stopped her and brought out a small bag with white powder. He started to use the cards to spread it out into five lines.

"Is this . . ."

"Yes," Hawk answered proudly. "My brother is a high-ranking member in the Gray Elephants. Girls like you might not know them, but they are one of the gangs in Slough who have a say in how things are run. It's easy for me to get my hands on this type of stuff, thanks to him. Come on, try it out. It's hard to explain just how good this feels!"

A few seconds later, all the boys had snorted their lines, and then they shook their heads for a few seconds. While Stacy had played along with the alcohol, hard drugs crossed even her line. Amy could see that this was far beyond what she had been expecting.

"Thank you very much, but I think I shouldn't. I haven't been feeling well for a while. Maybe it's the alcohol. I think I need to lie down. Stacy, I'm staying at your house tonight, right? Maybe we should go," Amy insisted.

"I think you're right," Stacy instantly agreed, happy that she had dragged Amy along. However, as she tried to stand up, Hawk grabbed her by the wrist.

"Hey, you can't just leave. We still have so much time left. We paid for this room, paid for your drinks, and we haven't even done anything yet. Don't you think we deserve something in return?" Hawk smiled mischievously.

Seeing this, Amy immediately stood up and was planning to grab her best friend and make a run for it, but Pierre grabbed her hand. He had a surprisingly tight grip.

"What are you doing? You're hurting my wrist! Let go!" Amy shouted. "I'll scream if you don't let go now!"

Then Ben went over and plugged the karaoke machine back in before turning it on at full volume. Now even if they did scream, nobody would hear them, or they would just think it was the music.

We're in real trouble.

Amy put her free hand in her pocket and hit the send button. She wasn't sure if he could come, but they needed someone who could help them out of this situation.

CHAPTER 6

PERFECT TIME

Gary knew that the smart thing would be to keep on watching, waiting for both sides to weaken each other further, so he could swoop in and finish off the losing side. This way he wouldn't use a lot of Energy, while still being able to get some Exp.

However, he had decided to take some risks. Given the content of the quest, it seemed wiser to get involved in the fight before any surprise backup could arrive. He didn't know how long this gang war would last, since it was just a matter of time until the Underdogs sent out their muscle.

If he waited too long, the gang war might escalate to the point where it would be too dangerous for him to get involved. At the moment, Gary was dressed in all black, so he could only help out and pretend to be a part of the black color gang.

It's two gangs against one, so I have to join in while the black color gang still has some members standing, Gary thought. He ran across the top of the bridge and waited for a few moments. Below him, the group were fighting at an underpass, and the black color gang members were slowly being pushed back, making their way out of the tunnel.

He could see three members still standing. They were hunched up together, obviously hurt but still fighting. It was clear that at this point they were basically running on fumes. Unfortunately, running away wasn't an option. Turning their back on the other color gangs would just seal their fate. They wouldn't get far before the other members caught up to them.

Damn, I was hoping they would be in better fighting condition so they could help me grab some last hits. I know my skills have improved, but without the boost from the moon I'm not too sure I can handle all of the others on my own.

In his hesitation, he thought back to his fight with Billy, at least what he could remember of it. Fighting a bunch of humans seemed a lot easier. Just then, he saw multiple people run from under the bridge.

One . . . two . . . three . . . four . . . five. They just keep coming, and there could be more.

It wouldn't stop him; he saw that the black color gang members had engaged with the others, and this was his chance. Two more people ran from the bridge, and with no fear, Gary leapt from above.

He was on a trajectory to land directly on them, and that's exactly what he did; stretching out his legs, he made sure his feet hit the backs of their heads, causing them to fall over and their heads to slam onto the concrete.

Your opponents (2) have been knocked out
100 Exp received
205/628 Exp

Such a move would knock anyone out, yet Gary was also a little afraid that he might have hurt them too much. Just as he considered checking their condition, someone swung a bike chain from behind and struck him across the face. Fortunately, it only cut his cheek, around his mouth.

−4 HP

"There's another one of those black color fuckers over here!" a young man dressed in red called out. "That bastard knocked out Stan and Kenny! Get him!"

Behind him, Gary saw seven more people, but on top of that he noticed something else that his nose was able to detect. Several gang members had been left on the side of the road, some of them bleeding, while others looked to be in much more critical condition.

If this really was a gang war, then ambulances would be hard to come by today. The police must have already been told about what was happening right now, and they would tell ambulances not to enter the area until things had calmed down. It was very possible that a lot of people would die tonight . . .

I almost felt sorry for the two that I hurt . . . but you're all just the same, Gary thought, as the red color gang member swung the bike chain again.

Skill activated: Charging Heart
All stats have temporarily been doubled
–10 Energy

At the right moment, Gary used his bare hands to grab the chain, and then the next second he pulled on it. The person holding it hadn't even recovered from the shock that someone had managed to grab his makeshift weapon, yet the next moment, his face connected with Gary's elbow.

As his head flung back, he let go of the chain. Gary knew he wasn't done yet, because the system had yet to notify him. Lifting his leg, he quickly spun and hit the red color gang member right on the neck, sending him to the ground.

Your opponent has been knocked out
50 Exp received
255/628 Exp

"Hey. Who is that guy?" one of the black color gang members asked his companion. They were still in the middle of their fight but had noticed what had happened.

"No idea. I can only see the back of his hood, but with him here, maybe we can get out of this thing," another answered, as he barely avoided the strike of the gray color gang member in front of him.

After taking on that one member and seeing the others back off, Gary noticed something. He had been around gangs for a while, but the person he had taken out appeared to have some authority among them, most likely one of the better fighters out of their group. Since Gary had dealt with him so effortlessly, as well as his imposing entrance, they were afraid of him.

He quickly changed his plans.

"I'm sorry," Gary said, having overheard the earlier conversation. "I'm on no one's side. I'll be taking everyone out!"

Gary had been forced to use another Charging Heart, but with his power boost, he had managed to defeat them all. Innu's lesson had proven quite effective, allowing him to have an easier time defeating them. It had been easy to tell which ones had trained and which had not, and thankfully all of them had already been tired after fighting beforehand.

It had become clear to Gary that they all were mostly relying on their makeshift weapons and lacked actual skills. After the first three, he had knocked out all remaining ten, granting him an additional 500 Exp, enough to level up.

I've finally gained another stat point! Argh, but still no new skill. I don't get it, do I need to fulfill some special conditions or something? Or are you just a miser, system? I know that you at least have that Hardened Will skill saved up!

Oh well, I will just have to keep grinding today. It's not every day that I get to beat the shit out of gang members without having to fear any consequences, so I should make the best out of it. Gary checked his status.

Name: Gary Dem
Level 6

Exp: 127/765
Health: 68/100
Energy: 92/120

I got hit way more in that last fight than I needed to. I guess some of my Energy will be used up to heal my wounds while I'm not fighting. Shoot, I should have grabbed something to replenish it. If only I had more money . . . looks like I might have to grab a bite on the way.

Gary's enhanced hearing allowed him to hear the sounds of fighting in other areas. Judging by how faint it was, he would probably have to run over to get there in time to actually have anyone left to fight, though. However, before he could even decide between searching for some food and heading toward the sounds, he felt his phone vibrate.

He instinctively grabbed his secret phone. It should be either Kai or Innu who might want something from him, but to his confusion the screen only showed him what time it was. There was no new message or missed call.

It took Gary a moment to put it back into his pocket and grab his regular one. Just as he had suspected, he had received a message, but the most surprising thing was the sender. It was from his sister, of all people.

Me and Stacy are on the main street at the Kobo Karaoke Club. I got dragged along to meet up with her internet boyfriend and he brought two friends along. If you get this message, then we're in trouble. Please bring help!

CHAPTER 7

NO ONE TO RELY ON

The police station was currently busier than ever, receiving nonstop calls from residents living in a certain part of Slough. All of them reported that they could hear fights, moans, and groans, with some even testifying to have seen teenagers in red and gray beating up others dressed in black on the street.

It didn't take long for the police to figure out what was going on, but just as Gary had predicted, because of the scale of the gang war, they couldn't respond immediately. The police force simply lacked the numbers to contain large-scale fighting like this.

Chief of Police Anton Millstun was in charge of the people's safety. Right now he was sitting behind his desk, grabbing his head in frustration as he didn't know how to deal with this situation.

"Those damn White Rose agents! They're only interested in their stupid Altered, yet when we have a situation like this on our hands, the only course of action they're willing to take is to 'let things play out,'" Anton complained, though more to himself than to Roo, who was with him in the room. The rookie was nervously standing in the office waiting for his superior to give out orders.

"How is it possible for such a situation to break out without any prior signs? All our informants have been telling us that the black color gang has been getting into more fights with the red color gang, but what does that have to do with the gray color gang?

"We know the black color gang is controlled by the Underdogs and that the Gray Elephants are behind the gray color gang. We still have no clue who is behind the red color gang. Could it be that the Gray Elephants found out before us and took over?" Anton spoke his thoughts out loud. It was one of his tics and his subordinates had gotten used to it. They knew why he did so: in case anyone wanted to chime in on his thoughts.

"I don't think it has always been the case, sir," Roo said. "I looked into them, just like you've asked, but while not as numerous, there have also been many incidents between the red and gray color gangs, the last one only a few days ago."

Anton thought this could be due to one of two things. Either the Gray Elephants had approached the red color gang's backers to pull off this stunt to massively piss off the Underdogs, perhaps some retaliation for something yet to be determined . . . or there was an even bigger figure behind it all. Someone who the Gray Elephants had no choice but to listen to.

"I just hope that none of those Kings are involved in any of this. If they are, then this town will become a battlefield before it's all over," Anton mumbled before he stood up from his seat, ready to move out.

"We might not have enough hands to stop the color gangs from fighting, but we can at least prevent them from going after the other areas. I want every available officer placing barriers around Chavley.

"Call in those who might have taken a day off, and maybe even those who have just retired for the day. Make sure that no one enters or gets out for the time being. As soon as things settle down, that's when we will make our move, understand?"

Although Roo did understand, he had a concerned look on his face.

"Sir, does that mean we won't be acting on the reports? What about the public places being attacked? Or the request for ambulances? This is a color gang war we're talking about, not the big gangs!"

What Roo meant by this was the difference in crimes. The bigger gangs, such as the Underdogs and Gray Elephants, actually acted more like businesses. Of course they both laundered their illegally obtained money through their businesses, but even if the police knew that, it was impossible to catch them without evidence.

At some point, a tacit agreement seemed to have occurred between the two parties. The gangs tended to stay out of the way of the public, not causing them any trouble, and the police didn't try to make life hard for them.

However, while the big gangs seemed harmless at first glance, the same could not be said about the color gangs. Those were filled with young frustrated teens and tweens who found it hard to get jobs, hoping to prove themselves out on the streets to rise in the ranks and get accepted into one of the bigger gangs.

In the past, when situations like this occurred, the color gangs tended to get a bit wild, drunk on power, and they started to rob stores and plunder and steal from the civilians. They all felt like they were unstoppable in those moments.

"I'm afraid that is a sacrifice we will have to make. Trying to save a few will just risk us getting dragged into this mess and the color gangs spreading throughout the whole town." Anton slammed the table. He didn't like that this was the only choice they had, but with their limited power, what else could they do?

"Roo, believe me, I wish it were different, but I have a feeling that this fight will push the Underdogs to act. If that's the case, this little war will be over far quicker than you might imagine. Let's just hope they will be the only ones to come out . . . otherwise, I'm not sure what it will mean for Slough."

Just as Anton had predicted, after the red and gray color gangs managed to overwhelm the black color gang on multiple fronts, they started to become a little wild. One group in particular was getting particularly crazy. It was full of mostly new recruits, one of them being none other than Gil.

The dropout had just picked up a trash can from the side of the street, which he promptly dunked on a black color gang member's head before kicking him to the ground. The others were impressed by the new member's ruthlessness; he seemed to be even better at fighting than before.

I was a little worried about him after what happened last time, but it seems like it just gave him an extra push, the group leader thought.

Around thirty gray color gang members were on a rampage—attacking everyone on sight, no longer differentiating between black color gang members and regular civilians—and that was when their group came across a certain twenty-four-hour supermarket.

Its lights were still on, yet it appeared the employees were in the middle of closing the shutters down for safety. Seeing this, Gil picked up another large trash can and ran toward the supermarket.

That guy looked at me like I was a loser! I'll show you who the real loser is! Gil thought, reaching the man and swinging the trash can before he could completely close the shutters. Gil didn't stop there, as he lifted the can and began whacking the man again and again.

"Hey, everyone, the store's up for grabs!" another member shouted, and soon the other members of the gray color gang were storming the supermarket. Once Gil was done, he entered as well, leaving behind a no-longer-moving man lying in a puddle of blood.

Inside the supermarket, seeing what was going on, the employees immediately ran toward the supply room in the back. Five of them had saved themselves, yet the last one, a frightened large woman, had slammed the door shut behind her, locking out three of her colleagues.

They banged on the door, again and again.

"Let us in, please, they'll kill us if you don't!" one of the women begged from the other side.

"We can't! They'll get us too, just hide for now!" the large woman cried out, holding on to the door.

Meanwhile, the pet food aisle was empty compared to the rest of the store. Pet food was toward the bottom of the priority list for looters. Two female employees were hiding out there. One was a middle-aged woman, while the other looked to be a young university student. The student had her head tucked into the older woman's stomach; both were on the floor shaking, doing their best to be as quiet as possible.

"Calm down, it's okay, we will be okay, the police will arrive and get us out of this place," the older woman whispered to the other one to calm her down. But no matter what she did, the student was still scared, and honestly, she herself was as well. She imagined the girl as her own child and knew she had to put on a brave act.

"They might come, but they'll be a bit slow." A male voice spoke above them.

The middle-aged woman looked up at the person who had spoken. A teenage boy who couldn't have been much older than her son stood there, covered in blood. He walked forward toward them.

"What a couple of pretty-looking girls. I should have joined a gang a long time ago. Out here, there are no rules." Gil licked his lips as he considered whether to start with the student or the older woman, whose name tag read *Maya*.

CHAPTER 8

200 BPM

Pierre still hadn't let go of Amy's hand, so she let out a scream. Unfortunately, the loud music from the karaoke drowned out her cry. Even if there had been no music, Amy doubted anyone would come to help them and not just because the room seemed to be pretty soundproof.

This is a public karaoke place, right? There has to be a camera in here or something! She desperately looked around and that was when she noticed that the camera in the corner of the room had been turned around to face the wall.

These guys . . . I should have known when they brought out the drugs. They must be in cahoots with someone from this place. They seem to have planned this from the very beginning. Oh, Stacy, what kind of mess did you get us into?

No matter how much Amy thought about it, she didn't see any way out. It seemed impossible for two high school girls to overpower three bigger and older young men. Even now as she tried to wiggle her arm free, she could feel Pierre just tightening his grip to the point that she couldn't move it at all.

"Hey!" Hawk shouted from the other side of the room. He held up a phone, but it didn't look like the one he had been using; instead it was one with a pink case. Now that she took a closer look, she recognized it as Stacy's.

Her best friend's makeup was completely ruined by now. Tears and snot were all over her face. Stacy felt the worst out of everyone there. Her internet boyfriend had turned out to be a complete douche, and he had hurt not only her but also Amy. She had never wanted to drag Amy into any of this.

"I'm sorry," Stacy cried. "I'm sorry, Amy, I'm so sorry!" She continued to sob, yet Hawk seemed to have had it with her. He slapped her right across the face. He hadn't held back, either; Stacy's face turned bright red, leaving the imprint of his hand.

Stacy fell silent, her eyes wide open. She had gone into shock and didn't know what to do. She looked at Amy, but in the next moment, Hawk pulled her up by her hair, making her scream in pain again.

"Shut the fuck up, will you?" he shouted as he brought her up to his eye level before letting go. "You two, make sure to confiscate the other slut's phone. We don't want them to call the police on us!"

Following the order, Pierre used one hand to pull Amy's arm out of her pocket, restraining her while Ben came over, searching for her phone. As he did so, he made sure to press his body against hers.

This . . . is so disgusting! What are they going to do with us? Hundreds of thoughts were running through Amy's head. She already had a very bad idea about what they were going to do; the real question was what they would do to make sure the girls wouldn't go to the police.

She had heard cases where victims were filmed, and the videos would be shared around if they told anyone.

"Shit! The bitch seems to have already messaged someone. Some guy named Gary!" Ben reported, after checking the messages. Although the phone was locked, they could see the preview of the reply from Gary, claiming he would be there in a second.

"Who did you message?" Hawk asked. "Tell me!"

Amy didn't answer him, trying to think of the best response in this situation. Hawk took that as a sign of mental deficiency, so he decided to make her talk. Instead of going after Amy, he grabbed

Stacy by the back of her head, pulling at her hair and making her scream once again.

"Ahh, it hurts! Please stop, it hurts!"

"Did you not hear me? I told you to shut up!" Hawk shouted as he pushed her head down. Everyone in the room heard her skull hit the table. Her teeth pierced her lips, causing a small amount of blood to spatter onto the tabletop.

Pierre and Ben looked at each other; despite being high, even they began to question their actions. Hawk, however, didn't stop there, and he continued to slam Stacy's face against the table.

"I can do this all day! I won't stop until you tell us who that guy is!" Hawk looked at Amy, hitting Stacy once more to stress his point.

"Don't! Gary's my brother!" Amy confessed.

Pierre and Ben laughed at this. They had already asked her about him, so they knew he was just some random nobody going to a no-name high school. Even if he were to come, what was he going to do? Hawk gave them a thumbs-up.

"Feel free, guys!" Hawk said as he started to unbuckle his belt, and the two boys next to Amy were about to do the same.

No . . . they can't! I have to get out of here, I have to save myself! Amy thought.

Pierre was still holding her arms up. She considered kicking him between his legs, but she was afraid he might see it coming, so she used the only body part she could at the moment. Opening her mouth, she bit down hard on Pierre's arm. He immediately let go, and without looking back Amy ran for the door.

Alas, before she could get far enough away, Ben, his trousers already dropped, grabbed the back of her hair, pulling her back in.

"It looks like you need to feel some pain as well!" Ben shouted as he pushed her up against the table. Her thighs hit the edge as a large force hit the back of her head, slamming it against the table and sending a shooting pain across her face.

She didn't quite know what had happened, and her eyesight was slightly blurred. Desperate to get out of the situation, she kicked behind her, hoping to hit Ben in the shin.

"Just stop trying to resist!" Ben shouted, banging her head on the table, not once, but twice, and continuing on. But Amy kept struggling and kicking; her eyesight was getting more blurry by the second and she wondered if she was about to pass out.

"*Amy!*" a voice shouted, as a green-haired boy suddenly entered the room.

"Gary! . . . But why . . . are you alone . . ." Amy thought before completely passing out.

Ben lifted her face up, and Gary saw his sister's face banged up, bloody, and bruised. His younger sister, who he had promised to protect . . .

The others laughed as Gary entered the room and strode toward them. They could see that he was far smaller than them, making them even less afraid of him. Even if he could fight, there were three of them and just one of him.

Not saying anything, Gary swung a fist toward Ben's face, too fast for Ben to react. It hit him right across the face, knocking several teeth out and forcing him to let go. In that second Gary grabbed Amy before she could fall to the ground.

His body was shaking from head to toe.

"What the fuck did you do to my sister?" Gary shouted.

You are heavily enraged
You have exceeded 200 BPM
Partial transformation has begun

His eyes narrowed, and his teeth and fingernails started to sharpen; the rage had taken over Gary completely.

CHAPTER 9

JUDGE, JURY, AND EXECUTIONER

When Gary read his sister's text message, he went into a panic. Amy wasn't the type to joke around, nor did she usually ask him for help. Since she had, it could only mean that the situation was seriously bad.

Gary's heart started to beat faster, to the point that there was no need for him to use the Charging Heart skill. His heart rate was currently at 169 BPM, making him twice as fast and twice as powerful with no Energy spent.

He didn't think about anything else, but just ran toward the Kobe Karaoke Club, where the two girls were supposed to be. He no longer cared about the gang war happening at the moment, nor did he care about gaining Exp. His only wish was to get there in time to prevent anything bad from happening to his sister.

Please be safe, Amy! Please be safe, Amy! Gary kept repeating it like a prayer in his head as he ran, ignoring all the fights happening around him. Eventually he found himself in front of the right place on the main street.

He ran up the stairs to the reception area. It was dark, and he heard the loud thumping of music behind the doors. Originally he had planned to use his enhanced senses to find out where Amy was.

Unfortunately, his enhanced senses proved to be a detriment for once. It took him a few moments to get used to the—to him—incredibly loud noise. However, in the end he pushed through because of his sister.

Behind the reception desk stood a young man wearing sunglasses. Gary thought it was a little weird since they were indoors, it was dark, and it was already late, yet he would be lying if he claimed that it didn't fit the image of this place.

"Hey," Gary called out. "I'm looking for two girls who came in here earlier today accompanied by three guys. One is unnaturally blond, and the other has brown hair and looks a bit like me?" He pulled his hood down, revealing his face.

Usually he wouldn't show his face, but right now he wasn't thinking things through, too preoccupied with getting to Amy.

"Sorry, kid, I can't just tell you what room people are in. Customer privacy and all, I don't even know who you are," the man replied, shrugging.

Were it not for the severeness of the situation, Gary might have tried again by politely asking the man, or he might have argued with him to convince him how important the matter was. Right now, though, he didn't have any time whatsoever.

The man was wearing a necktie, another fashion statement. Dangling in front of Gary's face, it was the perfect thing to grab. Gary yanked it and pulled the man down to his level so fast that his sunglasses fell off.

"Listen here, one of them is my sister and she asked me for help!" Gary practically growled at him. "Now tell me where they are!"

"You think threat—"

Gary didn't let him finish, just pulled harder on the tie, to the point that the man was starting to suffocate. Seeing how determined the green-haired teenager was, the man quickly pointed down the hallway. Gary immediately let go and ran in that direction.

Gary didn't like what he had just done; he had behaved like a real gangster, using violence to get his way, but this was an emergency, he told himself. He rushed down the hall, looking through the small window in each door.

Finally one room caught his attention, not because he could see his sister but because he could make out the smell of blood. Opening the door, he saw that one guy had his trousers down and was holding a girl by her head.

"Amy!" Gary shouted as he recognized her.

"What the fuck did you do to my sister?" he shouted, punching her attacker in the face, sending him off to the side as he carefully picked up his sister and held her in his arms.

You are heavily enraged
You have exceeded 200 BPM
Partial transformation has begun
All stats increased to 125%

His eyes narrowed and his teeth and fingernails started to sharpen as the rage took Gary over completely. His body had changed slightly, but he had yet to notice since the change wasn't on the same level as during the full moon.

"Stacy!" Gary shouted, as she was still conscious. "I want you and Amy to get out of here. Grab a taxi and get to the hospital!"

Although Stacy had just seen Gary send one of the boys across the room, she still felt he was outnumbered. She was afraid to move, as Hawk was directly next to her and Ben was already recovering, holding the side of his face.

Pierre was still pissed from having been bitten by Amy, so he ran over to Gary, but before he could do anything Gary kicked him in the stomach, sending him flying. His back hit the table so hard that his body flipped over on top of it, knocking all of the bottles onto the floor.

Gary quickly placed Amy next to the bench, then jumped on the table himself, stepping on Pierre's body along the way. Hawk, seeing that the situation was getting out of hand, let go of Stacy and pulled out a pocketknife.

He attempted to stab Gary, but the green-haired boy dropped down from the table and grabbed the knife, allowing it to pierce right through his palm. Gary was bleeding, yet the knife was stuck.

Looking into his eyes, Hawk was seriously scared. No sane person would ever try to stop a knife by sacrificing their own body. Clenching his fist, Gary started to crush Hawk's hand, and he screamed in pain. He could feel his fingers breaking.

"Get going, Stacy!" Gary shouted once more. She didn't need to be told again as she rushed over to grab Amy. Luckily, Amy had somewhat woken up, yet her vision was still blurry.

"Come on, Amy, let's leave it to your brother. I think he's got this," Stacy said as they stumbled out of the room.

"Do you have any idea who my brother is? You screwed up bigtime, Gary!" Hawk shouted, yet his voice contained a hint of hesitation. "My family are part of the Gray Elephants, and we will hunt you and your sister down! I will return this favor ten times worse."

Just then the door opened behind them, and the man who had been at the reception desk came in.

"Hawk, do you need help, bro?" the man asked. Gary had initially felt bad about how he'd treated the man earlier, but now it looked as if he had been in on this all along.

Remembering what Hawk had said, he pictured his sister's face, so bruised that he could hardly recognize her.

"That girl . . . she is the best sister in the whole goddamn world! She never complains, and she works hard . . . she's only fucking fifteen years old! What the hell were you planning to do to her? All of you are guilty!" Gary shouted as he looked at Hawk.

Bloodlust has been detected
Forced Bond has been activated
4/5 Marks have been assigned
Skill activated: Claw Drain
–15 Energy

His hand transformed slightly, and Gary swiped it along Hawk's chest, causing a deep wound with blood gushing out everywhere. As he felt the blood on his clawed hands, a strange refreshing energy rose inside him. The effects of the Claw Drain were working. The next second, the receptionist, Ben, and Pierre charged forward.

As for the events that followed . . . it all became a blur for Gary. A blur of red.

When it was over, he stood in the center of the room, glad that the music from the karaoke machine had been so loud. The entire room was now covered in blood, with the lights from the TV screen flashing once in a while, revealing the scene.

None of the four men would ever move again.

CHAPTER 10

FOR FAMILY

As he stood in the middle of the karaoke room, it took a while for Gary to process what he had just done. He looked down at his blood-covered hands; most of the gore was on his still-sharpened fingertips, which currently resembled the claws of a wild beast.

I've gone and done it now . . . only this time it was no accident, Gary thought. *I was just so . . . angry.*

His view was blocked at the moment, by none other than the system screen, which had "rewarded" him for his deeds. Gary wasn't sure how to feel about it. Usually someone would get punished for what he had done, yet here he was being actively encouraged to keep doing it.

527/765 Exp

Gary was still at Level 6, but killing each person had granted him 100 Exp, which was double the number he would get for just defeating any color gang member. It was the most Exp he had ever received for beating someone, and yet he instinctively knew why that was the case. It was because he had gone far beyond knocking them out . . .

On top of that, while in the middle of his rage, he had created a Forced Bond with Hawk and the receptionist, turning them into hunting targets. He was pretty sure that the other two would have also been marked, if it had not been for him hitting the limit at five.

Gary would have liked to blame everything on his rage, yet he knew exactly what he had been doing. He hadn't even tried to resist, his thoughts being filled with a desire to punish those assholes for what they had done to his sister.

My mind was clear enough for me to make that decision . . . which means I could have . . .

Gary had been assigned two random stat points for forcefully hunting down both of his targets.

Strength 7
Dexterity 6
Endurance 11

While checking his stats, he noticed that the additional points had been split between his Dexterity and Endurance. He had some-what been hoping that they would go to Strength, since that ability seemed more useful compared to the others. Especially if he was to compare his strength to Billy's.

As for his Health, he noticed that he was completely healed after using the Claw Drain skill on those four. Gary had also figured out that because of the transformation of his hands when using the skill, it turned out to be stronger than when he had tested it in the past. It was like having his own pair of blades, but even better.

However, on the downside his Energy was rather low after all the fighting. Although he hadn't needed to use Charging Heart, his heart rate had actually gone up so much that he had been granted additional stats, similar to the moon's effect, yet it had ended up consuming more Energy in that state.

Energy: 28/120

After he stood there for a while, the seriousness of the situation finally got to him.

I have to do something about this . . . I can't just leave them like this! If I get caught, who is going to look after Mom and Amy? How would they react if they found out I became a murderer? How would everyone react?

He looked around the room and noticed that the camera had been turned away, likely because of the evil things the trio had planned to do. The only person who had seen Gary enter had been the receptionist, and he was dead too.

He would have to check if there were cameras in the hallway, but since the receptionist was involved in this mess, it was a safe bet that those cameras might have been tampered with as well. Heck, in a scummy place like this, it wouldn't surprise him if most of the cameras were just there for show, but Gary couldn't risk it; he would need to check.

Amy should be okay, but I need to clean up the room and get rid of the bodies. Then it will take them a while before they find out that these guys are dead. They'll just think they ran away.

If he left the room in its current state, it was guaranteed to make the news. Stacy and Amy were smart enough to put two and two together and figure out that Gary must have done it.

The last thing he wanted to do was get them involved. He could perhaps trust his sister to keep a secret, but the same couldn't be said about Stacy.

How do I get rid of the bodies without anyone seeing me, though? Should I call Kai again? No, this time I was involved myself, and anyone he might send here will surely ask questions if they have to do so much overtime . . .

As if answering his question, the system popped up.

After a successful hunt, a predator consumes its kill.
Consume human flesh to gain additional stat points.

After reading the message, Gary walked toward one of the bodies. He turned it over so he wouldn't have to look it in the face.

Four bodies . . . am I really going to do this? I might have changed, but how much might I be able to eat? . . . Even if I do this, will I be able to get rid of the bones?

Gary kept repeating certain thoughts to himself, closing his eyes. *The worst part has already been done . . . they are already dead. They can no longer feel anything.* He tried to think of them as just bodies. Rats . . . only much, much bigger.

On top of that, because his Energy was low he could feel his stomach growling, and before he knew it, he was already digging in.

Human flesh of Ben Cuman consumed
+50 Exp
Strength +1
Human flesh of Pierre Cousant consumed
+50 Exp
Endurance +1
Human flesh of Hawk Et Dante consumed
+50 Exp
Endurance +1
Human flesh of Warmer Dudefun consumed
+50 Exp
Endurance +1

Name: Gary Dem
Level 6
Exp: 727/765
Health: 68/100
Energy: 92/120
Strength 8
Dexterity 6
Endurance 14

From head to toe, their bodies were gone.

I have to remember, I'm doing all of this for my family, Gary told himself.

CHAPTER 11

FADING

Gary felt like his body had become a bottomless pit; no matter how much he ate, his hunger didn't seem to get satisfied. On the plus side, he discovered that with his sharp teeth and strong jaws there had been no need for him to worry about bones.

After each bite he felt the human flesh energizing his body in unique ways, and after a while, all the bodies had disappeared. Alas, his supernatural devouring turned out to be limited to flesh. Once Hawk's hand had disappeared, Gary tried to bite down on his sleeve, but to his surprise he found it hard to swallow, forcing him to strip all of the bodies naked.

Leaving the karaoke room, he quickly searched for the cameras. Fortunately, all of them had already been turned around, which was a huge relief since he wasn't exactly a whiz kid with technology. He wouldn't even have known where to start if he had needed to delete some evidence.

With that out of the way, Gary headed to the supply closet. It was locked, though given his strength, breaking the door had posed no challenge. Grabbing the strongest chemicals and cleaning supplies he could find, he returned to the room.

With the help of Charging Heart, Gary was able to clean the room in record time. He knew that it wasn't perfect; heck, he was well aware that at least the door, the chemicals, and the tools would have his fingerprints on them, but since Gary had never been brought in for criminal charges, the police didn't have his fingerprints or DNA on file to outright identify him.

When the room no longer looked like a murder had just taken place, Gary put all of the victims' clothes in a large black trash bag, and he put personal items like phones, wallets, and keys in a separate, smaller bag.

I guess I should bury their clothes somewhere deep in the woods or something. I can't just throw them away in a garbage can, or the police will just find them. I can't bring them back with me either, since I already have enough evidence of other things hidden in my room.

After returning the cleaning supplies, Gary decided to leave a note on the reception desk, stating that the sunglasses guy had quit, effective immediately. This way, anyone who arrived would assume the receptionist had rage-quit and that the club was closed for the day. To top things off, he turned the *OPEN* sign to *CLOSED*, making it less likely that anyone would enter. Another reason for doing this was so the owner of the club wouldn't ask any questions, thinking he just had a bad employee.

As Gary left the Kobe Karaoke Club, he was happy that Amy and Stacy were nowhere to be seen, and he took a deep breath, still holding the trash bags.

Good, no one saw me go in. That Hawk guy claimed he was linked to the Gray Elephants gang. If that's the case, the police probably won't take a missing-person report seriously, and if they do find out that they have been killed, as long as they don't link it back to today, they'll just assume it's another gang. It will be okay.

Although he was still worried about Amy, Gary had no way of following her. He had been unable to mark his sister today, and her phone was currently with him. So he chose to trust that Stacy had gotten her out safely and that they had gotten to a hospital.

Gary made his way back to Chavley, where the war was taking place between the color gangs. He was shocked to see that the police had barricaded the entire area.

That wasn't there when I left! Well, I guess trying to contain it to just one area is the best they can do in this situation.

Gary placed a hand on his chest. For a second, when he first saw the police, he had feared that they had come to arrest him, but seeing all the vehicles and the police just standing there, he understood the situation.

It didn't matter to Gary, though; he just needed to find another way in. Using his newfound talents in jumping and climbing, he easily used the alleyways between the buildings to get over a fence and into the area where their apartment was.

Once he got in deep enough, Gary destroyed all of the phones he had retrieved. It took him a while, since he first needed to figure out whose phone was whose. Stacy's was easy enough to identify thanks to the pink case.

He didn't want to destroy the wrong ones by accident; he hadn't just destroyed them on-site and dumped them somewhere because if the police had a way to track the last known GPS location of those phones, it would have taken them to the karaoke club.

However, if the police figured out that the last time the victims had been seen was today—the day the gang war had happened—and tracked their phones to this area, they would assume they had gotten involved in the gang war. Gary just hoped that the police would be too lazy to run a more thorough investigation of all the victims' locations.

I guess being in the Underdogs helped me out quite a bit, Gary thought. *All that time, I was thinking what would I do if they told me to do something dangerous. Or what would happen if I needed to avoid being caught. So they taught me a lot.*

Kirk taught me a lot.

After disassembling the phones and spreading them around in different places, the last thing Gary needed to do was get rid of the clothes, which led him to the trusty forest he had been visiting more often than he ever had thought he would be doing.

Skill activated: Charging Heart
All stats have temporarily been doubled
–10 Energy
Energy: 98/120

Gary activated Charging Heart once more and started digging with his hands. He needed the hole to be deep enough so no animal or person would accidentally stumble upon the clothes. While doing so, he thought about many things, none of which were the lives he had taken.

No, he was worried about his sister and how he could protect the rest of his family, using the powers of the system.

If it hadn't been for this Werewolf System, could I have helped Amy today? What if it had been the Underdogs who captured her? My Energy got too low. I need to learn how to control my heart rate so I don't need to spend the Energy on activating Charging Heart.

I can't believe this thing doesn't have a reserve! I mean, with how much I ate earlier, I'm surprised I didn't increase it naturally. Just where did it all go, if after using Charging Heart my Energy is already down slightly?

Eventually, Gary finished burying the clothes. What felt like a very long night seemed to finally be over. Originally, he had planned to rejoin the fight, hoping to gain more Exp, but after what had happened, he just wanted to see if his sister was safe.

But then he noticed something strange. One of the green marks was fading in and out. This was the first time something like that had ever happened, so he wasn't quite sure what it meant. Nevertheless, that wasn't important, because from the smell of it he knew who it belonged to.

"Mom!"

CHAPTER 12

DON'T GIVE UP

The streets of Chavley had become chaotic, and it was getting worse by the second. Multiple shops and businesses that were open late had no choice but to close up. Unfortunately, some had failed to react in due time and incurred quite a loss in the process.

However, as a result, Chavley, although not one of the most affluent areas, was nevertheless under the control of the Underdogs. Many of those businesses either directly belonged to the gang or were at least affiliated with them. For the latter group, the owners had no other choice but to pay the Underdogs a percentage of their profits to keep operating.

Usually this was a big enough deterrent for anyone else to mess with their businesses, but today that clearly wasn't the case. The red and gray color gangs had come to wreak havoc, so they naturally didn't care about any such conventions.

Of course, this had led to many angry business owners picking up their phones to contact the one group they had never believed they would, asking them for help. For once, they were about to demand that the gang hold up their end of the deal and deliver on the protection they were forced to pay for.

One of the businesses that was most affected by this was a local twenty-four-hour discount store. It was modest in size, with several aisles that sold all the necessities. It even had its own bakery section. However, today it looked nothing like it usually did.

The electronics aisles were mostly empty, raided by the members of the color gang. The same was true for the alcohol aisle as well as the snack aisle. The theft seemed to be limited to what the looters could carry, as that the looting was clearly done on a whim, not planned beforehand.

Inside the store, the employees had followed protocol and tried to flee into the supply room. However, one panicked employee had refused to wait for her colleagues and had sealed the reinforced door behind her, leaving the others to fend for their lives.

Three employees had been left outside the door. One of them was an older gentleman with speckles of gray in his hair and his beard. While his two female co-workers implored the others to let them inside, he ran to the cleaning supplies and grabbed a mop, which he swung wildly toward the color gang members, his back against the freezer section.

"Stay back, you fiends! I don't own this store, so take whatever you want, just don't hurt me!" the old man shouted. Alas, he could see the look in their eyes; they saw him not as a fellow human, but a toy. They were clearly on some type of adrenaline rush.

The color gang members didn't care about stealing per se; they were just caught up in the chaos, doing what they were not normally allowed to do. One of them threw a paint can at the old man.

When it hit him in the head, he let go of the mop and fell to the ground. In an instant, three color gang members were on him, kicking and punching him and going through his pockets.

The two women came running, and the young university student was shaking.

"They're going to kill him! And they'll do the same thing to us!" she sobbed.

The older woman, Maya, grabbed the girl's hand and ran the other way to hide in the cereal aisle. They couldn't see any other gang members here, but they looked around to see if the creepy guy was following them.

"I'll protect you, Amalee! I promise it will be okay. I won't let that guy do anything to you," Maya said with a forced smile to calm her colleague, but it only frightened her more. The poor girl had started working part time less than two months ago. Who could have known that she would find herself in such a grim situation?

The young girl could see the lump on top of Maya's head. Just moments ago, the person they had met in the pet food aisle had attempted to grab her.

It had been obvious what the teenage boy had been about to do. Although Maya knew that it might have been her best chance to try to escape, she had been unable to leave the poor girl there. Amalee wasn't much older than Maya's daughter Amy, making her motherly instincts kick in.

She had attempted to fight the person off. Alas, he had proven to be bigger and far stronger than her. The back of his elbow had hit her face, just above her eyebrow. It had been a big blow, causing her to fall into the aisle, knocking over some of the pet food.

At that point, Amalee had been frozen with fear, terrified that if she fought back, even worse things would happen to her. If she had to go through . . . *that* and it meant he would let her live, then she would happily do it.

Seconds before the teenager could do anything else, though, something heavy whacked the top of his head and dropped to the floor. It turned out to be a heavy bag of dog food, of all things. While he was dazed, Maya rushed over and grabbed her co-worker and started running. That was when they saw the older man attacked.

"Amalee, never give up like you did back there, you hear me!" Maya berated her, placing her hands on her shoulders. "If that happens again, just run. You can't give up like that!"

"She's right." A familiar voice spoke with a pained groan. "It wouldn't be fun if you just let me do what I want."

Both of the women's hearts were beating frantically, and they looked left and right to try to see where the person was, but neither of them could find him. The next second, a hand came out from behind one of the cereal boxes and reached for the two of them.

Without even giving it a second thought, Maya pushed Amalee away, and the large hand grabbed the middle-aged woman.

"Didn't you hear me just now?" Maya shouted. *"Run!"*

It seemed like a hard choice for the young girl to make, but eventually she ran off to hide somewhere else, leaving Maya in the hands of Gil.

CHAPTER 13

DON'T BE A HERO

Although Gil had grabbed Maya, he was unable to simply walk over to her side because of the metal framework between the aisles. As an employee of the supermarket, Maya was naturally aware of that, and she dug her nails into Gil's hand.

"You bitch!" Gil shouted as blood trickled down his skin. Unwilling to let go, he pulled on Maya's shirt, slamming her into the metal frame and banging her head on one of the higher shelves. At that moment, she used all her strength to push away.

Maya managed to break free, but the top part of her uniform had torn slightly, revealing her bra. However, showing a bit of skin was the least of her worries. She just wanted to get out of this hell-hole, now that she was free. But a dark shadow loomed above her as several cereal boxes fell to the floor.

Turning her head, she saw that Gil had kicked the shelf as hard as he could, toppling it over. Maya flinched as she braced herself, but then the top of the shelf to her right hit the one to her left.

The whole supermarket underwent a domino effect as the shelves fell over, until it eventually stopped around midway. Fortunately Maya had quickly dropped down, narrowly avoiding being crushed. Once she was sure that she was relatively safe, she crawled toward one end.

I'm going to get out of here! I need to survive . . . for Gary and Amy. They both still need me to look after them! Maya thought as she dragged herself forward.

Just as she reached the end, two large hands grabbed her by her forearms and dragged her out. Her eyes met Gil's; he had been waiting for her.

"Look what you did to my hand, you damn hag!" he shouted as he stomped his feet, aiming for her head. Maya covered her head with her arms, but it did little to stop the force behind his kicks.

Suddenly the kicking stopped, but Maya was afraid to look up, worried that it might be a trick. But the newest gray color gang member had stopped because he had noticed something far more interesting.

After kicking Maya repeatedly, he had finally caught a glimpse of her ripped top. Now that the teenager had noticed her bra and how a certain part of her body was bouncing up and down, he felt something between his pants growing harder by the second.

"Why don't we take a closer look at these goods, huh?" Gil placed his hand on top of Maya's breast. He could feel that it was bigger than what could fit in his hand. Instinctively, Maya grabbed his forearm and dug her fingernails into it.

The horny teenager screamed, pulled his arm away, and kicked her in the ribs as hard as he could. He readied himself for another kick but detected someone running toward him.

"Ahhhh!" Amalee screamed as she ran forward with a knife in her hand. But Gil wasn't as afraid as she had expected him to be. Instead, he waited for her to come closer, only to sidestep her attack before grabbing her by the wrist.

"Nice try, but it's obvious that you've never used a weapon on someone before," Gil harrumphed, twisting her wrist to force her hand open. With his free hand, he took the knife.

"I bet you've never been stabbed. When you tried to stab me, you should have been prepared to get hurt as well, so here, have a taste of your own medicine!" Gil showed her a sick smile as he swung the knife toward Amalee's arm. However, before it reached her, another arm came between the two of them. Maya's arm.

"I said I wouldn't let you get hurt! Don't try to be a hero, just get the hell out of here!" Maya shouted.

Amalee was shocked, to the point that she was unable to do anything. She had been ready to run, but when she saw how that pervert had stepped on her co-worker who had always been nice to her, who had just sacrificed herself for her sake, the young woman couldn't leave her there.

She had stopped right at the aisle with all the kitchen tools. Taking it as a sign, she grabbed one of the knives, intending to repay her colleague. But she had just made the situation a whole lot worse . . . for both of them.

"You deserve this too, bitch!" Gil proclaimed, pulling the knife out of Maya's arm, blood gushing all over the floor, as she felt an even sharper pain. She looked up just in time to see that the psycho was planning to do something else with the blade.

He thrust it toward her, aiming right for her chest. She tried to move out of the way, but before she could, he grabbed the top of her shoulder, holding her in place.

The knife came forward . . . but a hand came out from the side, stopping it with two fingers.

"How could you make such a mess here?" a male voice said. "Has the name Underdogs suddenly lost all of its meaning? I've already had to clean up after a couple of your friends this evening, but your group has somehow managed to stir up the most shit.

"All of this area is our territory, which means your group has no business here whatsoever. The ones who are here, on the other hand, are all people who indirectly work for us. If you mess with them, it's the same as messing with us. And trust me, you don't want that . . . and I will make goddamn sure that it will be a lesson you'll never forget!"

The next second, by slightly rotating his hand, the stranger managed to bend the knife's edge as if were made out of paper rather than stainless steel. Gil felt a certain kind of pressure emanating from this stranger in a black suit with his yellow-spotted tie.

"Now before I deal with you, I'm going to ask you a question. You didn't happen to see a green-haired kid in this area, did you?"

CHAPTER 14

A REAL GANGSTER

To be able to bend a knife so easily, and to do it without a hint of fear, the man who had appeared out of nowhere was clearly far from normal. Every fiber of Gil's being was telling him that the stranger was dangerous. His appearance was unexpected, so it had taken Gil a moment to understand what the man wanted from him.

Underdogs . . . shit, Bowden warned us that there was a good chance they might come! But why would they come out just for a color gang? And how the hell am I supposed to know who they're looking for? Hell, a bunch of the guys in our group have green hair! Gil thought, frustrated about how this person had suddenly interrupted his fun.

Seeing the lack of a reaction from the gray color gang member, Kirk let out a big sigh.

"Yeah, I guess there are quite a few people who have green hair these days, huh? Since we're chasing him, he might have already dyed it another color. Or maybe he kept it green, thinking that we would expect him to change it?" Kirk was clearly not fazed at all by the seriousness of the situation.

For Maya, who had just been saved, when Kirk mentioned a "green-haired kid," only one boy instantly came to mind. She still vividly remembered the day when her teenage son had come home insisting on hiding his head under a hoodie. However, since it had been a rare free night for her, Maya had decided to have dinner with her children, as a family. Naturally, Gary had not been allowed to eat with his hoodie on . . .

That day was filled with tears of joy and laughter, all at Gary's expense.

Is he talking about Gary? No, that can't be it. It must just be a coincidence. This person is an adult who belongs to a gang. Why would Gary have anything to do with someone like that?

"The kid we're looking for should be around your age, which is why I'm asking on the off chance you might know him. He's a little on the small side, hotheaded, energetic. Does any of that ring a bell?" Kirk added some details, hoping that they might finally end up with a clue.

At this point, Gil let go of the knife. His frustration at not being taken seriously had started to outweigh his fear of this stranger. He might be a member of the Underdogs, but weren't they part of different gangs in the first place? Why should he answer him when there was nothing for him to gain by doing so?

"Maybe I do, maybe I don't. Why the fuck should I tell you anything?" Gil shouted as he threw a fist toward the man. But the man didn't lose his temper. Just like with the knife, he grabbed Gil's fist and quickly twisted it.

This wasn't the first time he had asked this question, yet somehow all these color gang members had the same reaction when he did, unable to comprehend that they were no longer in control. By now, the Altered was a little tired of their bravado, forcing him to get rough with them.

His nails started to stretch out, getting thicker, longer, and sharper. Fur appeared on his forearms, and his teeth started to grow as dark spots appeared on his body.

"Answer me!" Kirk demanded, screaming at the teenager.

At that moment, Gil flinched and went down to the floor—not because of Kirk's actions, but because what he looked like now had reminded him of an event that had happened not too long ago.

"You think you can just cower like that?" Kirk shouted at the frightened dropout. "Wasn't it you who was spouting some bullshit about being 'prepared to get hurt as well?' After all you did to these poor people, you nearly piss your pants when someone stands up to you?"

Whether Gil wanted to fight or not, Kirk had already been beyond angry with him. He hated these types of people the most: those who were happy to torture those weaker than them but became meek in front of those more powerful than them.

The Altered kicked Gil right in the stomach. The kick was so powerful that it lifted the teenager two feet off the ground. His eyes were watering, and it took a few seconds until he finally managed to breathe again. The first thing he could think of doing was calling for help.

"Help!" Gil whimpered, as he turned toward where the other color gang members should have been. "Help me!"

At that moment, five adult men wearing black suits similar to Kirk's came out. Each one held a couple of unconscious color gang members by the scruff of their clothes and were dragging them over to Kirk.

All of the gang members who had been busy raiding the supermarket had been dealt with. Seeing this, Gil began to realize the danger that he had gotten himself into.

"Do you understand now?" Kirk asked with a dangerous smirk. "Being in a gang is not all fun and games. You might think you're like family, or that you are untouchable by the law because of people backing you up, but this is the reality.

"All your actions still have consequences. You should remember this scene, because it will become something that you will see every day." Kirk crouched down to Gil's height; he was still transformed, and Gil wanted to look away.

Kirk's eyes looked like those of a lion or tiger, striking fear into his body. The Altered grabbed the teenager by his hair and forced him to turn his head.

"Look at me!" Kirk demanded as he stared into Gil's eyes. "Look at what you did!" He shifted him toward the two sobbing women behind him. "Do you still think this is fun?" Kirk asked, yet there was no response.

"Answer!" the Altered shouted, and he slapped Gil across the face. It was a heavy slap, and not just that, but his fingernails had transformed to claws, scratching the boy's cheek and causing blood to fall.

Meanwhile, running as fast as he could, doing his best to avoid all the chaos around him, Gary had passed countless fights, the unconscious and bloody bodies of color gang members lying on the streets, and other horrific scenes. Finally he reached the supermarket.

He had seen the destruction of the other shops, and with each one his worries about the state of his mother had increased. To top things off, his one remaining red mark was seemingly intertwined with the green mark of his mother.

Mom, please be safe!

CHAPTER 15

PROTECT HER

Blood was dripping from Gil's face, yet he garnered no sympathy from those present. After repeated slaps from Kirk, the teenager's face was guaranteed to end up scarred. The Altered had stayed in his partial transformation state, and the two women could see that he was clearly upset.

This was the first time either one of them had ever seen this man, so they weren't quite sure why. Eventually, Kirk let go of Gil, who had refused to say anything. The teenager had passed out, be it from pain, exhaustion, shock, or something else.

"Sir, they killed one of the employees before we got here and heavily injured two others. One will likely succumb to her injuries, whereas the other might survive if we get her to a hospital. We have beaten all the gray and red color members in the area. What would you like us to do with them?" one of the members asked.

Given the amount of respect the gang member had for the help-ful stranger, it became obvious that he was the leader of this group. Before Kirk gave his subordinates an answer, he looked at Gil on the ground, then grabbed a phone from his pocket. The display had multiple messages, which he browsed through.

"The other groups also seem to have gotten things under control. Looks like this little war is finally coming to an end." The Altered let out a big sigh before he started to give orders. "If you haven't already, notify the cleanup group to take care of the deceased. We'll round up some of the guys to try to get some information out of them back at the base. Hopefully the professionals will get them to sing."

"Yes, sir," the men replied in unison, and they started to drag the color gang members out of sight of the women. A few moments later, cries resounded throughout the supermarket as the gang members woke some of the less injured gang members in a brutal manner to ask them who their superiors were.

As for Kirk, he decided to take Gil with him. Although the large teenager seemed too young to have any important role in the color gang, the Altered was unwilling to just let him go.

Seeing that her savior was about to leave, Amalee wanted to thank him. To her, Kirk was a knight in shining armor who she would never be able to forget. Not only was he strong and brave but good-looking as well, but before she could say anything, Maya spoke up.

"Wait! Thank you! Thank you so much for saving us!" Maya called out, covering her exposed body with one hand while the other grabbed her head. She felt like it was about to explode. Over the evening, her head had been hit by Gil's elbow and banged against one of the shelves, and later the teenager had attempted to stomp on it a few times.

"There's no need to thank us." Kirk spoke with his back to them. "This time we were on your side, but it could have just as easily been us who attacked you. Unlike your colleagues, you were lucky that we made it in time to save you."

With that the Altered kept walking, but there was still one more thing Maya needed to ask.

"Hang on, you were looking for a green-haired teenager, right? There are a lot of people who come to shop here every day! Please, let us return the favor. If you could leave your name and number we can notify you if someone matching your description ever comes here. By the way, why exactly are you looking for him?"

Of course, Maya wasn't planning to tell Kirk anything about Gary at all. She wasn't even sure whether her savior was looking for her son in the first place, but if he was, then she needed to know what exactly they wanted from him. She had just seen just how dangerous a man he could be.

At the same time, Kirk didn't fail to notice that her offer had been worded in a very weird way.

If she just wanted to repay my kindness, then why is she so concerned about why we're looking for that kid? Could it be that she actually knows him?

It was then that Kirk took a closer look at the middle-aged woman.

Hmmm, agewise she might be old enough to be his mother, if she had him a little young. Should I question her? Kirk thought about it for a moment before he came to a decision.

"Should you find someone who fits that description, just tell them teens shouldn't be in this business, it's not a life they should want to live." With that, he walked out the front door.

"We . . . w-we're a-alive. W-we s-somehow s-survived." Amalee was so happy that tears of joy came out of her eyes. But then the two women heard footsteps. For a moment, they thought that the Underdogs might have forgotten something—but the sound came from behind them.

Whoever it was had entered through the supermarket's side entrance instead of the front. It didn't take long for them to see a hooded person in black clothes.

"A-another one." Amalee was frightened, and her body was shaking again. Now that Kirk and his men had left, who would protect them? However, to her surprise the hooded boy ran right past her and went straight toward Maya instead.

"Mom! Mom, are you all right?"

Looking under the hood, Maya saw that it was her own son, which made her smile. Gary took a second to look at her condition.

Her head was badly swollen, her clothes were ripped, her lip was split, and her arms and sides were badly bruised.

"Who did this? Which asshole is responsible for this?" Gary almost shouted.

However, instead of answering, his mother just opened her arms and gave her son a hug.

"I'm so glad to see you. How did you even know I was here?" she asked.

After realizing that Maya knew him, Amalee could finally relax.

Just then, Gary started sobbing. He had been through a lot. This one evening could have easily destroyed the entire Dem family. His entire reason for wanting to get stronger was to protect his mother and his sister.

All of the emotions that had swelled up inside him as he had hurried to rescue her were coming out. Although he was with her now, he hadn't managed to get there in time to prevent her from getting harmed. Nevertheless, he was just happy that she was still alive.

"Please, Gary . . . don't cry." His mother eventually pulled away and wiped some tears off his cheek. "Let's just go home," she said as she touched her still-hurting head. "This was the single most stressful eveni—"

Her voice drifted and so did her body as it swayed. Gary grabbed her before she hit the ground.

"Mom! Mom! Are you okay? What's wrong? Please, say something!" Gary shook her lightly, afraid to hurt her even more, yet there was no response.

CHAPTER 16

BAD NEWS

A minute had passed, and no matter how much Gary shook his mother, she refused to wake up. He helplessly looked at her colleague, but Amalee didn't know what to do either. She offered to call an ambulance.

Gary knew that with the color gang war still going on, neither the police, ambulances, taxis, nor anything else would be able to enter this area. Left with no other choice, he took it upon himself to take her to the hospital.

He didn't hesitate to use Charging Heart to get an extra boost. As long as he could get there even a second faster, he didn't care how much Energy he had to spend. However, there was barely any need for him to use the skill. He could hear his mother's heartbeat continuously weakening and slowing down, further increasing his heart rate to the point where he entered his partial transformation state.

Mom, please hang in there! You can't leave us! We still need you! Gary thought as he ran through the streets. *You made a promise, remember? You promised me that you would never leave us! You have to survive so I can give you and Amy the best life possible! So we can get out of this city, away from all the gangs! You still haven't even lived your life yet!*

Eventually, Gary arrived outside Slough's central hospital. It was quite a distance away from Chavley, where the gang war had occurred. Fortunately, thanks to his special situation, the teenager took less than twenty minutes to arrive. Even better, the hospital didn't seem to be overrun with other casualties just yet.

Unwilling to put his mother down, Gary ran through the double doors, pushing them open head first with a loud bang.

"Anybody, please help! My mother's been attacked by gang members! She's not waking up!" Gary began shouting the moment he entered the reception area, not caring what type of disturbance he might be causing. His little stunt proved to be immediately effective, leading the security guards as well as the few nurses on duty to come over.

Initially, the guards had been about to tell Gary off for his entrance, but then they noticed how exhausted he was. He had obviously carried his mother a great distance to come here. Seeing the condition she was in, the guards didn't know quite what to do until a nurse pushed them out of the way.

"How long has she been like that?" the nurse asked as she led Gary into the emergency room.

"I don't know, a while. She's hurt, please save her!"

The nurse gave him a determined look, one that made him believe that she would do everything in her power to help.

After handing his mother over, Gary followed the nurse's instructions and remained in the waiting area. His mind was racing, imagining what life might be like without his mother: how he would deal with it, and what would happen to him and Amy. Disrupting his wild fantasies, another nurse came over with a clipboard.

"I can see that you're going through a tough time, but we still need some information. Is there a father, partner, or boyfriend that we should inform?"

Gary shook his head.

"Ah, I see . . . For now, please just fill out what you can, but if possible contact an adult to help you and us with the paperwork. I'll leave you to it, and I'll let you know as soon as we know more."

After she left, Gary looked at the form, which was asking for details about health insurance and an emergency contact. He knew that their family couldn't afford health insurance. With more and more people out of work, most people had lost this privilege. Nowadays it only existed for Tier 1 and some Tier 2 cities.

An emergency contact, an adult. We don't have anyone helping us. Who could I contact to even help in this type of situation? Gary thought, as he gripped the pen so tightly that it snapped, causing the ink to burst all over the form, making him curse.

It's useless anyway; there's no information I can fill in. How did this happen? I made the Bond Mark so I could protect her, but I still failed! Was it the gang war? It had to be . . . I saw some of the members as I was walking through.

It had to be them! Those damn color gangs. I'll find them, I'll find whoever did this! With nothing else to hold on to, Gary was gripping the clipboard tightly, and it was close to almost snapping.

"Gary!" A familiar voice called out to him. Turning, he saw someone he hadn't expected, but at the same time it made sense for her to be here.

"Amy, you're here!" Gary said, standing up, and once again tears filled his eyes as he went to hug her, grabbing hold of her tightly. "I'm so happy that you're okay. I'm so happy that nothing happened to you."

A bit embarrassed, Amy pushed her brother away.

"Well, I'm not okay, look at my face," she said; it was partly covered in bandages, and even her nose was encased in something. "What are you doing here? Did Stacy call you? No, we left our phones with those jerks. I'm so happy to see that you made it out. Are you okay? They didn't do anything to you, did they?"

Amy clearly had a lot of questions, and so did Gary. For one, he wanted to know who had paid for Amy's treatment; it was horrible that the thought of money had to always be on his mind, yet at the same time, how could he explain what had happened to their mother? Would telling Amy make the situation worse, causing her to worry for no reason?

"Is there a Gary Dem present?" a doctor called out from the emergency area. Gary raised his hand, knowing that it must be news about his mother, but the look on the doctor's face wasn't promising.

"Gary, I don't exactly know the best way to say this, but it's about your mother. Unfortunately, I have some bad news."

CHAPTER 17

A FRIEND

For a second it seemed like everything around him had gone quiet. Gary was looking at the person in front of him, yet at the same time, his eyes weren't focused. The words *bad news* rang in his head again and again, drowning out the noise around him.

It felt as if someone had submerged him underwater, making him unable to breathe. The thoughts he'd had just moments ago could very well become a reality.

"Gary!" his sister called out. "Gary, what's going on? What is he talking about? What happened to Mom?" Amy shouted, panicked because she had no idea that their mother had been brought here as well.

The doctor waited to explain, because he could tell that Gary was still out of it. He had seen many people react like this before, and the young girl by the boy's side seemed to be a relative as well, most likely a daughter, who wasn't dealing with the sudden news any better than her brother.

Wait a second, the mark! Gary suddenly thought. *She can't be dead; if she died, then the system would inform me, right? She's not dead, she's still alive.* He checked the air and saw a faint but still-visible green mark coming from the emergency room.

"Please, tell me how my mother is," Gary said.

The doctor took a second look at the high schooler; there was a clear change in his eyes. Usually information like this wouldn't be passed on to a kid, but there was no one else here. He felt sorry that these children had to grow up in a world like this.

"You seem to be a brave young man, Gary; no matter what happens you should keep that determined look," the doctor said. "First, let me alleviate your worst worries; your mother is still with us. Her vitals are fine, and the bruises on the outside of her body will heal given time. The bones also seem to be only bruised, none broken.

"However, the issue is that your mother isn't showing any signs of waking up. There seems to have been some sort of head trauma that has caused her to go into a permanent sleeplike state."

"You mean a coma?" Amy shouted, holding on to the doctor's arm. "Our mother is in a coma? How did this happen? How long until she wakes up again? She will wake up, right? Right?"

Once again the doctor paused. His profession meant that he often had to deliver news like this, but seldom to relatives who were so young.

"We . . . don't know," the doctor answered with a sigh. "If we're lucky, she might wake up as if nothing had happened in a few hours or a few days. However, it may take weeks for her to regain consciousness, and in very rare cases it may even take years. I'm sorry, but it's too early to tell at this point in time.

"The next step would be to talk to your guardian, so that we can talk about accommodations and such. Now we can hold the bills for a week, but after that if nothing has been paid . . ." The doctor didn't continue there, as the cries of the girl next to Gary became louder and louder.

It was obviously too much for her, yet her brother had stayed strong.

"If you need any more information, or when your guardian arrives, feel free to come see me. I will try my best to make some time for you," the doctor said, taking his leave and heading back to the emergency department.

"Gary, what are we going to do? How are we going to pay for her care? What if she never wakes up again?" His sister continued to cry, while he was left with his own thoughts.

There were more problems than the bills; because of Gary's age, he wasn't classified as an adult, and if the hospital learned that their mother was their only guardian, they would likely inform the authorities. That could possibly mean that Gary and Amy would be split up, to be taken care of by foster families or put in orphanages.

In a Tier 3 town like Slough, that would be a worse life than they currently had.

"Amy, don't worry, I will get us out of this situation. We won't be leaving home, and Mom's going to be okay. You have to trust me, okay?" Gary said, taking her back to the waiting area and having her sit down. He also handed his sister her phone, as well as Stacy's.

Hopefully her phone would distract her from this mess. In the meantime, Gary now had another worry on his mind: what would happen to the two of them?

Mom's away most of the time anyway, and if this thing works out with Kai, then I should have some money to cover the expenses. The most important thing is to make sure that they don't find out we don't have another guardian.

Me and Amy can live together until you get better, Mom. I promise you that I will protect her.

In this situation, there was only one person who might be able to help him, and he decided to send them a message. All he could do now, though, was wait, but even then he was nervous, because he wasn't sure this person could help them this time.

While waiting, Gary glanced at his sister. She was currently on one of her old phones. Luckily, Amy was the type to never throw anything away, so she had something she could use after losing the other one. Well, "on her phone" wasn't exactly right; Amy had placed it on her lap, but she didn't seem to have the energy to lift it.

I have to stay strong in this situation, for Amy.

"Amy, I promise I'll make sure things are okay, but I want you to make a promise with me. When I think about what happened to Mom today, and what happened to you. If I hadn't arrived in time . . .

"There is a chance that it could have been you in there with Mom . . . You know how dangerous Slough can be, so I want you to promise me that if you ever feel like you're in trouble again, just like you did today, you will contact me immediately, okay?"

Before now, Gary wouldn't have made this type of promise, worried that his sister might try to hide something from him. However, since Amy had contacted him today of her own free will, especially after what she had experienced and learning what state their mother was in, he was convinced that she would never break that promise.

He held out his pinky finger, and Amy wrapped hers around it and nodded. Then, using their thumbs, they touched their pinkies at the same time. This was something that they had done ever since they were little: a pinky promise matched with a stamp of approval. Their mother had taught them how to do it, and they had found it cute how their thumbs acted as a little stamp, like they were entering some type of contract.

A spoken deal has been made, would you like to mark "Amy Dem"?
Yes.
4/5 Marks have been assigned

Now Gary could keep an eye on Amy whenever he needed to. As they waited, Gary watched the entrance. After a while Stacy came in, wondering where Amy had disappeared to. Initially she had been happy to see Gary, but she had trouble looking him in the eye, not that he was in any condition to care about it.

She tried to talk with Amy, but it became obvious that Amy was in no mood for idle talk. Eventually she left after thanking Gary for helping out and retrieving her phone. She briefly told him that he didn't have to worry about the hospital bill; she said it was the least she could do, since she knew it was all her fault. Fortunately, her parents had agreed to that.

Finally, Gary's eyes became more lively when he saw the person he had been waiting for come through the door. For once Kai seemed disheveled and bruised. Behind him was a beautiful older woman that Gary had never seen before.

"Who's that?" Amy asked as her brother suddenly stood up, looking toward the two newcomers.

"He's . . ." Gary wasn't sure what to say, because originally he had only come to Kai out of his own selfish need, but recently he had been forced to ask him for help over and over again. Surprisingly he came through every time, no matter how crazy Gary's request might be.

If he could fix their problem once again, Gary was ready to earnestly do his best to help Kai out; a person like that wasn't a stranger in his mind.

"He's . . . a friend," Gary answered with a smile.

CHAPTER 18

RISE TO THE TOP

After telling Amy to wait in her seat, Gary headed over to Kai. He hadn't been sure that Kai would actually come through, since his only reply had been, "I'll see what I can do." He wasn't a magical wish-granting genie, after all, and with what had happened in Slough, it wouldn't have surprised Gary if Kai had been occupied with something else.

Seeing him come through the door, especially with the older woman, made Gary feel hopeful. As for why he had told Amy to stay behind, it was because he definitely didn't want her to be involved in any of this mess.

"Be honest, do you get a kick out of ignoring all my warnings?" Kai asked in a slightly annoyed tone as he scratched his head. "I mean seriously, it's not like I ask you to stay put in a cell or anything. Yet here we are. Not only have you gone out but you somehow managed to end up in the hospital, even though you have a match tomorrow."

Gary had only told Kai what he needed and that he was at the hospital, rather than explaining the whole situation. It would have been hard to go over everything via text. On top of that, if only Kai knew what Gary really had been through, perhaps he would give him some slack . . . or maybe an even bigger earful.

"I'm sorry, Kai. I just . . ." Gary stopped there. It was undeniable that he had initially gone out despite the risk of being caught by the Underdogs. It was only later that he had hurried to save his family. "It's my mother . . ."

He went on to explain the details: how his mother got attacked in the supermarket, what condition he had found her in, how he had carried her over here, and the hospital staff needing an adult to take care of him and his sister and sign off on a few documents.

After telling the full story, Gary had half expected Kai to make some snide remark, but instead the look on his face had changed to one of sympathy. Surprising him even more, Kai placed a hand on Gary's shoulder.

"My condolences. I would have done the same if it had been my mother." Kai continued, "You're the gang leader, so of course I'll do whatever I can to help you out. Since I'm one year away from being an adult myself, I brought her here to act as your guardian."

Kai pointed to the woman standing next to him. She was around the same height as Kai, which was quite tall for a woman. She wore heavy black boots and red lipstick; her hair was jet black and straight, which was beautiful in a way and made her look more confident.

She didn't seem to resemble anyone from the Underdogs that Gary knew, and he didn't think that Kai, after everything that had happened, would bring one of their members here, so he wondered what their relationship was. At least the others could be explained as members of the Underdogs.

However, Gary chose not to pry. As long as the woman was willing to help them out, that was enough for him. The three of them walked over to the counter, where they received another form. Essentially, the woman had to agree to act as a guarantor. If payment wasn't handled in a timely fashion, the form gave the hospital permission to go after her and make her pay the bill.

This was something people would do for their most trusted family members or friends. Which raised the question once again:

who was she to Kai? She seemed too young to be Kai's mother, but looks could be deceiving. Still, the two didn't share many features on the surface, though she seemed somewhat familiar to Gary.

A few more details needed to be filled out, but the woman offered to handle it on her own, allowing Kai and Gary to move to the side. Neither one said anything for a while, yet Kai didn't miss that Gary was constantly clenching his fist. His face scrunched up a couple of times as well. It was clear he was thinking about something.

"I'll help you get the money to pay for the hospital bills," Kai offered. "If need be, we can just reach into the emergency funds for a while."

It was then that Gary realized Kai was trying to comfort him.

"Why me?" Gary asked as he looked up. "Why are you helping me so much? There's nothing special about me. I'm not as good a fighter as Innu, nor am I as cunning as you. You could have just sold me out to the Underdogs and looked for another teenager if you wanted a puppet for your gang. Why are you going out of your way to help me?"

"Does that mean you don't want my help, then?" Kai asked. For a moment there was an awkward silence, and then Kai let out another sigh. "Let me ask you this: what are you feeling right now? Anyone can tell that you're furious, so what is it you would like to do now?"

It felt out of the blue for Kai to answer his question with a question of his own, but Gary didn't mind getting it off his chest.

"I keep imagining those guys, those scumbags who did that to her," Gary answered. "It's not just her, though. My sister, a dead old man, injured and dying people out on the street. Why does everyone have to live in fear?"

"And the answer you came to?" Kai asked.

"Gangs," Gary replied. "It's because of the gangs who rule this place. They've gotten too big. I saw it; the best the police could do was quarantine Chavley off, hoping that the damage would be contained. The mayor and his government are unable to handle them. I hate them, I hate them so much. I want to get rid of them all!"

Kai looked at Gary again, and from the look in his eyes, he too had felt the same thing at one point.

"There's your answer, Gary. The more I'm around you, the more I come to realize that we aren't too different. The sad reality is that it will be impossible to get rid of them in any legal way. The new mayor might be against them, but either he will be bought off by them or they will just get rid of him if he doesn't play ball.

"It's not just Slough. Every town and city has these kinds of problems, only some hide it better than others. At the top of all the Tier 1 cities you have the Kings. However, even they have gotten so big that it has become impossible for them to act on their own. They're too afraid of stepping on each other's toes, since fighting among themselves will just weaken them, giving others the opportunity to potentially take them out.

"Until this day, there hasn't been a force that has been able to go to the very top, or strong enough to get rid of them all. If you want to get rid of the gangs, Gary, that's your answer. Make your own gang, climb to the top with me, and protect the ones you care about.

"That's the only way for guys like us to make any change in this godforsaken place. Nothing will ever change unless we can somehow get rid of them. It's up to you what you want to do once you're at the top, but let me warn you. You need to do this before you lose the people you care about, so that today becomes the exception and not the rule," Kai explained, holding out his hand.

"We already made a deal once, but now that we're both on the same wavelength, let's shake on this . . . leader."

Just then, Gary saw that the woman at the reception desk was done with the paperwork and was walking over. He somehow felt like he was suddenly under some type of time limit. Something was telling him that if he didn't take Kai's hand right now, the two of them would never see eye to eye again.

At the same time, shaking meant agreeing to create a gang, forcing him to create the one thing he had grown to hate. Was this really the only choice he had?

In the end, Gary reached out and grabbed Kai's hand, shaking it on the spot.

"I'll do it. I'll help you."

"Help *us*, you mean," Kai said with a smile.

CHAPTER 19

BEHIND THE ATTACK

In a Tier 3 town, crime was quite rampant. The police force was limited in these areas, budgets were low compared to the higher-tier cities, and there was overall less control from the gangs in the first place.

However, Slough could still have been considered a moderate town to live in. The Underdogs had been a threatening force in the area. Because of this, the police usually just had to deal with small disputes between the color gangs rather than the larger ones.

Until tonight. For the police force and the whole town, this had been one of the worst days in its history. Three of the biggest gangs had practically had a war in Chavley, and it had caused so much chaos. When it eventually settled down, the police were able to move in, as planned by Chief of Police Anton Millstun.

However, the results weren't pretty at all. Several gang members were now in intensive care or had an injury of some sort. Thankfully, not all of them went to the hospital, because they also had their own underground doctors who could treat them.

But the main concern of the police was the civilians who had been involved in the mess. At the moment, police reports claimed that fourteen suspected gang members had lost their lives.

Four members of the public had died, and two were in intensive care, including Gary's mother. Although the numbers might not have seemed high, there was also everything else the police would have to deal with, such as tracing stolen goods and gathering everyone's testimony about the events that had occurred.

To top it off, since the police weren't able to act at the moment, it would be very hard for them to even prosecute any of these gang members, and it was a waste of time in the first place.

Anton knew that if a large attack like this one took place, they would be ready. Someone was backing them, and when it came to the trial phase they always got off. It had happened so many times that Anton knew there was nothing that they could do.

Along with Roo, he had successfully made it back to the police station after a tough day. His eyes were red and he was busy rubbing his face up and down.

"Sir, you have worked hard, why don't you get some rest?" Roo said.

"What's the point?" Anton replied. "Eighteen lives lost, multiple people missing, and there are probably more. Did I ever tell you that I became a police officer to stop events like today from occurring? When I was young like you, the chief just sat back and did nothing. So I worked hard and rose to this position. Now I'm here, yet in some ways I feel even more useless than my younger self!"

Roo knew he didn't mean it that way, but the police force knew they were pretty much useless, especially for large-scale things like this. However, he liked how Anton cared; he knew he was working for a good person.

"Then change it," Roo said. "You reached this position, right? If the police and government are corrupt, let's rise to the top and change it, getting rid of the bad from the inside."

Anton just sighed; Roo displayed the same naivety he had in the past. Did he think people hadn't tried to do that before? There was a reason: anyone who had attempted to clean up the police force or government would be dealt with. The problem was that the gangs were already involved with the police force, even if the public didn't know it.

"I wish I were still like you," Anton mumbled, shaking his head and picking up another report in front of him. "Huh . . . of all things, we have a business owner complaining about his employee leaving midway through work! Do they seriously think we have the time to deal with a missing employee when a gang war just took place? This isn't even a matter for the police to solve!"

With the small war ending, members of the gray and red color gangs eventually returned. They had been informed of the attack, and the leaders were to report what exactly was going on.

The leader of the gray color gang, Buffin, and the leader of the red color gang, Riv, were walking together as they headed to an abandoned warehouse. In the past they would never have been seen standing side by side, but they had been called to explain the situation.

At the warehouse, members were standing outside wearing gray suits. It was the mark of the Gray Elephants. Both of the leaders were a little nervous, and they each took a deep breath before going inside.

The warehouse was full of shipping crates. It used to be the gray color gang's hangout, but the leader of the Gray Elephants, since they were in charge of the gray color gang, used it as they wished.

A large figure stood on top of a crate at the very back. He looked like a wall of muscle, built on top of muscle. If one saw him with normal clothes on, they might think of him as fat.

However, he wore a large open fur overcoat that showed the middle of his stomach, revealing a defined six-pack. By his side were two others who looked small when compared to the leader, but they were not small people at all.

These three were the leaders of the Gray Elephants gang, and the one thing they had in common was the fact that they all wore strange-looking gloves on their hands. The one in the center wore gray gloves, while the other two wore red and blue.

The two color gang leaders stopped walking forward; the room was filled with over a hundred people, and unlike the color gangs, these were all real gangsters. One wrong word or move, and Buffin and Riv knew they were done for.

They were waiting for some type of order, and that was when the large leader in the center turned to the man on his left, who was wearing red gloves.

"Raven, we have guests, don't you think it's polite to put your phone away?" he asked.

"I'm sorry, I've been trying to get hold of my stupid brother. He said he would be here for this meeting but he's not answering," Raven replied. "I told him to stay away from the Chavley area, and he's one of those guys who's a phone addict, so usually he replies to me straightaway.

"Damn you, Hawk, what are you doing?"

CHAPTER 20

ONE WHO NEEDS NO INTRODUCTION

Raven knew that his brother had a tendency to be reckless and do stupid things, since he wasn't afraid of any consequences because of his older brother's position. However, he also knew the importance of not tarnishing the Gray Elephants gang's name.

He was supposed to keep his phone on him at all times, in case he was called for an important matter, like right now. What's more, Raven had informed Hawk beforehand and had stressed the importance of this meeting, so he had no idea what possible reason his brother might have had to turn his phone off.

In the end, he had no choice but to leave a voice message and hope for the best. He might be one of the leaders of the Gray Elephants, but that didn't give him the right to stop the meeting, especially since all three leaders would be present today. The young man swore to beat some sense into his younger brother later.

"We heard the reports; it seems you guys caused quite the stir." The one who was speaking to them all now was a man in his mid-thirties. His name was Brandon Trunk, and he was one of the three leaders said to have created the Gray Elephants. Their gang quickly rose to prominence because of their strength in hand-to-hand combat.

As for who was the strongest among the three, that was a question that didn't have to be asked. Although all three held the rank of leader, everyone knew that the real boss was Brandon. Some even speculated that the gang name had been chosen solely by him because of his last name.

"However, it looks like you didn't last as long as you assured us you would be able to. It's been a couple of hours, whereas I recall you promising me it would be easy enough to last until sunrise. I hope you have a good explanation for this?" Brandon looked at the two men. His tone didn't have a hint of aggression, yet in a way this scared Buffin and Riv even more.

The two color gang leaders gulped hard as Brandon waited for an explanation. They were clearly nervous for more than one reason. Both of them had been aware of how important their task was, and that it would have been the perfect opportunity to allow them to join the ranks of the Gray Elephants as high-ranking members.

In the first place, they held a higher position than the average Gray Elephants member. After all, they controlled their respective color gangs. Although the gangs were filled with teenagers and university students, there were still over a hundred people who listened to them.

The leader of a color gang needed to be strong, and they had to have a good eye. Many of them would also accept those who were known as loners. On such a leader's recommendation, it would be easy for someone to enter the Gray Elephants gang behind them.

It was an important job that couldn't just be given to anybody. However, these two had both been leaders of their respective color gangs for a long time. Completing their task today should have been easy enough, and life as a high-ranking member of a large gang like the Gray Elephants would mean riches beyond their wildest dreams.

"Working together with the red color gang, we were easily able to deal with the black color gang like you asked us to," Buffin explained. "We outnumbered them, but some of our newer members went a little too wild, which led to the Underdogs getting involved far quicker than we had anticipated."

Brandon stomped his foot on the top of the shipping container, a loud echoing bang. The two flinched at the sound.

"Is that so? Then how come the two of you look to be in perfect condition? Many of your subordinates, on the other hand, appear to have received quite a beating. From the looks of it, the moment you heard that the Underdogs came out, you decided to run. Surely, that is just a misconception on my part . . . right?"

Riv was worried. He had personally seen the power that the three men in front of him held. Just like the gray color gang, the red color gang used to be under another group like the Gray Elephants.

However, these three leaders alone had changed the whole situation and taken over the group. Riv knew there was no point fighting back, and as someone who was leading a color gang, he knew the smartest thing he could do was to join the strongest faction.

"I have reason to believe that the Underdogs were actually already out," Riv said. "They reacted too fast, like they were out before the attack. I'm not saying that there is a leak among us . . . but from what I've been told, they appeared to have already been out looking for someone! Those who were caught but let go reported that the Underdogs were asking around about someone with green hair, a young adult or teenager.

"I'm sure that this boy must be someone of great importance to them! They sent out the Cheetah Squad, and their leader Kirk Summerfield was there as well! That's why we had to come back earlier than planned."

"That's it? That's all you can tell me?" Brandon jumped down from the container and walked over toward the two of them. At the sound of his heavy footsteps, the two braced themselves for a beating.

"There was a gang war happening, yet those Underdogs were more interested in some random green-haired boy? How very peculiar," a voice sounded from the back. A man walked in, and when they saw him the other members were ready to attack. That was until they saw the marking on the back of his giant overcoat.

In an instant all of them stayed in place and kept their arms down. They didn't bow, as they had no reason to respect this person, but not a single one would dare to attack him. Riv, having turned his head slightly to see who could have stopped Brandon in his tracks, was utterly shocked.

He was a lean man with long red hair, tied up in a ponytail. He had a feminine-looking face, yet no one present would dare to point that out. After all, he had the emblem of a phoenix on his coat.

Sin Mutav was the leader of one of the top gangs in the entire country, the Phoenix gang. The Kings were well known among the gangs, because they ruled with an iron fist, and Sin was one of the more flashy leaders.

What is he doing here? Why would someone like him be in a town like Slough? This doesn't make any sense! Everyone who saw him was thinking the same thing.

As he walked into the room, the gang members noticed a burning look in Sin's eyes. They weren't sure if they were imagining it, but ever since he entered the room they had begun to feel as if it was getting hotter. They then realized, with each step, that the heat was actually coming from none other than this newcomer.

"Please, give me more time." Brandon stopped what he had been about to do and immediately got down on his knees to plead.

It was a strange scene. For the first time in their life they actually witnessed their almighty leader displaying fear in front of someone else.

Just how strong was this guy to make a man like Brandon act in such a manner?

CHAPTER 21

A GIFT

Sin was still standing about five feet away from the two color gang leaders. At first they believed that they were sweating because of nerves. Now, though, they could tell that their bodies were actually feeling hot because of the immense heat radiating from Sin.

How can someone produce so much heat? It looks like the ground around his feet is being seared a little . . . is that smoke? Riv thought. *It must be his Altered powers, but he's not even in his Altered form yet. Is such a thing even possible?*

Knowledge about the Altered was limited to what the public had seen broadcast on TV: competitions, celebrities, and so on. However, those at the very top were wise enough to keep the best DNA of the most powerful ancient beast to themselves.

Of course, their forms would remain a secret to the general public. If anything, one might be privy to some tales of their great feats, but even that would require a certain amount of influence.

Sin reached into his large overcoat, which looked to be three sizes too big for him, causing the two color gang leaders to flinch, but he merely brought out a cigarette. He placed it in his mouth, and Riv instantly reached into his pocket.

It was a custom between gang members to always have a lighter on them, purely to light cigarettes for members in a higher position.

So far Riv had wanted to suck up to Brandon, but right now might be the only opportunity for him to get in the good graces of a dragon, compared to a large fish.

As he stepped forward and reached out, though, Sin held up his hand, palm out, indicating for him to stop. The next second, like a magic trick, the cigarette lit on its own. The King took one large puff before proceeding to speak.

"Now, I'm wondering why you still haven't gotten what I asked you to get. Was the reward not enticing enough?" Sin asked, looking toward the two nervous color gang leaders.

"Do you really have to use these scraps to fight your battles for you? Why don't you just fight them yourself? Don't tell me I was wrong in asking the Gray Elephants to take up this job, because I hate being wrong!"

"No, of course you were right!" Brandon replied, a little flustered. Seeing Brandon nervous was making the other two leaders by his side nervous as well. "We will get it soon and will deliver it ASAP. It was just that we didn't expect the Underdogs to get involved so soon."

"I fail to see where the issue is. The Underdogs should be nothing more than a Tier 3 gang like yours. When I made a request I didn't expect it to take this long. Do I really need to explain to a gang leader that time is money? It wasn't exactly easy to appear here without the others noticing, so you better get what I need!" Sin said, walking forward past the color gang leaders. He looked down at the still-kneeling Brandon, then toward Raven, and lastly at the third leader by his side.

"Are you saying the Underdogs are stronger than you?" Sin asked.

"Yeah, right," the third leader chuckled. "If it weren't for Kirk, we would have just taken them over already. Do you expect most of us to die just because of your request? Then you might as well be the one to—"

Before he could finish his sentence, Sin grabbed him by the mouth, clenching it so hard he could no longer move it. Immediately the leader grabbed Sin's arm, trying to claw it off, but it wasn't working.

"Then I might as well be the one to kill you? Fine, I shall grant your wish, but I assure you it will be far more painful than any death those Underdogs would have given you!" Sin said, his eyes burning with passion.

Muffled screams emanated from the Gray Elephants leader. His legs kicked out, and his face appeared to be melting. Boils were appearing on his skin, large blisters popping by the second and gushing out blood.

All the Gray Elephants members had seen death before, and this held true for most of the color gang members as well, but none had seen anything as gruesome as the scene in front of them. The worst part of it all was that even now, with the leader's skin having practically melted, he remained alive, and boils were still appearing on his body all over, literal steam coming from his head.

It looked as if the man had been placed in some type of microwave, and eventually the struggling came to an end. The King just dropped him onto the floor before pulling out a handkerchief and wiping his hand with it, then throwing it onto the dead body.

"Now, does someone mind telling me who this Kirk fellow is?" Sin asked.

The others looked at the body on the ground. They couldn't even imagine the type of pain he must have suffered with this kind of death. The worst part of it all was the fact that a loyal and important member of their gang had just been killed in front of them, and they could do nothing about it.

It made them feel small and insignificant in comparison to the King.

"He was talking about the Underdogs' Altered," Brandon answered while watching the lifeless corpse. "They somehow scrounged enough money to have one of their men receive the Altered treatment. He's also very proficient and won one of those rookie tournaments not too long ago.

"He's the only real troublesome one of the group. It's not that we aren't confident we can't beat him, but it would cost us too many lives.

"I apologize, but I have to agree with what Yovan said. I don't wish to risk my whole gang for this whole mission. Not when we stand no chance of winning against them."

The other members were now worried for Brandon. After the way Sin had reacted to what the other leader said, they thought Sin would take him out next, but at the same time they respected him for at least saying that much.

The cigarette in Sin's mouth was nearly finished, and he spat it out on the floor and stomped on it, then reached into his coat pocket once more. They thought that perhaps he would pull out another one, but instead the King pulled out a small box.

Opening its lid, he took out one of two large syringes that were filled with a dark liquid. Strangely there appeared to be something moving inside it.

"That's it? Your only problem is that you lack an Altered? Well, I guess today's your lucky day, then. With this you will be able to match them. Now which one of you always wanted to be an Altered?" Sin asked with a sinister smile.

CHAPTER 22

PAYDAY

After hearing Sin's offer, the members couldn't help but excitedly talk among themselves about it. They couldn't believe that a King was actually offering them something so valuable. However, Brandon didn't seem to be nearly as pleased as his gang members. He looked at the strange syringe and the liquid moving inside.

I've never heard of someone becoming an Altered through a simple injection. Is this something that the Kings have developed? He must be planning to use us as lab rats, but I can't exactly decline.

"Thank you! With this great gift we will definitely give you the answers you are looking for!" Brandon promised as he grabbed the box with both hands, accepting it. With that, Sin left, but his short stay would forever be burned into their minds.

All of them could now attest that the Kings were dangerous and not to be messed with.

"What are you all waiting for? The meeting is dismissed!" Brandon shouted. He waited for the other members to leave. Some headed back out into the night, while others stayed in the warehouse, as they had been sleeping there, though they wouldn't disturb whatever it was Brandon wanted to do next.

As for the two color gang leaders, they were patiently waiting for their next order. They had been hoping for a promotion, but with everything that had happened, it seemed like they might be lucky to not get demoted now.

Brandon crouched down next to Yovan's body on the floor. He took a closer look, but there wasn't much to look at. He no longer looked like Brandon's friend with whom he had started the Gray Elephants.

"I'm sorry, my dear friend, but I won't even be able to get revenge for you. The least I can do is make sure you will receive a proper burial," Brandon said to the corpse.

"Who would have ever thought that the leader of the Phoenix gang himself would come all the way to a Tier 3 town, just for a job like this? I mean, if he's here anyway and the Underdogs gang has what he wants, why doesn't he just do it himself?" Raven complained. Now that Sin was gone, he could finally get all his frustrations out.

"It's probably because of the other Kings," Brandon answered. "You heard him say that he came here without the others noticing. Whatever he was doing, he clearly wants it to remain a secret from the others.

"That's the entire reason he came to us. I imagine if news spread that a King came down to a Tier 3 town, the others would come to investigate what he was doing here, and that seems to be bad news for him."

Raven scowled at this comment, because he knew it was true.

"Which means they're basically just using us in their little game of chess. I hate it! And what do you think of that syringe? I've never heard of Altered DNA being injected into someone before."

"Me neither." Brandon shrugged as he looked at the box. "However, who knows how much things have advanced in those Tier 1 cities. Still, I can't help but think that it doesn't make sense. If the stuff inside can really make us into Altered, then we could just sell it off for millions, which is far more than what he was going to pay us.

"He should know that as well, so I think it might be some new prototype. I don't know about you, but I don't want to be their guinea pig."

"But an Altered would help us on our side, and we can't just give it to someone who isn't loyal to the gang," Raven said.

Brandon handed Raven the box.

"You keep it for now. I'm not telling you to use it, but maybe you will find the right person who can. Perhaps that useless brother of yours might be a good choice. As for you two . . ." Brandon turned around.

"The color gangs lost a lot of people tonight. I know one of you was looking to get promoted, and as you can see, a very high position has just been opened. We have a lack of members, and I'm sure this beating that they received will be a wake-up call and a lot of them will decide to quit.

"Tomorrow, there's an underground fight happening. Both of you head there and look for some recruits. Raven will tag along with you."

"Thank you, boss!" the two of them said in sync, and they quickly got up to leave the place. They would remember this day for the rest of their lives.

The next morning Gary stretched as he woke up far earlier than usual. Ever since he had gotten the system, his nights had been very restless, yet now that the full moon had passed, he was finding it far easier to sleep . . . even despite everything that had happened just hours ago.

Too many things had happened, but only when he looked at his sister in the bed next to him did he realize how much would change now. He quickly got out of bed, planning to make her breakfast. With her injuries, as well as their area having suffered from the gang war, the school would surely understand the need for them to take a few days off.

The fridge is empty . . . and there are bills to be paid. However, it's just me and Amy until Mom wakes up. I will have to look after everything now, Gary realized as he opened the fridge only to find two measly pieces of bread.

There wasn't really much he could make with them, so he decided to just leave them for his sister, so Amy could enjoy them with some jam. Gary could always go out and find some food to replenish his Energy. Reaching into his pockets, he pulled out a wallet that wasn't his, and it reminded him of the events that had happened at the karaoke place.

He pulled out a twenty-dollar bill, and his hands hesitated. It just felt so wrong, using the money of the dead, like he was committing a crime stealing from them. They deserved to die—Gary could live with that—but this just felt criminal to him.

Why am I being stupid? Amy is the most important person right now, and she doesn't even have food, Gary thought, placing the bread and the money on the table.

Just as he was about to leave a note, he heard his sleepy sister wake up and head for the bathroom.

"What are you doing up so early?" Amy asked as she let out a yawn.

"Oh, I planned to make you some breakfast, but there's only bread and jam left," Gary answered, before he headed toward the door. "Don't worry, I left you some money to order some food, and I'll bring back some food tonight for us to eat. Oh, and I'll be back quite late tonight, so don't stay up waiting for me."

"What will you be doing?" Amy asked, now that she was a bit more awake. She still hadn't really worked through what had happened yesterday, and the last thing she wanted was to be alone in the empty apartment.

"Remember that money from the job I told you about? Mom won't be here for a while, but don't worry, Amy, I got things covered. Just rest for today, all right?" Gary said, leaving through the front door and closing it behind him.

He stopped for a few seconds as he suddenly heard Amy's crying from behind the door.

I'm sorry, Amy. I will look after us. I promise I'll make lots of money today so I won't have to leave you on your own. I hope that you can forgive me for lying to you.

Today was the big day, the day of his fight with Innu, and the debut of the Howlers.

CHAPTER 23

ONLY WORTH . . .

Since he had woken up so early, Gary was in no hurry to get to school. In the worst case, he could always use Charging Heart to get there faster, but even at his lackadaisical pace he would arrive with plenty of time to spare.

On his way, Gary checked out his stats. The first thing he noticed was that just as his system had promised him, he had gained 10 Exp for every Bond Mark he had placed on a person, for a total of 30 Exp.

When he shook Kai's hand, the system had asked him if he wanted to mark him. However, the "promise" they had made seemed a bit too weighty. He would have much more preferred something that he wouldn't have to worry about, like the promise he had made with his mother.

Although Gary had felt that he had gotten closer to Kai, there was still too much mystery surrounding the older student. Nevertheless, Gary truly did consider him a friend, yet he wasn't too sure about Kai's end goal. Aside from that, on the off chance Kai might break the promise, it would turn him into one of his hunting targets . . .

So he had decided against marking him.

There were actually more reasons for it, such as the fact that Gary's Mark skill only had five slots and four of them had already been occupied. Making a bond with Kai would have left him with zero. While 10 "free" Exp each day might seem nice, he had only recently enjoyed the benefits of hunting a target.

Whoever had attacked his mother, Gary was determined to hunt them down!

Unfortunately, he was now missing exactly that one little boost of Exp.

757/765 Exp

He would have to finish both of his Daily Quests to gain enough for a level-up. It was seriously bugging Gary, as much as it did when he saw someone leave an unread notification on their phone, the little red dot indicating that they had not yet read the message.

People who do that are crazy . . . I'll never understand them. If there were only a way for me to get a few Exp.

"What am I supposed to do now? I'm totally ruined! You police are completely useless!" Gary heard an angry man shout at two police officers.

As usual, Gary was wearing a hoodie, and he had it on even tighter than before. This was because of the fighting yesterday; he was afraid that the Underdogs might have sent out their members to patrol the area, but the police were there instead.

The police were being bombarded by not just one man. The entire area seemed to put the blame on them. They needed to shout their frustrations at someone, and some of them were scared while others looked to have been hurt in the chaos yesterday, not just his mother.

Just then he heard voices coming from an alley.

"What is wrong with them . . . I thought this area was okay because it was protected by the Underdogs. What the hell were they doing yesterday?"

"Come on, man, let's get out of here. The police are down there; if they see you in those colors they're going to arrest you! Heck, after yesterday you might get attacked on the street!"

The voice was only an angry whisper, but Gary's sensitive ears had picked it up. Heading toward the sound, he wondered who would be afraid of the police, and he could only think of a few people. It certainly wouldn't have been the Underdogs.

Quickly turning down the alleyway, he saw two teens getting rid of their clothes. One of them was midway to pulling off his sweater. It was gray in color, but not only that, there was blood on it as well.

"Hey, someone saw us! What do we do!" the one who was in the midst of changing asked.

"It's just a high school brat, let's just get out of here!" the other one answered.

When he saw the blood, something from yesterday clicked in Gary's head.

"Wait!" Gary shouted, but the two teens ran away from him. A few seconds later, they heard something strange; one of the teens turned around, and he couldn't believe his eyes. The kid wearing the hood was somehow gripped onto the side of the wall like Spider-Man.

Before they knew it he had leapt into the air, grabbed the two of them by the backs of their heads, and slammed them onto the ground. Their foreheads hit the concrete, bruising and grazing their skin.

"I told you to wait!" Gary shouted. "Why did you attack this place yesterday?"

Both of them were still dazed by what had just happened.

"Answer me!" Gary demanded as he slammed one of them down harder onto the ground.

"Stop, you'll kill him, you crazy bastard!" the gray color gang member shouted.

"Oh, so it's okay to hurt someone as long as it's not somebody you know, is that what you're saying?" Gary shouted again, and slammed the teen's head back onto the ground.

"I'll tell you anything you want, just please stop! Our gang's leader Buffin and the red color gang's Riv coordinated that attack.

We just followed the orders we got, all right? That's it, we know nothing else!"

The teen seemed to be telling the truth, but there was one more thing Gary had to ask.

"That blood on his shirt. Whose is it? And you better not lie to me." Gary looked him in the eyes.

Right now this teen was scared for his life. His friend had passed out with blood dripping down his face. One wrong word and he would be punished for it. He was unable to make up a lie, too afraid to risk it.

"It was . . . one of the shopkeepers."

Gary looked down for a second.

"You guys are only worth Exp," he muttered.

CHAPTER 24

SLIPPERS

Level 7
Exp: 32/882
Health: 100/100
Energy: 120/120
Strength 8
Dexterity 6
Endurance 14

Gary's mood had become a lot better after knocking those two guys out. Not only had he done a good deed, he had even been rewarded with a level-up. Although the system had once again only granted him a stat point to allocate without any new skill, it was nevertheless one level closer to Level 10.

Besides, his stats had upgraded immensely after his little incident, and unless Billy had killed more victims that the media had not reported, it looked like the teenager had vastly closed the gap between the two.

Billy's stayed quiet for a while, although who knows if he was doing the same thing as I was during that gang war. I still have no clue if he has a system like me or not, but at least I have two unassigned stat points. For now I'll save them until I need them.

Having consumed the bodies in the Kobe Karaoke Club, Gary didn't know if the additional stat points the system had granted him had been as random as the ones he got for killing his hunting targets, or if it depended on things like their blood type or perhaps his own composition.

Unfortunately, his gains had mostly come in the form of increased Endurance, which would do bupkis against Billy, who, at least from what he could remember, had been faster and stronger than him.

How's Endurance going to help me in a fight? Admit it, stupid system, you just wanna watch me get pummeled for longer, don't you?

Alas, the only way to figure out how the system worked would be to eat more bodies, and Gary didn't have any plans to do that in the foreseeable future. Seconds ago, he had thought about it again, but it was a dark road that he didn't want to go down.

Well, there was one person that he perhaps would consider, but for some reason his mark wasn't visible, indicating that he was too far away right now.

Eventually Gary arrived at school, and everything felt strange to him. He saw Innu and Tom sitting at their desks talking peacefully. Although everything that had happened to him just hours ago would be with him for the rest of his life, for the rest of the world it had been mostly a normal weekday.

"Are you okay, bro? You look a bit like death," Innu asked, a little worried. Unlike yesterday he had cooled down some, especially since he had enjoyed a good long rest, and it looked like Gary had not. "You know Kai told you to get some good sleep today, right?"

Judging from the way Innu was speaking, it didn't seem like Kai had told him anything about Gary's situation, which he was thankful for. After all, it wasn't their business and it was a problem that he needed to solve himself.

"Are you guys going somewhere today?" Tom asked. Previously he might have ignored these actions, but it was starting to get on his nerves a little. Ever since the day before yesterday, it had become apparent that Gary had some connection to Kai's group, yet he didn't admit it.

At the same time, after briefly hearing some news about Chavley, he wondered if Gary had done something—after all, it would explain his tiredness—but he also didn't think his best friend was stupid enough to get involved in that.

They had four more weeks to figure out how to avoid a repeat of the incident from two days ago. Gary didn't miss Tom staring at him, so he was left trying to come up with a reasonable excuse, but what could he say this time?

"Gambling," Gary answered in a hushed tone, once he made sure nobody else was paying attention to them. "I think you know that money is tight at my house. Kai was actually the one who recommended me to my last job, but . . . Since I still need money, I asked him if he had a way. That was actually why they were looking for me after the rugby match. Kai makes most of his money that way. He's going to be our 'in' person tonight.

"I'm sorry, Tom, I was sure you would want to come along, but I'm telling you now, you can't. Unlike me, you have good parents and you get good grades. I just don't want you to risk your future by tagging along.

"If anyone sees you, you could get in serious trouble, and I'm not talking about school. Just imagine what your parents would do if they found out their precious son was doing something as illegal as gambling! I mean, you've told me about the slippers, but I bet it would be a hundred times worse!"

Before Tom could reply, Gary put his head down on the desk, clearly indicating that he didn't want either of them to talk to him.

I nearly lost Amy yesterday, and I can't even speak to Mom anymore. No matter what, Tom, I'm not letting you get involved in any more of my mess than you already are.

The rest of the school day was as boring as always, with Gary seemingly ignoring everyone around him; he just wanted to get through the day. Even at lunch he stayed out of sight of the others, though that was mostly because he had climbed onto the school roof, where seagulls had built their nests. It had allowed him to catch them without anyone seeing him.

He ate them to build up his Energy, and he was also getting faster at tracking and hunting. The more he thought about it, the more he realized that he had become something akin to a wild beast.

After an uneventful rugby practice it was finally time. Gary left the school gates and headed to the gym. He had some time before he needed to meet up with the others anyway. After his workout, he changed into the black-and-gold-trim outfit that Kai had given him.

Then he ran to the park where he usually practiced with Innu, and he found the others waiting for him. Kai, Marie, and Innu were all dressed in the same color scheme, only Marie was wearing a skirt instead.

"Clothes really do make people. We finally are looking like a proper gang," Kai stated with a satisfied grin, and he pulled on his jacket a bit, straightening it out.

"Are you sure it's okay to be out like this? Won't the gangs pick a fight with us once they see us?" Gary asked.

"Aaahhh, I really need Marie to give you a crash course on how to behave like a proper gang leader." Kai let out a sigh as he disheveled his hair. "As of now, nobody even knows who the Howlers are. If anyone sees the five of us in matching clothes, they will just think that we're part of a volleyball team or something. Anyway, this time the place is a drive away, so . . ."

Kai pointed toward a car that was parked on the street. The window was rolled partway down, and inside the car the woman Gary had met yesterday was enjoying a cigarette.

"She'll take us there. It will be a bit of a squeeze in the back, but you'll just have to endure," Kai explained.

They all got inside, and Gary was pleased that even Innu didn't seem to know who this woman was, though he noticed something strange. All the boys were sitting in the back, whereas Marie sat in the front.

Well, I guess it's a bit rude to make a girl sit in between two boys. Kai's quite the gentleman . . . or is he just that much of a ladies' man? Gary wondered.

The woman started driving, and eventually she attempted to make some light conversation to clear the awkward air.

"I'm happy to see you have made so many friends. So how was school, pumpkin?"

It was clearly a nickname for one of those in the car, but Gary thought *pumpkin* was a little too cute for Kai.

"The usual, boring and not really worth it. Can we just turn on the radio and drive in silence, Mom?" Marie requested, clearly in no mood for conversation.

"Mom?" Innu shouted out in shock, which was exactly the reaction Gary had, yet he managed to keep it in. Right now there were countless thoughts going through his head. He had been wondering what the relationship was between Kai and this woman, for the two of them to appear that late at a hospital.

He would have been far less surprised to learn that she was Kai's mother, but Marie's mother? Well, the resemblance was there, but how did she fit into all of this?

Was she part of a gang? Was she part of the Underdogs? She clearly seemed to know where they were going!

A slight panic was setting in as Gary started to suspect that all of this might be a huge trap!

CHAPTER 25

A LITTLE TEST

Gary started looking out the window to see where they were and how fast the car was moving. He tried to decide whether he would survive jumping out of a moving vehicle.

Maybe increased Endurance is good for something after all. If I double it through Charging Heart, it shouldn't hurt too much . . . right?

I can't let them take me to the Underdogs gang! Without the package, Damion will make mincemeat out of me! This system might make me stronger than an average human, but Kirk is still an Altered!

At that moment, Kai noticed that Gary was acting strangely and looked at him, shaking his head.

"What's got your panties in a twist? If you're worried, there's no need. Marie will stay with me, and her mother won't stick around. She is actually a big part of our plan going forward; for now, just think of her as a sponsor.

"Now, if you're starting to get nervous, how about you catch up on some sleep? I can't blame you for not getting enough after what happened, but we'll need you in tip-top shape for your match. As long as everything goes well, this one event will kick-start our whole gang," Kai explained, before he leaned in to whisper.

"I borrowed some money to use for betting on you. As long as you win, you won't have to worry about your mother's hospital bills for the next few months."

Gary realized he might have been panicking for no reason. Still, one day, he would very much like an answer from Kai as to why Marie and her mother were both helping him out so much.

The sun was starting to set, and speeding on the streets on a motorbike with no helmet was a certain high school student who had used far too much gel in his hair. Even with the wind blowing it back, it was staying put with only slight movement.

This place is a little far and I don't even know why I'm trying so hard to get there, but that guy just rubs me the wrong way for some reason, Austin thought as he twisted the throttle to speed up. Of course Austin was riding illegally, but he didn't care; it wasn't as if someone would ask him for a driver's license where he was going.

Eventually, following the instructions on his phone, he reached his destination. It looked like a giant park in the middle of the woods. At the entrance was a large sign with the center's name, and beyond the sign were large fields of open grass. It was clearly a place where people went camping, so he wondered why he had been sent here.

Fortunately, another car was just pulling up, entering the park. With nothing better to do, Austin followed along on his bike as the car drove directly on the grass, and it looked like something had been temporarily set up on the field.

It resembled a makeshift boxing ring, made from hay bales of all things.

Several cars were also stationed on the outside area, and hundreds of people were present. Since there were too many people up ahead, Austin had decided to park his bike a little farther away and off the green.

All this nice grass and they're ruining it, he thought, but the car ahead of him stopped in a similar place. When he saw who exited the vehicle, Austin was surprised to recognize them.

It was two men, one dressed in red and the other in gray.

The color gang leaders . . . if they're here, is this one of those "underground" fights? Austin thought. The two figures seemed to be busy arguing with each other. It was strange to see two leaders of a color gang together, yet Austin had heard some of the rumors of what had happened yesterday, and if these men had come here, the rumors might very well be true.

Not paying any attention as they argued, the two didn't even notice that they were on a head-on collision course for Austin. They walked right into him, yet the loner stayed firm and even stopped them from going any further.

"Hey, what the hell?" Riv complained, looking at the muscular student in front of him. "What are you doing just standing there? Get out of the frigging way!"

The red color gang leader wasn't satisfied with a verbal warning alone, though, so he threw a fist, but Austin moved his head out of the way, easily avoiding the punch. However, he didn't expect the other color gang leader to attack him as well. But before he reached Austin, his hand was stopped by someone behind him.

"What the hell do you two think you're doing?" Raven asked sternly. "Don't tell me you aren't aware of the rules at these types of places! We've come here with a purpose and I have no desire to babysit the two of you!"

Riv was about to complain, but Raven was holding two fists. One was Buffin's, and the other was Austin's—which was about to connect with the gray leader's ribs. It looked like the stranger was just as fast as the color gang leader.

"I apologize for these two knuckleheads. Let's all just enjoy today's fights." And with that, Raven let go of Austin's hand. The loner decided to let go, though his main reason was that he didn't think he could take three people on his own. Not in a place like this, where he hardly knew anyone.

What's more, Raven had managed to catch his fist. Austin took pride in his strength, so it had come as a real surprise to him.

Most of the guys here are dropouts and there aren't really a lot of adults around here. He must be someone really important if two color gang leaders are actually listening to him, Austin thought.

At the same time, Raven was impressed by Austin's performance.

That kid doesn't seem to be affiliated with anyone. Not only was he fast, but his punch was quite heavy as well. If only those two idiots hadn't attacked him. Oh well, it can't hurt to make him an offer later. Worst case, he refuses.

Now, I still need to find someone to use this solution on. Hawk might be a bit of a useless dolt, but he's still my brother . . . just where the hell has that bastard disappeared to? I don't want to use any of our gang members as guinea pigs, so it would be best if I could find someone promising.

Should I just make one of these two idiots take it? No, they were there when we had our conversation earlier . . . Isn't there someone strong but gullible here? Raven looked around, but aside from Austin no one else caught his attention.

If only I knew for sure that whatever's inside these syringes works without any side effects, I would just use one myself . . . Hmmm, maybe that's not such a bad idea. But first I will need to test it out. It would certainly cause quite the stir . . .

If it can really make anyone into an Altered, then I might actually be able to get revenge on that bastard for what he did to Yoven!

CHAPTER 26

PLACE YOUR BETS

"Ladies and gentlemen, the first fight of the evening will soon begin!" the host shouted, and two large speakers echoed the announcement out to everyone, allowing them all to easily hear. "The board to my right has all of tonight's fights and betting odds! You will now have a few more minutes to place your bets on the first fight! We accept cold cash and digital currency only!"

The crowd looked intensely at the gang names and started talking with each other. They were seeing if anyone had heard of them or seen them fight before. Gathering information would give them the best chance of making the winning bet.

Austin was a little familiar with how these events worked, even though he had never been to one. The only thing he really cared about was being the strongest fighter. He had already become top dog at his own school, so he had been planning to challenge those in the surrounding areas.

Although he didn't want to get involved in real gangs for now, he still felt like he was in the middle of a crossroads. Looking at the board, he searched for a name he might be familiar with, but it only displayed the group names, not those of any individual fighters. He had never heard of any of them, making him believe that they must be from either small-time gangs or those trying to establish one. Nevertheless, there was one name he did recognize.

Eton High? Is someone actually crazy enough to use their school name for such an event? . . . Well, if they're really from that school, perhaps it shouldn't be surprising. They've got an even nastier reputation than my own school. The guys have also run into them a couple of times, and I remember them saying they were a bunch of tough bastards. Come to think of it, maybe I should participate in one of these as well. Might be a good way to spread the school's reputation. A shortcut to make it to the top and then . . .

"Well, well, well, looks like my sales pitch was enough to get you to come here after all." Austin heard a teasing voice behind him. Although he had only heard it once, it had been memorable enough to make the teenager clench his teeth almost instantly.

He turned around to see Kai with his trademark grin on his face, though this time he was accompanied by a black-haired girl Austin didn't know. Judging from their matching outfits they were clearly together, though.

That chick definitely looks out of place, but him . . . I still don't know if he's one of us or just some bored rich kid. I mean, can he even fight? Austin thought as he looked at the older teenager. It was difficult for him to get a grasp on who or what Kai was. He didn't seem to be yet another delinquent, one whose future seemed predestined to be tied to some gang, yet at the same time, he did have a dangerous aura around him.

Just what would happen if someone decided to attack him?

"Why did you invite me here? I fail to see what part of this whole event is supposed to give me a better future, unless you wanted me here to either bet on these outcomes or turn me into a fighter," Austin said. "But let me make something clear to you, I would never listen to someone I could beat in a fight."

"Well, I suppose if you bet on the right fighter you could strike it rich today, which would lead to a better future for you, but that's not why I called you here. If you recall, I promised to show you something very interesting.

"That green-haired kid who saved your ass is actually here as well. Right now, he's placing his own bets, but you'll see him sooner than you might think. After that, we can still talk about your better future," Kai replied.

"That's it? In essence, you invited me to watch a match? I think that's kind of stupid." Austin was about to walk away, at least from Kai. He had driven all the way out here, so he would at least stay long enough to watch the fight, yet talking with the bleached-blond teenager just pissed him off. However, Austin knew better than to start a fight at such an event.

"But you're interested in him, right? I mean, why else would you have come here? We'll talk after the fight and if you want to make some cash, place a bet on the Howlers!" Kai shouted after him, yet Austin just kept walking until he found himself at the front of the crowd, with a better view of the fights that were going to take place.

I had a plan in mind to take over all the nearby schools . . . and from there I would continue on, but for some reason his words that day . . . I can't get them out of my head! What was I planning to do afterward?

This was the real reason why Austin was so annoyed with Kai: because deep down he knew the older boy was right. Austin didn't have a plan beyond that, and part of him knew that even if he took over all the schools, once he graduated it would amount to nothing. However, he didn't want to join any gangs either.

Just when he was considering whether he should follow Kai's tip and put some money on that team, he heard a ringing sound.

"The betting period has officially come to a close for the first bout!" the announcer stated. He was a bald man with sunglasses and a sleeveless shirt. Given the temperature outside at this late hour, he must have felt cold, yet he looked menacing enough to simply endure it.

"Don't worry, ladies and gentlemen, after the first fight has finished, a new round of betting will continue for the subsequent fights, but let's not waste any more time and give you what you've all come for!"

CHAPTER 27

A FAMILIAR FACE

The fight was about to begin and the crowd cheered in response, some toasting with the alcohol they had either brought or bought here, while others took harder drugs, even though most of them were clearly underage. However, nobody really cared; the ones selling were just happy to make their profit.

Others looked more serious and refrained from taking any substances. Those were the scouts sent out by bigger gangs, looking to recruit some promising new members.

"Today's event is a little special, as we are going to have several tag team matches. First up we have Team Eton High. A school known to have no leaders, with things so bad that even the teachers had already given up on their students, until these two came in and changed *everything*.

"Please give a big round of applause for the Vicious Twins!"

The announcer really knew how to get the crowd excited, and they immediately made room for the two fighters, who ran through and entered the stage by doing a flip over the hay bales. They were dressed in dark red with straps along their arms, and on their clothes were images of two snakes. One of them had short red hair, and the other had long red hair.

"Hey, those guys are . . . it's those two from the rugby match!" Marie pointed out, having recognized Sren and Leng.

"I expected something like this to happen when I heard the rumors." Kai seemed far less surprised to see them here. "These guys aren't just normal students. After hearing about what happened to our Westbridge team, I decided to look into them more. There aren't many who can do what they did to all of our school's regular rugby players."

Marie nodded along, clearly wanting to know more.

"Well, it all starts with why they filmed that entire rugby match. After all, why would they want to film a match if their usual winning strategy is to take out their opponent's ace players, especially seeing that they had gone the extra mile against us?

"To give credit where credit's due, you gotta admire them for brazenly setting up a betting gig and then livestreaming the entire event. From what I found out they have quite the following, so they must have made a lot of cash that way.

"Their scheme seems to revolve around offering a large payout in case the opposing team wins, enticing people to bet on them winning. They give good odds to the other side. Now you understand why whoever they go against finds themselves injured before the big day. That was until a certain team forced them into a draw.

"If anyone actually bet on a draw that day, the payout they had to make must have been huge, and I'm sure them not winning has majorly pissed off their regulars, who would usually bet on them as the safe choice. The things they have been doing, they're not just normal high school thugs."

Hearing this, Marie was a bit worried; she had seen how fast and agile the twins had been during the rugby match, and their flashy entrance was further proving that fact. However, Kai seemed to really trust in Gary and Innu, as he had bet a lot of money on them winning . . . money he had "borrowed" from the Underdogs, from what he had told her.

That kid . . . I don't even know where he got that money from, yet this time he's willing to bet it all on himself, Kai thought. *Someone who lacks skills and confidence is going far to protect what's important to him. I'm really looking forward to this, Gary. If my intuition is correct, it will be something none of us will ever forget . . . the fight of a desperate person.*

"Next, let's welcome their opponents. For the first time registering, making this the debut of their gang, we have the Howw-wlllerrrs!"

From the other side, Innu stepped from between the hay bales into the ring. His sleeveless black-and-gold uniform showed off his muscles and the scars on his shoulders. His hands were wrapped up as usual, and since he wasn't exactly new to fighting in these events, he received quite a reception from the people who recognized him.

"That guy's Innu the Warrior? Looks like he finally joined a gang, but with how skilled he is, why do you think he would join such a no-name gang? I'm sure he could have gotten into one of the more prominent ones," a teenager said to his buddy.

"Beats me, I just know he always refused those offers. Maybe none of them were good enough for him, so maybe he became fed up and just created his own gang? Well, let's just see who his partner is. If those Howlers are powerful, it wouldn't be the worst idea to join. Being a founding member sure beats having to kiss ass to rise up the ranks," his buddy replied with a shrug.

Following Innu in his black-and-gold jacket was Gary. However, his entrance was a bit problematic, as he had to push one of Innu's fans to the side to even get in. The crowd broke out in murmurs as he climbed over the hay bales, revealing his small frame and then eventually his green hair.

"Hey, I know that guy! He's that newbie who beat up Billy Buster! Green Mutt! . . . or was it Green Dog?" the first teen said, as he had been there that day.

As Gary stood up, everyone saw his face, and several people were shocked; most shocked of all were two adults who had come to the match in disguise.

"Correct me if I'm wrong, but isn't that green-haired kid the one we spotted snooping around Billy Bruntin's home that day?" Frank whispered to his partner.

Sadie nodded with a satisfied smile. At the time, they had believed Gary when he said he was just a curious kid, but seeing him here, they realized that White Rose might have possibly found someone who would be able to help them solve this Altered murder case.

She didn't know why, but the wound on her leg felt like it was pulsating. It had taken a little longer to heal compared to her other wounds, but she just took it as a sign from above that they were on to something.

CHAPTER 28

DON'T BE A FOOL

The two White Rose agents were currently undercover, following a lead to track down the missing student and suspected Altered murderer that had brought them here, to an underground fighting ring. The police had apprehended someone who had testified that Billy Bruntin had been participating in these events under the stage name of Billy Buster.

Unfortunately, the venues where these events took place were constantly changing. Even going to the place where Billy Buster had last appeared had given them no results. It looked as if some professionals had come and cleaned up the place pretty well. Whoever was in charge of organizing these things knew what they were doing.

It had taken them quite a while, but they had eventually been given a location and were hoping that they would find someone who might know Billy. If possible they hoped to learn what had happened to him on the day his parents died, if not before.

Of course, they had to stay undercover to gather information. Luckily, nobody really cared about who was who at this type of event, as long as they didn't create a scene. Even though the two agents were well aware that everything that was going on was illegal, this wasn't the time for them to act, nor was it their concern.

The police would have to take care of this, while Sadie and Frank were merely responsible for dealing with Altered. If they were to try to catch every single gang member, their job would never end, and they knew they needed to be professional and concern themselves only with Altered cases, like the one they were currently on.

But they had never expected to see someone that neither of them would forget. However, after checking Westbridge's school register and finding that the high school did indeed have a student by the name of Gary Dem, they had stopped bothering with him. Since he hadn't lied about that part, they had chosen to believe him about just having been there.

That kid told us he didn't know who Billy was, yet now he not only comes to this type of event but is even actively participating in it. If he just happened to start fighting, this would be the biggest coincidence in the world. Whatever the case, he'll have some serious explaining to do, Sadie thought. *He knows something about Billy that he's kept hidden from us, I just know it!*

"If we approach him here he might run off and alarm those around us. Let's not risk blowing our cover and just continue watching for now. We've already checked in with his school, so we can always find him later," Frank suggested, and Sadie was inclined to agree.

Why trouble themselves trying to catch him in this mess, when they knew where he would be five days of the week. Sadie was seriously looking forward to finding out why that Gary kid lied to them. Was he covering for Billy, or were the two of them related in some other way?

So that guy didn't lie about the green kid being here. Didn't think I would see that loner Innu here as well, but those two against those Eton High guys I heard so much about . . . well, this should indeed be interesting. That guy didn't overpromise in that regard.

I never did get to test out how strong either one of them is, so let's see what they've got.

As Gary stood there looking at their opponents, he was very thankful. He wanted to believe he was better than the average bully. So far, he had mostly fought against gang members, and knowing what they did he had little to no sympathy for them.

However, just fighting for the sake of fighting wasn't something Gary was used to. Even in his official fight against Billy and Steven, he had had his reasons. In the former case, he fought because he needed the money, and Kai had sorta forced him into it. In the latter case, he had believed that fighting was a quick way to gain Exp, and his system had even sweetened the deal by issuing him a quest.

Of course, seeing the smug faces of the twins in front of him, Gary was more than happy to repay them for what they had done to Tom during the rugby match.

"What a nice surprise, not only are our opponents a couple of weaklings, but we'll even get the chance for some payback on that onion head." Sren sneered as he looked down on the green-haired teenager. He was still pissed about how much money they had lost because the game had ended in a draw. He had even considered finding a way to make Gary and Blake pay up the money.

"If you think I'm the same as in that rugby match, you're in for a surprise!" Gary replied confidently. "This time there won't be a referee to save you once I have you pinned down. I haven't forgotten what you bastards did to my best friend!"

As for Innu and Leng, they just looked at each other without saying a word, both aware that their fists could do all the talking for them in a moment. Both teams took their positions, with Innu and Gary standing on one side, while the twins stood opposite them.

"All right guys, you know the rules! Let's get ready to *rumble!*" The announcer started the match with a gong.

New Quest received
Honorable Fight 2.0!
Many people are watching, so don't make a fool out of yourself.
Win the match!
Condition: Knock out or kill your opponents

Reward: 500 Exp
Failure: ???

Considering how the two color gang members today had only been worth 20 Exp each, it seemed like the match would be a hard one.

CHAPTER 29

AN EXPERIMENT

Gary had decided that he wouldn't use Charging Heart right off the bat but keep it as a game-changer. His stats had vastly improved since yesterday and his "fight" this morning had been more of a beatdown, so he wanted to use this opportunity to check how much he had grown. It would also allow him to attempt to learn how to control his heart rate without having to spend his Energy.

Still, there was one thing that he didn't have that he did have before, and that was the power of the moon. Even with Charging Heart he had been having trouble catching up to the twins and had needed to focus on his Strength.

The twins immediately started to run toward him and Innu, and they were just as fast as Gary remembered.

"Green Fang!" Innu shouted, making sure to use his stage name. Quickly coming over to his side, Gary placed his back against Innu. To be honest, they hadn't focused on teamwork during their training session. The time they had spent training had been too short to realistically get used to fighting together, especially since they fought in different ways.

So they had concluded that their best shot at winning a tag team match would be to force their opponents into one-on-one fights.

———

Sren was the first to attack by stepping to the side and throwing a kick, but Innu easily blocked it with his arm. The attack wasn't too heavy, but it stung a bit as the kick had been fast and sharp. Looking straight ahead, though, he had lost sight of the short-haired teenager. Or so he thought.

Sren was holding on to his brother's arm and was swinging his brother's body; he was kicking mostly so he could balance better. There was a reason why it was light; with the momentum, the kick from Leng went around Innu, heading toward Gary's stomach. It was too quick for him to block, but he was able to tense his stomach before it connected. As a result, it didn't wind him, but it still hurt.

−4 HP

The kick was strong, and many people in the crowd saw that it should have been quite a heavy blow; they were not surprised that Green Fang fell to the ground.

Hahaha, seems like I was wrong, having a high Endurance stat isn't that bad! Gary thought, as he went to grab Leng's leg before he could pull it back, but just like in the rugby match, they were far too fast and slippery for him.

Yeah, looks like there's no need to worry about Gary, he can take hits better than a punching bag, so I'll just focus on doing my part! Innu decided, attempting to grab Sren's head, but Sren pulled back just in time to avoid the grab; Innu's fingertips had missed Sren's face by an inch, and then Sren quickly leaned forward and ran ahead.

Innu braced himself again, planning to knee his opponent with good timing, but nothing came his way, because Sren had gone behind him and was aiming once more at Innu's partner. This time the punch came toward Gary's face; he managed to block it just in time, but then another blow hit him in the ribs again.

−2 HP

He blocked that hit, but suddenly he was being pummeled from two sides. Eventually, not really knowing what to block, Gary was being hit more than he should.

–2 HP
–3 HP
–2 HP

Crap, even with all this Endurance I can't do anything unless I catch him. Do I really need to use Charging Heart so soon?

Whenever Innu tried to help, their opponents would split up and run away. It was a hit-and-run tactic, with Gary as their target. If Innu tried to chase after one of them, he just tired himself out running around the ring. He was quite good at trapping his opponent in a corner if it was a one-on-one, but this match wasn't.

Unfortunately their tactic was proving to be quite effective.

Come on, Gary, I'm going to have to rely on you for this one! Innu thought.

Gary was concentrating hard, focusing on the twins' movements. They were running across each other and had split him and Innu up. If Gary tried to get close to his partner, they would just come in between and attack. He knew that he was the only one who could break through this vicious cycle.

They can't be that much faster than me, right? I know my Dexterity is low, but it shouldn't be impossible to catch them!

Since the attacks were hurting him only a little, he gave up on trying to block them; instead he was trying to find a pattern or something that would allow him to exploit them.

They kicked his thighs and his sides, and the only thing Gary had done was turtle up, using his arms to block his face while staring through a small gap. Seeing this, the crowd started to boo loudly. After all, to them it looked like Green Fang was doing nothing but just standing there and taking the beating.

Whatever, do you think I care about you people? The only thing I care about is beating them and earning my rewards!

Finally, Gary noticed something that might help him turn things around. He brought his hands down, but one of the twins was already there to punish that action.

"You're just a sitting turtle who will eventually fall!" Sren taunted him as he threw a punch to Gary's face, flinging his head slightly to the side.

−4 HP

"You guys . . . are just like those annoying squirrels." Gary smiled as he looked at Sren, and for some reason his smile caused the hair on Sren's arms to stand up.

So they've decided to target him, Austin concluded as he watched the match. *His punches might be powerful but that doesn't mean much if they don't connect. On the other hand, it looks like Innu can't use his techniques because of them running all over the place. This seems like a bad match; good thing I didn't bet on it.*

Hmmm, but that guy came looking for me . . . Did he just overestimate these two? And why does it seem like the green-haired kid is far slower than on the roof?

Unbeknownst to him, someone was slowly approaching Austin from behind. He was unfortunately so engrossed in the fight that he was unaware of it.

You look to be the most remarkable person around, and we don't exactly know what this will do, so I'm just going to test a little bit on you and see what happens, Raven thought as he pulled out a syringe.

CHAPTER 30

SCREW THIS

When Sin handed them the box with the syringes, he had told them nothing about how to use them: whether to inject all of the liquid into one person or if it was supposed to be used multiple times. None of the gang members present had ever heard about a syringe with a liquid being used to turn someone into an Altered.

So the first thing Raven wanted to do was test out how effective just a little bit of the unknown substance was by injecting a stranger. After the earlier exchange he had a good estimate of Austin's power, so he considered him the perfect test subject. This way, he could gauge for himself how much more powerful Austin was after the injection.

He slowly crept his way up to Austin. It was pretty crowded but not so packed that moving was impossible. Fortunately, everyone's attention was still on the first fight.

Now! Raven thought, thrusting the needle forward . . . only for someone to grab him by the wrist at the last second.

"What do you think you're doing?" a voice asked him.

Hearing someone close behind him, Austin turned around to see that Kai had grabbed the wrist of a man who held a large syringe . . . aimed at him. Looking up, he recognized the person holding it.

"What the fuck did you just try to do?" Austin was beyond mad. He had just bumped into Raven's two goons, but was that really a reason to drug him?

Not wanting to lose the precious syringe, Raven threw a kick toward the teenager holding on to him. Kai jumped back to evade it but let go of Raven in the process.

"Why don't you let us take a look at what's in your hands?" Kai asked, having noticed that Raven clearly seemed to value the syringe. Whatever was inside looked strange to him, and using such a thing in a place like this, especially at a time like this, clearly wasn't good.

Austin was lucky that Kai had kept an eye out for him, curious to see how he would react to Gary's fight. That was when he had spotted Raven getting closer and closer.

"I'm going to pound your head in!" Austin shouted, yet Buffin and Riv hadn't been too far away and were now standing by the Gray Elephants leader's side. It looked like a fight might take place outside the ring as well as inside.

Damn it, those two are with him. They're quite strong, and if it's three against one . . . actually, that guy avoided his kick from earlier. I guess he actually is a fighter after all. Maybe with him—

"Ohhh!" The crowd suddenly cheered loudly as something happened in the fight. Instinctively Kai and Austin turned around for a second, yet when they looked back they could only see that the trio had disappeared into the crowd.

With the small problem dealt with, they preferred to concentrate on the match to see what could have happened, and to their surprise, they saw Gary on the ground with his nose bleeding.

Gary thought that he had figured it out. The problem with the twins wasn't just that they were too fast. No, they were behaving like the annoying squirrels that he had tried to catch in the forest. They were agile and nimble, but most of all, they were flexible.

A few times while getting hit, Gary had tried to throw a few punches of his own, but the twins had easily avoided them, only to retaliate with more. At the same time, a kick or punch seemed like it was going straight ahead, but then it would suddenly change direction.

This was true even for their running movements, constantly changing direction. Now, thinking about them as if they were the animals that Gary regularly hunted, he could keep track of them. The next problem was to catch them.

Just then, Gary let a punch go right through, hitting him in the face, and he knew what to do next. His Health hadn't gotten too low yet, and with his high Endurance he could afford to get hit. Quickly Sren pulled his arm out, and just like he had been doing this the whole time, he moved it left and right, making it hard to see exactly where it would go.

For the first time, Gary managed to grab it with one hand, gripping it as hard as possible.

"I've been waiting to do this all day!" Gary shouted, throwing a punch of his own, holding on to the twin so it was impossible for him to retaliate. Unfortunately, Gary had overlooked the fact that there were more fighters to this match than the two of them.

Just when he was about to get a good hit in, a leg came toward his face. With Gary propelled forward and Leng's leg coming toward him, the impact was twice as hard, and Gary's head flung back with blood flying through the air as he fell to the ground.

−10 HP
44/100 HP

Despite Gary's strong Endurance, his Health had now dropped to half.

"What are you doing, Innu?" Gary shouted in frustration. "I finally got one of them, and then the other one hits me. Didn't we agree that each of us would occupy one?"

Innu was standing by the side, watching the fight like a spectator. He had been waiting to join in, but just like Sren he hadn't expected Gary to catch the twin's fist. When the chance had finally come, he had blanked out, forgetting that he was actually also a fighter in this match, allowing Leng to save his brother.

"Let's stop playing around and get rid of this onion head. It looks like we've hurt him enough!" Leng said as he went to stomp on Gary's stomach. But Gary managed to roll away, avoiding the blow before quickly jumping to his feet.

"Screw this!" Gary shouted.

Sren charged forward again, clearly being the more aggressive of the two brothers. He went for a kick again, moving far faster than any of his previous attacks.

Don't tell me they've seriously been holding back against Gary? Innu thought, surprised. However, this time he was ready to help in the fight. He just hoped it wasn't too late.

The kick went toward Gary's head, and the spectators expected Gary to go down . . . but Gary caught the leg with a single hand. His body didn't recoil, and Sren stood still like a statue.

I don't give a crap about getting better anymore. I'm just going to win this fight!

Skill activated: Charging Heart
All stats have temporarily been doubled
−10 Energy

Pulling Sren forward by his leg, he threw him off balance. Next, Gary threw a fist, faster than any he had thrown before. He planted it right in his opponent's face, and Sren's body flew back several feet and fell to the ground.

CHAPTER 31

AN UPGRADE

Unlike a few moments ago when Gary had fallen, the crowd went silent for a few seconds. It had been obvious that the Vicious Twins were winning the fight so far. The whole fight had been pretty one-sided in favor of Team Eton High. Gary had been too slow to react, and nearly everyone believed that it would only be a matter of time before the Howlers lost.

So this sudden turnaround came pretty much out of the blue.

They had never seen anything like it before. The twins had done their best to remain elusive throughout the fight, so how did the green-haired teenager suddenly manage to catch what looked like the fastest kick of the entire match?

Goddamn, this hurts! What the hell are his fists made of? Sren cursed internally, rubbing his face but quickly getting up off the ground. *His grip strength is the real thing; I couldn't move my leg at all.*

Then Sren remembered something. During the rugby match, Gary had also shown great feats of strength. Since the fight so far had been going their way, they had completely forgotten that this green-haired teenager was far stronger than he seemed to be.

"Innu, take out the short-haired one!" Gary ordered. "I need to punch the other one!"

"What, so now I'm just here to pick up your scraps?" Innu shout-ed, yet he quickly got in front of Sren.

For the first time, thanks to Gary's hit, the two brothers were quite far apart, something the Howlers intended to put to good use.

Finally getting a hit in just felt good to Gary, especially after the beating he'd suffered at the hands and feet of the twins. He just wanted to win the fight now; getting better would have to wait for another time.

With Charging Heart active and a lot of Energy to spare, Gary rushed over to the long-haired brother, Leng. His speed surprised everyone but him, but when Gary threw a kick, the twin leaned back, avoiding it just by a few inches.

Gary's body flipped over, as he had too much strength in his kick; his back was now facing Leng. Seeing this, the fighter quickly punched him, picking a painful spot just under the ribs.

Usually when Leng made such an attack, his opponent would at least flinch slightly, but not this time. Gary swung around, trying to get Leng with the back of his fist. Unfortunately, the twin ducked and took a few steps back, wondering what was going on.

–1 HP

It's my own fault for taking this whole "honorable fight" thing so seriously! Gary chided himself. *I should have just used Charging Heart since the beginning to double my stats. With 28 effective points of Endurance, their attacks barely hurt!*

Now that Gary knew he could take dozens of hits before having to worry, he started to swing his punches and kicks quite widely. Without any technique behind Gary's attack, Leng had a relatively easy time avoiding them, and once in a while he found an opening to attack Gary.

–1 HP
–1 HP

What's going on, Gary? Did all that adrenaline rush to your head, making you forget everything I taught you? Why are you swinging like that? Innu thought as he watched Gary from the corner of his eye. Unfortunately, he had his own problem to deal with.

Innu had avoided the attacks but backed Sren up against the corner of the hay bales. Whenever Sren tried to escape or run to the side, Innu repositioned himself so he couldn't get out.

Sren tried one more time, and this time Innu swept his leg against the ground, kicking up the dirt into Sren's eyes. As Sren charged in, his fist connected with Innu's chest, yet Innu pushed forward, not letting Sren's arm fully extend, weakening its power slightly.

At that moment, Innu went for the grab and locked his arms behind Sren's neck.

"Now I've caught you. This whole thing is done," Innu announced.

With both fights at a critical point, many of the spectators didn't know where to look. As for the two White Rose agents, they hadn't taken their eyes off Gary for even a moment.

"You noticed it too, right?" Frank asked.

"Of course I noticed it. His speed, the look on his face, everything is different from before," Sadie replied. "It doesn't make sense. That Gary kid was clearly having a difficult time, and if he was holding back, then he's the best actor I've ever seen."

Others might be confused about his sudden change, yet since Frank and Sadie were both Altered, their eyes were more perceptive, and working in the police force, they knew how to watch for things like this.

In this fight, just like with the rugby game, I can't catch them even with Charging Heart. Yeah, sure, my Endurance is great, but eventually, even Leng will beat me, Gary thought.

He was starting to suspect that Leng might actually be the faster of the brothers, or that the only reason he had caught Sren had been the surprise effect.

Wait a second, surprise? Gary suddenly got an idea.

He threw a punch again and Leng moved to the side, narrowly avoiding it and striking back, hitting him on the shoulder. Gary then swung out a kick, and the twin stepped back, avoiding that as well and retaliating with a kick of his own.

I was right; the way these guys attack, they're fighting me at my own speed. So much so that Leng has been avoiding me just enough to attack back at the perfect time. Otherwise, even he would be too slow to hit me. Damn . . . I hate to admit it, but these guys are seriously good if he is avoiding me narrowly on purpose.

Gary was right about that. The twins could theoretically move faster than they were moving now, yet their style seemed to be to match their opponent's speed and then win by being slightly faster. It was how they had been able to take down most of Eton High by themselves.

However, Gary was about to use their skill against them. Stepping forward, he positioned himself perfectly and was ready to throw out his right arm. It was a finishing move, with all his strength behind it.

I can see his arm coming. I'll move to the side and counter, giving him a harder hit. I can dodge this one as well! Leng thought.

He was wary of the green-haired teenager as he knew that not only did he have great endurance, but he also had enough power in his punches and kicks to seriously threaten him. He needed to come in at a counter point. When Gary was attacking, Leng needed to attack so he could use Gary's forward momentum against him.

Leng moved forward, getting ready to move out of the way at the right time; however . . .

1 stat point has been allocated into Dexterity
Your base Dexterity is now at 7
Dexterity 14

Suddenly, Gary's punch sped up midswing. With all his strength and with Leng running forward, the fist connected with the twin's face, causing his body to flip around before falling on the ground.

It was obvious to everyone that Leng wouldn't be getting up on his own.

Looking on, the two White Rose members shared the same opinion.

"Sudden bursts in power and speed like that . . . it's the sign of an Altered state," Sadie stated. "Frank, I think we'll have to reevaluate the importance of this kid in this entire case."

CHAPTER 32

AN INTRODUCTION

Gary's arm was still extended. All his training had been so short that he had almost forgotten it in the fight, but still somehow he was able to win. He was expecting his opponent to get back up, but before Leng even lifted his head, something else happened.

He was greeted with a nice little surprise: a message from the system.

Quest reward: 500 Exp
542/882 Exp

The quest was complete. Honestly Gary hadn't expected a single punch to end it all; he had also expected to have to use his little stat boost one more time if necessary, but with two forces of Energy, the blow was just too much for Leng to handle.

However, the system message meant that Sren must have also been defeated. Gary looked up and saw that Innu's face was in bad shape; he was huffing and panting, but Sren was lying on the floor.

"That damn slimy guy, he was like a snake. I couldn't hold him down and his body was so damn flexible, but still after a couple of knees to the stomach he sure did slow down a bit," Innu said, looking up and half expecting that he needed to help Gary, but to his surprise his friend had won his fight as well.

Although Gary's face didn't look to be in the best condition either. They smiled at each other as the realization hit them.

"Ladies and gentlemen, you've all seen it. The winners for tonight's debut match are the Howwwwlllerrrs!" the announcer shouted.

There were cheers among the crowd, as quite a few had made good money on the odds given, while others complained; they had clearly decided to play it safe and bet on the twins. Although they were annoyed about losing money, they could still respect an entertaining fight, so they joined in on the cheering.

Surprisingly, a few howls were heard as well. They sounded like some type of war cry; clearly people had had too much to drink and were trying to imitate wolves because of the gang's name. However, Gary and Innu thought it suited them well, and maybe it would become a tradition after one of them had been through a tough time.

Meanwhile, Austin was still trying to make up his mind about Gary.

The green-haired kid eventually won, but it looked a bit sloppy. But I also liked the look in his eyes when he threw that punch. Austin smiled. It was the first fight of the evening, yet after coming all the way out here, the loner was debating whether he should stay or just call it a day. After all, he had seen what Kai had wanted to show him.

"Well, what do you think?" Kai asked. "Can you see a better future for yourself by joining our little gang?"

Austin continued to look at Gary as Innu wrapped his arm around Gary's neck and ran his fingers through his green hair. Innu was showboating and enjoying every bit of his hard-earned victory as he bowed to the crowd.

Meanwhile, Sren and Leng were recovering and getting up from the fight. They didn't even shake hands and were already leaving the arena. Not that Gary ever expected them to be respectful in the first place, but after a fight like that, Gary's anger toward them seemed to be leaving his body.

"Based on what you asked me before, I'm guessing you want me to join this gang of yours?" Austin concluded. It was a good way to introduce the Howlers, especially since Austin already had an interest in Innu.

"Don't you think it will be more interesting than what you had planned?" Kai replied.

"I told you my answer. I don't follow anyone who's weaker than me, so if you really want me to join your gang, then tell me when you want us to fight." Austin was getting excited, especially since he had seen Kai's form earlier, which convinced him that Kai wasn't the pretty boy he had suspected him to be.

"That's reasonable, but if that's the case, you should fight the leader, not me," Kai replied with a smile. When Austin heard this, a memory clicked for him. Back when the police had questioned him about Billy's sudden appearance, he had asked Innu who the green-haired boy was, and the transfer student had told him that Gary was his leader.

"Very well." Austin nodded.

"All right, but you'll have to do that another time. After this match, he'll need some rest. Tag along with us for a little bit; I have something to show you after this."

The two White Rose agents were in a similar state of mind. They figured there was a good chance that Gary would leave after his fight, so they had a quick discussion about whether they should go after him or stay around longer.

Ultimately, they agreed to treat Gary as a potential lead. Since they knew where he would be tomorrow, they decided the smarter move would be to stay and start questioning people about Billy once the event was over. Since Gary had been in the debut fight, it shouldn't even be suspicious if they asked if someone knew if there was any connection between the two.

"If not, we'll just have to pay a visit to his school tomorrow," Sadie suggested.

CHAPTER 33

NOT ENOUGH

After leaving the fight, Gary and Innu went to a little area that had been set up a small distance from the host, where tables were laid out with money processing machines, laptops, and more.

The people here looked older than the fighters and spectators, and Gary could clearly tell that they were gangsters.

"They look scary, right?" Innu whispered. "But you know, someday we might be running something like this as well. Do you know why no one fights at these things? Outside of the ring, I mean. It's because the people who organize these types of fights in the smaller-tier cities and towns don't belong to the gangs in this area; they belong to the gangs in the cities above, the higher tiers.

"If anyone causes a fight, messes with the guys who organize this, or is crazy enough to go after their money, the entire gang would likely get involved," Innu explained.

Eventually Kai and Marie headed their way, but what came as a big surprise to both Gary and Innu was the person who was following them.

"Austin? What is he doing here?" Innu asked, shocked.

"Say hello to our newest member," Kai answered with a grin.

"I haven't agreed to anything!" Austin corrected him immediately. "It's just an interest."

With a closer look, Austin realized that Gary didn't look as bad as he thought. Although he had been hit a lot, the marks on his face, even from the kick, hadn't bruised up.

This was all due to Gary's Energy. Now that he was no longer fighting, his Energy was passively healing his wounds. He had plenty of Energy this time, not using a lot of skills or breaking his bones because of his strong Endurance.

Unlike after his fight with Billy, the system hadn't issued any emergency healing, which was why the markings were now less visible than before.

Kai went to the desk, and after a little bit of talking back and forth, he returned with four bundles of cash. Gary couldn't even imagine how much he was carrying right now.

"All right, I have good news and some bad news," Kai said, approaching the gang. "Let's start with the good news. You're now looking at four thousand dollars."

Straightaway, dollar signs appeared in Gary's eyes. With this much money, he could pay for his mother's hospital stay, food, electricity, and other bills they were behind on!

However, it did make him wonder just how much money Kai had put up in the first place. Although he had ended up spending the money from those he had eaten at the Kobe Karaoke Club, their total cash had amounted to around only a few hundred.

"The bad news is it won't be as easy to make this much cash from fights like this again. For one, you've managed to defeat a well-known and skillful pair of opponents, so after today our gang's name will be known, so our future odds will be far less generous.

"As for the other reason, after talking to the guys for a bit, I've learned that these venues aren't meant to bring in this much cash in the first place. There are a few hundred people here, and with how much we bet and won, they won't be making any money from your fight, and only off the others. We could go to bigger events . . .

but we're not ready for that yet. Unless one of you is an Altered, or thinks you can face one."

Gary remained silent.

"At the end of the day, this event is still like a business. Luckily for you all, my silver tongue managed to get them to pay our share for today at least," Kai explained.

It was pretty bad news, but still, if Gary could make a stable income through these fights, he was fine with that, though perhaps Kai had another way to make money. The first thing Kai did was keep one of the bundles for himself.

"This one's for the gang moving forward. We need seed money so we can start investing in ourselves. Besides, all these clothes didn't come for free," Kai said. He then handed some cash from another bundle to Marie and kept the rest for himself.

"Wait, why does Marie get cash when she didn't even fight?" Gary asked. He felt bad about complaining, but at the end of the day he desperately needed money, while the others looked less needy. Most of all, he felt like he had rightfully earned that money with his sweat and tears.

"Gary, you're the gang leader, but as a leader you also have to reward those that follow you. One of your most important duties is to make sure that you keep everyone happy in our group. Everyone here has helped you out somewhat today.

"You wouldn't have known about this place if it weren't for me, and if I hadn't put up the seed money we wouldn't have won as much as we did. Without Marie and her mother, we wouldn't have been able to come here without problems. Also, Marie has many uses for it. Trust me, you won't regret paying her her share."

Gary felt a little guilty after that; he had been thinking only about himself, yet Kai was right. If it weren't for Marie's mother, then he and Amy would have had a lot of problems at the hospital. He might not like it, but he owed them.

Finally, Kai threw two of the bundles to him and Innu. The four thousand had quickly gone down to one. All of those hopes he just had—paying for rent, food, electricity, the hospital bills—all seemed to be down the drain.

"It's not enough," Gary mumbled. He held his head down, and everyone could tell that he was somewhat down now, compared to his mood from before. Whatever his situation was, they could tell that he needed the money; the problem was that it was the same for them as well.

"Come on, before I take you guys back, I want to show you something. Maybe it will make you all feel better. Austin, you come along as well," Kai said.

Sren and Leng felt completely defeated. Trying to make up the money that they had lost from the betting ring, they had bet on themselves to win tonight's match, leading them to lose their pride as well as their money.

This was the second time that the green-haired boy had gotten in their way.

"What should we do, Leng? We could call up everyone from Eton High and raid their school. Or get all the guys to beat every Westbridge student they see!" Sren suggested.

"What's the point?" Leng replied. "He can beat us. If we can get some guys, what's stopping him from doing the same? Unless we get some extra help on our side, going after him would be useless."

"Maybe I can be the help you guys need," Raven offered as he approached them. "You two seem to lack the extra little bit of strength you need to beat those Howler guys. I just happen to have something that can provide you that boost."

CHAPTER 34

A SURPRISE

Leaving the venue, the group returned to the car, where Marie's mother was busy waiting for them. She had stayed behind the whole time, though it would seriously surprise Gary if she was unaware of what was going on at such a place.

To be honest, he felt a little strange seeing her there. He had always imagined that if he joined a gang for real, not just as a transporter but as a full-fledged member, one who would do whatever his superiors told him to do, he would do his darnedest to keep it from his family. Gary had even been prepared to take it to the grave with him, just so that his mother and sister could keep him in their memory as the good boy and brother they remembered.

Yet Marie's mother was actively supporting her daughter and her friends by driving them around. It made Gary wonder how his own mother would react. Would she also be this supportive? He seriously doubted it, and if it were up to him he would very much like to never find out her stance on it.

While the five of them took their places in the car, Austin followed on his bike. The loner had agreed to accompany them for now, since Kai claimed he still had a little more to show him before he left for the night.

"Hey, Kai, how come you invited Austin along? I know he's strong and all, I mean he might be just a tiny bit weaker than me, but I'm like really, really strong, so that means he's somewhat strong. But if you're just looking for strong people for our gang, wouldn't those twins be a better fit?" Innu inquired, now that Austin couldn't hear him. "I mean, they're already involved in these kinds of activities, so I don't think they would have refused."

Everyone in the car heard the question, and all of the teenagers were interested in Kai's reason for going after Austin, especially since he seemed to have gone the extra mile to invite him.

"Well, let's ignore for a moment whether they would have actually wanted to join us after the two of you defeated and pretty much humiliated them in public, but before I answer, let me ask our leader a quick question here. Gary, how would you feel if those twins joined our gang?"

Gary didn't even have to answer; his face said it all. He was obviously against the idea. It wasn't just the fact that they had hurt Tom, but he was sure that they were also the ones who had sent out their goons to take out the Westbridge rugby players.

From what he had seen, they had no shame and would do whatever was needed to achieve their goals, not caring in the slightest who they might end up hurting. In a way, they acted like the color gang members had during the gang war. Gary had no respect for these types of people at all.

"Easy there, Green Fang, you've already defeated them. It was just a hypothetical question." Kai teased Gary, whose dislike for the idea had been very open. "Now I want you to imagine Austin joining us."

Gary hesitated for a bit, but he realized that he didn't actually have a problem with it at all.

"I can't quite picture it," he replied eventually. "When we met on the roof, the first thing he did was try to pick a fight with me, but somehow I can't fault him for that. I have a feeling that that's just the type of person he is.

"When Billy attacked Innu in school, he could have easily run away. After all, he had nothing to gain, yet he valiantly stayed and helped us fight him off. Overall, my impression of him is that he isn't a bad person and that I wouldn't mind hanging out with him."

"Just like with you, I had a feeling about him being . . . Let's call it 'special.' Since our leader likes him, there should be nothing to complain about, right?" Kai gave his usual smile that captured girls' hearts in seconds. "Although there are other reasons, getting him to join will push us into the next step."

In the middle of Kai's explanation, everyone heard an incredibly loud growl from the corner. They turned to a red-faced Gary holding his stomach.

"I'm sorry, but I'm really hungry after that fight. Is there any chance that we can stop somewhere to eat first?" Gary asked. After using Charging Heart, fighting, and then healing the sustained damage, his Energy was slightly above half capacity. He was getting the hunger pangs that he had grown accustomed to, yet that didn't stop his stomach from reminding him.

A short while later they found a diner that was open at this hour on the side of the road. Before they entered, though, Gary stopped outside for a few seconds. He felt kind of bad. When was the last time he and his family had gone out to eat? It had been a long time since they were able to afford it, and here he was about to spend this precious money.

If they hadn't been on the road, he would be looking for wild animals, but he couldn't do that while in the company of the others. This made him feel incredibly guilty.

"Don't worry, since I wasn't fighting, I should at least treat our fighters to a meal." Kai patted him on the back before he placed something in his hand and whispered, "And this here is something you've earned."

Kai had given him another bundle of cash.

"That's what you earned from your own bet. I just wanted to give it to you away from the eyes of everyone else. You put in a hundred, so you got two-fifty back, and I added another fifty on top since I know it must be hard for you and your sister right now.

"Use it however you like, and Gary . . . sometimes you're allowed to be a little selfish and look after yourself before you can look after others. If something happens to you, then who is left to look after your family?"

With this said, the group went in to eat, and two of them surprised the rest with how much they were able to stuff themselves without getting full. It was a cheap place and Gary had ordered multiple burgers, but he wasn't the only one. Austin did the same, and they both filled their trays.

"You said you were paying, right?" Austin looked at Kai as he bit into a burger, devouring half of it in one bite. While doing so he never took his gaze off Kai, staring into his eyes intently with each bite.

Strangely, Gary was keeping up with him, despite being half his size. It was a strange group of characters, that was for sure, but Gary was enjoying his time with them.

"So where are we exactly going?" Innu asked with his mouth full.

"That . . . is a surprise," Kai replied.

CHAPTER 35

A HOME

After their impromptu meal, they drove on and soon reached a part of town that wasn't in the best shape. It was between the borders of Chavley and Cipher, two territories belonging to two different gangs, making it a problematic area. Most of the fighting between the two color gangs would be in this area, meaning any type of night business would struggle.

The car eventually stopped outside what looked like a boarded-up bar. The windows were covered with plywood and spray paint. It was hard to tell what the business was because it had no sign. Any letters that used to be there had been removed or stolen.

The group got out of the car, looking left and right for any signs of trouble, and they were happy to see that it seemed to be a silent night. Perhaps the gangs were being a bit more cautious because of the rising tensions.

"So what exactly are we doing here?" Innu asked.

Kai walked forward and stood in front of the bar, turning to all the others.

"Don't you remember asking me about our hideout? At the time, we didn't have any, but every gang needs a starting place, a place that they can call home and regularly meet up. What you see behind me will be our base from today onward.

"Right now, it's all under Miss DeGrace's name." Kai looked at Marie's mother. "We're just renting it, but soon enough we should be able to buy it. This business now belongs to us, making this our territory! It will be from here that we'll grow, and today is the day the Howlers become a real gang!

"Welcome to the Howlers' base!"

Walking up to the door, Miss DeGrace pulled a key out of her pocket. It looked like everything had been planned beforehand. The door swung open, letting out a musty smell. Gary immediately covered his nose and sneezed a few times.

His nose was far more sensitive compared to the others. Seeing this, they were even less inclined to go inside, but ignoring everything Kai walked in. Not wanting to stay out in the cold, the others had no choice but to follow behind.

Upon entering, they saw that the place had been completely ruined; there was broken glass on the floor and dust everywhere. It was hard to say when the last time someone had been inside. However, at least it was quite large, and there were some things they could use.

There was a large bar area that was surprisingly intact; all it needed were some stools and a supply of alcohol, and there were eight pool tables.

"Looks like this used to be a pool club," Innu said. "Pretty neat, if I say so myself."

"Well, maybe in the past, but right now I'd say this place is a dump," Marie complained, kicking a glass bottle across the floor. "It will cost a pretty penny to renovate all of it."

"It might be a dump, but you guys need to use your imagination a bit." Kai smiled. "We have some seed money, and we have hands. With a little work we can clean up this place. Purchase a few things to make it look nice.

"Miss DeGrace will be the bartender. She has some experience and is quite a beauty, to get the older customers in. The deal is that after rent and all expenses get paid, the Howlers will get ten percent of all the profits."

"What about the area?" Gary asked. "You should know that this isn't exactly the most ideal place."

Of course Kai knew that, and it was probably why the rent was so cheap and why it had been abandoned in the first place. Whoever owned this dump would need good protection from the other gangs. From the look of the place, there had probably been a few fights before the last owner gave up.

"For now, the business will only be open during the day. I think it might be best to just use it as a pool club for young university students or high school students to go to after school. We all go to schools and know people, just invite them along.

"Heck, Austin's the top dog of his school, so he can just pretty much force them to come here, meaning we would have guaranteed customers. Then later on we can open up the business at night, further expanding our streams of revenue."

"And when would that be?" Innu asked.

"When we are confident enough to stop anyone from touching this place. When the name of the Howlers is known not only among those who go to underground fighting events, but all the other gangs and I don't mean color gangs. It might be shabby right now, but don't worry, this is just the start!" Kai clenched his fist.

It was the first time the others had seen him so passionate about something. Every word he spoke was filled with excitement. This guy's dream was to rise to the top, and it looked like he would do anything to get his way.

"Every day, we will come here. You and Innu can continue training, and it should be a safe place away from Billy. Marie will be in charge of finances, handling our money among other things. Think of her like the accountant of our business."

"Hey!" Austin shouted. "I think you're forgetting something. I haven't agreed to anything yet. You remember my deal. This is all great and all, but your plan doesn't work if you don't have the strength to back it up . . . If you can't even beat me, how can you beat all those gangs out there?"

Kai looked at Gary.

"Well, Gary, you wanted to rise to the top with me. You want to change your situation, right? To do that, we need Austin. So what's it going to be?"

Gary knew what Kai was asking him to do.

"Austin, don't you think that's a bit unfair? Gary was in a fight not too long ago; can't you have your stupid fight tomorrow?" Marie asked.

Gary was debating internally. His Energy was full, his Health was full, and he was actually in perfect condition to fight Austin.

New Quest received
A person wishes to test your strength
Task: Knock out your opponent or make them submit!
Reward: ???

CHAPTER 36

A BRICK WALL

After seeing the quest message, Gary had made up his mind. He would defeat Austin to make him join the Howlers. So far, listening to Kai had always worked in his favor.

And now, after listening to Kai's speech about this place, Gary was more convinced than ever that his friend had already planned out the next dozen steps. He intended to truly change the status quo.

If Kai claimed that they needed Austin in their gang, then Gary was sure that there might be more than just one reason for it. So Gary would fight like he meant it. The only thing he was curious about was the quest reward. Unlike his fight against the twins, the system kept it a secret from him.

The only other time this happened was when I fought that Altered Hunter. The system might let me choose another skill, or the reward might be something as good. Who knows, maybe the system hasn't decided yet and it will depend on my performance? Argh, Tom would be the better person to ask about this type of thing, Gary thought, making a mental note to pretend to have found a game in order to ask his best friend some questions.

He walked across the room to stand on top of a few pieces of broken glass and took a stance. Austin understood that this meant

Gary had accepted the challenge, so he went to the other side of the room to do the same.

The others moved over to the bar area, which wasn't as messy as the rest of the place. Now they were out of the way and could carefully watch the fight. Meanwhile Marie's mother, Miss Degrace, was standing behind the bar, already filling her role as she sorted through whatever bottles were left. It was almost as if the fight weren't even happening behind her; she was that calm about it.

"I just don't understand you boys; why do you need to solve everything with your fists?" Marie said, leaning on her elbow with her hand pressed against her face, clearly not interested in the fight at all. She was paying more attention to what her mother was doing, mentally calculating how much money they would have to put into the place to fix it.

"You're not wrong; not everything needs to be solved using your fists," Kai said as he playfully ruffled her hair, earning him an annoyed look. "However, certain things just can't be solved with words. Besides, we're in an area where the only universal language is violence.

"Just let them talk it out with their fists today. It's also important for our gang to know each member's strengths so we can rely on each other."

On the other hand, Innu was very interested in watching the fight, and honestly he was also quite nervous for Gary's sake. After all, despite having taken a break, it was undeniable that they had just been through a tough fight, and Innu hadn't forgotten how many punches their leader had taken.

There were bound to be some bruises, and taking too many hits from bare fists wasn't good in the first place. Although Gary's endurance was praiseworthy, unlike the twins, Austin seemed to be a heavy hitter rather than a speedster.

"Come on, then!" Austin challenged his opponent with a smile on his face. He walked over, not taking a real fighting stance or anything, yet the amount of confidence emanating off his body was frightening.

I've learned from my mistake, so I will meet you with all I've got! Gary decided.

Skill activated: Charging Heart
All stats have temporarily been doubled
–10 Energy

The green-haired teenager thought that maybe now Austin would take him more seriously, but the loner had been taking him seriously from the very beginning.

As Gary ran toward him and threw a fist, Austin stepped to the side. He swung his own fist, hitting Gary right in the ribs. It was a short and compact blow, but he had twisted his body to put all his weight behind it.

–4 HP

What the hell? How strong is he that he can do this much damage against 28 points of Endurance? Fuck, this seriously hurts, and it didn't even seem like he used his full strength! Gary lost a bit of his earlier confidence. He'd been convinced that he would be able to ignore whatever Austin could dish out and subdue him in a fight.

"Looks like you're using your full speed against me from the start." Austin's smile got bigger. "I'm glad you're taking me more seriously than you did those twins. I might not be as fast as them, but if you can see your opponent's attacks and time it correctly, you don't need to be fast to dodge them, and guess what, I can see yours perfectly!"

The way Austin was talking was a little strange, but Gary didn't have the leisure time to care about that.

Hmm, that's certainly an interesting approach, Kai thought, since he had no such problems.

There was no need for Austin to explain what he was doing. It was clear that he had spoken out loud on purpose, as if he wanted his opponent to hear. It was almost like Austin was trying to teach Gary how to deal with an opponent who was faster than him, or what he would have done if he had gone up against the twins.

Regaining his composure, Gary charged in, trying to remember what he and Innu had practiced. There weren't two opponents attacking him this time. It was one-on-one.

I can do this!

CHAPTER 37

A HEAVY FIST

Austin stretched his arms out wide, waiting for Gary's next move, a thigh kick he had practiced with Innu countless times. But Austin whacked the green-haired teenager's foot away and stepped forward, quickly throwing a fist of his own at Gary's stomach.

−4 HP

Gary lurched forward from the heavy blow. Austin grabbed the back of his opponent's head, holding on to his hair, and pulled him up. He swung his fist into Gary's face, sending him down.

−6 HP

"Hey, isn't that a bit much, grabbing his hair?" Marie worriedly asked.

"Does that matter in a street fight?" Innu responded.

The girl had nothing to say to that. She was well aware that people used weapons and all sorts of dirty methods to win, not caring in the slightest whether something was fair.

As Gary landed on the floor, one of the glass shards pierced his hand. It was shoved in quite deep, and blood was already flowing.

−1 HP

You are suffering from minor blood loss
Foreign object detected in body
Unable to perform emergency healing

Gary quickly stood up. Gritting his teeth, he pulled out the glass shard and threw it across the floor. Marie grimaced a little bit, imagining how much pain she would feel, but Gary didn't even flinch; instead he clenched his fist as if there were no pain at all.

Emergency healing now in progress

"I've been through a lot worse!" Gary shouted, remembering the two times he had been stabbed by a knife; a glass shard through his hand simply couldn't compare to that. As for the pain, compared to the emotional pain his family had gone through and the stress he had been through these past few days, this wasn't even worth mentioning!

The fight so far had been pretty one-sided; Gary hadn't managed to land a single blow, while he himself had received several. It was beginning to look like a repeat of the fight against the Vicious Twins. Only this time, Gary had gone all out using Charging Heart from the beginning, meaning he had nothing else to use to gain an advantage over his opponent.

This is what I was worried about. Innu sighed. *For someone like Gary, this matchup is the worst. Our leader seems to be blessed with natural speed, strength, and endurance that allows him to take quite a beating.*

He also knows a few basic skills, so he can take down the average thug. Even if they are trained, his endurance and strength can make up for that.

But with Austin . . . he's a natural street fighter. You can tell he doesn't have any training at all. There's no pattern to follow, and he just does whatever his instincts tell him would be the optimal move.

Gary hasn't fought enough to deal with this type of unorthodox fighter.

Kai was of the same opinion. It would have been far more favorable if they had sent someone trained like Innu, who could use his skills to support his fighting style to deal with Austin. The thought of watching a fight between these two interested him as well.

That or it would take someone who was a lot faster or a lot stronger than Austin. Unfortunately, Gary was neither of those things.

Come on, Gary! I know you have it in you. For the first time, you agreed to a fight yourself. I can feel it, you are also starting to see the goal, aren't you? Kai thought. *In the grand scheme of things, Austin is just a small pebble on our long and bumpy road. If you want us to reach the top, you need to take him out!* Even for Kai, fighting the loner wouldn't be easy, and he wasn't 100 percent sure that he would be able to win.

Gary's kicks and punches were unable to reach his opponent. Austin's style wasn't like that of the twins, who had been dodging narrowly, yet it was as effective, if not more so. The green-haired teenager still had one unallocated stat point, yet he wasn't sure that a stat boost alone would help him win, no matter which stat he chose.

He's not countering me because I'm too slow, but because he has keen eyes. Dexterity won't help me change that, and what's the point of putting it in Strength if I can't hit him? My Endurance is already stupidly high, yet his punches hurt.

Come on, Gary, use your brain, there's gotta be something you can do to beat him!

Charging forward again, Gary let his body do what it had trained to do many times before. Austin had been expecting a lot of desperate measures that Gary might resort to at this point, but trying to tackle him as if they were playing rugby wasn't on that list. The green-haired teenager gripped the loner's waist tightly.

"You got me, but what are you going to do now?" Austin shouted as he clasped his hands together and slammed them down on Gary's back like a hammer.

−4 HP

Gary held on, though, not letting go of Austin's waist. He started to squeeze him tightly.

I don't even know what I'm doing, but what else can I do? Gary wondered, hoping he could make use of his doubled Strength.

Meanwhile, Austin continued to slam both hands down Gary's back.

−4 HP
77/100 HP

"Did you guys hear his back click?" Innu looked around to the other two, whose faces showed that they were mentally sharing Gary's pain.

What do I do, I can't just keep holding him. Should I use Claw Drain? No, I can't. Not with everyone watching . . .

CHAPTER 38

YOUR BODY IS SPECIAL

Another attack hammered down, even harder than the last.

–6 HP

Then Gary attempted to lift Austin into the air. The loner could feel it, but he could only laugh.

"Do you really think that will work, while you let me continue to slam down on your back? If you don't give up soon, I'll break it!" Austin shouted, swinging his hands down again.

–7 HP

Gary didn't know if Austin was getting stronger with each hit, or whether his Endurance was weakening. But it was clear that Austin's attacks were doing a lot more damage than before.

When I try to lift him, I can tell that I'm close. I just need to be a little stronger. Should I dump that stat point into Strength now?

With Charging Heart, one stat point would be as effective as two.

No, that's still not enough. I need more Strength.

Gary remembered a time that he had managed to summon more strength than before: when he had seen his sister's injured face. When he had seen what those people had attempted to do to her. He fought against the pain as Austin slammed his back; he thought about the people counting on him, his sister and his hospitalized mother.

If only I were a bit stronger! Why don't you help me out for once, you shitty system?

BPM is rising rapidly
160 BPM
170 BPM

Austin wasn't sure if he was imagining it, but he thought he could feel Gary's body pulsing at an unbelievable speed. If it really was a heartbeat, then what was going on in Gary's small body?

190 BPM
200 BPM
You have exceeded 200 BPM
Partial transformation has begun
All stats increased by 125%

Once again Austin lifted his fists, and when he swung down this time, Gary knew it was his chance. He quickly moved to the side, making the swing hit nothing but air, and now Gary was directly behind him.

"System, put one point in Strength!"

1 stat point has been allocated into Strength
Your base Strength is now at 9
Strength: 20.25

Thanks to his partial transformation state, Gary's Strength was now over 20, giving him a 25 percent increase in power over the previous 16 points he had from Charging Heart.

Austin could immediately tell the difference. His body was being lifted off the floor. It was as amazing as it was comical having Gary lift him without thinking about what he was doing. It looked like he was about to do a suplex, until the green-haired teenager slammed his opponent onto the floor, sending the glass shards flying.

44/120 Energy

Gary looked at his downed opponent. His Energy was going down a lot faster now; his heart rate was above 200 BPM, and it looked like it was already calming down. At the same time the Charging Heart skill had also deactivated, bringing his Strength back down to 9.

Don't get up . . . please, don't get up, Gary silently prayed. He didn't want to beat on Austin anymore. After all, they were supposed to recruit him, and after all that beating Gary needed a moment to just catch his breath.

I guess Energy and Stamina aren't one and the same after all.

However, Austin was slowly getting up from the floor. He wiped away some spit that had come out of his mouth and then stared into Gary's eyes.

This guy is a freaking tank! I can use Charging Heart again, but I might not have the Strength or Energy to beat this guy! Gary thought, getting ready.

"I . . . admit it's my loss." Austin smiled. "You . . . really are one little warrior, aren't you . . . I can see now why you're the leader. If I have to follow someone, I believe you wouldn't be my worst choice."

With that said, Austin walked toward the door. Before he went out, though, he stopped for a moment.

"I'll see you guys tomorrow," Austin mumbled, closing the door.

"What . . . just happened?" Gary asked, confused.

"Didn't you hear him? You, our mighty leader, won," Kai explained, slapping him on the back, causing Gary to let out a little yelp.

"Why . . . of all the places," Gary whined, feeling the pain run through his body.

As soon as Kai said those words, the system also confirmed his victory.

Quest reward: Instant Level-Up
Congratulations, you have now reached: Level 8
A new skill has been unlocked
A stat point has been granted
542/1024 Exp

Current list of skills:
Marks: 4/5
Charging Heart
Claw Drain (Level 1)
Full Transformation (new)

From a glance at his previous rewards, an Instant Level-Up was impressive after fighting one person. It was in a way the hardest Gary had ever had to fight before. Usually beating down random goons on the street only gave him 20 or 25 Exp, or 50 Exp at the most.

Gary was most happy to see that the Instant Level-Up hadn't just given him 340 Exp, which he needed to reach the next level, but seemingly 882, so that he was already halfway to Level 9. He was very much looking forward to reaching Level 10 and fulfilling the only Main Quest the Werewolf System had issued him so far. Hopefully, it would give him the power to beat Billy.

When he thought about the other omega wolf, he recalled that not even Austin's blow had been able to hurt Billy, and that was when he had still been in human form. Was Billy doing the same right now? Was he out there getting stronger just like Gary?

Perhaps the other werewolf would always be just a bit ahead of him. Still, there was one thing that possibly might turn the tide if Gary and Billy were to meet again, and that was the last reward for completing the quest.

Full Transformation . . . does this mean what I think it does?

Just as Gary was going to check out the description of the message, Marie ran over and grabbed his arm.

"Come over here," she demanded as she pulled him along. She quickly pulled up one of the fallen barstools, one of the few that weren't broken, and got Gary to sit down on it. On the bar were a bottle of alcohol and a first-aid kit.

"Apparently no one ever used this. The owner must have bought it shortly before going out of business. Now show me your hand, we need to get that cut checked out! Depending on how deep it is, we might even have to go to the hospital. If we don't do something it could get infected," Marie said as she opened his hand.

Gary couldn't even say anything; Marie turned out to be a force that couldn't be stopped, and before he realized it, it was too late. She cleaned the wound, but there was no pain when she cleaned it with alcohol.

Marie had experience with nasty cuts like this, and the normal reaction would be to scream like a little girl, yet Gary was as silent as when he pulled the shard out.

That was when she noticed the reason for his behavior.

"What the—? Did I see wrong? Was it your other hand?" Marie asked in confusion, looking at Gary's other hand. "No, but all this blood . . . how can there be no cut?"

CHAPTER 39

FINDING OUT THE TRUTH

More and more often, Gary found himself being put in situations that forced him to lie because the truth was just too bizarre, and there were things he needed to hide no matter what. Making matters even worse, he had more than one secret, and all of the people around him only knew certain parts or had been lied to in regard to others.

His mother was currently in the hospital, and when she woke up he would have to explain where he had managed to acquire the money to pay the bills. Gary had told Amy that he had been helping out another friend of his with their family business, yet he had deliberately avoided mentioning that this "family business" had him working as a transporter for the Underdogs.

As for Tom, his best friend still believed that Gary had become a werewolf because of a strange package, yet he knew nothing about where it had come from. Overall, Gary had done his best to keep Tom away from anything gang-related, such as him having been in one and being the active leader of another.

Then there was Kai, who was the only one aware of the situation with the Underdogs, and now that Gary thought about it, Kai also knew about the Dem family problems, as well as about Billy. He knew pretty much everything except that Gary wasn't exactly 100 percent human anymore.

Gary worried about how the others would react if they learned the truth. It would be one thing if he was an Altered, yet his situation appeared to be something else entirely. He didn't want them to know, for fear he would lose them. Aside from his family and Tom, the Howlers were all he had right now.

The worst part of it all was that Gary was a horrible liar. Often he said the first thought that came to his mind, which this time was *Whoa, it really healed, I must have superpowers.* Thankfully he bit his tongue this time before saying anything.

When Marie tried to look at his other hand, he hid both of them behind his back.

What the . . . am I an idiot? It's not like if she can't see my hands, she will now believe whatever I say, Gary chided himself.

"You two also saw that glass shard pierce his hand, right?" Marie asked the two boys who were still behind the bar. "I'm not going crazy, right? Heck, he even took it out and right here I have a rag full of blood!" She lifted it up, seemingly to convince herself as much as Innu and Kai. Meanwhile, Gary scooted around to reposition himself so his fellow gang members wouldn't be able to see his next action.

Innu looked at the floor and saw the large shard with blood on it. There was no doubt in his mind that they had all seen the same thing.

What do I do? Should I just confess to being an Altered? No, that will just open another can of worms, meaning I would have to come up with more lies to hide it. There's only one thing I can do.

Instead of adding to the web of lies he had already spun, Gary decided to do something more drastic.

Skill activated: Claw Drain
−15 Energy

His fingers started to grow slightly, and so did his sharp, hard nails. It would hurt, but Gary had no choice, and with his hands behind his back the others wouldn't be able to see. He used the claw to dig into his hand, creating a large cut across it.

–2 HP
You are suffering from minor blood loss
If too much blood is lost it will continue to lower your HP

Shit, this hurts way more than that stupid little piece of glass. The things I do to keep up this lie . . . maybe it would have been easier to tell them the truth.

However, Gary worried that since he wasn't in a fight, his passive healing or perhaps even his emergency healing might take effect.

Claw Drain only lasted two seconds at Level 1, and while that might be detrimental during a fight, for his current purposes it was perfect. By the time everyone looked from the rag back to him, his hands had already reverted to normal. He lifted up his hand with blood dripping down it.

"Sorry, I just didn't want you to put alcohol on the wounded hand. Alcohol on an open wound seriously hurts, but you're right, it needs to get disinfected. I just put some blood on the other hand hoping you wouldn't find out. The cut is still there, it's just on the other hand."

Marie let out a big sigh.

"Just come over here, you big crybaby." She shook her head while Gary went over and put his hand out. She got to work, not even questioning why the cut looked so fresh. Gary didn't even have to act to let out a cry when the alcohol came into contact with his wound. He just hoped that the emergency or passive healing wouldn't kick in so quickly that Marie could see it healing on the spot.

In the end, Marie bandaged it up, and it looked like she hadn't noticed anything strange. However, the other two boys weren't as convinced. Marie might not have paid enough attention to the fight, but both Kai and Innu were more than 90 percent sure that the shard should have gone through the other hand. To top it off, Gary's strange actions were definitely because he was hiding something.

Why the need to cover it up, Gary? Kai wondered, as he thought back to certain events. *Wait, could it be possible . . . it seems too crazy to be true, but if I put everything together—your fast improvement and what happened in the park with Tom and that wolf-type Altered—but how . . . is that it? Was that what was inside the briefcase Damion is so crazy about, and is that why you're running from the Underdogs?*

Of course, Kai had no way to test the conclusion he had reached. Confronting Gary directly wouldn't yield much. He would have to either wait or find a way to make Gary confess, though he didn't know how close his thoughts were to the actual reality. For now, he intended to keep their gang leader's secret a secret.

This is getting exciting. If that's really the case, we'll be able to seriously accelerate the progress of my plans. And a large grin appeared on Kai's face.

CHAPTER 40

FULL TRANSFORMATION?

Miss Degrace offered to drive everyone home, but Gary declined, claiming that just as Marie wanted, he would head straight to the hospital to get himself checked out. Of course, there was no way he was actually going there to waste his hard-earned money when his body could naturally heal. Heck, it would probably get even better than whatever a doctor would do, especially since there would be no wound by the time he arrived.

The group had agreed that they would meet at the pool club tomorrow once classes and club activities were over. They intended to go every day to work on cleanup and repair. On the way home, Gary stopped by a convenience store to grab what he needed for himself and some other items.

Does Amy even know how to cook? Maybe I'll need to learn how while Mom is away. Let's not risk it; better just get some instant noodles and microwave food to be safe. I know it's not the best, but it will be better than me burning the house down, Gary decided.

He looked at the cash he had earned. He could pay the hospital bills for a while with this, allowing his mother to stay, and he could perhaps pay rent. Other than that, there was still a mountain of bills that he wouldn't be able to cover.

Money was still on his mind, and it didn't seem like these events were a reliable source of income, nor could he earn as much from them as in the past.

He recalled a scene he saw frequently while walking around—delinquent students extorting money from other students—but he never wanted to be that type of person.

One day I hope I'll be rich enough to hire a personal chef. I won't have to worry about anything, just do whatever I want and enjoy tasty food. Gary daydreamed for a while. *Maybe by then, I can enjoy some normal food, and although I was never a big chocolate person, now that I can't have it, I do kinda miss it.*

The streets were mostly empty, with a few strange adult men in black suits on street corners now and then. These were members of the Underdogs, and Gary understood that he had to be more careful than ever. He pulled his hood even closer over his head.

Since the gang war, it looked like a lot of the black color gang had been injured, so now the Underdogs gang members were monitoring the area so a second attack wouldn't happen . . . at least not so soon. The good thing was, this led to a significant decrease in the local crime rate.

Those bastards! If they had just protected this place from the beginning, or if the police had protected us, then my mother wouldn't have been hurt in the first place!

Before heading back, Gary decided to check out one thing: his newly unlocked skill.

Full Transformation
When activated, the user's body transforms into its werewolf form. The skill will take 20 points of Energy to use.
After activation, the skill will consume 10 points of Energy per minute.

Warning: Skill will forcefully be canceled when Energy reaches less than 10 Energy!

Gary had to read the description a couple of times, just to make sure he was understanding it correctly. When he saw the name of this new skill, he believed that it would be far more limited, perhaps allowing him to transform an entire part of his body; he hadn't thought it would actually turn him *entirely* into a werewolf.

Come on, system, can't you elaborate a bit more? Gary pleaded, to no effect as usual. *I kinda need to know if I will stay conscious or whether this will make me pass out and act on autopilot! I have no desire to become a wild and feral beast, especially when Blake's family might have it out for me, you know?*

It was because of this possibility that Gary wasn't so keen to test the Full Transformation skill right here, right now, though it did look like it would have some differences from when he had forcefully been changed into a werewolf because of the full moon.

For one, he could see that it had a clear time limit, one tied to his Energy. It appeared that the maximum duration of Full Transformation would be nine minutes, and that was assuming he activated the skill with a full Energy bar. It would probably end far sooner if he used any skills as a werewolf or if the Energy he expended for anything was separate from the 10 Energy points required to uphold the skill.

I mean, unless I'm constantly eating while in that state. Because then my energy would be restored while I'm fighting. But a situation where I would want to eat all those around me . . . is not something I want to think about.

Based on the information Tom had given him, he had been in his werewolf form for a long time. Perhaps he would have stayed until sunrise if it weren't for his Energy getting low at an incredible rate, which he assumed was due to his fight with Billy. He also still didn't know if he would have transformed back into a werewolf if he had eaten his fill during the full moon.

It might be for the best if I consider this a last-resort skill, but even then . . . I would have to know if I couldn't beat my opponent at all. If I fought someone for a while, then my Energy would be lower, meaning the time limit would be shorter. That's not the only problem, though; it doesn't even tell me what type of boost I get for going full werewolf.

Where are the improved stats? Where are the exclusive werewolf skills and all that shiz? Gary complained, yet all he got was silence. Just then a member of the Underdogs walked past him on the street.

His heart was thumping loudly; he worried that the gang member might notice him or ask him a few questions. Gary continued walking until he saw an alley nearby.

If I use Claw Drain a few times to lower my energy, and then use Full Transformation, it should only last a minute at most, right? Gary glanced at the Underdogs member behind him.

CHAPTER 41

NO MORE DRAMA

In the end, Gary decided against the idea of testing Full Transformation, not now and not in this area against a person he didn't even know. Sure, gang members were mostly bad, but he had no right to punish a random person who might have similar circumstances to himself, especially if all he was doing was making sure that the neighborhood was safe.

Alas, it appeared that Gary would not find out what would happen until he tested it out. Maybe when he transformed he would get all these benefits, provided he stayed conscious, of course. Right now he would have very much preferred a Partial Transformation skill over the full version.

Wait . . . can Billy do this too? he thought suddenly. *I got this reward from the system, and maybe he hasn't done anything that allows him to do this stuff. If that's the case, isn't this an easy way to take him out? If I can somehow get me and Billy together in an empty room . . . he might be strong, but surely my werewolf form should be enough to beat Billy in human form, right?*

There was no way to confirm whether Billy could do this, but the only reason he thought he couldn't was because he hadn't tried to attack Innu or Gary since that day.

Of course, Gary wouldn't just gamble everything on that without trying it out first, but this wasn't the time or the place. Someone had been waiting for him the entire day. When he entered the apartment, his sister came out of her room to see who was there.

"Gary!" Amy ran over to give her big brother a large hug. Her eyes were puffy.

She must have been crying since this morning . . .

"Sorry it took so long. I hope twenty dollars was enough to order something nice. I've also brought some food like I said I would." Gary handed over the shopping bag, and Amy immediately began to unpack the groceries.

It was strange how something so regular and boring put a smile on Gary's face, and he went over to do his part. As thankful as she was, Amy did give him an earful about two things: the amount of meat he had purchased as well as the amount of junk food. When he was shopping, his instincts must have taken over for the former; as for the latter, he had just wanted to avoid burning down their apartment, which he confessed.

They joked and laughed about it, and Gary believed that he and Amy would be able to get through this hard time. As long as they stayed together, everything would turn out fine.

28 days until the next full moon
30 Exp received due to active Bond Marks
572/1024 Exp

Once again, Gary woke up before Amy, though there were a few reasons why he didn't just go back to sleep. Now that he would be heading to the pool club after school, he needed to go to the gym in the morning before school.

He still needed to improve his body and get his daily Exp, even if it was a pittance, and then he would do his morning routine of hunting in the forest. He was getting better at using his skills. In particular, his Claw Drain had allowed him to catch birds and squirrels thanks to his suddenly longer reach, and it was good for his footwork as well. The fights had also improved his hunting to some degree.

For once, when he got to school, he felt like there were no immediate problems. Of course there were still many problems, but he would have enough time to deal with them all.

"I feel like I finally got a break," Gary mumbled to Tom as he took his seat.

"Oh, did you overexert yourself? Here I thought you must have been having fun with your new friends," Tom commented, a bit snarkily. He was clearly annoyed. To be fair, Gary hadn't even bothered to talk to him or text him after simply disappearing once rugby training was over.

When was the last time he had gone to Tom's house, or the two of them had watched an Altered match together? Lately, Gary had been obsessed with rugby or going out with the others after school. It was starting to feel as if they were drifting apart, the only glue holding their friendship together being the secret the two of them shared about his sudden chocolate "allergy."

"Hey, Tom . . ." Gary began, unsure about whether inviting him to the pool club would be a good or bad idea. *As long as it's during the day and it's just about helping the place out, it wouldn't be too dangerous . . . shit, but that would mean that I would have to ask the others to avoid openly talking about any Howlers business . . .*

"I'm sorry, man, I'm just really busy these days. I promise everything will be back to normal soon, and I think I might need your help with, you know"—Gary leaned in and whispered—"my 'special problem.'"

Tom wondered what type of questions he could ask him.

Just as the first period was about to start, someone knocked on the classroom door.

"Come in!" the teacher called.

Two people barged into the classroom, flashing their badges toward the teacher, who immediately took a step back.

"We have permission from your principal to look for one of your students, a boy by the name of Gary Dem," the woman explained as she looked over the class, stopping when she spotted a green head.

Gary immediately gulped because there was no way he could forget the two White Rose agents who had found him snooping around Billy's place.

Shit, did they find out anything? Gary wondered, lamenting his fate of not even being allowed to get one day off without any drama.

CHAPTER 42

EVERYONE'S BUSINESS

When Gary heard his name, his heart immediately started to beat more rapidly. With all this added pressure, he worried that he might have heart problems one day, but perhaps being a werewolf would make him immune to that.

It would have been one thing if they had been looking for a "green-haired teenager," but the agents had specifically called him out by name, which of course made everyone turn around and stare at him. Gary didn't know how to handle this kind of unwanted attention.

"Do you think this has anything to do with Steven? I've heard that his mother wanted to sue the school for not expelling Gary. Maybe she called the cops on him?" one of his classmates whispered to his neighbor.

"I seriously doubt it. If it were that, they would have come ages ago. Doesn't Gary live somewhere in Chavley? I believe they might want his testimony because of what happened there recently," the other student answered.

"You think so? Didn't you see their badges? They aren't the regular police; those guys are from White Rose. What relation could Gary have with Altered?" another student said, joining in their theory crafting.

Since turning into a werewolf Gary had gotten used to filtering out all the noises he could hear, but right now he was unable to, either because he was too flustered in the current situation or because of his subconscious desire to know what his peers thought about him. Either way, it was seriously getting to him.

That's it, they must have somehow found out that I know Billy. They've linked me with him, and even if they haven't, I have no idea how I could lie my way out of this one! Gary was panicking, until he felt someone touch his back.

"Dude, it's going to be okay," Tom whispered. "Just relax. If they had any clear evidence to bring you in, they wouldn't have had to ask the principal for permission. Just remember, you have the right to remain silent, although it may cause them to investigate you more, but whatever you do, don't mention anything about what you are . . . you need to look after Amy, right? . . . and your mother in the hospital."

Gary looked at Tom and saw the gentle smile on his face. He didn't remember telling his best friend about his mother's condition. More than that, why would he even care? Tom's words gave Gary a boost of confidence, and he stood up and walked over to the two agents, who would take him to another room to start their investigation.

Gary . . . what exactly happened that earned you the attention of White Rose? Tom wondered. *Was it the fight with Billy? Well, they did arrive that day, but they shouldn't know that you were there . . .*

Did they find some of your blood at the scene? They shouldn't have you on file to link you to the case, since you never did anything criminal . . . at least nothing that you've told me . . . could it be something else? Are they maybe linked to the suitcase that made you into a werewolf?

Innu was also worried about Gary. After all, he was the Howlers' leader, so if he got into some sort of trouble it would be bad for all of them. Innu didn't know what to do, so he decided to inform the one person who might be able to help.

Two White Rose agents just came into our class and asked for Gary specifically. Thought I should let you know.

Kai had been sitting in class, not in the least looking forward to another boring lesson with Mrs. Bedford, when his phone vibrated. The sudden news came as a shock to him, and he abruptly stood up. Although class hadn't begun yet, he excused himself by saying he really needed to go to the restroom.

Why now of all times? Shit, was I right with my assumption yesterday? Is Gary really an Altered . . . or something else? If so, do they just suspect him, or did they manage to link him back to the Underdogs? Either way, this could be major trouble . . . I need to do something!

As Sadie and Frank walked down the hallway on either side of Gary, they noticed that he was being awfully quiet. This was quite the norm when they captured criminals, but they had expected Gary to be different, especially given how wordy he had been the last time they had met.

"Don't be so nervous." Frank spoke to break the awkward silence. "We're not here to arrest you or anything. We're just going to ask you some questions. We've already met you at the apartment block where the Bruntins lived, so we're just going to continue along with that."

"Okay, yeah, that sounds good," Gary stupidly replied, his voice almost cracking. It was clear he was hiding something. However, neither agent had any idea that he was hiding far more things than they suspected.

As they walked through the halls, they passed the windows of the other classes, who all were intrigued about why a high school student was being escorted by two well-dressed adults. Some of them pointed and looked up, and one was particularly interested.

Those guys, Blake thought, as he recognized the two agents as members of White Rose. *Why would they go after him? Did they figure out that he was an Altered? I need to . . . I . . . no, I shouldn't get involved.*

He gripped his pencil tightly, while everyone talked about Gary. Eventually Blake's pencil snapped in his hand.

No, I need to know . . . for the sake of the Altered Hunters!

While everyone was still distracted, Blake snuck out and followed the trio. Eventually they entered the teachers' lounge, which he guessed would be empty right now. Blake continued down the hallway, entering the next room, the printer room. He placed his ear against the door, trying to eavesdrop on the conversation, but the noise was far too muffled.

If I stay in here, then I'm bound to get caught as well.

Blake looked at the window and slid it open. Outside was a ledge that connected to the window in the teachers' lounge. That was one option.

He then looked at the ceiling to see if there was a way he could go from above . . . no matter what, he was going to find out what was going on in that room!

It should be okay. As long as I do it for the sake of Ga— the Altered Hunters.

Inside the teachers' lounge were several desks with computers and stacks of paper, yet nobody was inside. Since it was first period, the teachers were already in class, and those whose lessons started later had yet to arrive.

A table on the right side of the room had been cleared off, and three chairs were set up around it: two on one side and one on the other side.

"Please take a seat, Gary. We are glad that you are cooperating with us," Sadie said, hoping to make him less nervous. Sitting down, Gary placed his hands down at his sides. He didn't want them to see how much they were shaking.

"Do you mind placing your hands on the table?" Frank requested. "It's a little nerve-racking not seeing them. While you don't really seem the type, we've had encounters with others who were hiding something."

Gary naturally complied; all he could think about doing was following their orders and listening to what they had to say. He hoped that everything would turn out to be far less serious than he thought. He intended to answer as much as he could, hopefully without sounding suspicious.

"All right, just to let you know, our little talk is currently being recorded via the school camera, and we will also be recording it on this device here," Sadie explained, placing a recorder in the middle of the table. "Now before we begin, you're entitled to know that you have the following rights."

The investigation was starting, and Gary could tell he was in trouble; he wasn't so sure this time if he could get through it alone.

CHAPTER 43

NOT ENOUGH

Having a White Rose agent read him his rights just stressed the fact that Gary was in a very serious situation. He wasn't sure whether to be happy that the two were pursuing things the legal way, and that included the recording in front of him. Just as Tom had said, they seemed to be treating him as a suspect. The only question was, for what? Was this about Billy . . . or something else entirely?

The two White Rose agents sat down, Sadie staring at him far more aggressively now that they had moved on to official business. She seemed to be the type who would much rather beat information out of him than waste her time questioning him. Just like last time, Frank was playing good cop, a friendly smile on his face, yet his body was leaning away from his partner, as if he himself were scared of Sadie.

They told me I could call an attorney, but I don't have any numbers. Do I really need one, though? Shit, but what if I say something really bad? Should I ask them to refer me to one, but how would I pay for it? Argh, I spent a good part of the money for groceries yesterday, and I need the rest to pay the hospital! This was one of the most stressful situations Gary had ever encountered, and it seemed as if the two adults were deliberately stretching time before asking him any questions.

"Let's establish some simple facts first. Gary Dem, today isn't the first time you've met me or my partner, Agent Nimper, is that correct?" Frank broke the silence, and Gary just nodded. "For the audio recording, please consent or disagree verbally," Frank instructed him before repeating the question.

"Yes, that is correct." Gary played along, earning him a satisfied nod from Frank.

"The first time we had the pleasure was when we found you in the vicinity of the apartment block where the Bruntin family used to live. Can you confirm this statement?"

"Yes, I happened to be around that area," Gary admitted, as it didn't seem to be to his detriment.

"All right, see, it's not so hard. Now, could you please state your reason for being in that area?" Frank asked, his friendly smile suddenly appearing far more sinister.

"I was just . . ." Gary paused for a moment, even though he knew that wasn't a good sign. Unfortunately, with how much he had been forced to deal with recently, he had long since forgotten the lie he had told them that time. This was the problem with lying; you have to keep track of your lies, and for someone like Gary who wasn't used to it, that wasn't easy.

Nevertheless, this brief moment allowed him to think about why they had wanted to talk to him. There were many things he had been afraid White Rose could ask him about. The gangsters at the construction site, the Underdogs, what he had done recently at the karaoke place, but out of all of them it turned out that they had come because of Billy.

Did they find out he's a werewolf like me? No, if anything they would probably treat him as a wolf-type Altered. However, why did they come to me? If I listen to Tom, as long as I don't talk about that I should be okay . . . I hope.

"Can we stop with these stupid games?" Sadie interrupted even before Gary had a chance to come up with an answer, revealing herself to be the impatient type. "You were there to meet Billy, weren't you? What other reason could you have had to go there, knowing that a murder had taken place?

"At the time you told us that you didn't know him, but we now know that to be a lie, so why don't you just tell us the truth?"

Her words gave Gary an idea. He was terrible at lying anyway, so why not just tell the truth? Of course, he planned to skip certain hairy details, but apart from that, wasn't he a victim in all of this? Ultimately, the one thing that would be almost impossible to trace, unless they found Billy himself, was the fact that Gary was the reason for Billy's supernatural powers.

"All right, I'm sorry I lied about not knowing who he is, but I swear I barely know him," Gary confessed. "I'd only met him once before that tragedy happened to his family! And . . . and I'm pretty sure he's after my life now! Because of certain reasons, he's pissed at me, and I had been hoping to find him and talk things out!"

The words sounded truthful, and Gary's voice was less shaky than before, but Frank didn't miss that he had omitted certain details. Was he worried about implicating himself by admitting to having participated in those illegal fighting rings, or was there something more to it?

It would make sense for a teenager to worry about those things, but the White Rose agents didn't really care about any of that.

"When you say that you knew Billy . . . was it due to the—" Frank stopped there as he felt a breeze hitting him. He looked up and noticed that the window was slightly open. He hadn't been paying attention before, so he wasn't sure if it had been open when they entered the room.

Regardless, he continued his questioning.

"Look, if it's about Billy Buster, we already know about his fight against Green Fang, so you might as well tell us the whole truth, Gary. Please don't try to deny it, we saw yesterday's fight against the Vicious Twins, and we questioned the people there. The last time anyone saw Billy just happened to be during a certain someone's debut."

Once again, Gary's heart felt like it was going to jump out of his throat. This was getting too close to the truth.

They know about the underground fights, and they were even there yesterday! If they know I was the last person who saw him, then maybe they will link him back to me.

"Look, if you know that much, then you should also know that I don't actually know him!" Gary said, trying his best to sound frustrated. "I coincidentally found out about those events and I needed the money. That's it! I wasn't lying about only ever having met him once!

"How was I supposed to know that he was a psycho? Not only did he kill his parents, he appears to be after all those he lost to in a fight! I've asked around; that university student was one of them and I bet so was the high school student, which means he's after me as well! Please, you gotta help me!"

It was a panicked answer, but it also was a part of how he truly felt.

The two White Rose agents looked at each other. The story added up and sounded plausible; of course, they would have to do their research and dig deeper to see if this was a coincidence or if Gary had actually revealed something they and the police hadn't known. If it was true, then they might even be able to use the green-haired teenager to lay a trap for Billy!

At that moment, Sadie felt a pain in her leg again. She started to rub it slightly. It didn't usually bother her, but because she was an Altered it was strange for an injury to take so long to heal. Even stranger was that it had acted up right now in front of Gary, just as it had yesterday during his match.

"We'll have to investigate to see if what you say is true. Still, there are a few more things that are . . . unclear. We were originally called here because of another killing, which had to have been done by an Altered. However, we suspect that our original killer is not Billy.

"Either Billy has been going on a rampage, deviating from his 'hit list' that you just revealed, or, if my suspicion is correct, the more likely answer is that there are actually two Altered killers in Slough," Sadie said as she placed a photo of Billy on the table and pointed it toward Gary.

The second reason why they had come here was to find out whether Gary might be that other Altered!

CHAPTER 44

A GUILTY TEST

After Blake briefly deliberated whether he should try to use the vents to listen in, an idea that he quickly dropped because of the noise it would create, the young Altered Hunter decided to go with his original idea. He looked outside to make sure there were no students out there, but since the teachers' lounge and the printer room faced away from the main road, he wouldn't have to worry about people mistaking his actions for a suicide attempt and shouting out, creating a scene that would reveal his location.

Blake opened the window and dropped down to the windowsill. He held on with his fingers, using his strong grip strength.

This reminds me of my early childhood training . . . I still don't have any idea in what circumstance this would help deal with an Altered, but it's definitely proving handy right about now, Blake thought as he moved along the edge slowly, his legs hanging down.

There was a gap between the windowsill he was on and the one outside the room where Gary was. Blake easily swung his body from side to side, and at the right moment he let go of the edge. Reaching out, he quickly grabbed the next windowsill and held on tightly. His strong fingers, which had calluses on top of calluses, had served him well and were holding out.

Now that he was in the right place, all he needed to do was listen to what they were saying. The problem was, even from his current position he had trouble making out the words clearly, so the only thing he could do was lift one hand up slowly, reaching for the window from the outside. He had to be careful; after all, they were on the third floor. Nevertheless, the young Altered Hunter didn't hesitate as he managed to maintain his grip with one hand and quickly pushed the window ever so slightly open with the other, allowing him to finally hear everything that was going on.

Billy? That's that murderer on the news! According to Dad, he's most likely one of the Altered we fought in the park, and he obviously wasn't the one I fought. Did they find something linking him to Gary? . . . Come to think of it, I guess I never did ask him, but the two of them . . . they were fighting, yet both of them were the same type of Altered.

From what I know, only the Kings and the big corporations should have a hold on specific types of Altered DNA . . . Damn it, why didn't I think of it before? Gary and Billy have to know each other somehow. I should have . . . Now that Blake had thought of it, he also wondered why he had refrained from asking Gary anything about how he became an Altered.

After all, it was pretty clear that he wasn't some rich kid, nor did the green-haired teenager seem special enough for someone to sponsor him. So what exactly had stopped him from learning more about that side of Gary? If it was only to protect the Altered Hunters, would he really be hanging down the side of the school wall?

"Two Altered killers? Are you serious? They didn't report anything like that on the news." Gary went back to his nervous self after Sadie made it crystal clear that she suspected him.

"You see, on the night of the full moon we actually had a little run-in with Billy Bruntin in his Altered form, and we were able to get some traces of his blood from our fight. According to the guys in the lab, it coincided with traces we found in the cases of the Bruntin family, the high school student, and the university student, yet there were a few other deaths that had no traces of him. However, all those other cases had another common denominator," Sadie explained.

The White Rose agent placed more photos on the table. The first one was what was left of the three men at the construction site. Next she showed a picture of Barry out in the alleyway and later in the hospital, and then she presented Gary with a few more photos.

Looking at them all, Gary was unable to recognize the others, and he was happy to see that at least there were no scenes of the karaoke place. It seemed that they weren't following his trail, just a trail of murders.

"At each of these scenes the same blood was found. Now after watching your little performance yesterday, we have reason to believe that just like Billy, you're actually an unregistered Altered. However, fortunately that's easy to clear up; all you have to do is take a voluntary blood test." Sadie smiled, as if she had caught her suspect right where she wanted him.

What do I do? I can't give them my blood! I have no idea if I will be recognized as an Altered, but if they take my blood, then they will be able to link me to Barry, the construction site, the karaoke club! If they lock me up, then Amy will be all alone!" Gary looked around to make sure there was nobody else in the room.

I've killed before . . . if I use Full Transformation now while they're still off guard . . . maybe it will be enough to get rid of them, and then . . . maybe no one will know . . . but . . . but . . . can I kill . . . again? I have to . . . it's for my family!

At the same time, Blake, who was still hanging from the window-sill, had heard everything and was wondering what to do himself. In the end, he concluded that there was absolutely nothing he could do. He had already done more than enough by not revealing Gary's secret, and if Gary had failed to hide his tracks, that was on him.

At that moment, the door slid open and a bleached-blond teen-ager confidently walked in.

"Sorry, but if you're looking for a teacher, try somewhere else. This room is currently in use," Frank told the newcomer, assuming that he had merely entered by mistake.

"Oh I know, I'm here for him," Kai said.

Seeing Kai at this moment gave Gary hope. He was especially thankful that it would save him from having to take a suicidal gamble by fighting against two White Rose agents.

"I heard what you did." Kai spoke confidently, as if he were telling the police off. "Gary, you don't have to say anything, you know that, right? I guess you agreed to talk just so that these guys would leave you alone.

"It's not called a *voluntary* blood test for nothing! They can't force you to take a blood test; for that they would need a warrant from a judge. My guess is they don't even have anything that puts you as the suspect, which was why they came here and asked you to 'volunteer' your blood to them. I bet a judge would never grant their request with what little they have."

Kai walked over to Gary's side, assuming a position as if he were his legal guardian. He then looked at the photos on the table. He hadn't heard the whole conversation, just the end of it.

"What the hell are these photos? Are you trying to traumatize my buddy here? Has White Rose stooped so low that they're trying to create a scapegoat to pin all the blame on? Tell me, what grounds do you even have to ask him for a blood test?"

The agents looked a bit startled, but they soon regained their composure, and Sadie started to laugh.

"You really think you're so clever, don't you? I didn't know that they were teaching law here at Westbridge, but I have met enough male Karens like you before who thought they knew everything," Sadie said.

"You're right, we aren't able to force him into a blood test without a warrant from a judge. However, as members of White Rose we enjoy certain privileges. According to Section 5 of the Altered

Investigation Force Act, 'agents are permitted to enforce a test in cases where they have sufficient reason to believe someone to be an unregistered Altered.' We have a special test to verify whether your friend here is a normal human."

Gary looked at Kai, and it was the first time he had seen a worried look on his face.

CHAPTER 45

AN ALTERED TEST

Kai had gone behind Gary and was tightly gripping the chair. It was a clear sign that he had been backed into a corner. This was the first time he had ever heard of something like the Altered Investigation Force Act, so of course he had nothing prepared to counter that. He had hoped that he could use his meager legal knowledge to get his friend out of this situation.

Seeing that Kai was speechless, Gary could only assume that the White Rose agents' claims were true. He wouldn't be surprised if they had special privileges, but he naturally had no idea that they would be so extensive.

Shit, isn't there anything I can do to get Gary out of this situation?... If this whole case went to court, I could probably help him out then, but there's even more of a chance for things to get out of hand. Kai chewed on his thumb, unsure what to do.

He only knew that Gary was a suspected Altered, but he had no idea that Gary wanted to avoid being brought in for completely different reasons. If they got his blood, all the cases he was linked to would come to light! However, since Kai had come here to stand up for him, Gary didn't want to give up, so there had to be another way.

"What exactly is the test?" Gary asked confidently.

The White Rose agents found this a little strange; during the whole interrogation Gary had been pretty much an emotional mess, so why was the boy acting up now? Was it because of his friend? If that was the case, shouldn't he be more nervous just like his friend clearly was?

"We test your blood," Sadie began to explain, which only put a confused look on Gary's face. He was sure he had just heard that they were unable to just take his blood and that it would be a special test.

"I can see your confusion, so let me explain. I'm not sure how familiar you are with Altered and how they came into existence, but I assume you at least know that the procedure uses the fossils of beasts that used to roam our planet.

"There is a little-known fact about these beasts, and that is that unlike us, their blood was black. Now, since beast DNA runs through the bodies of us Altered, it means that we too no longer have normal blood like the average human."

Frank pulled a small tube out of his coat and handed it to Sadie. There was a bit of light blue liquid inside. Sadie opened the lid slightly, and one of her fingers turned into a type of claw.

She pricked a finger on her other hand, allowing blood to fall into the container. Strangely, the blood from her hand looked quite red—at least it was impossible to tell with the naked eye if there was any difference at all from normal blood.

"There is a reason why the Altered Investigation Force was established, and why White Rose is looking for unregistered Altered. There are things that aren't publicly told on the news.

"The color of one's blood varies from person to person. In my case you don't really see it, but in other cases the blood of the Altered has darkened to the point where you don't even need this test. In extreme cases, the blood is completely black, which indicates that the beast DNA has mostly repressed the human DNA.

"In these cases we have found that their human nature starts to change; they start to attack others, they exhibit a lust for rage and anger, and worst of all they may even assault their family and friends."

This was the first time Gary had heard anything like this. He knew a little about the blood from watching the Altered fighting matches, but not about black blood being a sign of a dangerous Altered. Now he knew why the White Rose agents were so involved in this case.

Billy had killed his parents, and his other murders had led them to believe that he was on a killing spree. From the sounds of it, those Altered weren't humans who had just gone angry because of a new power they had obtained, but something inside them had fundamentally changed them.

Gary gulped, because that sounded very similar to what he had experienced. At some point the system had begun warning him that his bloodlust was rising, and the closer it had gotten to the full moon, the worse it had become. He now worried whether he might have become this last type of Altered.

"Regardless of all that, this test will bring us clarity about exactly what you are, Gary," Sadie said, shaking the small tube until the liquid inside the tube slowly turned from red to black. On a closer inspection, the two substances had actually split, with the black liquid on the bottom and the red blood, a bit brighter than before, on the top.

"As you can see with my blood, it looked bright red, just as you would expect normal human blood to look, but this little thing inside lets us break down the blood. If you are an Altered, like us, then the same thing will happen with your blood.

"You're clearly unregistered, so if the test works, that will be our grounds to get a warrant from a judge to get our blood sample." Sadie smiled.

The only thing Kai could think was that they were screwed. There was no way out of the test at all, and there didn't seem to be any way to trick it either. On the other hand, Gary felt like somebody had thrown him a rope.

Ever since I got this thing, I wondered whether I would technically count as an Altered. Was there really an ancient beast in the past that was a werewolf? It's a risky test, but . . . I don't think I've ever seen that my blood was black. All I can do is take the test. If there's no way out of it, then there's no way out of it. There is nothing else I can do, but . . .

"I'll take your test," Gary agreed.

"Good, not that you had a choice anyway," Sadie pointed out.

"However, as I understand it, you're only allowed to do this because you think I'm an Altered, right? I'll do the test now in front of you, but I will only show you the result. I keep this tube, and I keep it with me."

The two White Rose agents looked at each other, and while they didn't like his commanding tone, they didn't really see a problem with it either. It wasn't unusual for people to not want to consent to things that had to do with the police or the government.

Nevertheless, they had done this job long enough to know that people refusing to cooperate wasn't necessarily because they were guilty; many of those they had wrongfully accused simply hadn't wanted to be on file.

After a nod from Sadie, Frank pulled out another tube and handed it to Gary, who started to open the lid.

CHAPTER 46

THE RESULT

Kai was watching Gary carefully, assuming that he might try to switch the tube out at some point, but seeing him do nothing was causing sweat to run down his face. Seeing Kai so nervous only strengthened Sadie's belief that they had caught their suspect.

Since the test needed his blood, Gary asked the agents if they had something for him to prick his finger. When Sadie offered to do it with her claw, he naturally pulled his hand back. Then Kai pulled out a small pocketknife.

Technically students weren't supposed to have such an item, but given the situation, no one cared. However, before Gary could prick his finger, Frank inspected the blade carefully, even going so far as to clean it with a disinfectant before handing it to Gary.

This whole thing seemed absurd to Gary. He was only a teenager, and yet two adults from the Altered Investigation Force were telling him to cut his hand to prove he wasn't an Altered. The world had truly gone crazy.

Why were they here instead of looking for Billy, who had tried to kill them? Why weren't they doing something more useful, like handling the gangs who had put his mother in the hospital?

Fueled by anger, Gary pricked his finger with the pocketknife and dropped the blood into the tube. He didn't even attempt to play any tricks, as he was sure they would force him to cooperate until he did it properly anyway.

Once the blood was inside the tube, he carefully shook it, slowly, so they could all see everything. With bated breath, they waited for the result. Even Blake, who had overheard everything, had lifted himself up so the top of his head peeked over the windowsill.

He had gambled that their attention would be completely on the tube, and he was partly right. Sensing something, Frank turned around, but the Altered Hunter dropped before he got caught.

Eventually, Gary let out a big sigh of relief.

"It . . . it didn't change color . . . As you can see, I'm just a normal teenager," Gary said softly. "I'm not an Altered, so I didn't kill those people!"

Stepping in front of him, Kai thought it would be better if he was the one to do the talking from this point forward, since he was a little worried that Gary might slip up in these final moments.

"The evidence is there; you all saw that he didn't tamper with it. We all saw the results, so you no longer have any grounds to question him! If you want to pursue this, then you will have to do it through legal means!"

Sadie looked beyond annoyed, and the frown on her face clearly showed it. Still, she accepted that they had made an honest mistake. Based on what they had seen so far, their culprit had to have been an Altered, and while Gary's sudden increase in strength yesterday continued to baffle her, it wasn't something she could fault him for.

"I apologize. We thank you for your cooperation. If you have any more news about Billy, then please tell us as soon as you can. Perhaps a police officer might come by and ask you a few questions if you can help us." Sadie bowed her head, completely changing her tone, and Frank bowed also as the two of them left.

In the hallway, Sadie walked up to a window that faced the center of the school. A large tree stood in the middle of the courtyard, surrounded by students sitting on benches.

"Hey, just because your instincts were wrong this time doesn't mean it was all a waste of time. We can still try to use him as bait," Frank said, trying to cheer his partner up. "Besides, if what that kid claimed is true, then we may have a lead on where Billy will strike next."

"It's not that," Sadie replied. "That kid . . . he definitely knows something, but if he's not an Altered . . . I'm not sure how he is related to all of this."

"What makes you say that?"

"The photos. When we placed the photos down, I purposely mixed photos from different Altered cases in there that were completely unrelated to cases here in Slough. It was a test to see how he would react. I paid close attention and could see it in his eyes. His pupils got bigger when he saw the first three photos, and after going through the others, he went back to look at them.

"On top of that, the three photos he looked at were those where the same traces of blood were found . . . so he definitely knows something, but I don't know what."

"Maybe he just recognized that guy from the second and third pictures? I believe he went to this school as well."

Frank still had a lot to learn about his partner's tactics. He didn't even realize why she had done such a thing. Not all White Rose agents were there because of their smarts, but more so their strength, yet Sadie was a bit different.

"So, what do you want to do?"

"What can we do? Let's try to get the judge to give us a warrant with what evidence we have. It's unlikely, but it's the only thing we can do while we continue to investigate," Sadie answered as she walked down the hallway.

Back in the teachers' lounge, Kai and Gary wrapped Gary's finger with a bandage, making sure that none of the blood spilled anywhere. They were worried that the agents might return for another sample, but they appeared to have left, and Gary's nose told him the same thing.

Kai picked up the tube, staring intensely at it. The blood was completely red; there was no sign of black at all.

"Did you trick them?" Kai eventually asked.

"No . . . of course not! Do you really think I had any idea they were going to come after me today?" Gary felt more tired than when he had taken the test. It was something he never wanted to experience again.

Kai still had the tube in his hand, and while he looked at the blood, he had only one thing on his mind.

"Gary, if you're not an Altered, then what exactly are you?"

CHAPTER 47

WHAT'S HIS STORY?

Gary's head was drooping and for some reason he found it incredibly hard to take another step forward. He stood outside the boarded-up place that the group had recently taken ownership of.

As for why he was unable to walk forward, Even Gary didn't know. Perhaps it was because he was avoiding seeing a certain someone.

"Why? . . . Why do I feel so guilty?" he wondered, clenching his fists.

"Gary, if you're not an Altered, then what exactly are you?"

When Kai asked him that question, Gary responded with what he had considered the most natural answer.

"What do you mean, what am I? I'm human, just like you. That tube in your hand isn't black, so doesn't that prove that I'm not an Altered?" Gary replied with a nervous smile.

Kai didn't say anything, just looked from the tube to Gary, back to the tube, yet Gary could clearly see the pained look on his face.

"I see . . . so that's your answer . . . that's how you still see me." Kai let out a sigh as he left the tube on the table and exited the room.

Gary still wasn't sure why, but he felt extremely guilty for having lied to Kai. Perhaps he felt as if he had betrayed his trust somehow.

Earlier in the day, when he had so desperately needed someone to help him, Kai had appeared.

What's more, Kai had helped him time and time again ever since he had become a werewolf, but how did Gary reward that kindness? By lying straight to his face.

He already seems to know that there is something . . . but Kai, I'm sorry . . . it just seems that whenever I try to say anything about it, the words just can't seem to leave my mouth. I'm scared . . . scared that if I tell you the truth, maybe . . . maybe you'll betray me, and not just me . . . it could affect everyone around me as well . . .

Right after dealing with White Rose, Gary had naturally been hounded by his classmates about why he had been called out, by agents no less. Since Gary had returned to class, instead of being escorted out in handcuffs, they could only assume that he had been questioned about another case.

Unsurprisingly, Gary had been in no mood to tell them anything. He had decided that he was done with lying at that point . . . but then he was forced to face Tom. During the lunch break, he had confessed to the truth . . . at least partially. He told Tom that White Rose had found a connection between him and Billy, but after doing a blood test, they had deemed him not to be the killer.

Once again, although this hadn't been a complete lie, he nevertheless had omitted a lot of the truth . . .

"Are you going to walk in, or are you planning to just stand out here all day?" a familiar-sounding voice asked him from behind.

Gary turned around to see the large student he had fought the previous day, Austin Foster. Apparently, he had been dead serious when he told them he would join if Gary managed to defeat him. Now, as the leader of the Howlers, he had no excuse to continue waiting outside the door any longer.

They entered the pool club together, and inside they found Innu, Kai, Marie, and Miss Degrace already busy. Each one had a bucket of cleaning supplies, and at the back were also several boxes containing orders that the group had made, improvements for the bar.

For a second, Gary's and Innu's eyes met, but Gary immediately looked away. Gary and Innu were in the same class, so he must have known that Gary had been avoiding him since their last talk.

"Looks like you two finally made it," Kai said with his usual grin. "First order of business, we need to clean this place. Be careful, there are a lot of needles, glass, and all sorts of other things here, so make sure you put some gloves on.

"After we've cleaned, we can start getting everything else sorted out, and then it won't be long until we're open for business. So grab a bucket and get to work!"

The two did as Kai ordered. The place was large, and it needed a lot of work, so they estimated that it would take at least a few days just to clean it. Perhaps a couple of weeks before they could officially open, and even then it would require a few more improvements so the place could operate as more than just a bar.

Gary and Austin had picked one of the corners of the room to start from, which happened to be opposite from the corner where Innu and Kai were.

"You know, when I said I would help out, I thought my muscles would be put to better use than this," Austin grumbled lightly as he scrubbed at the dirt on the wooden floor. It didn't seem to go away, so he scrubbed harder. Gary began to worry that any moment now a fire might start.

"So, tell me a bit about yourself. You don't exactly strike me as the type who would choose to live the life of a gangster. What made you come up with the idea to start a gang of your own? And how exactly did you get someone like him on your side?" Austin asked. As for who he was referring to, he didn't even try to hide it. His sponge was pointed toward Kai, who was busy texting someone on his phone.

"It wasn't my idea. I-it was his," Gary said softly.

For a moment, Austin gave him a funny look, but then he just shrugged it off. Somehow, that scenario made more sense to Austin than anything else. Gary didn't seem like the leader type, and going so far as to rent a place to make it a hideout didn't feel like it was something an ordinary kid could come up with either.

"Well, at least he is on our side. I wouldn't want to know him as an enemy, but let me give you a warning," Austin said as he resumed cleaning. "I don't exactly like his kind. With sly ones like him, you never know what exactly they're scheming, making them the hardest ones to trust."

Hearing Austin speak made Gary think about what had happened this morning. Could he be right? Did he not want to confess his biggest secret to Kai because Kai was smarter than him?

"However," Austin continued, "I can see it in his eyes. The two of you seem to be somewhat alike. I feel like he won't hesitate to do whatever it costs to achieve his goal . . . although that could be a good thing or a bad thing.

"Will he drop us all to the curb if we're no longer useful, or is part of his goal bringing us all out of this shithole with him? What can you tell me about him? If he wants you to lead us, the two of you have to be close, right? What's his story? Why is he doing all of this?"

It suddenly clicked in Gary's head. *This* was why he hesitated to tell Kai more than he already knew. It was because he had no clue what Kai's story was.

Sure, the blond teenager had told him that he wanted to leave the Underdogs as well and that he wanted to change the status quo . . . but Gary had no idea about Kai's past. He still had no clue what his connection to Marie or her mother was.

Most importantly, he didn't know how Kai had ended up working with the Underdogs and why he would want to leave the life of a gang so bad, just to create another one.

Looking toward Marie and her mother, who were with Kai before even he was, he thought he might get his answer.

CHAPTER 48

HAVING TRUST

Right now, Gary couldn't help but feel a little awkward when trying to approach Kai. He believed his next best bet would be to ask the two women who seemed to always be by his side. In a way, their background was just as mysterious as Kai's.

Slowly, Gary inched his way over to the bar, cleaning away from where Austin was. Marie had taken a break and was sitting on a stool with a notepad. She also had her phone out, and from what he could see, she was busy using a calculator and writing things down.

"Hey, Marie—"

"Shhh!" She didn't even look up, shooing Gary away as if he were a pesky fly. It was clear that she didn't want to be disturbed. His only other choice was to question Miss Degrace, who was doing a few finishing touches on the place.

How . . . do I start this conversation? Gary wondered.

"Is something troubling you, dear?" Miss Degrace asked. She hadn't even turned around. It reminded him of his own mother, and it made him question whether having eyes in the back of their head was a common trait shared by all mothers. Still, this was his chance.

"How did you know?" Gary chuckled as he moved closer and started to wipe the shelves where the bottles were. This way, his back was facing away from the others as they talked.

"You see, I was wondering if you could tell me more about Kai . . . we've only started getting to know each other better over these last few days, but I recently realized that I really know nothing about him. On the other hand, it seems like you and Marie are quite close."

"In other words, you're interested in your friend? Well, I can kinda understand why, he isn't exactly your typical kid," Miss Degrace replied, opening one of the whiskey bottles that still had a bit of liquid on the bottom. She sniffed it a few times and screwed the cap back on.

"However, if you're really interested in him, why don't you simply ask him yourself? I'm sure he would answer your questions as long as you don't ask anything overly personal."

Unfortunately, Gary didn't think it would be as simple as that. Now that Kai at least suspected that he was hiding something, what right did Gary have to learn anything about Kai's secrets?

"If you want my advice, and I don't mean to insult you, in hindsight most of the problems I had as a teenager turned out to be far less problematic than I initially believed. Nevertheless, I also tended to make things harder for myself than they needed to be." Miss Degrace sighed as she seemed to be reminiscing about her own youth. "To be fair, it doesn't seem to be exclusive to teenagers. Sometimes, I believe that if people around the world just spoke more to each other about their feelings and their issues, then we could help each other more than we do now.

"Think about it: if nobody knows what your difficulties are, how can they help? While I could share a few things about him, it's really not my business to tell. I can tell you about myself, though. Marie and I both owe him a lot. It may be hard to believe, but I owe him my life. So I'm more than happy to help him when he needs me. If only things hadn't ended as they did, perhaps he could have led a normal life . . ." It sounded like she diverted a bit around the end, but Gary hadn't heard her, as he was still busy thinking about her last piece of advice.

"Let me tell you one thing, Kai is the type of person that as long as you put your trust in him, he will put all of his trust back in you as well. Think about it: why has he been helping you so much? Was it only because you agreed to help him with something in return?"

Multiple images of Gary and his first meetings with Kai flashed through his mind. It had started out as a deal, but Gary felt like he had hardly done anything to repay Kai. Still, Kai had helped him on multiple occasions without asking too many questions.

"I think you have your answer: he thought you already trusted him, which is why he was happy to help. Trust me, with the way he's been talking about you, I can assure you that talking with him will only help."

The talk with Miss Degrace didn't reveal a lot about Kai's past, but it did help Gary get his head back on straight. Over the next few hours, the group continued to clean up, and they made more progress than any of them had anticipated. What they had estimated to take an entire week had taken just a single day.

Most of it was actually due to Gary and Austin. Gary had demonstrated seemingly endless stamina, allowing him to work at a steady pace. At the same time, he had been working extra hard, regarding it as a form of penance for having acted so stupid. In Austin's case, he had seen Gary put in the work, and he hadn't wanted to lose out to him. So he had done his best to keep up with Gary, and he succeeded.

"Great job, everyone! With this tempo, it will only be a couple more days until we might be able to open for business! It will take a while for the windows, but we can just make this like a private club of some sort." Kai looked happy and decided to call it a day.

However, as everyone left and Miss Degrace was ready to lock up, Gary informed her that there was something he wanted to tell Kai. She put on her coat, gave Gary a thumbs-up, and left him the keys.

With Marie having left before her mother, only Gary and Kai were left in the former pool club.

"I'm sorry" were the first words out of Gary's mouth. "I felt like crap all day because of what I said earlier. You've helped me out so much, so I decided that I want to tell you the truth . . ."

There was a pause between the two. Kai didn't say anything as he waited for Gary to continue.

"As you've seen, I'm not an Altered, at least I don't think I am one . . . but I believe I'm not exactly completely human anymore either . . . Remember that suitcase that went missing? The one that is the whole reason the Underdogs are after me? I swear to you that I'm not joking, but . . . whatever was inside, it turned me into a w . . . w-were . . . werewolf!" Gary finally blurted out.

As he said these words, he kept his head down, worried about Kai's reaction. When he heard a chuckle, he looked up to see a giant grin on Kai's face.

"Gary, I believe you; I believe every word you just said. I'd already guessed as much after what happened in the park with Billy. However, before the test, and your confession just now, it seemed purely crazy.

"You actually being a werewolf, rather than an Altered, is a thousand times better than I thought. Now, because you have told me the truth, I think we are ready to move forward, I have a little gift for you."

CHAPTER 49

THE NEW SKILL

A week passed, and eventually the next weekend arrived. Gary wasn't as worried as usual. For one, he had about three more weeks until the next full moon. His mother's condition had also stabilized, and while it hadn't improved, at least it hadn't worsened either.

Progress on the business that Kai was planning to implement for the Howlers was going smoothly, and it would be ready to open soon. On top of that, Gary and Kai had made up and cleared their misunderstanding, bringing them a little closer.

Gary also hadn't had any more run-ins with White Rose agents or the police force. His stress levels had pretty much been reduced to normal. Of course, there was still the constant worry of money on his mind. Nevertheless, after he had paid the hospital bill for his mother, he wouldn't have to worry about it for the time being.

Kai had assured him that once the business was running they wouldn't have to rely on underground fights any more.

Name: Gary Dem
Level 8
Exp: 892/1024
Health: 100/100
Energy: 115/120

Today was a bright and shiny day, and Gary was waiting for Tom, who he had neglected quite a bit over the last few days. While he waited, he was checking out his system to see how close he was to getting stronger.

Aside from the money issue, one major problem stayed in the back of his mind, and that was Billy. There hadn't been any reports about him on the news for some time, but he had killed more than once before. While the omega wolf appeared to have limited himself to only killing people he had a grudge against, there was no telling how long he would stay true to his principles. The more time passed, the higher the chance that more deaths would occur and the stronger he would get.

"I finally made it, but are you sure all of this is necessary?" Tom asked, as he arrived with two shopping bags full of food. He wore a large backpack as well.

"Yeah, trust me, we're going to need all of that," Gary replied as he picked up his own share of food and his backpack. They headed into the forest near the park, but Gary had yet to explain what they intended to do today.

The two boys went deep into the forest, as far as they could go. Tom flinched every time he heard an animal move. Ever since the night of the full moon, he hadn't been in a forest. Although the one they were in wasn't the same one where they had been attacked, it still scared him.

The only reason he was able to put up with it was that he felt it should be relatively safe during the day.

"Whoa, thank the heavens you're not a vampire! Otherwise, I'm pretty sure you would have turned to dust from all this sun."

Gary wasn't really appreciating his best friend's jokes right now. He might not be a vampire, but he wasn't sure whether being a werewolf was any better. However, he didn't say anything. Gary had known Tom long enough to be aware that this was just his way of coping with things.

"This tree looks like it will do, and I think we're far enough away now," Gary said, as he pointed toward a large tree with a thick trunk that was nearly the same width as an average person's height.

"Are you going to finally tell me what we are doing here?" Tom asked, panting. Unlike Gary, he didn't have an endless supply of stamina, nor had anyone ever described him as physically fit.

Gary took out a pair of thick chains, the thickest ones he had been able to purchase. Tom had brought along several similarly strong locks, at Gary's request, that he had borrowed from his parents' storage unit.

"I'm going to try turning into my werewolf form," Gary finally revealed. "I know it sounds crazy, but I need to learn how to control it, Tom. If I can learn how to control it, then we might not have to worry about the next full moon. It will also allow me to get rid of the other omega wolf before he attacks again."

"Get rid of him? What do you mean, 'get rid of him'? Are you saying you plan to kill him, Gary?" Tom was completely baffled. Gary didn't answer, yet his silence spoke volumes.

"Tom . . . I don't want to keep lying to you . . . the truth is I was the one who created him. Outside of school, I got into a fight, and during that fight I bit him. I know that I was the reason that he turned into a werewolf as well. Do you understand now? . . . I'm the one responsible for everything he has done! It's because of me that you guys were in trouble that day! And it's because of me that people have already died!

"So I have to do whatever I can to stop him. Yes, even if it means I have to kill him!"

While Tom was happy that Gary had finally decided to be honest with him, he still felt that he was hiding something. For one, Gary hadn't mentioned anything about his mother ending up at the hospital. Tom had only found out after doing his own research.

Because of this, he had quickly forgiven Gary for doing something risky like gambling to get money. Fortunately, the fact that

Gary had chosen to confide in him made him hopeful that eventually he would tell him everything.

When we're out of school, Gary, I'll help you. I'll create a company of my own, and I'll use all that money to help you! Tom swore to himself.

Aside from the fact that Gary lacked the money to buy everything himself, he had called Tom over because he couldn't tie himself up on his own. He also couldn't lock himself up, and in case they survived, he couldn't unlock himself either.

Having learned from last time, they used far more chains than on the night of the full moon. They wrapped the chains around the whole tree, then put cuffs around his arms that linked to chains with spikes that were hammered deep into the other trees nearby. Finally, they set up Gary's phone on a tripod at a safe distance, so everything would be filmed.

CHAPTER 50

A NEW STATE

The preparations were complete, and with a few tugs it looked like Gary was secure.

"I'm not so sure about this, Gary; you broke out of my parents' storage unit with ease. I'm worried you might be able to break out of this as well," Tom said.

"It won't be like last time," Gary stated confidently. "I'm not sure how to explain it, but I feel weaker now that the full moon has passed. I should still be able to use its power to transform me, but it shouldn't last too long."

None of that was true. Gary was actually going to test out his newly acquired Full Transformation skill. There was one thing he had sworn to himself, and that was that he wouldn't tell Tom anything related to the Underdogs, which included the system. Who knew if this system was created by them as well? In the worst-case scenario, they might kill anyone who knew even the tiniest bit about it.

Gary's plan was to use his Charging Heart and Claw Drain skills to lower his Energy down to around 35. Using Full Transformation cost him 20 Energy points, and since it took 10 Energy points for every additional minute in his transformed state, he was sure his transformation should automatically be canceled after thirty seconds once his Energy value reached 10, thus reverting him back to his original form.

These chains don't need to hold me for long, they just need to buy me thirty seconds, Gary thought.

Tom then placed the bags of food, which were filled with raw meat, a short distance away from Gary. He would use it after the transformation. The distance was based on these thirty seconds. If he broke out, it was possible that he would reach the food, giving him more Energy and lengthening the transformed state, which was why the food needed to be a certain distance away: so he wouldn't reach it in time.

"Are you completely sure about this, Gary?" Tom shouted. "What if you can't control it? You said last time that you didn't know what was happening! That could easily happen again, right?"

"That's what I need to find out, whether I can turn and still stay in control," Gary replied. "Just trust me, everything is set up so even if I can't remember everything or my werewolf instincts take over, I'll turn back into a human before anyone gets hurt . . . I hope."

Tom turned on the recorder on Gary's phone, then headed back into the forest. Gary waited a good ten minutes for Tom to be far enough away.

Finally, it was time. Gary had used Charging Heart on his walk here. He'd realized that whenever he used the skill and he wasn't actually fighting, a rush of adrenaline entered his body. It was hard for him to even walk. All he wanted to do was run, but he was holding himself back because of Tom.

Now, with his Energy down to 35, it was time to act.

Skill activated: Full Transformation
–20 Energy
Transformation has begun

Gritting his teeth, Gary braced himself for the unbearable pain that he still vividly remembered. Unfortunately, it hadn't been a onetime thing, and everything was happening all over again. The strong heartbeat, the bulging of his muscles, and more.

He wasn't sure if it hurt more or less than last time, but he was determined to stay focused, so he could remember everything.

I have to keep conscious! There's a good chance that if I pass out, my mind will be taken over by my natural instincts . . . or however it works. I need to learn to resist it.

His skin quickly started to fall off; as his fur grew in through his hands, he wanted to claw and rip at his body, but the chains seemed to be doing their job. As he strained forward, they dug into the tree, pulling it back and forth, ripping off the bark. However, one of the spikes that was digging into the other tree had ripped out.

Stay focused! Gary told himself, feeling even his face changing, and eventually the transformation came to an end.

Gary felt like he was slightly taller than before. When he looked down, he saw a hairy pair of legs and clawed hands; he could not recognize any sign of his old body, yet he could tell that it was his by the feel of the wind blowing through his hair.

It . . . it worked! I've transformed and I'm still conscious!

"Rawr rawr!" Gary tried to say *It worked!* out loud, but only growls came out. It didn't sound even remotely like human speech. His large tongue and his roughened vocal cords were foreign to him.

His system was displaying an Energy bar, and it was going down rapidly. This was a good thing and a bad thing; he'd imagined that it would be a distraction, but it also served as a warning of when he would turn back.

Still, as it was going down, Gary wanted to check one more thing, and that was his status. He needed to know just how much stronger he was at the moment.

State: Werewolf (Omega)
Grade: Pawn
Strength 18 (+5)
Dexterity 14 (+5)
Endurance 28 (+5)

The stats displayed corresponded to his own during Charging Heart, yet that much should have been a given. However, he also benefited from an extra 5 points in all of them while in his werewolf form.

This looks even better than when I got strengthened by the power of the moon. I wonder if those stack. I might actually be even stronger when I turn at the full moon as well. Still, just because I'm still conscious for this doesn't mean it will be the same on that day. The turning back . . . I don't think this one's the same; that day it felt far more aggressive.

While he was thinking about this, his time ran out. Gary started to transform back to human. His body was shrinking and, thankfully, there seemed to be no pain associated with reverting to his normal self.

Unfortunately, the sensation on his skin when he came back was a little weird . . . what he hadn't accounted for was that his clothes had stretched to the point where they had ripped off him . . . leaving him pretty much naked once again.

Screw me, I just hope Tom comes back soon. If someone happens to pass by and see me in the woods chained up like this, they'll think I'm some kind of super pervert! Gary would have loved to facepalm himself, yet he was unable to reach.

Nevertheless, this was definitely a step in the right direction!

Now . . . it's time for me to hunt you, Billy!

CHAPTER 51

AN ENEMY IS A FRIEND

Tom came back after a short while and was surprised to see that the chains were all still intact and that Gary stood there buck naked. He deliberately avoided gazing at a certain area of Gary's body, instead hurrying to unlock all the locks.

"So what happened?" Tom asked. "Wait, before you tell me, please change into these!"

Fortunately, Tom had brought an extra set of clothes.

As soon as he put on the boxers, Gary ran toward where the bags had been placed. A few minutes later, Gary came back; the bags were practically empty. He was happy that Tom hadn't followed him to see how he had gobbled everything up.

"How did you know?" Gary asked, heading toward his phone. "About bringing the clothes, I mean?"

"Did you forget that I was the one who had to clean up the storage unit after you? Your clothes were ripped to shreds! Given all the food you had me buy and the locks you asked me to bring, I was assuming you would want to do something werewolf related; I just didn't know you could actually change," Tom replied, still a bit stunned. "Hang on, since your clothes ripped again, doesn't that mean . . . Holy shit, it worked, didn't it? Did you really do it?"

There was no need for Gary to say anything; he had a big smile on his face as he turned his phone around for Tom to watch. The screen showed a large brown hairy wolf. Without a doubt, it had worked.

They talked about Gary's experience and discovered a few things. For one, Tom was sure that the werewolf in the recording was the same one he had seen that day.

Tom went on to describe what Billy looked like and how he and Gary had different colored fur. According to Tom, Gary's Full Transformation form seemed a little smaller than his natural state, but Tom wasn't 100 percent sure as he only had the video to go on.

"I guess what I thought before might be right, then. The werewolf version of me during the full moon should be bigger and stronger," Gary concluded. "The only thing I can't figure out is what Pawn grade means. It's not there at the moment, so it must be exclusive to werewolf form."

"So, what do you plan to do now?" Tom asked, sitting down on the leaves as Gary did the same.

Gary's Energy was refilled, but he wasn't going to try to transform again anytime soon. He was happy that it all worked out the first time, otherwise it would have been expensive to keep purchasing meat.

"I . . . I need to find Billy," Gary answered.

Tom had thought as much, that the other werewolf was Billy from the news, the suspected murderer. It was all making sense, but what didn't make sense was how Gary had met up with Billy.

They got into a fight, but how? I guess I shouldn't try to pry too much. Gary has been revealing more information to me bit by bit. As long as I'm patient, he might tell me when he's ready.

Aloud, Tom said, "That might be a bit of a problem. How do you plan to find him, if even the police can't? Come to think of it, I wonder how those Altered Hunters knew where he would be? I mean, they were there that day, right? So they must have somehow tracked one of you down. It's too bad you don't have their skills."

Tom's words gave Gary a brilliant idea. He might not be able to find him, but wasn't there an Altered Hunter in their very school? Gary couldn't help smiling. If he could somehow convince Blake . . . he might get a head start on finding Billy!

The day was coming to an end, yet Slough's police station was as busy as ever. If one stood outside, they would hear an intense conversation coming from inside. It was clearly a yelling match.

"I've been back here three times already, and each time you tell me the *exact same thing*!" a young man shouted, slamming both hands on the desk. "My brother has been missing for over a week now, and it's not just him! His useless friends that he usually hangs out with have gone missing as well. Admit it, you're not even trying because of who I am!"

The worker behind the desk looked uncomfortable; he didn't know how to handle the situation. The person opposite him didn't have the best temper either. Some people might have found this situation strange, but it was actually quite normal for gangsters and the police to deal with each other.

"How often do we have to tell you the same thing until it gets through your thick skull?" Anton thundered as he came out of his office. He had been hiding in there for a while now, but since the nuisance had shown no signs of disappearing on his own, the chief of police felt like he had no other choice but to deal with him.

"For the last time, it's nigh impossible to find out *any* information from that day. All we know is that your brother and his friend weren't among the list of dead or injured that night.

"You're lucky we even looked that far, when *your* gang was mostly responsible for that entire shit show!" Anton poked the young man's chest with his finger. "If scum like you are off the streets, then that's fine by me."

Not willing to discuss the matter any further, he returned to his office, making sure to slam the door extra hard to send out the intended message, leaving Raven in anger. He knew he was getting nowhere and decided to walk out of the building. Frustrated, he sat down on the front steps with his hands in his hair.

Goddammit, where could you have disappeared to, Hawk? I've tried looking for you everywhere! Not only that, but I tried looking for your stupid friends and everything, but I couldn't find any clues whatsoever.

Raven heard the door opening again behind him, but he didn't bother to turn his head. Eventually he could tell that someone was standing over his shoulder, and that person shoved a paper in front of his face.

He looked up and saw that it was a young officer.

"Chief might not like you, but we've really tried finding your brother. I spent some of my free time looking over his case," Roo revealed. "Unfortunately, we only managed to get hold of the cell phone provider. Here is the transcript of some of your brother's last messages.

"It looked like he was talking with some girl. It's the only thing I can do without being put under investigation myself. I wish you luck in finding your brother and his friends." With that, the young police officer went back inside, leaving Raven with the paper.

Shuffling through them, Raven saw that he had possibly found his first clue to finding his brother.

CHAPTER 52

THE GRAND DAY

Today was Sunday, and in the past, Gary would have slept in until close to noon. However, today he woke up at seven a.m. sharp. He had gotten used to waking up early ever since his mother was hospitalized, so he could prepare Amy some breakfast . . . even though it was usually just a sandwich or some cereal.

As usual, the first thing on his morning ritual's agenda was to check his status.

Name: Gary Dem
Level 8
Exp: 932/1024
Health: 100/100
Energy: 120/120
Strength 9
Dexterity 7
Endurance 14

The Bond Marks continued providing him 30 Exp a day, and with another 10 Exp from the Daily Quests he had been accumulating a good amount of Exp each day. With the current tempo, he would reach Level 9 in just three more days, meaning he would be only a single level off from earning himself a class . . . even though he had no idea what that would entail as a werewolf.

His plan of asking Blake to help with locating Billy would have to wait until Monday. Gary had no idea where Blake lived. Besides, it wasn't exactly the best idea to enter the home of a family of Altered Hunters, considering what he was and how they would treat him.

Why should he enter the lions' den, when he could meet Blake on school grounds?

Picking up his phone, Gary looked at the latest message.

Be there tomorrow morning, 8 AM. Last check before the grand opening

This was the main reason for Gary waking up early. Yesterday, all members of the Howlers had received the text. On Friday, Kai had given them Saturday off, and apparently he had finished the last of the renovations, allowing the establishment to open today.

According to the agreement, Miss Degrace was supposed to take care of things during the week, but Kai had insisted that the members would help out on the weekends. Once the Howlers grew as a group, Kai planned to have future members work there. Right now, though, there were just the five teenagers and one adult. These were the only people they could really trust until they made a name for themselves.

For the time being, they would be open only on weekends and on weekdays a few hours before school started and after school ended. That way, once they finished they could help out with extra work until it got busy, closing in the late evening.

Gary was ten minutes late. He had tried to surprise Amy with a home-made omelet, only to discover that watching the Poutube instruction video while he made it had turned out to be a very bad idea.

To his surprise, the other four were standing outside the place, impatiently waiting for him. He had hoped that at least Austin might be late as well, yet nobody said anything. All of them were too excited to get inside. They all wore beaming smiles as the hard work that they had put in was finally paying off.

"What are you doing standing outside?" Gary asked.

"Waiting for you, of course," Kai said. "We all worked on this, so it only felt right to enter when we're all together."

Gary could see a significant difference from the last time he had been there. He had no clue how Kai had managed it, but the building was now adorned with gray metal letters, making the building look a lot more professional.

"I can see you've noticed my finishing touch." Kai chuckled. "Everyone, welcome to the Wolf's Pool Club!"

"That's kind of a cool name. I like it, wolves are cool animals," Innu said, only to suddenly remember a particular creature that had constantly chased after him. "Actually, scratch that, wolves are assholes! They're pure assholes!"

Kai gave Gary a meaningful wink, which made him believe that the name of this establishment had been chosen because of him.

Entering the place, they all experienced a drastic difference. For one, there were ambient lights that actually worked. Green neon lighting snaked across the walls, giving it a nice warm feeling.

The pool tables had been refurbished, the balls polished, the pool cues replaced, and the bar finally had stools for people to sit on. The only thing that seemed missing was an assortment of alcohol behind the bar. Right now it was rather empty, though they did have drinks and snacks ready, and the windows still hadn't been fitted.

Gary had to pinch himself, unable to believe his eyes; he'd never thought such a dump could be turned around, especially in so little time.

"Man, it's beautiful; I think I'm tearing up." Innu spoke for them all. "All that scrubbing, and building all that crap . . . now I can see it was all worth it. This is ours! I can't believe this is our place!"

Gary had the same feeling; he never in his life thought he would feel this way, but this belonged to all of them, the gang known as the Howlers.

The club was set to open at two p.m., just a little after lunch, and then they would stay open until eight p.m., just when the streets started to get dark. Marie went to the front and started going through the cashier system, checking that the prices of everything had been set up correctly.

There were so many things the group had to learn: the various membership cards they were offering, monthly payments, snacks, and food. Between them, they thought they would be okay as each person decided to remember one thing, but alone they held no chance.

"Look, just come to me if you don't understand anything, I've got it all right here," Marie said as she laid her thick notepad on the table, a big grin on her face.

After doing a few practice runs, Austin made some calls, informing his underlings and friends about the place. Gary and Innu wanted to do the same, but they quickly realized that the contact numbers on their phones were next to nonexistent.

"Great . . . Mom, Amy, and Tom . . . people I don't want to invite here at all." Gary sighed.

Of course, that hadn't been the only advertisement. Kai had actually paid some paperboys to distribute their flyers this morning. Eventually the area would come to learn of their presence, so why not sooner rather than later?

One of the flyers happened to end up in the hands of a gray color gang member, who had immediately informed his leader, Buffin.

"What should we do, boss? It looks like that business will open up today. They don't have protection from the Underdogs or any of the other gangs yet. Should we inform the Gray Elephants?" The gray color gang member rubbed his hands, imagining that this information might be valuable enough to earn him favor in the gang.

The first thing Buffin did was check the location. He noticed it was a troublesome place. It had a lot of foot traffic during the day, but when night came, there would be a lot of trouble in the area since it bordered on the territory of two gangs. Businesses like that only lasted a few months at most, having to constantly pay for repairs and protection.

"There's no need to bother the Gray Elephants with something like that; go and call on the new guys. Let them check it out!" Buffin ordered.

CHAPTER 53

THE OPENING

The Wolf's Pool Club was finally open for business, yet it was hard to say whether it was a success. The place was busy, and Gary was hardly able to catch a break as he was busy serving people and answering their questions. There was a good flow of income at the same time.

Gary found it difficult to call it a successful opening because 90 percent of the customers were from Austin's school. At first, when some of them arrived, they looked worried. They had even asked who they were facing and what school they were going up against now.

It quickly became clear that Austin hadn't actually explained the situation to them. Since their school's top dog had ordered them to be here, they had naturally expected a fight. After they realized that it wasn't a call for a big fight, the teenagers decided to stay anyway, playing a few games of pool and buying some snacks. They seemed to be enjoying themselves, but all the Howlers could do was hope that they liked it enough to decide to return.

I guess that's the power of a real leader right there, Gary thought. He looked at the room, filled with around twenty high school students who had all come just because of Austin.

The cash register was constantly going off, and since it was busier than they had expected, even Marie had to help out as a waitress; she had a couple of Cokes and some snacks on a tray. She placed it on a table between two sofas. As she bent down, two boys sitting on either side were eyeing up her legs and the skirt she was wearing.

The boys exchanged looks, and then one of them imitated hitting her backside, leading the other to giggle at the gesture.

"Here's your food, I hope you enjoy it," Marie said with a smile. To those who knew her, Marie seemed like a completely different person. She was all smiles, talked politely, and was generally a pleasure to be around. It was the complete opposite of the commanding girl who had drilled them on what they needed to know.

As soon as Marie turned around, though, someone whacked her on her backside. Immediately the boys behind her started to laugh and whistle. Marie froze, clearly unsure how to react.

The boys continued to laugh until one of them felt someone grab him by the wrist, lifting him off the seat to a standing position. It was so forceful that he thought his shoulder was going to be dislocated.

"What the hell did you just do?" Gary asked.

"Are you crazy, man? You're hurting me! Let go! I'm a paying customer, you have no right to treat me like this!" the student yelled, and the others turned, looking like they were ready to jump in at any moment.

"So what? That doesn't give you the right to do that! What . . . what if that was your sister, or your mother?" Gary asked. Just thinking about it made the his blood boil. Marie's small frame was similar to Amy's, and this incident reminded him of an unpleasant scene.

"Are you her boyfriend or something? If you want to simp for her, don't get me involved. It was just a little tap, she wasn't hurt or anything. She can just ignore it, and I didn't hear her complain either!" The harasser didn't show any signs of remorse.

However, it was clear from her reaction that she didn't like it at all, and the student's tone was just annoying Gary further.

"Get out!" Austin's voice resounded throughout the pool club. The other guests were making way for him to get through.

225

Seeing this, the high school student grinned. "You're dead now."

Gary was unsure what to do; though he wanted to teach that guy a lesson, Austin was the one who had invited them all over. Not to mention, it would cause a big problem if the two of them were to fight.

When Austin arrived, he grabbed the student that Gary had held up by the collar.

"Not him, but you, dipshit!" Austin said, pushing his forehead up against the student's.

"As for the rest of you, no one is allowed to treat our staff like this! These people are a part of my group, you understand? What he did was no different from harassing my little sister!" With that said, the latest member of the Howlers dragged the offender by the scruff of his neck and opened the doors.

"You can come back once you know what you've done wrong! You better have a sincere apology ready for her!" Austin clapped his hands as he threw him outside and slammed the doors shut.

There was silence in the room when Austin turned around. No more laughter and cheer.

"The show is over, everyone; go back to having fun again. Let's forget that idiot!" Austin shouted.

It took a while but eventually things returned to normal, except that Kai told Marie to stay behind the counter as the rest of the boys picked up speed. After everyone got served, things started to quiet down.

By the time new customers came in, they had somewhat gotten used to the process, making things quicker, and there was no need for them to go back and forth to ask Marie for help. The initial impact of a full house made the place look popular, attracting even more customers.

Eventually Gary got a chance to take his first break. He sat down by the bar, where Marie and her mother were working, and watched the rest have fun.

Kai, Innu, and Austin had started playing against the others, and it looked like the blond teenager was making some bets. To nobody's surprise, a few minutes later, money was being exchanged, all of it going to the Howlers.

"Thank you," a soft voice said. It was so soft that it was barely audible with all the surrounding noise.

"What did you say?" Gary asked, as he hadn't been sure he had heard correctly. Although he wasn't far away, the voice had been faint even with his enhanced hearing. Having already found it hard to muster the courage to say it once, Marie was turning red.

"I said thank you!" Marie repeated, slightly louder this time, her eyes fixed on the glass she was cleaning. "And I don't just mean today. I've yet to thank you for saving me that time with the black color gang. Sorry it took me so long."

"Oh, that. Well, yeah, I mean, those guys deserved it and so did that pervert," Gary said, a little embarrassed himself now. After all, this was the first time he had ever been praised for doing something heroic.

Now that she had reminded him, the first time he had seen Marie had been when those black color gang members had been picking on her. Usually, Gary wouldn't have thought twice about color gangs picking on anybody, but the strangest thing had been that it had happened during the day.

Maybe I should ask?

CHAPTER 54

A MONSTER

However, before Gary could ask about that day, Marie surprised him with a question of her own.

"Are you an idiot?"

Now he was really confused. One moment, Marie had been thanking him, yet the very next she was insulting him?

"I'm sorry, that came out wrong. I just don't get how you can not get scared in these situations. Back then, the black color gang members seriously outnumbered you. There was also a good chance that everyone could have jumped you earlier as well."

Now Gary understood a little more what she meant.

"Well, I guess I am a bit of an idiot, then. I dunno, but it just felt wrong to stand there and watch it happen. In the past, I guess I never acted when I saw something like that. Now, though, people around me are getting hurt, and no one is doing anything about it.

"So I thought, what would happen if I became that person, who took action instead of just watching and wishing for help. Man, when I say this stuff out loud, it seriously sounds lame . . . Like weird superhero film crap . . . only I'm far from being a superhero.

"I mean, for one, I'm not good-looking, I'm scrawny, and my personality sucks balls. Well, not actually balls, but you know what I mean . . ." Gary said, trailing off, and eventually he looked toward Kai, Austin, and Innu.

"When I look at them, they fit that role a lot better than me."

Somehow, Gary's rambling only ended up depressing him. He hadn't had the time to talk with anyone about all the things he was going through. Tom used to be the closest person he had.

He heard a thump and when he looked up, a Coke in a pint glass sat in front of him.

"It's on the house . . . huh, I guess since you're kinda the boss of this whole place it's a given . . . Anyway, you deserve a free drink," Marie said as she handed him the glass.

"Just remember what I said, you're the boss, not them. Who's to say that when they look at you, they don't think the same way? Did anyone else come forward before you did, Gary? No, they might have come forward, but you were the first one to act, and that's what makes you you.

"And besides . . . you're not that bad-looking. In fact, you're kinda cute."

Gary was in the middle of drinking the Coke when Marie said that, and it nearly made him spill it all over. Before he could react, though, she had already run off to the far end of the bar to serve another customer.

I guess she's kinda cute herself . . . Gary thought, yet he wouldn't dare to say that out loud.

After a successful debut, it was time for them to count how much money they had made. Surprisingly, the club had managed to earn around three thousand dollars after the cost of the drinks and food had been subtracted. It was far more than any of them would have imagined in a single day.

It sounded like a huge amount, at least until Gary did the calculations.

"Wait a second, ten percent of that is three hundred, and then that would need to be split between all of us . . . that means I hardly get anything . . . it's far from being enough."

"I can see that look on your face," Kai said as he put a hand around Gary's shoulder. "If it were easy to get rich, do you think anyone would remain poor? This was just the first day, and the business will grow. We will be able to open for longer and possibly at night as well.

"Once that happens, we should easily be able to earn double that amount. Besides, this is just the first of many priorities, and most of that money needs to stay with Marie and her mother, so they can deal with all the bureaucratic stuff such an establishment requires.

"They are working the hardest out of all of us, after all. Eventually, we won't even have to lift a finger and all of that income will turn to passive income."

In the end, Kai pulled out a hundred dollars and handed it to Gary. Part of it was from his share of the 10 percent; the rest was from the bets he had won earlier.

"Making money can be quick, and it will be, but we can't make it appear overnight. Trust me, we will get there. For the time being, just be glad that I can't bear the thought of you making your cutie of a sister starve. You earned that, and good job standing up for one of our members back there. You're becoming more of a leader every day."

Gary instinctively grumbled a bit at Kai's teasing, but he still thanked him for the money, and he also appreciated the compliment. He did trust Kai, so if he claimed this was a step in the right direction, Gary believed him.

Nevertheless, this meant that for now whenever an underground fight took place, they would probably have to join it, unless something drastic were to change.

On Monday, Gary's attempt at an omelet for Amy turned out far better than the day before, even though the end result became scrambled eggs. With that done, he hurried to the gym to complete his Daily Quest.

Unfortunately, even after all that time, he had seen no more improvement to his stats, to the point that he began wondering whether those 5 Exp were really worth the effort. The fact that it would start to cost him money at some point didn't make it any more appealing. After a quick bite to replenish his Energy, he checked his progress.

982/1024 Exp

Damn, I'm so close to Level 9 . . . Argh, I will have to wait until Wednesday for it to naturally occur. System, why do you have to taunt me so much? Can't you give me 2 extra Exp tomorrow? Please, just once, give me that small extra bit! Gary's begging was met with the usual silence.

When he arrived at school, a few students were already inside; one of them was Xin, who seemed to be staring at Tiffany for some reason. Gary wasn't sure how to interact with the new girl. He still somewhat fancied her, but given their last interaction, he didn't know how to behave around her.

On the other hand, things seemed to be back to normal with Tom after their little experiment. While Gary had been busy helping out at the pool club on Sunday, his best friend had been busy trying to find out more information about Altered and werewolves.

When it was time for lunch, Gary excused himself by claiming he needed to go to the restroom, leaving Innu and Tom to their own devices. However, the real reason was that he saw a certain someone walking down the hall.

"Blake, wait, do you have a moment? I need to talk to you," Gary said.

Oh crap! Blake thought. *I still haven't processed everything I heard the other day, and now he wants to speak to me? I could live with you being an Altered, Gary . . . but since the test was negative . . . if you're not an Altered . . . are you a monster?*

CHAPTER 55

THE HUNTER'S TROUBLE

Hanging outside the school from a windowsill wasn't exactly a normal thing for a student to do, yet Blake had done exactly that. He'd done so out of great concern for his fel— No, he had done so because it was his duty as an Altered Hunter who was worried about an Altered possibly being at his school!

Seeing White Rose agents at their school meant that there could be even worse things roaming around the school than Gary. Which was why he needed to act fast. However, after listening in to their entire investigation, the only thing the young Altered Hunter had learned was that Gary was not an Altered . . . It was a head-scratching moment for Blake.

For the rest of the day, Blake had been very absent-minded. Hurrying home after rugby practice, he felt strangely relieved. His heart was no longer beating fast, but he had a lot on his mind.

I definitely saw him transform from a doglike beast back into a human. Human-to-beast transformation should be something that only Altered can do, right?

But then why did that test fail? Even if the test was faulty, it usually comes down to human error, otherwise White Rose and the Altered

Hunters wouldn't use it for verification. However, it's impossible for two experienced agents to make such a rookie mistake. But then, how was it possible? It was clear that this puzzle was beyond what Blake could figure out on his own, so he was hoping that a certain someone might help. Someone who could give him answers.

Right now, he had finally arrived home. On the side was their clinic. It wasn't a large hospital, just a small place that treated the locals, typically for small wounds here and there; they also sold medicine at their pharmacy and occasionally helped out the local hospital.

The clinic was owned by the Hunt family, but next to it was where Blake and his family lived. There was a large wall blocking the house from public view, so onlookers would be unable to see inside.

In the wall was a wooden gate that could be slid open once a passcode was entered, and Blake did just that. On the other side was a garden, and toward the back of the garden was a traditional Asian-inspired house made out of wood, with only one story. It was a large house, but it was hard to tell whether the family was wealthy as the building was a bit run-down.

Blake took off his shoes as he slid the front door open, and in an instant he heard something striking the air. Blake immediately jumped to the side, rolling, and his father stood there holding a baton.

"Although you avoided the blow, you were slower than usual," his father chastised him as he stood there in his white robe. It looked like he himself had just gotten off work at the clinic. "If I were an Altered based on some speed-type beast, you might be dead now. You should always remain vigilant and do your best to be active rather than reactive."

His father paused before going back inside. "I'm guessing something's on your mind, for you to slack off like that. Come in, let's talk."

Inside was what looked like a standard training room, similar to those in traditional dojos. He and his father regularly trained with special weapons, but of course these special weapons were illegal under the No Lethal Weapons Pact; hence they had made sure that nobody could see inside.

His father walked toward a table at the back, on which sat three monkey statues. The one on the left was covering its eyes, the middle one was covering its ears, and the one on the right was covering its mouth. After his father touched them in a particular order, he heard a click.

The wall to the right slowly spun around until it stopped halfway, revealing a staircase that led downstairs. Blake and his father walked down, small lights by the side illuminating their path.

Eventually, they reached the bottom and the secret Altered Hunter room. Blake warily stared at the shelves filled with old books. He still remembered the countless times that he had been told to read them over and over again as a child.

They contained a trove of information regarding the family's history and why they did what they did. In addition, they had information about all the different beasts of old their ancestors had hunted, knowledge that proved invaluable when going up against any Altered.

Farther along was a workbench, with an experimental table next to it. On the other side were the weapons and sets of armor their predecessors had used. Each weapon was unique, and it was the same with the armor sets; there were different ones that had been made centuries ago, although each subsequent generation had improved on them.

"I thought you might feel more comfortable here discussing what's on your mind," his father began. "Are you still hung up about what happened? You know, if you really want to hurry up and become a one-star Altered Hunter, we could move to one of the higher-tier cities once we've taken care of Slough's Altered. After that we'll be able to meet the others, and you won't feel so . . . left out."

Hearing this reminded Blake of who he was. His father, Ozacas Hunt, was a three-star Altered Hunter, which meant he had killed more than fifteen Altered, while Blake hadn't even killed a single one yet. In fact, he had actually let what would have been his first kill go free.

His father often talked about meeting others, but so far Ozacas had been the only Altered Hunter he had ever met. His father didn't want to introduce him to the others until he had at least earned his first star.

Blake loved his father, but he hated that side of him. He had read that the past generations of the Hunt family had enjoyed a lot of prestige among their own kind, yet Ozacas hiding his son made Blake feel as if his father was ashamed of him.

"It might be slightly related to that matter," Blake confessed. "I was just wondering, the books talk of beasts that used to roam the earth long ago . . . and I know that their fossils are being used to create the Altered, but . . . is it possible that those beasts still exist today?"

"That is actually a popular topic among Altered Hunters," Ozacas replied, scratching his chin. "While there has yet to be a definitive answer to that question, I personally believe that there are. Although I have never met one, there are rumors of certain special Altered being out there.

"Do you remember reading that there were beasts that had attained a humanoid form? These were the most dangerous during their time, since they were said to display clear signs of intelligence. I suspect that some of those special Altered are exactly that, hiding among us today."

Was that the answer? Was Gary actually some type of humanoid beast who had taken on the appearance of the naked teenager to invoke some sort of sympathy from Blake? However, if that was the case, his blood should have been black . . . yet Blake was certain it had been red. He was quite sure of it; after all, he had been the one who had to wash it off his outfit.

His father went to put the baton away and started toward the staircase. While it was a good tool to prepare his son for surprise attacks, if the police caught him with such a thing, it would lead to a very bad outcome.

"Then . . . have you ever heard about a beast not bleeding black blood?" Blake asked.

Just as he reached the top of the stairs, his father froze when he heard this question.

"Why does it sound as if this isn't a hypothetical question?" his father asked, slowly turning his head, making Blake gulp down hard.

CHAPTER 56

TRACKING THE OMEGA

After Gary told Blake that the two of them needed to talk about something, they made their way outside to the bench next to the art block. This time, Gary was the only one to sit down, while the young Altered Hunter insisted on standing.

"Hey! Earth to Blake, are you with me?" Gary waved his hand in front of Blake's face. "Is everything all right with you? Were you out and about with your dad yesterday or something? You seem a bit out of it."

"Huh? My bad, I've just got a lot going on, and . . . honestly I still don't think it's a great idea for the two of us to meet outside of rugby practice," Blake replied, and it looked like he was ready to leave again.

"Wait!" Gary grabbed Blake by the arm. "It's important, it's about the other Altered from that day!"

He had deliberated how much he should tell the Altered Hunter. After all, Blake had already discovered Gary's secret, only he believed that Gary was actually an Altered, an honest mistake Gary wasn't too keen on correcting. However, if it meant gaining his trust and cooperation, he was somewhat ready to tell Blake the truth.

"That Altered . . . I think I know who it is. I'm sure you heard about White Rose coming to Westbridge and asking for me the other day. They came to ask me a few questions about Billy Bruntin, the guy that was on the news a while ago.

"Anyway, last time you and your dad were there to stop us. Somehow, you were both able to track down the Altered before even White Rose could. Could you tell me how you did that?" As long as he had the method, he could do it himself, allowing him to face Billy alone.

"And what do you plan to do when you find the Altered, Gary?" Blake asked. He had a plethora of other questions in his head, like what exactly was the relationship between the two. They looked to be the same type of Altered or beast, so surely there had to be something connecting them. However, Gary had indirectly admitted that he was unable to find or contact the other person.

Gary could see it in Blake's eyes, that he wasn't going to budge until he heard a satisfying answer. Fortunately, the one person who Gary believed might be all right with the answer to that question was the young Altered Hunter.

"I want to get rid of him!" Gary answered with no hesitation. "He's hurting and killing people. He might be laying low right now, but I know he hasn't stopped. You know Innu, the guy who transferred here not too long ago? I'm convinced he's being targeted by Billy.

"That's why that guy was in the forest that day. I know your situation, which is why I'm not asking you for help, I just need to know how you did it."

Blake wasn't sure whether Gary was telling the truth, but he knew he could use the current situation to his advantage. Gary needed something from him, and he had questions only the green-haired teenager could answer. "All right, I'll tell you how to find him . . . if you can tell me how you're connected to Billy. And I want the *actual* truth, Gary . . . I'm aware that you're not really an Altered, so first I need you to tell me what exactly you are, then," Blake demanded.

This was not the reaction Gary had expected from Blake. How did he even find out that Gary wasn't an Altered? Was it some sort of sixth sense that Altered Hunters had? Did they perhaps have some type of mole in the police force, updating them?

Ultimately, it didn't matter. The important part was finding Billy. The longer he waited, the stronger the other omega wolf could become, and the bigger the risk would be for everyone around Gary to get hurt.

"I . . . I'll tell you . . ." Recently, Gary had been telling others the truth a lot more often, and it felt good to get things off his chest. Of course, there was no need for him to explain to Blake how he had become a werewolf.

At the same time, he made sure to leave out one critical piece of information: that he was the one who had turned Billy into a werewolf. If Blake or the other Altered Hunters were to learn that all it took for Gary to turn others was a simple bite, he was sure they would do everything to hunt him down.

After Gary had confessed to everything, Blake's reaction was not what he was expecting at all. The young Altered Hunter merely let out a big sigh of relief.

"Thank goodness, so you're just a werewolf." Blake smiled, but the smile soon changed as he came closer to Gary and placed a hand on his shoulder. "I'm sorry, but I lied. There's really no easy way for us to track down someone like Billy. Altered Hunters use a lot of tools that help us, but we don't have a guaranteed way.

"Unfortunately, there isn't some sort of secret I can just share with you, and those instruments require some in-depth knowledge, so I can't just lend them out. You understand that, right?"

Gary was upset, and he had every right to be. Just when he thought there might be a way to get one step closer to getting rid of one of the biggest problems in his life, it turned out that his only lead had disappeared. He also didn't appreciate being lied to like that, even if he hadn't been totally honest with Blake either.

"However, there is something I can do for you. If anyone ever finds out what I'm about to propose, they'll probably excommunicate me . . . Why don't the two of us try to take him down together?

"I mean, I'm an Altered Hunter, and even if he's a werewolf, he's kinda like an Altered who needs to be taken down, right? No offense, but if I managed to deal with you, you'll have a hard to impossible time going in by yourself.

"He's managed to go up against my three-star dad and survive, so calling him tough seems to be an understatement. While we might not stand a chance on our own, together we might just be enough to pull it off. What do you say?"

CHAPTER 57

BETTER TOGETHER

Gary hesitated to accept Blake's offer. Billy was his responsibility, and he hated the thought that his friends might get involved. The fact that the omega wolf had attacked them still haunted him, especially since it had boiled down to dumb luck that none of them had gotten killed that night.

However, Blake was different from the rest. In the first place, he was an Altered Hunter, belonging to a group of people who risked their lives to kill Altered on the daily. Even if he refused, chances were that Blake and his father would be looking for Billy anyway.

But is working with an Altered Hunter really the best thing? I can trust Blake, can't I? Gary wondered. *He did let me go that night, even though I was too injured and too weak to resist. He could have easily killed me . . . well, I guess he could always tell his father about me if he wanted to . . .*

Then an idea popped into his head. Instead of worrying about things he couldn't control, why not use his system? At least that way, he would get a warning if his trust turned out to have been misplaced.

"You're right, the two of us stand a much better chance to take down Billy together. However, I have one condition. I want you to promise me that you won't try to kill me," Gary said as he held out his hand for a handshake.

Strangely, Blake was now the one who hesitated. However, in the end, he shook Gary's hand.

"Seems fair . . . I promise I won't try to kill you." Blake answered, yet he remained careful with his words. Although he might not make an attempt on Gary's life, he couldn't promise that others wouldn't.

A spoken deal has been made, would you like to mark "Blake Hunt"?
Yes
5/5 Marks have been assigned
Please reach a higher level to increase the number of available Marks

Oh! So that's how I can get more marks.

Gary was pleased to find out that information. He had kept one mark free, just in case he needed to make a bond with anyone else he cared about. Of course, it could have also been used to initiate a Forced Bond with anyone he might have needed to track down in the future.

Fortunately, he had already created Bond Marks with those close to him, and this promise with Blake also had another nice benefit. With the additional 10 Exp he would gain, he would only have to finish one of his Daily Quests tomorrow to reach Level 9.

Maybe then I will finally gain that Iron Body skill I saw a while ago. It might be too much to ask for more marks to assign that early, but possibly Level 10 will do the trick. It seems special enough, seeing as the system called it a Main Quest.

"Do you mind if we start looking for Billy tomorrow?" Gary asked Blake. "I still need to get some things sorted out today." As much as he wanted to take down the omega wolf, that extra stat point he would get tomorrow might end up playing a vital role.

"Not at all." Blake shook his head. "It's going to take me a couple of days before I can gather the things I require anyway. Just to let you know, we'll probably only get one shot at this. Honestly, I don't like doing this stuff behind my dad's back. If it doesn't work out, or it turns out to be too dangerous, we should leave it.

"Worst case, I can just pretend to have found him on my own, without mentioning you. With all the leads, he will probably be able to take care of it."

Gary nodded, although he didn't completely agree to the deal. He wanted to make sure Billy was truly gone, rather than leaving it in the hands of others. As long as the quest was still there, he was sure the omega wolf would be after him.

The two went their separate ways, and Gary now had a new contact in his phone, adding Blake's number to his small list. Gary considered inviting Blake to the pool club. Kai did say that they should invite their classmates since it was a business, after all, and if they were working together, it wouldn't be bad for their relationship to be closer.

Maybe after all this Billy stuff is taken care of, Gary thought, not wanting to stop his friend from making the preparation he had talked about.

After the lunch break, afternoon classes continued as usual until it was time for them to go to their club activities. Right now, Gary and even Tom were on the field. Ever since the last match where substitutes had been used, Mr. Root had started involving them more in practice, just in case a similar incident occurred.

"Say, do you plan to do more werewolf stuff later? Since we know you can control it now, it might not hurt testing out your limits and such," Tom suggested, while pretending to kick a ball.

"Ah, actually I'm busy . . . Hey, how about you just come along after club practice instead?" Gary had been about to decline his best friend's suggestion, but then he offered to take him along. "I recently got another part-time job. The atmosphere is relaxing, and you actually already know the others. It shouldn't be a problem, and it will let you see what I'm doing. Stay there for as long as you like, or leave if it's not your thing."

Tom couldn't quite believe his ears; Gary was actually inviting him to his job. He gulped slightly, wondering what it could be, but if his best friend was inviting him it had to be safe . . . right?

Gary didn't want to further distance himself from Tom, who had always helped him out. After their first day of business at the club, Gary didn't have to worry about the members talking about any gang stuff, simply because they would be far too busy taking care of things in the Wolf's Pool Club. It had become nothing more than a hangout place, so there was no reason to keep it a secret from Tom.

"Sure, that would be great!" Tom agreed enthusiastically.

When practice was over, Tom, Gary, and Innu were all waiting outside the school gate. Gary had explained to Tom that all of them worked at the same place, so they were all currently waiting for Kai, who according to Tom's knowledge was the one with connections to the place.

Tom didn't really like that Gary was hanging around Kai and the others, especially since he still assumed that Gary had gone gambling with them. He was simply worried that they might influence him to do other, potentially worse things. However, he also hadn't forgotten that without them, he might have ended up as a snack for the other werewolf he had initially mistaken to be Gary.

"Customer or another pair of helping hands?" Kai asked teasingly, as he joined the three boys.

"Where's Marie?" Innu asked, noticing that Kai was on his own.

"Ah, as far as the school knows, she got injured recently, making her unable to participate in club activities for a while, so she gets to leave earlier than the rest of us. In other words, she should already be there," Kai answered.

Gary's face was feeling a little hot as he recalled yesterday's conversation with Marie. Rather than enjoy her free time, she was diligently going to the pool club and working hard. In fact, Marie had diligently been working while everyone else was cleaning. She hadn't even taken a single break, working at the cash register and the bar simultaneously.

They started to walk together, and Tom couldn't stop asking questions about the place. Luckily, after Gary answered the initial questions, Kai took over and answered all of Tom's concerns.

"I can't believe you're working at a place called the Wolf's Pool Club, of all things," Tom said while glancing at Gary. This didn't go unnoticed by Kai, who made a mental note that he might not be the only one to know Gary's secret.

"Relax, man, it's just a normal pool club!" Innu finally said, placing his arm around Tom. The two of them were more comfortable with each other since they were in the same class and seat neighbors. "Your boy is okay, you don't have to worry, and none of us are going to get in trouble. It's one of those under-the-table things. As long as no one reports it, nobody gets hurt, and we all profit."

When they finally arrived at the place, the door had been left wide open, which seemed unusual, and not just because it was supposed to keep the heat in. As they rushed into the pool club they couldn't believe their eyes.

"What the fuck? Who did this?" Innu shouted, as he looked around for a perpetrator.

CHAPTER 58

WHAT NOW?

Innu let out his frustration by shouting and yelling at the scene in front of him. The other two boys were too shocked to say anything, while Tom remained silent. He had never before seen such a look on Gary, who was beyond mad. His fists were clenched so tightly that the veins on top were showing.

"Who did all of this? Screw me, this place looks even worse than before!" Innu continued to yell, and rightly so. The place had been completely wrecked. The pool tables, the cues, and even the barstools had been destroyed. Glass shards were everywhere, surrounded by the liquid that was once inside the bottles. All of their hard work had been ruined just like that.

"This . . . has to be intentional," Kai said slowly. "Shit! They were supposed to come to us to talk first! . . . Why didn't they send out their representatives? . . . I made a mistake . . . Fuck! I never thought they would act this fast."

It was clear that Kai wasn't his usual self, yet all of them turned around as they heard an incoming motorbike. Austin could tell that something was wrong when none of the other boys greeted him and Gary stayed in the doorway. Getting off his bike, he entered the pool club, and his reaction was similar to Innu's.

"Who did this? Who dared to touch our place? Tell me their names, so I can pound their heads in!" Austin shouted, punching his fist into his other hand.

Tom was just baffled, wondering who this new scary figure was that he hadn't seen before. He could only assume that Austin was another employee, but now didn't seem like the best time for an introduction.

What he also didn't understand was why everyone was so upset that their place of work had been destroyed. Their employer should have insurance that would cover all of this damage. Sure, they had every right to be upset about being unable to work for a while, but they were all taking this really personally.

He hadn't been told that they were actually the owners, nor that they had invested their own time and sweat to transform it into a working establishment. It had only been open for a single day, yet someone had come in and destroyed all of their hard work . . .

While the others were still coming to terms with the grim situation, Gary remained standing at the door.

"Tom . . . I smell blood," Gary finally said. "Why do I smell blood?"

Tom suddenly understood why his best friend had been more than just a little angry about his place of work being destroyed; if he smelled blood, it could only mean one thing.

"Guys! Where is Marie? Didn't Kai say she was supposed to be here already?" Tom loudly asked, having connected the dots.

Another one of the group was standing frozen by the bar area, looking down. Gary noticed that was where the smell of blood had come from and rushed over. Kai fell to his knees and held Miss Degrace up. She had been beaten and there was a cut on the top of her head.

Seeing Miss Degrace in this condition brought back images in Gary's head from when he had found his own mother like this.

"No! No! No! Not again!" Kai screamed, holding her. "Wake up! Can you hear me?"

The others gathered behind him to see the state she was in—and the state Kai was in. The normally calm person was startled and clearly out of it.

Eventually, though, through the shouting, Miss Degrace had opened her eyes and seemed to have regained consciousness.

"Kai, you're here . . ." she said as her eyes immediately started to well up. "I'm sorry, I tried to contact you . . . I tried to stop them." Her voice sounded very weak.

"They took her . . . they took Marie. I'm sorry . . . I really did try to stop them."

"I know you did!" Kai held her hand, tears running down his face. "Don't worry, I'll get her back! Just tell me who did this to you!"

"They were wearing . . . gray . . . I think it was the gray color gang . . . but there were another two with them," Miss Degrace answered in a weak voice; the act of speaking was clearly exhausting.

Kai's main suspects had naturally been the black and gray color gangs who fought over the area. Normally they would have sent out their scouts to visit the business and offer their "services." However, two things didn't make sense to him.

Why did they outright attack them rather than try to force them to pay up? With the pool club in its current state, there was nothing to be gained from it. Nevertheless, the more pressing matter was why did they take Marie with them? *I can't . . . think straight*, Kai realized.

Gary put his hand on Kai's shoulder, giving him some reassurance. "Let's get her to a hospital first. They'll make sure she will be okay," he said, concerned that her condition might worsen. "Tom, can you take her there? Get a taxi and make sure she's all right. An ambulance might take too long."

"Wait, what are you going to do? Aren't you guys going to come with me?" Tom asked as he dialed the number.

Gary looked at the faces of the other teenagers. Everyone seemed to feel the same, and he couldn't get the image of Marie from yesterday out of his head.

"We'll go and find Marie. Please, Tom, take care of her for us," Gary said.

Tom had heard who had attacked this place. It was the gray color gang, and while they might not be as dangerous as the main gang backing them, he couldn't imagine what Gary and the other three could do on their own. He wanted to stop them, but Gary's words seemed firm.

"All right, but promise me, Gary, don't do anything you'll regret," Tom said, as Austin helped lift Miss Degrace and the three of them went out to wait for the cab. When Austin returned, Kai was standing there in place, still looking at the spot where the woman had been.

He's too angry, his head isn't in the right place, but who can blame him? Usually, he would be the one to tell us what to do in this situation, but since he's out . . .

Austin turned to Gary. "So, boss, what are we going to do now?"

Innu also turned to Gary, and even Kai had looked up. All eyes of the Howlers were on him.

"Isn't it obvious?" Gary asked aggressively. "This is our place . . . and Marie is part of the Howlers. They've messed with us and our place, so we're going to storm their fucking place, get her back, and *make them pay!*"

CHAPTER 59

KAI'S GIFT

Gary had been ready to go on his own in the worst-case scenario. He wouldn't have blamed any of them, since what they were about to do was crazy for any normal teenager, yet not a single member of the Howlers hesitated. They were all willing to go along with their leader's decision and rescue one of their own.

In the short amount of time that the group had spent together, they had formed a bond that couldn't be explained with just words. On top of that, they all seriously wanted to punish those who had destroyed the pool club.

If anything, now is the perfect time . . . I'm sure the gray color gang should still be suffering from the fight they had with the black color gang and the Underdogs. There shouldn't be as many of them active as they were before, Gary thought.

Now knowing who their target was, Kai began making some calls to find out where they needed to go. However, in case he couldn't come through, Gary already had a pretty good idea where the gray color gang's hangout was.

He had followed Gil's scent to an abandoned warehouse and watched his former schoolmate go through some type of initiation, and the leader was there as well. He was sure that if they needed answers, that was the place to go.

Still, it might mean we'll be going up against the entire gray color gang if they're at their hideout, but Marie could be with them . . . who knows what they're doing with her? She could end up getting hurt just like Amy . . . or Mom . . . If it comes to it, I'll have to use everything.

"You guys prepare yourselves, I need to get something first." Gary excused himself and headed to the back, where a staircase led underneath the pool club. The group had used the cellar to store supplies and equipment. The door had been kicked in, so Gary wasn't surprised to find their supplies stolen and most of the equipment destroyed.

How much damage did they cause? Gary wondered, yet he was thinking about who had been affected the most by this, and it was clearly Kai, Marie, and her mother.

Walking through the cellar, Gary eventually found what he was looking for, lying on the floor. It was Kai's gift for telling him the truth. It wasn't really anything special, which was why the gray color gang members hadn't bothered taking it. Bending down, he picked up the item and thought back to his conversation with Kai that day.

"As you know, the leader is the most important figure in any gang," Kai had said after leading Gary down to the cellar. "You've heard of the Kings, I assume?"

"Of course," Gary answered. Even before he had done any research into gangs, that had been a name anyone would know. The Kings were a different thing entirely. They were beyond untouchable by their local government; in fact, they were working hand in hand with them.

"Since you were part of the Underdogs, I'm sure you already know that as grand as they might sound, they are pretty much just the biggest gang of the Tier 1 cities. However, how many of them do you actually know by name, and I don't just mean what gang they belong to?" Kai asked. Yet after naming two of them, Gary was already scratching his head.

"Exactly!" Kai pointed out with a slight grin. "Aside from those two, who act a bit more flashy and whose faces are already well known, the others hide their identities. The unknown is always scarier than anything you can put your finger on.

"Rumors of their exploits continue to spread, allowing their names to strike even more fear. I thought it wouldn't hurt if we start doing the same, even if we are only small-time right now. I've prepared this for now, and I think it's important you use it. Now that I know what you are, even more so.

"I'm sure you would like to continue going to school as usual, with your family and friends being none the wiser about this part of your life, right? This should make it easier for you to live that double life."

"Thank you," Gary said, yet at the time he had left the gift in the cellar, and not just because he was worried Amy might find it and start asking questions. He truly did want to separate the two lives that he had, but perhaps in the future the line between the two would come closer and closer.

Gary wiped the dust off the item before he put it on. It fit surprisingly well.

It was a mask to hide who he was. A handcrafted accessory that covered the top half of his face, from his forehead to the tip of his nose. It was painted black, with a few details in gold trim, matching the Howlers' gang colors. There were stylish claw marks on either side, coming toward the face, and on the top of the forehead.

Kai . . . this should be the perfect time to use it. You gave this to me . . . so I didn't have to hide from others. I will use this well, Gary thought as he stood back up.

He changed into his gang clothing, the black and gold blazer with black trousers underneath, and his white shirt from school. He walked up the stairs and saw that the others were ready as well, and even Austin had changed into the uniform.

252

The others were surprised to see their leader wearing a mask. Innu was obviously biting his tongue not to ask what was up with that, but because of the tension in the room, none of them commented on it.

"Did you get the information?" Gary asked.

Kai looked at his phone one more time, shaking his head.

"I found out that a few people saw the gray color gang come to this area, and I know where their hideout is, but we can't be sure that Marie is there."

"Let's go there anyway," Gary replied. "Even if she won't be there, we should be able to find someone who might lead us to her."

"Wait, you want us to take on the whole gray color gang? With just the five of us?" Innu asked. He wasn't afraid of anyone in a one-on-one fight. He had also seen the strength of his fellow gang members, so he wouldn't have minded fighting off a larger force, but this . . . this just seemed suicidal.

Color gangs had hundreds of members. Their hideouts would naturally have at least a few dozen members present, no matter the time. They would practically be walking into the lions' den.

"I called for help, but it might take them a while," Austin said as reassurance. "I'll share my location with them as soon as we get there."

"We will go there first," Gary insisted. "We don't know what they've done to her, or what they still plan on doing to her. Whatever it is, it can't be good, and I don't want her to be scared."

The others nodded and left the establishment. The sun hadn't quite gone down yet, and it wasn't dark enough for the color gangs to wander the streets, but it didn't matter. Since the pool club was between the two areas, the gray color gang's base wasn't too far away.

Walking the streets they hardly ran into any trouble because of the hour, but when they got to the docks where the abandoned warehouse was located, they found that a fence went around the entire place.

Standing in front, four gray color gang members were acting as some type of guard, and Gary had received a message.

New Quest received
When You Mess With The Bull, You Get The Horns!
Your enemies have abducted someone close to you.
Show them the consequences of going against you!
Quest reward: 30 Exp per defeated person

"Hey, what the hell are you kids doing here?" A tall, lean man walked toward them. "This is the gray color gang area; do you guys have some type of meeting?" he asked again, frowning at all the kids in front of him.

"What's with that stupid mask? Does he think he's some kind of superhero?" Another one laughed as he pointed at Gary.

"Charging Heart, activate," Gary mumbled to himself.

"Hey, what did you say?" The man leaned forward and tried to grab the masked teenager by the collar. As he reached out, Gary threw a fist as hard and fast as he could. Blood gushed out of the man's nose as his head flew back and his body dropped to the ground.

"Where is she?" Gary shouted, his fist now covered in blood.

CHAPTER 60

SPLIT UP

The large warehouse, located by the docks, used to store boats. However, it had been ages since it had been used for that purpose; now it was just another abandoned building. The only evidence reminding anyone of its past function was the empty shipping containers that had been left behind.

They were one of the reasons why the gray color gang had chosen to use it as their base. Many of their members were runaways, homeless, or just had nothing else to do, so they used the shipping containers as their sleeping quarters. They were filled with quilts, sheets, and small cooking units here and there.

These containers could be found not only inside the warehouse but outside as well. The ones inside were filled with the more high-ranking members of the gray color gang. The better-equipped ones were reserved for those with more say. The most luxurious one, the one at the very back, had a steel door, so the gang leader could enjoy his privacy.

However, right now, he had three visitors: two teenage boys and a teenage girl. Her arms were lifted above her and tied to the corners of the room, strapped to large iron nails. Her wrists were red and her skin rubbed raw from her repeated escape attempts.

"One of you explain to me how a simple scouting mission, which I assigned you *yesterday*, resulted in *this*!" Buffin pointed at Marie, as he looked at the red-haired twins, Sren and Leng. "Not only that, but somehow you decided that it was a good idea to *trash* the whole place! How do you suppose we'll be able to make any income off them, huh? For two newbies, you already have had a bad start."

The two looked to be holding back their anger. It was the first time they had been in a gang other than their own, and they weren't used to receiving orders rather than giving them.

"Sir, the establishment was actually being run by a new up-and-coming gang," Sren answered. "They didn't accept your offer, and it looked like they weren't going to accept the other gang's offer either. Their owner seemed to be away, so to remind them and to let them know that we were serious, we decided to bring one of them here to call out the others."

Buffin let out a big sigh.

These two . . . they really are great liars. I would be inclined to believe them, if Bowden hadn't told me what really happened. They probably ruled their school with their smarts and think they can do something similar here . . . Shit, why couldn't Raven dump them on Riv? Why do I have to be the one to look after them?

"All right, but when they come to collect her, you'll have to be the ones to deal with them!" Buffin declared. "If it comes down to it, you better not hesitate to take those."

The twins looked at each other and reached into their pockets. Each one had a small container with a special syringe inside. It contained a very small amount of the liquid that Raven had given them.

Surprisingly, the Gray Elephants leader had been more up front with them than they had expected, claiming that it was an experimental drug that could turn them into Altered. They didn't take it there and then, but he said that if they wanted to beat the green-haired teenager who had defeated them, it would be an option.

The idea was to eventually send the twins into a dangerous situation like scouting out the Underdogs until they were forced to use it. The only thing was that he had asked Buffin to keep an eye on them to verify the effects of the medicine.

He really must have lost his mind if he believes I'm going to tail them into the Underdogs' den and get myself hurt. Pfft.

"Just get out of my sight. I'll call on you once you're needed. Make sure not to create another mess," Buffin said as the door closed behind him. He looked at Marie. She was conscious and wriggling about; her mouth had been sealed with tape, so she didn't make too much noise.

"Hey, you better hope that gang of yours comes soon." Buffin crouched down and stroked the bottom of her smooth face. "If they don't, we won't be able to strike a deal and then . . . well, I guess we could always send you back as a warning, but I guarantee you won't be in as good a state as you are now . . ."

Marie struggled toward the man, trying to do anything to hit him. The pathetic attempt just made Buffin smile. He leaned in closer to see the look in her eyes. Marie took the opportunity, swung her body forward, and managed to headbutt him, hitting him in the nose.

Wiping his nose to check for blood, Buffin saw that there was none, but his mood was clearly soured.

"Let me show you what a headbutt is like!" Buffin said, grabbing the back of her head and holding on to her hair. He then swung his forehead forward and smashed it against her face, hitting her jaw and lips. The soft tissue hit her teeth, causing her lips to swell and bleed.

"This will be your only warning! I never gave a crap about all that chivalry garbage! Don't think you'll get any special treatment. Right now, you're nothing but a hostage," Buffin said.

Outside, the twins were making their way to their room, thinking about what they had done. They had trashed the place with some gray color gang members that they had brought along.

They had actually scouted out the place yesterday, at which point they saw Gary and the others. Seeing that they had a connection to this place, even though they hadn't discovered that it belonged to them, they hatched the plan to attack it during school hours.

The two brothers had lost a lot of money, not once but twice, and everything was going downhill for them ever since they had met a certain green-haired teenager. So they had used today's opportunity for some payback.

CHAPTER 61

THE HOWLERS ATTACK

"Hey . . . that guy isn't getting up . . . I think the masked guy just knocked him out with one punch!" one of the gray color gang members reported, as he shook his friend who was on the ground.

"Come on, he's not bald, how is that possible!" another said, looking at the small figure who had hit his friend.

You have successfully knocked out a gray color gang member
30 Exp received
1012/1024 Exp

These aren't the Gray Elephants, they're not real gangsters, and I've gotten stronger.

Even if the gym hadn't given him extra stats, Gary could still tell that his body had improved from the workouts. Perhaps his Strength hadn't increased enough for the system to grant him another point, but it was as if he was between stages somewhere.

"Hey . . . you knocked him out cold, now that is quite the entrance." Austin cheered.

"That bastard's trying to start a fight with us, get him!" one of them shouted, and the other two guards immediately ran forward, charging toward the strange person wearing the mask. Gary was ready to deal with both of them again.

I need to conserve my Energy. Who knows how many are inside? Gary thought. Before he could act, though, he saw two figures whiz past him, one large and the other small.

A large fist hit one of the gray color gang members in the gut. The punch was so strong that spit came out of his mouth and he fell to the ground. Following up with a strike on the temple, Austin knocked him out.

Meanwhile Innu had jumped with his knee forward. The movement was so fast and sudden that the other gang member was unable to react. Innu's knees dug right into his opponent's chest, knocking him to the ground.

"What? Did you forget that we were here with you?" Kai asked as he undid his expensive watch and placed it in one of his pockets. It seemed like for the first time he would get involved personally in their matters.

"Hey, in a gang, we need to protect our leader at all costs," Innu said with a thumbs-up toward Gary.

"Thank you," Gary said, looking at them all. "But as a leader, I also need to make sure all of you are okay."

The four of them walked forward toward the last guard, who had picked up a pot and a pan. He ran back, scared, and started bashing the two items furiously.

"We're being attacked! I repeat, we're being attacked!" the man shouted to warn his companions.

Those who had been sleeping or hanging out in their containers started to come out to see who was attacking them.

"Is it the black color gang? Maybe they are here because of what happened last time?"

"It might be the Underdogs as well."

About thirty people came out to meet the intruders. They looked younger or the same age as themselves, which ruled out the Underdogs; at the same time, the Howlers saw only a single group.

"Really? You got us all worked up for this?" one of the gray color gang members complained. They had been on their toes ever since the attack, afraid that the others might come at them at any time.

The one who had run away froze. He didn't really know what to say that wouldn't make him seem weak, but these guys weren't normal kids. They had knocked out the other members so quickly.

There are about thirty of them . . . everyone here is strong . . . actually, I have no clue about Kai. He must have come here just because he was worried about Marie, but I might need to protect him. If it's all of us, we can deal with these guys and then head inside. Gary was trying to come up with a plan.

He felt a familiar hand on his shoulder. He looked up to see Kai shaking his head.

"Don't waste your time on this riffraff. We may not be able to defeat them all, but we can at least buy you some time. Worst case, we might get beaten up, but we'll live. Just head inside and make sure Marie is okay. There should be more of them inside," Kai advised.

Was it the right thing to do? Was Kai just being brave, or was he placing Marie's safety above their own?

Gary honestly wasn't too sure, but since none of the gang members before them had come out of the warehouse, there might be even more inside waiting.

"Gary, I trust you more than anyone to find Marie and help her. Once you do, concentrate on getting her out. We can always get back at them later, but first we have to save her! Don't hesitate to go wild, and get her for me, will ya?" Kai asked as he patted him on the shoulder.

As the leader of the Howlers, he estimated that if he was quick, he might make it back in time to help them out. They knew the risks when they agreed to come here. Gary started to run ahead, and several gang members looked like they were about to pounce on him, but once again both Innu and Austin were there to stop them, show-ing off their skills.

Suddenly a third person was running after Gary. Before he could grab him, though, a foot reached around his neck. The next second Gary's assailant had been pulled back, and a sudden *thud* announced that he had fallen to the ground.

The gray color gang member looked up and saw a pretty blond boy looking over him with his hands in his pockets.

"No one is disturbing him, he has a job to do," Kai declared.

Austin smiled. "I knew he had some skills."

Thanks to the commotion the others had made, Gary easily ran to the warehouse and opened its doors. He closed them behind him, and now that he was inside the building, he saw a few people walk-ing around.

"Huh, who the fuck is that? Was the boss expecting a visitor?" one of them asked as they spotted Gary.

Well, they've already caught me, so no need to try to be sneaky, Gary thought.

"Marie!" he shouted at the top of his lungs. *"I'm here to get you! Just wait for me!"*

CHAPTER 62

ONE AT A TIME

Gary let out a powerful shout that seemed to come from deep within his belly. If he had been in his right mind, he would have also noticed that this yell was incredibly loud, but at that moment he only cared about one thing.

His war cry had done exactly what he had expected it to do. Several gang members came out of the containers inside the warehouse, and they were now all looking at the intruder.

"Hey, some of us are trying to sleep! Can somebody please take care of this masked idiot? How the hell did he even manage to get in?" one member complained, as he was still groggy from the rough awakening. Those who had just been chilling had come out expecting to see a good show.

It was just one person, after all.

"Fine, I'll take care of him. Can't wait to see how Buffin will punish all those slackers outside." One gray color gang member decided to come forward.

Meanwhile, Gary sniffed the air. He hadn't marked Marie, so there was no visible scent trail leading him to her. Fortunately, he had another way of tracking her. Ever since he had used Tom's bloody shirt to find whoever had beaten him, he had been training his nose.

One of the benefits of becoming a werewolf was that all his senses had drastically improved, including his sense of smell. He had been slowly memorizing his friends' unique scents, just in case of a situation like this one.

"I can't smell her on any of you, so where is she?" Gary asked.

The others just laughed, and the young lad took a swing toward Gary. The attack wasn't as fast as Innu's, and he was sure it wasn't as strong as Austin's either. Gary moved his head, avoiding the punch, and before the attacker could do anything else, he grabbed him by the arm.

You guys are the ones that attacked Chavley, and now you are hurting me again! I'll make sure you can never use these hands to hurt anyone! Gary thought as he pulled on the trapped arm, straightening it, and lifted his own arm in the air, slamming his elbow down.

He barely felt any resistance as he heard a loud pop, clearly indicating that the joint had been broken. The lad screamed in pain, and the next second a fist hit him in the head, knocking him out.

"I have no sympathy for you guys; I can't even feel bad for you any more," Gary said as he looked at what he had done.

Your opponent has been knocked out
30 Exp received
Congratulations, you have now reached: Level 9
A stat point has been granted
18/1228 Exp

Seeing such a brutal example made out of one of their own, the others no longer regarded this masked intruder as a joke but as a real threat. They stayed back slightly, wondering who this person was, until one of their leaders shouted some sense into them. "Get him, he must be from one of the other gangs!"

They all decided to come at Gary at once, though this was exactly what he had been hoping for. He only had so much Energy he could use, after all, and it didn't help that Charging Heart's duration had deactivated after the last attack.

Skill activated: Charging Heart
All stats have temporarily been doubled
–10 Energy
88/120 Energy

The first attacker came in with a kick, but Gary moved to the side, planning to retaliate. Unfortunately, he didn't get a chance, as someone kicked him from behind. His Endurance was high, but he wasn't exempt from the laws of physics, and he stumbled as another fist landed right in his face.

Damn it, fighting multiple opponents is harder than I thought.

–2 HP
–1 HP

Now on his knees, Gary could feel a few of them stepping on his back, but he reached out, grabbing the leg of the gang member who was standing in front of him. Using all his strength, he pulled on it, making the teenager fall on the floor next to him.

Gary immediately climbed on top of him. The others tried to pull the masked person off their friend; some continued to hit him, but Gary ignored his decreasing Health.

–1 HP
–2 HP
–3 HP

Instead, he concentrated on punching the person beneath him, until he received another message.

Your opponent has been knocked out
30 Exp received
48/1228 Exp

Gary stood up, ran through the crowd of people attacking him, and turned around. Now that he had gotten up, the others could see the state of their fellow gang member, and they were horrified to see his bloody face as he lay motionless on the floor.

"What is it with this guy? He didn't let go of him, no matter what we did." One of them was starting to be afraid of Gary. He didn't know if it was the mask or his lack of self-preservation.

"Come on, he has to be hurt by now! Let's get him!" another shouted, and charged forward.

That's two down. If they're only this powerful, I should be able to take them down one by one! Gary thought, completely focused on his goal.

Once again, the masked teenager charged forward, but with so many of them, he couldn't avoid getting kicked. Fortunately, he didn't take long to recover, so he started punching the closest person as hard as he could. He didn't knock him out, but Gary quickly pulled on the collar of his shirt, not letting go as he ignored the surrounding attacks.

−2 HP
−1 HP
−3 HP

Holding the gang member in front of him made it harder for his friends to attack. Gary used this opportunity to throw his fist into the face of another attacker, and thanks to the system, he knew that that one wouldn't be getting back up any time soon.

Your opponent has been knocked out
30 Exp received
78/1228 Exp

Suddenly, Gary felt a familiar pain emanating from his back. It was the sharp, stinging pain he had suffered far too often in a relatively short time frame.

You have been stabbed!
–7 HP
56/100 HP
You are bleeding!
Your Health will decrease by 1 HP per minute until you're patched up or healed.

Gary quickly turned around and looked at the person who had stabbed him. What's worse, he noticed that multiple gang members had picked up weapons: wooden planks, bike chains, and pocket-knives.

"You were the one who used a weapon first, remember that," Gary growled in anger as he took a swipe toward the young man who had stabbed him.

Skill activated: Claw Drain
All stats have temporarily been doubled
–15 Energy
73/120 Energy

Midswing, his hand started to transform, his nails elongating as he swiped across the attacker's shoulder. The force behind the blow was strong enough to push him back, banging his head against the one behind him.

+4 HP regenerated
Your opponent has been knocked out
30 Exp received
108/1228 Exp

The rest of the gray color gang stopped what they were doing. They were sure of it, they had just seen the intruder's hand transform . . .

CHAPTER 63

MEET AGAIN

The strange teenager had surprised them. The thirty or so gray color gang members had been hitting him for a while now, yet he still hadn't fallen. What's more, he hadn't shown any sign of getting tired or weaker.

Nevertheless, common sense told them that he had to have been hurt, so it was just a question of when the intruder would succumb. But it never happened, which was why a few of them had gotten fed up.

The gray color gang's members took pride in the strength of their fists. Then again, they were flexible; since their fists didn't work, there were plenty of things they could use to cause damage.

However, they had seen what Gary had done, and unless their eyes were playing tricks on them, they were sure of it; the person in front of them had to be an Altered.

"Who is this person? You saw him transform, right?" someone asked, just to make sure.

"Yeah, it like changed into something, only Altered can do that."

"An Altered? I thought the only gang in Slough that had an Altered was the Underdogs. Is this really an attack from them?"

"You idiot, does this person in front of you look like Kirk?"

While the others were arguing, Gary looked at his stats and saw a few worrying things. For one, he had used his Claw Drain out of anger after being stabbed. It had healed the wound on his back and given him a bit of Health back, but it didn't seem to be worth the Energy that it had used.

He had been getting constantly hit during the fight as well, and although that was all right at the beginning, now that they had weapons they were producing more damage.

I have two stat points . . . I could put them into Energy and use the Claw Drain a few times . . . but when I run out of Energy, then what? I could put it in Health and try to fight them off for as long as possible, but even then that wouldn't work . . . what's important right now is to not get hit.

Gary was unsure if he was making the right decision, but it was a gamble in the first place coming in; as a last resort he could always use . . . *that.* He was sure that would take care of them.

2 stat points have been allocated into Dexterity
Your base Dexterity is now at 9
Skill activated: Charging Heart
All stats have temporarily been doubled
−10 Energy
63/120 Energy

I can see their movements, I'm just not fast enough.

While fighting, Gary noticed that he could always see what the person was doing; his eyes were no longer human. But what he couldn't do was avoid them. Right now, he was gambling that the increased speed would be enough, and having one point still unused, Gary had placed them all now in Dexterity.

The gray color gang members seemed confused about whether they should attack a suspected Altered, but just like before, he was sure that the others would attack him again.

Taking this chance, he ran forward, and this time, one of the gang members swung a plank. Gary moved to the side, spinning as he readied his elbow and swung it right into the face of another attacker.

Your opponent has been knocked out
30 Exp received
138/1228 Exp

Another one tried hitting him, but he kicked their knee before they got closer and he ran again, trying to not get hit.

I learn a lot from Innu . . . I don't know if he knew something like this was going to happen, but if I can't fight multiple opponents, then I need to try to make it so I can fight them one-on-one!

His attackers' speed varied as they chased him, and it only took a few hits for him to deal with them. He quickly turned around and dealt a sweeping kick to the leading gang member, making him fall flat on his face.

The next second, Gary slammed his foot on top of the fallen one's head.

Your opponent has been knocked out
30 Exp received
168/1228 Exp

"What the hell is going on?" someone shouted as the metal door to one of the containers opened.

There . . . I can smell it! It's Marie! Gary's eyes were now locked on Buffin.

Outside, the gray color gang members were struggling just as much with the intruders, if not even more so. The three Howlers had managed to defeat a couple of gang members as they made their way to the warehouse.

Now, with their backs facing the entrance, they were going to make sure no one entered. They were able to cover their front, and since they weren't moving, there was no way for the others to get behind them either. That was, unless someone came out of the warehouse.

Yet Kai had told the others to trust Gary, that they wouldn't be coming out, that the next people coming out would be him and Marie.

"Who are these teenagers? They took out ten of our guys already . . . and there's only three of them," one of the gang members said, acting cautiously.

Innu peeked toward Kai.

Who is he? His skills aren't any less than mine or Austin's . . . heck, I don't want to admit it, but they might be even better. So why is he leaving everything to Gary? Innu wondered.

"Oh, what do we have here?" a voice said from behind the gray color gang members. "We didn't think you would turn up so soon, but where's the green-haired one?"

Two red-haired teenagers walked through the color gang members. It looked like they had come back from somewhere; they were carrying shopping bags, so they had probably been grabbing some food.

"Turn up so soon?" Kai said, clenching his fist. "Now I see, the gray color gang asked you to join them after the fight . . . you were the ones who wrecked the Wolf's Pool Club!"

"You guys have some balls!" Innu shouted. "We kicked your ass once, and now you decide to mess with us again? Well, now we'll just have to do it all over again!"

Innu looked ready for round two, and so did Austin, but before they could move, Kai stepped forward instead.

"No, please, I want to handle this one," Kai said.

CHAPTER 64

SECRET'S OUT!

As soon as the door to the container at the very back opened, the smell wafted into Gary's nose. He turned his head and saw a person standing outside it.

What was worse, though, was that just like in the pool club, Gary could smell blood.

No . . . no . . . not again! Why am I always too late!

There were still plenty of gray color gang members left standing, but Gary's feet were already moving before his mind caught up. He started to run toward the container; at the same time Buffin couldn't quite comprehend what was happening.

"What the fuck is wrong with you guys? You can't even handle one person! Why is it taking you so long?"

One of the members swung another wooden plank toward Gary like a baseball bat. Gary covered his head with his arms; the plank snapped but didn't slow him down at all.

He was like a cannonball, determined, with only one thing in his sight. But for some reason, the eyes of the person in front of him scared him.

Once again, Gary's heart rate was naturally rising on its own.

You have exceeded 200 BPM

Partial transformation has begun
All stats increased by 125%

Buffin had attempted to close the door. There was an iron lock on the other side, but as he tried to swing it closed, Gary leapt and reached it just in time, grabbing the handle.

"Where do you think you're going?" Gary said as he used his strength to pull it open and kicked Buffin onto the ground.

Quickly, as the others closed in behind him, Gary closed the door and slammed the iron bolt lock shut. Seconds later, constant banging started on the outside. Fortunately, this was a metal container; perhaps they could get in eventually, but it would take some time.

He turned around and saw Marie.

She had been tied up, and her mouth was swollen, blood still dripping from it. It looked like the noise had woken her up from the pain she was in.

Lifting her head, Marie saw a strange masked boy. At first, she didn't know who it was, but then she saw green hair sticking out the top.

"Yob bifiot!" Marie smiled and tried to speak, but her swollen, busted-up lips made it difficult.

After the other two had left, Buffin had been punching Marie even more. He had ripped the tape from her mouth and warned her not to scream or shout, but she didn't listen, and every time she had spoken, he slapped her across the face until she learned her lesson.

"Did you fucking do this?" Gary shouted.

Buffin had already gotten up from the ground, and he threw a kick.

"I'm not like those losers outside!" Buffin said.

Gary saw that Marie was exhausted. He knew that the gray color gang leader had to be strong; he would have only a little fighting ability compared to the leaders of the Gray Elephants.

Seeing Buffin's kick confirmed this.

If I fight this guy head-on, it actually might be a hard fight, so

I have one chance . . . Gary stopped clenching his fist, opened up his hand, and swung it again. *I want to hurt this person as much as possible!*

Skill activated: Claw Drain
–15 Energy
42/120 Energy

Instead of using his hand to block the kick, Gary attacked with a swipe instead, as his hands transformed. His nails dug into the leg Buffin screamed in pain.

+5 HP

Gary dashed forward and slashed at Buffin's chest, then jumped on top of him.

+5 HP

"You're an Altered! I'm sorry, I didn't—" Buffin tried to yell, but before he could finish, Gary swiped at him a third time, hitting his face and slicing his cheek and tongue. At that point, the transformation ended.

You have defeated the gray color gang leader
200 Exp received
368/1228 Exp

Gary looked at the leader beneath him. He wasn't sure if in his fit of rage he had killed again, but it didn't look like it. He had been careful with his sharp claws and had only cut open part of the cheek and tongue, nothing else. Buffin had simply passed out from shock.

Gary looked up and saw Marie in front of him, her eyes wide. Even though they were swollen, she had seen everything.

She had seen Gary transform his hands into claws, even if only briefly.

"Gawr, you're an Alded?" Marie managed to mumble. But honestly, she didn't care about what he was, she was just happy that he had saved her.

The banging on the container hadn't stopped, and Gary stood up and turned around.

"I'm sorry that they did this to you . . . I'm sorry that I wasn't here earlier . . . there's still a lot of those guys outside, so I'm going to need you to wait just a little longer. I promise you're going to be okay."

Marie thought Gary sounded a little cheesy, but she couldn't quite believe it; for some reason he looked very large, and she thought he looked a little cool.

Outside, Kai had gone to deal with the twins, while Innu and Austin continued to stop anyone from getting close, and they had done a good job, knocking out another five gang members.

They were quite bruised themselves, but they weren't going to fall. The number of gray color gang members had lowered dramatically, but what Kai had done was even more impressive.

In only a few minutes, he made it out victorious. What's more, there wasn't a single mark on his face. His hair was blowing in the wind while the twins lay on the ground.

I couldn't see everything properly because I was too busy dealing with the others . . . but he clearly managed to beat both twins at the same time. Austin wondered if he could do the same, and honestly he wasn't too sure. He didn't doubt his ability to defeat them, but doing so unharmed was a tall ask.

This guy . . . he's a monster, Leng thought as he struggled to get up. After this short confrontation, he and Sren were convinced that they couldn't beat the person in front of them. They had failed once again, and it was all because of these people.

Leng looked at his brother and reached into his pocket. Sren did the same.

Kai became wary, expecting them to take out some type of weapon. However, the brothers did something surprising as they distanced themselves from the blond teenager. While Kai tried to make up his mind who to attack, each one pulled out a small box with a syringe inside.

Without any hesitation, they injected themselves with the strange substance.

CHAPTER 65

INCOMPLETE

The syringes that the twins had used to inject themselves contained only a small amount of liquid. Honestly, Raven wasn't sure what exactly it would do, but as a leader of the Gray Elephants gang, he knew that testing it out on their loyal followers would be a terrible gamble.

If the syringes worked as Sin had suggested, he could always use them on himself or someone else later, but first he had to know their effects . . . especially the side effects.

The twins showed an immediate reaction. The veins around the puncture site started to bulge. Sren and Leng felt as if a foreign organism had entered their body and was now crawling through it, changing them by the second.

What the hell? Kai wondered as he carefully approached Sren. He had expected them to do something, but both of them just stared at their veins. He carefully approached Sren since he was closer to him.

"Hey, what did you just take?" Kai asked the red-haired teenager, but Sren's eyes indicated that he was in a trance or experiencing some kind of psychedelic trip. He was looking up at Kai yet at the same time not registering his presence.

What's more, Kai could see that Sren seemed to be burning up. He could even feel the heat coming from his body. Since both of his opponents seemed to be out of it, Kai looked at the syringes on the floor.

Didn't I see something like that before? . . . Could it be . . . was this the same stuff that strange guy tried to inject Austin with during Gary and Innu's fight? Kai thought as he figured the situation out.

"What was in the syringe?" Kai shouted at Sren once more, but he still didn't react. By now, the veins on the side of his forehead were bulging, and his head had turned slightly red. Without warning, Sren grabbed Kai's wrist, gripping it tightly, and Kai could feel him getting stronger by the second. Strangely, Sren still seemed to be out of it, as he tilted his head and looked at Kai with enlarged pupils.

"Get off me!" Kai demanded, as he used all his strength to kick his captor in the stomach. Fortunately it did the trick; Sren let go and fell to his knees, allowing Kai to step back and try to figure out the situation.

Slowly getting back up, Sren lifted his head, allowing Kai, and everyone else, to get a closer look at what he was changing into. His eyes had sunken in deep and his sclera had changed from white to black. There was no distinguishing between the pupil and the rest of his eye.

Sren's hair was falling out, leaving only the outline of his scalp. For some reason, Sren's lips were starting to fuse together. However, it wasn't one solid piece; there were small gaps in between, allowing him to open and close his mouth, and when he did, the inside resembled melted cheese.

What was in that liquid? We have to get out of here ASAP! I have an awful feeling. Kai started to back away even more. He turned around, running back to Innu and Austin.

"Hey, man, what freaky voodoo shit do they have going on over there?" Innu asked, though the main thing that scared him was the sudden hair loss. "What if that stuff is infectious? I don't wanna go bald at my age!"

"Didn't you see them inject themselves? Probably some enhancement drug gone wrong. Maybe something like a souped-up steroid?" Austin theorized.

Kai was thinking along the same lines, yet they could see that the transformation of the two was complete. It was hard to describe their current outer appearance, but they resembled monsters out of a nightmare, no longer human.

The twins' fingers had slightly elongated, and their nails had turned long and sharp, but on their faces and hands were patches of fur slightly green in color.

Did that injection change them into Altered? Kai wondered. Looking at them, especially at the way they behaved, there had to be something seriously wrong with them. It was almost as if they were incomplete.

"Haha, this is great! Buffin told us that he gave you guys an ace up your sleeve. This must be it!" a gray color gang member said with confidence as he approached Sren.

By now, the gray color gang was down to around a dozen members. Innu and Austin were showing signs of exhaustion, but the remaining color gang members weren't too keen on their chances of taking them down. Their best chance was to get the twins to fight them.

The gang member was a bit scared about their changed appearance, but he knew that the twins were on their side. If they were as strong as they were ugly, those three intruders would stand no chance.

Alas, the moment he came close enough to the being that used to be the short-haired twin, it snapped its head around. The dark, sunken black eyes frightened him, yet before he could escape he felt liquid filling in his throat.

He didn't understand what had happened as the life escaped his eyes, but everyone else saw the grotesque scene. Sren had shoved his monstrous nails into the gray color gang member's throat. Blood was slowly filling his mouth, and eventually Sren chucked his body to the floor, dead.

Unfortunately, Sren wasn't the only one who had changed. Leng looked identical to his twin. He leapt through the air, covering a distance no normal human would be able to cross, and pierced the throat of a different gray color gang member.

"What the fuck is going on?" Innu asked in a panic. "They're attacking their own side! Shit, what do we do, Kai?"

The blond teenager looked ahead. He wasn't liking their chances of getting out alive by trying to flee after seeing the twins' leaping power. At the same time, running into the warehouse wasn't exactly safe either. There should still be more gray color gang members inside, and it might endanger Marie further.

"Gary's there . . . and if the color gang members see those monsters, even they should understand that teaming up might be our only chance to take them down!" Kai made his decision and went to open the warehouse door.

CHAPTER 66

DON'T TOUCH MY GANG!

Do I just cover her with my body and charge out? No, they have weapons, so she might get seriously hurt. Gary considered what to do, now that he had found Marie.

42/120 Energy

Being low on Energy meant that he couldn't afford to waste much time in the container thinking about what to do next. He had untied Marie, allowing her to move on her own, but since there were still more gang members outside, there was nowhere she could really go.

Damn it, if Marie weren't here, I could have eaten an arm or a leg from the gray color gang leader to help me out of this situation! Gary briefly contemplated asking her to turn around. Since she had seen him transform, maybe she wouldn't mind.

However, the banging on the other side was getting louder. Looking around the room, he saw only one exit, so he would have to try his best. With one hand, Gary lifted Buffin's body off the ground. The gray color gang leader wasn't dead, but his body was dead weight.

"Marie, please stay back for now. If worse comes to worst, I promise I'll protect you. I'll open a path for you, and Kai and the others should be waiting outside. There's no need to worry about me."

Marie nodded; knowing what Gary was, she felt that if anyone could get them out of this situation, it would be him. With his hand on the iron lock, the green-haired teenager was ready. He quickly slid it open and yanked the door forward.

As he did so, a gang member fell through the door. Gary slammed his knee into his face, which knocked him out in an instant.

Your opponent has been knocked out
30 Exp received
398/1228 Exp

Gary let him fall to the floor so he would act as a hindrance for the others. When the next one tried to enter, the masked teenager swung the door as hard as he could, slamming it into the newcomer's face.

Your opponent has been knocked out
30 Exp received
428/1228 Exp

Gary's impressive strength was serving him well, but more than anything, the small opening was perfect to force a one-on-one situation. The only question was what would run out first, the werewolf's Energy reserve or the manpower on the gray color gang's side.

Maybe if I keep beating these guys I'll manage to level up . . . I could do something with it, help me fight a bit longer. Worst-case scenario, I'll just have to start eating some fingers! Gary decided. As the door opened again, he lifted the gang leader's body with both hands and hurled it at the group on the other side.

At first, they had no clue who it was, but as the first row of them was knocked over, they recognized their leader, Buffin.

He beat our leader... he beat him... but then... what do we do? was the thought that was running through their heads.

Gary was surprised that nobody else came at him. He decided to take a quick peek, yet when they saw him, they collectively took a few steps back. Because he had beaten their leader, the gang members seemed more hesitant than before.

I don't get it... When they saw my hand transform like an Altered, they continued to attack me... When they saw me easily beat up one of their members, they still attacked... but now they act like this?

Seeing the state of their all-powerful leader, a person they all looked up to, a figure that they considered stronger than all of them, in such a state had made most of them lose their remaining will to fight against Gary.

It was almost as if they knew they had been defeated. The negative energy of some of their members was passing on to the others, and when they looked at Gary, they started to share another emotion...

They were afraid of this person who had beaten the one they had all considered unbeatable. They had all heard about how powerful Altered could be, but seeing Buffin passed out just proved that none of them would stand a chance against the masked intruder.

On top of that, they had already lost a number of people because of this single person, and the magnitude of his strength was starting to set in.

Is this what Kai meant... how a leader always had to be strong? If I knew it could be this freaking easy, then I would have just gone for the damn leader at the start.

Since Marie could no longer hear the sound of fighting outside, she decided to follow after Gary. She saw that the gray color gang members were spread out, not really doing anything, just looking at Gary, seemingly waiting for him to do something.

She quickly went to his side and grabbed his arm. Gary felt her whole body shaking as Marie held on to him tightly. He decided that he should use this opportunity to get out.

"Listen up!" Gary shouted imposingly. "We're leaving this place! And no one is going to stop us!" He looked at Buffin, and the gang members looked at the state he was in. As Gary lifted his arm and made a fist, the gray color gang members flinched, expecting a fight.

"This is a warning to all of you as well: in the future none of you are to touch any members of the Howlers! If you ever hear our name, or anyone mentioning that they are part of our group, and you hurt them in any way, then I will personally hunt you down!"

Although Gary wasn't sure if his words sounded menacing, the others felt their effect, unsure if it was because of his strange mask or the bloody mess that Buffin had been left in. Gary strode forward and they stepped out of his way, making a clear path while Marie held on to him, until the door was only a few feet away.

The door slid open, and immediately Innu and Austin slid it shut. Kai followed right after, and all three of them shared a look of panic on their faces.

"What's wrong?" Gary asked.

The others didn't even know where to begin to explain, but there was no need, because the next second, they heard a bang. It was followed by another, and by the time the third one sounded out, a strange-looking hand had penetrated the metal door.

CHAPTER 67

BLACK BLOOD

Inside the warehouse, no one could comprehend the situation they were in. People they had never seen before had entered the warehouse and defeated their leader, and all of them had given up fighting. Yet there seemed to be a new problem.

Austin quickly found a metal pipe lying on the floor. Perhaps a weapon from one of the other members. Picking it up, he slid it through the door handles and used all his strength to bend it, which would make it harder for the twins to open the doors.

Austin was strong, but he didn't even know where he had found the strength to bend the pipe. Perhaps it was the fear running through him that his life could be over at any second.

Suddenly the strange long fingernails pierced right through the metal warehouse door. A screeching noise like metal against metal echoed as the long nails scratched down, leaving behind large claw marks.

For a brief second, through the gap that had been made, everyone saw the head of the figure on the other side, its black, sunken eyes staring in at them. In a blink, though, the head disappeared.

"What was that? First an Altered showed up . . . and now *aliens*?" someone asked, pinching himself to make sure this wasn't all a nightmare.

"It scratched part of the door as well; am I seeing things?" another one replied.

The three Howlers ran to Gary and stood by his side, but they soon turned around because they didn't want their backs facing the other direction.

"It doesn't look like there's any other exit from this place!" Kai shouted as he looked around; he also briefly looked at Marie, who looked to be badly hurt and not in the best shape to start running for her life.

"Guys, can you tell me what is going on? What was that?" Gary asked.

"You might not believe it, but it's those twins!" Innu answered, pointing at the door. "Kai defeated them, but then they freaking injected themselves with some shit. After that they started going bald, and before we knew it they had already turned into freaks.

"Those guys are out of their mind! They didn't even hesitate to kill their own gang members. If they had concentrated on us first, we would have been dead by now!"

They heard another loud bang, and the doors were pushed forward, revealing a small gap. But luckily the pipe that Austin had bent around the handles managed to hold them off a bit longer. But only until a hand with long nails came through; it sliced downward, splitting the pipe in half.

The doors were then pushed to the side, and the two strange figures emerged.

WARNING!
Beasts have been detected in the vicinity
Beasts are natural predators of humans

New Quest received
Predator or Prey?
Although you're a werewolf, in their eyes you're just another feisty treat

Defeat the beasts
Reward: ???
Failure: Death

They're beasts, as in those things that Altered are based on? How is that possible? I really don't like the "Failure" addition. System, do you plan to kill me if I run away? Or are you trying to tell me it's impossible? Why don't you upgrade me with some new skills?

Several gray color gang members were near them, and rather than looking for a specific target, the twins were just going for whoever was closest to them, latching on and digging their long claws into their bodies.

Gary watched the beasts stabbing the gray color gang members in the stomach, one after another, very fast, until each one died and fell to the floor.

They are even faster than before . . . and I don't have any stat points to increase my Dexterity further . . .

68/100 HP
40/100 Energy

I'm not at full Health, and I don't have a lot of Energy left either, but the Claw Drain seemed to stop the bleeding from the stab wound . . . How am I supposed to do this?

"Gary, I'm not going to lie to you, I don't think we can beat those things. I don't know how strong you are, and I don't know if putting pressure on you is the right thing to do right now, but if we can't kill those abominations, we'll all die. I can't afford to die yet!" Kai said.

"You can say that again! I ain't dying here in some crappy warehouse!" Austin shouted.

The gray color gang members had scattered after they saw the beasts kill their friends; some had run toward the beasts while others had run away, but it was mostly useless.

Gary could feel Marie shaking just as she had been before, and he looked toward her.

"It's going to be okay! Remember what I said? I will protect you," Gary reminded her. Marie nodded, trying to hold back her tears at their impending doom. He turned to Kai. "I'll be honest, Kai, I don't like my chances against the two of them at once. If you can distract one of them, I might be able to take the other one on."

Innu said, "Look, Gary, it's great that you take this leader thing seriously, but I don't think now is the time to act brave. You've seen what they're capable of. Once they get you—"

"We don't have time for this," Gary said, cutting Innu off. "Just trust in me. Austin, please take Marie, and I'll try to deal with them as quickly as possible."

Austin easily carried the small girl on his back, and the other boys got ready. Gary charged toward the beast on his left. He was scared. Of course he was scared; he had no idea how much his Endurance would do against their nails, which seemed to be sharper than knives. However, right now everyone was relying on him, and he couldn't just stand there shaking in his boots.

"Hey, assholes, look at me! I can't even tell you apart now that you've gone bald! I thought you were supposed to be twins; how come one of you is uglier than the other?" Gary shouted.

Both of them turned toward him, and it looked like his taunt had gotten their attention. Meanwhile, on the other side, Kai held something in his hand, and he threw it as fast as he could.

It was the small pocketknife he usually carried. It hit the back of one beast's head, penetrating the skin. Black blood spurted out.

That reminds me about what those damn White Rose agents said . . . about these beasts. Is that why they're attacking everyone? Gary thought.

Unfortunately, the light injury only pissed the beast off, making it shift its focus to Kai. It leapt toward him, while its brother charged at Gary.

The two boys ran away, each wishing the other luck.

CHAPTER 68

LOW ENERGY

The beast that still had the pocketknife stuck in the back of its head went after Kai. A few gray color gang members remained nearby. Seeing how the beast had decided to focus on someone else, though, they decided to make a run for it; some of them even ran out the door where the others had come in.

Of course that would happen, but the only way for all of us to survive was for someone to sacrifice themself, and none of them were going to do anything, Kai thought as he turned to run.

There was one good thing on their side about fighting in the warehouse, and that was the containers that were spread out everywhere. In some areas they were quite narrow, and they could also be used in other ways.

Up ahead, Kai had gone through between two of them and then taken a right turn. The beast was quick to follow, and the small gap had slowed it down somewhat, but it was still incredibly fast. When the beast turned the corner, though, it was in for a surprise as an iron bar struck it in the head, causing it to fall on its back.

"I don't usually use weapons, but against a monster like you, I think it's only fair to make an exception," Austin said, looking down. Marie peeked over his shoulder at the beast.

Behind the beast in the other direction was Innu, who also held a wooden plank. He swung it down, aiming for the beast's head, but before it hit, the beast threw out its arm, breaking the plank with ease.

"Crap, keep running!" Innu shouted, as he quickly escaped by running between the containers, along with the others and Austin, who had Marie on his back again.

The one thing Kai didn't want them to do was split up. If the beast found any of them alone, there was a zero percent chance of survival . . . apart from Gary, perhaps.

When the beast got up, it saw the others running through a small gap. It knew that its larger body would slow it down, so it used its claws to dig into a container and climb on top of it. The open space made it easier for the beast to chase after them, jumping from container to container and seeing them all from above.

Gary dealt with the other beast using the same method, running through the containers on the other side.

I don't exactly know how strong it is, and I can't use Claw Drain much either because I have a low amount of Energy, but I can't just keep running either.

After getting between two containers, Gary turned around and saw the beast in front of him. Seeing its claws up close, Gary couldn't help but chuckle. It was a forced laugh to make him feel better about the situation.

"You call those claws? I've seen worse! I'm much more of a monster than you!" Gary yelled, taunting it. He charged in as the beast swung its arm toward him. He ducked to avoid the hit, and the beast's claws pierced a nearby container. It was stuck.

Gary saw his chance and swung a punch toward its chest.

Do I use Claw Drain now, try to do the most damage I can . . . or do I save my Energy, in case I need to do that later? Gary contemplated his choices, but he couldn't decide quick enough, and his punch connected with the beast's chest.

Although Gary had more than doubled his Strength, his punch did nearly nothing; the beast hadn't even flinched. It kicked Gary in the chest, causing him to fall to the ground.

–5 HP
53/100 HP

Before Gary could get up, the beast's foot was on him. It was large and strong. No matter how much he struggled, he could not break free.

One of the clawed hands reached for his head, and Gary swatted it to the side, where it pierced the ground. But the beast aimed its other hand at Gary's ribs, and he was unable to avoid it with the beast's foot on top of him.

The sharp nails pierced his body, and he screamed in pain.

–15 HP
38/100 HP
You are bleeding!
Your Health will decrease by 2 HP per minute until you're patched up or healed.

Damn it, I can't die here! Gary thought.

Right now, he couldn't afford to worry about his Energy; he needed to do something to get free. He had to rely on his powers from the system. Gary swung at the leg on top of him with both hands.

Skill activated: Claw Drain
–15 Energy
25/120 Energy

Gary's hand transformed midswing, and his nails dug into the beast's leg.

+4 HP
+4 HP

46/100 HP
Your wound is healing

Gary hadn't noticed that his Claw Drain skill also helped heal injuries, like the one he had suffered earlier, even if he didn't have enough Energy to perform emergency healing. But now wasn't the time to appreciate this life hack.

In order to get Gary's claws out of its legs, the beast took a step back. It appeared startled that Gary had managed to injure it, but Gary knew that his transformation was only temporary. While Claw Drain had certainly done wonders for his Health, the same couldn't be said for his Energy.

Since the beast was only partially injured, Gary got up and ran back to the main area, where it was more open and there were fewer crates. He thought he might be able to see the others, but he couldn't; all he could see were dead bodies on the ground.

"Arghh!" A shout came from elsewhere. Gary could only imagine that something was going on with the others.

I have to hurry . . . I have to help them! Gary ran to one of the dead color gang members. *I'm sorry, but I don't have the luxury to care about a dead guy's feelings; hopefully you'll approve of the fact that your body will be used to get revenge on your killer.*

With that, Gary pulled up the sleeve of the shirt and bit into the human arm.

CHAPTER 69

A SACRIFICE

Gary had never imagined himself willingly chomping down on a person's body. They might be dead, but it still felt wrong. The fact that he could still feel residual body heat didn't help, but right now his life was literally on the line, as well as those of his friends.

If he didn't defeat the beasts that were chasing him, then who would? Perhaps White Rose or some other Altered might be able to do something about them, but how long would it take for them to arrive and deal with the twins? How many more lives would be lost because of their rampage?

Most importantly to Gary, if he died here, then who would look after his family? The answer to that question was no one.

Ever since he had become a werewolf, it was like his body knew what needed to be done. His teeth elongated to canine ones, making it easier to bite into flesh, and the thought of what he was actually doing went to the back of his mind. So it was easy and fast for him to wolf down his food and restore a good chunk of his Energy.

50/120 Energy
First-time bonus not in effect.
You have not consumed enough of the human to obtain a stat point.

As a werewolf you're supposed to be a predator, not a scavenger! If you wish to grow stronger, hunt down your own targets and feast on them!

Thanks for nothing, system! If you have the time for a stupid lecture, might at least throw me a bone and help out! At least human flesh seems to do the trick . . . but it's not like I can sit here for long, Gary thought, as he turned around and saw that the beast was now out in the open again.

On the other side, a little before Gary had enjoyed his impromptu snack, Kai and the others were trying to shake off the beast that was following them from above. It was smart enough to realize that moving atop the containers was much easier, and it was about to pounce on them at any second.

"What are we going to do?" Innu shouted from the back of the group. Given his position, he was the most likely target. Up ahead, Kai stopped running straight and took a turn, hoping to confuse the beast, but he quickly discovered that this was a mistake. A gray color gang member was blocking their path; Kai was shaking, too afraid to move with the beasts in the warehouse.

"Knock him out, we have to keep moving!" Austin shouted.

Kai understood that that was the right choice, even though it would likely doom the poor guy. However, they had to keep moving, so he prepared to kick him in the head. He didn't get that chance, though. The beast jumped down, landing directly on the gray color gang member.

The Howlers watched as the beast's victim let out a blood-chilling scream, while its claws stabbed him repeatedly. There was no chance of saving him, and no damage seemed to be able to kill the beast, so they turned and ran in their original direction.

But alas, now they encountered another problem. Having left the area with the containers, they were in an open space again.

"If you have a plan, now would be a bloody good time to share it with us!" Innu screamed.

Kai saw that the other beast was out in the open as well, but it was more toward the front of the warehouse; Gary hadn't defeated it yet.

I'm not even sure if he can defeat these monsters . . . Gary can't have been a werewolf for long, and how strong is a werewolf anyway? Kai thought. *But I promised I would keep them apart.*

So Kai shared the only plan he could think of. There was one container at the very back of the warehouse, the one where Marie had been kept. The doors were wide open and now Kai was standing in front.

After waiting a few seconds, they expected to see the beast leap down into the open space in front of them. Kai's body was shaking, but he took a fighting stance and waited for the beast. It was incredibly fast, especially when charging forward, but Kai was counting on that fact.

Soon the beast with the humanlike frame ran forward on its two legs, and then to pick up speed it started to use its hands as it charged.

Not now . . . just a bit closer . . .

The beast continued to advance, and then it leapt once more with its hands stretched out, aiming at Kai, who dodged to the side at the last second, like a bullfighter holding a red piece of cloth.

One of the claws still managed to scratch Kai's chest, but he had avoided the brunt of the attack. As the beast continued forward, pushed by its own momentum, it flew inside one of the containers.

You might be stronger and faster, but it looks like you lost all of your brain cells in your transformation! Kai thought as he shouted, "Now!"

The wide-open doors were being closed from both sides—Austin and Marie on one side, Innu on the other. They slammed the doors shut quickly and engaged the small lock on the outside, trapping the beast within.

Everyone took a step back as the beast banged on the container and dents appeared from the inside.

"What are we going to do now?" Austin asked. "We know that the container isn't going to keep it in there. It can tear through the metal with its claws."

As if to stress his point, the beast started to stab the metal container, breaking parts of it here and there. This was as far as Kai's plan had taken him. He didn't know what else to do; perhaps the best option would be to run.

"Open the container!" a voice shouted. When they turned around they saw Gary running toward them, with blood smeared across his mouth, and right behind him was the other beast.

"What? Are you crazy? What do you plan to do?" Innu shouted back.

"Just do it if you want to live!" Gary growled back. *"That's an order!"*

The first person who decided to listen was Kai, as he removed the lock. Then Austin quickly came to help and swung one of the doors open.

Gary ran into the container, and the beast followed right after him. "Close it!" he yelled from inside. *"Close it!"*

They locked the door, trapping Gary inside, and all they could hear were the sounds and cries of the beasts. Marie dropped to her knees, and so did Innu.

"Why the *fuck* did you guys do that? You just trapped him in there with them. How could you let him sacrifice himself? You're literally responsible for his death!" Innu grabbed Kai by the collar, but Kai didn't have the energy to explain anything.

Instead of fleeing, the group stayed at the container. Suddenly the sounds stopped, and then they heard a voice.

"You can open the door now." Gary sounded exhausted.

Immediately, Kai and Austin opened the door, and a bloody Gary walked out, his clothes mostly ripped off, covered in black blood.

CHAPTER 70

A BLOODY MESS

The beast in front of Gary was faster than him, and it looked like only his claws could do any real damage to it. Unfortunately, it cost a lot of Energy points to use them, and they only lasted two seconds right now.

The only way he could defeat it would be to prolong that time. Fortunately, his latest skill would allow him to do just that. With 50 Energy points, Gary would be able to stay fully transformed for two entire minutes, yet there was a reason why he hadn't used the skill yet.

He was worried it wouldn't be enough. Since he had never fought in that state before, he had no idea how long it would take him to defeat one of the twins. The time limit was also a burden. If they evaded him long enough, he might revert to human form, and that would be it . . .

As stupid as it sounded, what he needed to do was to fight both of them at once using his Full Transformation skill. Get them so close together that they couldn't run away and fight the hardest he possibly could.

As he pondered this, he saw that Kai and the others had trapped the other beast in one of the containers, and then it hit him. *That was the answer!*

He ran forward, and although he got hurt slightly on the way by the beast's claws, Gary didn't care. He picked up one of the bodies on the ground and threw it toward the beast as he continued to run.

A short while later, his plan had succeeded; Gary was in Buffin's container with the two beasts. As soon as the second one had entered, he activated his skill.

Skill activated: Full Transformation
–20 Energy
Transformation has begun

His transformation happened a lot faster than last time, though he wasn't sure if that was because he had been in his partial transformation state, his system was actually helping him, or something else.

Whatever the case, given his newfound strength and speed and his deadly claws, Gary was surprised to discover how easy it was to deal with the two beasts. He grabbed the wrist of the first one that jumped at him and crushed it. With his claws he shredded their bodies, and with his powerful jaws he bit them again and again.

During the Full Transformation, Gary remained in control. He knew what he was doing, but he felt like some type of battle instinct instructed him on what he should do, because he wasn't fighting like a human would, but more like a wild animal.

He also discovered that if he swallowed the flesh he bit, he regained a bit of Energy as well.

Not that he needed it; two minutes turned out to be plenty of time for him to deal with the twins. In fact, he had finished them off in one. Canceling his transformation afterward, Gary still had quite a bit of Energy to spare.

Error: An anomaly has been detected in the beast flesh!
Consuming the beast's body will not reward the user with any stats!

Back in his human form, Gary was naked again. This was a serious downside he needed to solve when using the Full Transformation skill. If there was one thing he was thankful for, aside from having survived this whole ordeal, it was that the system didn't require him to eat the twins . . . or whatever they had become.

He could have done it for Energy, but that was no longer needed. Still, he would have most likely done it if it had resulted in stat points, but since they weren't fully beasts, or fully Altered, he was happy to just leave them. Interestingly, their forms didn't revert, even after they had clearly died.

Gary picked up some clothes in the room that looked to have belonged to Buffin and put them on. He placed the mask he had chucked into the corner of the room back on his face, covering himself. He took a deep breath.

"You can open the door now."

Walking out, he was greeted with the faces of his friends, who displayed a mixture of emotions. One of them was confused as to why he was the one to make it out, covered in blood. How did he defeat the two monsters, and in such a short time to boot? What exactly did he do for them to end up in that state?

However, he also noticed the tears. Innu and Marie had shed tears for him while he was in that container. They obviously cared for him . . . and that was enough for him to have done what he had done to save their lives.

I killed . . . again, Gary realized. The first time that had happened still haunted him every so often. Barry had been an unfortunate accident. Of course, his schoolmate had stabbed him in broad daylight, so he had attacked him in a fit of rage, but he still felt guilty deep inside. But this time there was hardly any guilt.

Am I slowly losing myself? Gary wondered as he looked at his hands, tainted with black blood.

"Gary, thank you, you saved us all," Kai said. Austin gave him a thumbs-up, not asking further what exactly had happened in there.

This had become a far more serious matter than he had ever thought. Marie had gone to Gary's side and tried to find something to clean him up, but there was nothing in the room, other than the clothes on the dead bodies.

While the other Howlers outside were trying to figure out what to do, Kai went inside the container and took a long good look at the mangled bodies of the twins. There was black blood everywhere around the room.

On their bodies and all around the container were claw and bite marks. Stepping carefully around the blood, he bent over one of the corpses and pulled out the pocketknife that was still stuck in the back of its head.

He wiped off the black blood and inspected the knife carefully. Once he was sure there was nothing wrong with it, he let out a sigh of relief and placed it back in his pocket, observing the scene one final time.

When he walked back out, all eyes were on him, including Gary's. They were waiting to hear what they were supposed to do now. None of them had been prepared for things to escalate to such a degree.

"Our leader did his part," Kai said, patting Gary on the shoulder. "So now it's time for me to do mine. I promise that none of you will get in any trouble for this. It's the least I can do, after you guys came here to save Marie, and Gary saved all our lives."

CHAPTER 71

MAIN QUEST COMPLETE

At the time, each of them had been worried for their own life; they honestly would have all done the same since the only way to survive seemed to be to kill the twins. Otherwise, they would have been the ones added to the corpse pile. So nobody blamed Gary for what he had done.

While the teenagers might be okay with it, in the eyes of the law murder was a major crime. In fact, the warehouse as a whole would be a major crime scene, since multiple members of the gray color gang had been killed by the two beasts. The Howlers were all left wondering if they could get out of the place without any trouble.

"Say, can you call those guys over?" Innu asked, thinking back to when Billy had left him a special gift.

"They won't be able to cover all of this." Kai shook his head. "There are also too many witnesses. Not sure if they killed everyone outside, but a good number of those who escaped saw us already. We can't keep them quiet . . . However, we don't really have to worry about it.

"After all, we aren't the only ones who don't want everything that happened here to leak to the outside. Those syringes that the twins had . . . I doubt they came from the gray color gang, so most likely they got them from the Gray Elephants.

"By now they might already know that something is happening here, so they'll have to have started preparing the cleaners. They wouldn't want word of what happened here going out to anyone, like the police or the other gangs. So for once, we should be thankful that there is a group big enough to clean up this mess. In a way, these twins solved that problem for us."

"That still leaves one problem," Austin said, his arms folded. "Unlike our leader, the rest of us didn't have our faces covered. It shouldn't be too hard for them to find out who caused all of this."

Kai smiled as he went looking around for something. He had already looked around in Buffin's container and didn't find it. "You don't have to worry about that either. Who would believe that a no-name gang like us, the Howlers, would have the power to take out an entire color gang? Especially if they also had monsters like these?

"The only logical explanation is that we have someone backing us . . . and the only gang in all of Slough with that kind of power would be the Underdogs. They won't attack us anytime soon. I know I was wrong about the Wolf's Pool Club, but if I were to take a guess, that was all due to the personal vendetta of the twins rather than the gray color gang's order."

Eventually, Kai found what he was looking for: a small box that was hidden behind a small crate. He kicked the crate to the side and found what looked like a safe. There wasn't even a lock on it; some gangs used this method to test their members' loyalty. Of course, if anyone stole from the safe, they probably would never be found again, but this time, everything was there. The safe was filled with cash. It looked like the gray color gang had been paid quite well, or at least rather recently, by the Gray Elephants.

"I think we deserve this after what we went through. Don't you think so?" Kai asked, shoving some of it over to Austin since he was unable to hold it all by himself. "We'll use this money to restore the pool club and pay our medical bills, and of course you all deserve some for your troubles. I'll use my cut to try to expand our business a little more."

Austin found a bag in one of the containers and placed all the money inside.

"Let's get out of here." Kai smiled at them all. "I also want to congratulate all of you. In a way, this was the first real fight we had as a gang. Everyone survived and we came out on top. Think of this as a good thing if you can."

Outside, a few of Austin's friends had already arrived with their motorbikes. They had parked just outside the warehouse gate, unable to see inside. They were a little worried about heading into another gang's territory.

There were four of them, and one had only come along to bring Austin's bike for him. They gave everyone a ride home, including Gary, and not once did anyone ask him what had happened. The Howlers agreed that they would talk about what to do some other time, and Kai would contact them all.

Back at the apartment, Gary headed for his room. He gathered some clothes, since he was still wearing the ones he had borrowed from the gray color gang members, and took a long and thorough bath. He cooked dinner for Amy as if it were a regular, normal day, but it was far from it as he went to his bed and lay down.

His phone buzzed with a couple of messages.

A new group has been created
The Howlers

Kai: Welcome to the Howlers group chat! Here I will update everyone on events, duties, and more. Everyone, you might be happy to learn that so far it looks like we have nothing to worry about. No reports have been made about what happened today.

However, there is news of the gray color gang having been defeated. For now, I would say keep your mouth shut about what we did.

In other good news, Miss Degrace is doing well. She was released from the hospital and her injuries have been stitched up. As for Marie, she is already better. She will still be staying in the hospital for a couple of days, though.

I will handle the repairs of the Wolf's Pool Club with today's funds. Have a rest for the next couple of days, enjoy life, and I'll let you know once the club is ready to be back in action.

The message put a smile on Gary's face.

It's over . . . right? Those twins can't mess with us anymore, but that's just one problem out of what feels like a hundred.

Before going to sleep, Gary wanted to check one more thing. After defeating the twins, he had completed two quests and received a great reward; for one, he had reached Level 10.

Leveling up twice from this event meant he had gotten stronger and had two more stat points to use as he wished, but he had also completed another quest that he had long forgotten about.

Congratulations, you have now reached: Level 10

Main Quest completed

Look at you! You are growing into a fine werewolf and taking on this role well.

Now that you know what you're doing, society demands that you make yourself useful!

It's time to choose a path to go down on your werewolf journey.

Please select from one of the following classes!

CHAPTER 72

SELECT YOUR CLASS

There was a lot on Gary's mind after he killed the twins, and he didn't really have the time to check up on his rewards. However, as the day continued and he eventually saw Amy, his heart settled down somewhat from the events of the day. After receiving the group message from Kai, he decided that he should continue on with what he needed to do.

I remember it saying to select a class, but what does it exactly do? Gary wondered.

Ever since he completed the Main Quest, the system kept prompting him to make a choice. Even after he made the notification go away, every twenty minutes it would pop back up. It was clear that the system would continue to bother him until he made his choice.

"I guess this is just something I'm going to have to do," Gary grumbled as he looked over at his sister lying on her bed. He got up, went to their bathroom, and sat on the toilet. It was a strange place to be, but at least he was safe if any changes suddenly started to occur.

All right, so let's see what these options are again?

Please select from one of the following classes

Hunter Class

A Werewolf Hunter is fast, agile, and sneaky. He focuses on killing his prey quickly, out of sight and from the shadows. He is able to track his targets from a great distance and has excellent focus. Class perks include: More and better marks, improved tracking.

The first choice certainly is interesting; I could always do with extra marks. It would be great if I could create bonds with the others, and it would be a safe way to farm Exp . . . if that's how it still works . . .

So far the system gave me quests based on the situation I was in, but what if it starts to give me quests based on the class I've chosen? If I become a Werewolf Hunter, then the most obvious quest it would give me would be to hunt more. Why else would it give me more and better marks? I doubt the better marks will be like my Bond Marks; more than likely it will be improved Forced Bonds or something.

Gary decided to move on to the next class, which had a little extra text next to it.

Protector Class (Recommended)

A Werewolf Protector boasts one of the sturdiest bodies of his race. He uses his own body to shield his pack members from any harm, making sure that they will survive.
Class perks include: 1 extra point in Endurance upon each level-up, faster healing.

I can see why the system recommends this one. My Endurance certainly is way above my other stats. However . . . its strong point seems to be taking a beating. As useful as that is, I have seen time and time again that it doesn't matter if I don't have the strength or speed to defeat my opponents . . .

The Underdogs have Kirk . . . and the gangs in higher-tier towns must have Altered as well. They surely are a lot stronger than the fake ones I went up against today. Sure, I could just stand there and take a beating, but this role only seems to work if I have someone who can help me attack.

Keeping it as a maybe, Gary went over his last option.

Warrior Class

A Werewolf Warrior could be considered the vanguard of his pack. He leads his pack into battle with his strength. He has exceptional fighting ability and courage, but it is because of this trait, and his role, that this class boasts the highest fatality rate.

Before reading the additional perks, Gary gulped right there. The description had sounded great at the start . . . until he read the dying part.

Class perks include: Wide range of skills to select from, large Energy pool.

Hmm, I guess that's the problem with these additional perks: although it tells you a few details it doesn't tell you too much. Like how much is "large"? Will I have 150 Energy points, 200 Energy points, 500 Energy points? Is it the only class that increases it? Come to think of it, will my stats change depending on which one I choose? Honestly they all seem to have their advantages and disadvantages.

His finger hovered over the options, but he hesitated. For a moment Gary seemed to have made up his mind on one, then he changed to another, and then the last.

Damn it, this is just so hard. Should I trust in the system's recommendation?

Since Gary was struggling with what to pick, he decided to text Tom. He explained that he was playing a game, and these were the classes to select from. He asked Tom which class would suit him best in real life.

He waited and in the end got a reply.

I would say the Warrior Class suits you the best. You always do crazy things that get you in situations that might get you killed.

However, that's what makes you you. I always thought you had courage like a warrior.

Gary replied with a Thank you, as he had made up his mind. Something else was drawing him to this option: the part where it stated that this class leads the pack. He didn't know if his choice was influenced by Kai and the others, but he really did feel more like a leader as time went on.

> *Are you certain you wish to select the Warrior Class?*
> *Yes.*
> *Class has been selected*
> *Your grade has been upgraded from Pawn to Knight*
> *New skills are now available*
> *Changes to your status will now be applied*

The messages continued to arrive as Gary became a Werewolf Warrior.

CHAPTER 73

AN UPGRADE!

Apparently, selecting a class gave him more than just perks; Gary could physically feel that his body was changing. It felt similar to when he transformed.

Seriously? Right here, right now? You didn't tell me something like this was going to happen! What if Amy sees me? This is bad! Gary thought as sweat ran down his forehead. He quickly got out of his clothes, as he had gone through too many recently and he didn't want to waste money on buying more.

His arms and muscles were bulging, but his skin wasn't ripping off as it usually did. With each passing second he felt like his bones were growing slightly larger, and then finally it stopped.

Congratulations, your class has changed to: Werewolf Warrior
Class: Warrior
State: Human (Omega)
Grade: Knight

After taking a breath or two, Gary decided to check out the system; he had received multiple notifications, but he was unable to focus and tell what they were, so he just checked them all out.

What does Grade: Knight mean? It went from Pawn to Knight, so I'm guessing it's based on chess, but what exactly does it symbolize? Why is it separate from the class?

Alas, his system came and went as it pleased. Rather than focus on the things he didn't understand, he decided to look at the things he did understand.

The maximum number of marks available has increased
5/8 Marks

He had gained three more slots, which made Gary quite happy. He wondered what level he would have to reach to make them increase again, and he was also curious how many he would have gotten if he had selected the Hunter Class instead.

Error: One of your skills is incompatible with your current class
Charging Heart will be removed

Huh? Wait, what? I can't use Charging Heart anymore? What crap is that? Gary was getting really pissed at the Werewolf System's shenanigans. It was one thing to not give him a heads-up about his body changing, but his skills being incompatible with any of the classes should have warranted a warning!

He quickly went over to the Skills tab, and he could see that it had indeed disappeared. Charging Heart was the bread-and-butter skill that Gary had relied on the most. He could only hope that he could still enjoy the effect of doubling all his stats if his heart rate increased to or above 150 BPM on its own.

New skills are available; please select one skill from the following skills

Rather than stay down about it, Gary opted to look at the plus side; perhaps there was a skill compatible with his class that would benefit him even more than Charging Heart.

The first thing Gary noticed was that Hardened Will wasn't listed as one of the options.

Is this because it's also incompatible with the Warrior Class? Does that mean if I had selected one of the other classes, I might have kept

Charging Heart but lost the Claw Drain skill? He understood that at this point it would all be speculation.

Berserker
This skill can only be activated once the user falls below 50% of his Health. The skill does not require any Energy to use, but no other skills can be used while in effect. For one minute, the user's Strength will increase by 25%.

Controlled Transformation
This skill allows the user to transform different body parts to be part wolf as they wish. The Strength gained from this will depend on how much the user wishes to transform. While in this state, Energy will be consumed twice as fast as normal. Stats will increase depending on which body parts are transformed.

Out of the two skills, one was far more clear on what type of effects it would have. The second one seemed a bit wishy-washy at first, but reading it, Gary understood why and he was more inclined to choose that one.

When I was fighting against the twins, it was because of my claws that I managed to hurt them. Also, if I could change just part of my body, I could get away with being an Altered! What's more, I could permanently keep my claws to fight!

Full Transformation . . . just makes it too obvious that I'm not an Altered. However, the Energy consumption will be doubled . . . How much is my Energy now anyway? One of the class perks did mention a "large pool."

Gary bought up his status, and his jaw dropped wide open.

Name: Gary Dem
Class: Warrior
State: Human (Omega)
Grade: Knight

Level 10
Exp: 220/1456
Health: 100/100
Energy: 120 → 300/300
Strength 9 → 15
Dexterity 9 → 15
Endurance 14 → 15

My Energy is now at 300! I might actually be able to transform a lot of my body without having to worry. At the same time, I can use my skills a lot more easily now. On top of that, all of my basic stats have improved!

Now I don't feel too bad about Charging Heart. The Energy increase alone would have been the equivalent of eighteen levels! Gary thought excitedly. It looked like Gary still had one stat point to use as he wished, but as usual for now he decided to keep it.

Because of this newfound information, Gary decided to select the second skill.

Are you sure you would like to select the skill Controlled Transformation?

Yes

Current list of skills:
Mark 5/8
Claw Drain (Level 1)
Full Transformation
Controlled Transformation (new)

Finally, there was the last set of notifications for Gary to look at.

Daily Quests are no longer active
Exp gained from bonds will continue

The Knight grade cannot gain stats from eating humans
The Knight grade can still gain stats from eating beasts

Gary wasn't too upset. Lately, he had been finding it hard to head to the gym in the morning with how much he had to do throughout the day. The Exp requirement was also increasing with every level, so the little help he got from completing his Daily Quest had become very marginal.

However, he still intended to keep hunting. Not only did it save him money, but with his large Energy pool, he would have to eat more to keep it filled up. As for eating humans, now he had the perfect excuse not to. However, there was something on his mind as he read the last message.

"I can gain stats from eating beasts? It mentioned that there was an anomaly with the twins . . . was it because they weren't fully Altered? Or is it talking about beasts . . . because they still exist on earth?"

CHAPTER 74

A CHANGE

After checking out everything the system had to offer, Gary couldn't really say he was upset with his choice. For one, he had no way to find out what he would have gained, but the one thing he now did have was the skill called Controlled Transformation. In his mind, this was the biggest win out of them all.

Honestly, Gary wanted to test everything there and then, but he thought that maybe it wasn't the best idea for him to do so in the bathroom. What if he suddenly went from just controlling the change in one part of his body to controlling it fully?

There were also his regular worries that hadn't gone away, such as the other omega. If he could transform this drastically, did that mean Billy might have changed as well? Aside from that, there was also the fact that the message about the full moon hadn't disappeared. Only time could tell how his new class would affect that.

With all of these new skills and powers, I might actually be able to fight Billy on even ground . . . or even have the advantage.

When he put on his discarded clothes, Gary noticed that the shirt felt a little tight, and his sleeves came up a little short on his forearms. On top of that, his trousers had the same issues. Overall, it felt like his clothes were stretched a little more.

What the—? Gary thought, and he finally looked in the mirror. He was in so much shock that he dropped his trousers back on the floor, for he had to touch his face to see if something was going wrong.

It is me, but what happened to me?

His reflection was staring back at him. He still recognized his spiked green hair with short sides, his normal eyes and nose . . . only everything looked a little different. His face had grown a little longer and his jawline had become slightly chiseled.

That was when he caught on that not only had his appearance changed, but there were physical changes as well. He had grown a bit taller, his limbs were a bit longer, and overall his body was a little bigger. When he lifted his shirt, Gary saw well-defined muscles, and it was the same for the rest of his body.

Is this all because of the class change? I guess this is what it meant by "changes will be applied" . . . not only did it improve my base stats, it also gave me a body to match it. I have the body of a Warrior, Gary thought, and he immediately felt embarrassed that he had had that thought.

Then he made one last check, looking downward toward a certain area.

This is amazing!

19 days until the next full moon

The full moon was too far away for Gary to care at this point, and he had woken up even earlier than usual. He was slowly getting better at cooking, and he left some scrambled eggs out for his sister.

As for why he had chosen to leave early, it was because he didn't want to have a conversation with his sister. For one, his school clothes already looked a bit ridiculous on him, and he had to send a message to Kai, asking him to get him a different size for his gang uniform. There wasn't much to salvage after his transformation yesterday.

Man . . . this is going to be a strange day.

While Gary headed to school, just as Kai had expected, the news had reached the Gray Elephants. They had received multiple different reports, but because of how drastic the stories were, it was hard for the Gray Elephants to believe what they had heard.

The two leaders were meeting in an office on the top floor of a factory that made machine parts. It was one of the main businesses that the Gray Elephants protected from other gangs.

Raven opened the door for Riv so he could join him and Brandon. After what had happened yesterday, they needed to speak to the red color gang leader.

"Raven, it looks like you did the right thing after all," Brandon said with a smile. "Judging from the reports, the twins did change, but they acted like wild animals. I guess Sin really was trying to use us as his guinea pigs."

"You're right," Raven replied. He wore a sour expression because he recalled that Brandon had recommended that he use the syringe on his brother as a test subject. "I only gave them a diluted mix, so maybe it was that. There is still plenty of the solution, but we have no clue if more of it is actually better or worse. What should we do with it? We can't exactly give it back."

Brandon thought for a while and eventually came up with an answer.

"For now, let's talk about other matters. The remaining gray color gang members will join the red color gang. Get them to change their colors and if any of them won't comply, just give them the boot.

"As for that Howlers group . . . we should leave them alone. I imagine they're just bait, even though reports claimed that they had an Altered among them. The only Altered who works for a gang is Kirk. They say he covered his face, but it has to be him, which means the Underdogs are involved in all of this.

"Maybe we can use this to our advantage. Sin is getting impatient, and now we know what the solution does as well. Instead of risking it, we can dilute the solution to create some monsters to take care of them." Brandon smiled at his idea.

After the meeting was over, Raven looked like he had one more thing on his mind.

"Brandon, I might be away for a couple of days. It'll take a few days for you to set everything up, so I'll be by your side by then. But right now I have things to deal with. I hope that's okay."

It was clear from Brandon's look and his hesitation that it wasn't okay. However, the leaders were supposed to be equal, not one above the others. With Yovan dead, it was only him and Raven, so it felt like Brandon had no choice but to let him go.

"All right, I trust you to be back in time. Can you at least tell me what's so important?" the Gray Elephants leader asked as he lit up a cigar.

"I'm going to find out what happened to my brother!" Raven replied with conviction.

CHAPTER 75

CENTER OF ATTENTION

Arriving at school, Gary was happy to see that everyone was okay. He had been worried that Innu might run away after seeing what happened. Sure, they were all somewhat involved in the underworld, but Gary knew exactly what it was like to see a dead body.

It was a memory that he couldn't get out of his head, although perhaps Gary had it worse because he had gone through worse things. Which was why, although Innu was in class with his head down on his desk, Gary wasn't going to disturb him or give him a hard time.

When Gary came close, Innu lifted his head and took a peek before putting it back down again.

"How come I feel like shit, while you look like some type of golden boy . . . am I that tired?" Innu mumbled.

But it wasn't only Innu who noticed. Soon many of those in the room couldn't stop staring at Gary. Something seemed clearly different about him.

"Did he get a new haircut or something?" one of the students asked.

"No, he still has that same stupid green hair, but he really looks different. Did he get plastic surgery, maybe?"

"Nah, it's not plastic surgery. Look at his body, he's been working out. His clothes are bulging, I think you can see his muscles."

After hearing what everyone was saying, Innu lifted his head again and rubbed his eyes slightly. He wasn't imagining things; Gary really did look great after everything that had happened.

Did that black blood turn him into some kind of superhero or something? Innu couldn't believe it. *If I had known, I might have also taken some . . . although . . . no, his hair seems to be fine.*

Gary hadn't really expected that he would garner this much attention. He wasn't used to the stares—he was even avoiding their gazes a bit—but he would be lying if he said he didn't like all the praise he was getting. He looked over toward Xin.

For a second, he saw her glancing his way before quickly turning around.

Oh . . . I didn't expect that.

"Hey, Gary, right? The two of us don't talk much, but look at you." A girl came up to him and stroked her hair, putting it behind her shoulder to reveal her ear. It was Tiffany. She had gotten incredibly close, to the point where Gary was uncomfortable.

"The superstar of the rugby team, and now look at you. It looks like you've been working out, but how did you get like that so fast?"

Gary nervously chuckled as she pushed her body up against his and started to feel his arm. She stroked his biceps, and even Tiffany seemed surprised by how large and hard it was.

"I think it's just a growth spurt," Gary mumbled.

The door opened and Tom walked in. He had entered through the back door rather than the front door, which meant he was close to his seat and saw Gary, red-faced, being grabbed by what Tom would refer to as a leech.

"Hey, Tiffany, do you know my name?" Tom asked as he slammed his bag down on the table. It looked like she froze for a second as she tried to remember it.

"Ah, I'm a bit of a ditz," she said, knocking herself on the head in a cute fashion. "This brain of mine is freezing."

"Yeah, we sit next to each other in geography, and we've been in the same class for four years. Anyway, Gary's mine," Tom declared, licking his lips.

Tiffany let go of Gary's arm. "Wait, you mean he's . . ."

Tom just folded his arms, nodding his head, and eventually she decided to awkwardly leave. Which immediately made both Tom and Gary burst out in laughter.

"Well, I didn't expect you to come up with something like that." Gary wiped a tear from his eye as he pounded Tom on the shoulder, which made Tom flinch.

"Not my fault if she misunderstands. Anyway, what the hell happened to you? Yesterday you asked me about a game, not telling me anything about what happened, and now you look like a jock who never leaves the gym. Be honest, did you get transported into a game world, and then it spewed you out based on your class?" Tom asked skeptically.

"Nah, it's just a growth spurt," Gary insisted, although it was scary how close to the truth Tom's joke was. As his best friend, Tom had known Gary for a long time, and in the past Gary was only slightly taller. For him to experience such a growth spurt seemed somewhat ridiculous, and far too coincidental . . . but he assumed that it might have something to do with him being a werewolf.

The lesson went on, and now it was time for the group to have a bit of self-study. Innu was fast asleep, snoring away, and Gary believed it was a good chance to ask Tom a few questions.

"I remember you saying that your parents' work is related to Altered. That should mean they know a lot about beasts, right? Like the beasts that Altered DNA comes from and so on?" Gary asked.

Tom nodded, but honestly he knew little more than that about what his parents did.

"What I wanted to know was . . . are there still any beasts out there? I'm not talking about Altered, but real beasts."

At Gary's current grade, there was one way to get stat points, and that was to kill and eat beasts. This gave him more peace of mind than the prospect of eating humans or Altered. The problem was that beasts no longer roamed the earth, so where would he find one? He hoped that Tom might know more; if not, there was also Blake . . . but he doubted the Altered Hunter would share that knowledge with him.

"I have no idea. I mean, I've never seen one, have you? But I'll ask them, and I can tell you tomorrow. Now I want you to tell me something. What happened yesterday? After I took that woman to the hospital, I mean?"

There was a pause before Gary answered; he had forgotten that Tom had been there yesterday, but if he told Tom everything, would he believe him, and wouldn't that involve him with gang matters?

"We tried finding out who really trashed the club. In the end . . . we found Marie, but she was badly hurt, so we took her to the hospital afterward. Anyway, because of the state of the club I have no job for a few days, but I did want to test out a few things with you." Gary placed his hand over his mouth and whispered, "Werewolf."

This part was true, and since he wouldn't be going to the club today, he thought he could at least test out his new skills, which conveniently meant they would be spending time together.

His best friend nodded and got back to studying, but he knew once again that Gary had lied to him. This morning, Tom had decided to surf a section of the dark web, a special part of the internet that many criminal organizations used, and there were plenty of forums there as well.

He had been so late today because he had found a particularly interesting discussion of theories as to what happened that might have led to the apparent annihilation of the gray color gang in Slough.

Gary, was that you? Tom wondered.

CHAPTER 76

GROWTH SPURT

School had ended, and for once Gary didn't need to go searching for Kai to inform him about something, or go looking for Blake. Both of them had told him they would contact him when they needed to.

Earlier, Marie had sent them an update in the Howlers group chat saying she would be taking the day off school, and all of them could understand why. Until the swelling went down, she would be harassed with all sorts of questions, especially at school. Perhaps they would even assume it was her parents who had beaten her, so to avoid questions it was best to just pretend she was sick.

There was club practice as usual, and just like in class, his teammates as well as Mr. Root had noticed his "growth spurt." However, they had all seen radical changes in people who were Gary's age before, so they weren't too surprised. Instead they were proud that one of their star players seemed to be taking the sport more seriously now by working out.

After club practice, while the sun was still out, Gary and Tom headed to the park that was closest to the school. It was also one of the safer areas for that reason. It was the same one where he and Tom had gone three days ago to experiment with his Full Transformation skill.

When they finally entered the forest in the park, they sat down and drank some water.

"So, tell me, do you think your changing body is a werewolf thing?" Tom asked, seeing as no one else was around.

"That does seem to be the most likely explanation." Gary touched his own hard chest. "It's hard to explain, but it feels as if my body itself might have evolved. Like it's grown! That's why I wanted to invite you out here. You understand more about all this werewolf lore stuff, so I wanted to ask your opinion about it. Did you read anything about such drastic changes?"

Tom honestly had no clue. He had never heard about a werewolf evolving, and why had that change happened overnight? If anything, the most likely timing for any changes should have been either the moment he became a werewolf or after his first turning.

He could only think of a few things that would cause this evolution: an increase in strength and power, perhaps due to fighting, or maybe something else . . .

Gary took off his shirt, followed by his trousers, leaving him only in his underwear. Although he would need to get new clothes that fit him, he thought it was a waste to keep ripping clothes. Besides, he still had to go home somehow.

"I want you to tell me what I look like, because I think that change allowed me to control my transformation," Gary said as he looked at his arm.

Skill activated: Controlled Transformation
Transformation has begun

Using the skill, Gary could tell that the system had split his body into several parts. He understood it all in his head. It was so detailed that it was unbelievable. Gary could, if he wanted to, change just a single finger to grow out his nail, or change the entire hand.

It was the same for all the other parts of his body. It was as if he had a diagram in his head and all he had to do was select the body part that he wanted to transform. From then on, there was a slider of some sort, which he could move in his head as he wished.

As a test, Gary selected his whole arm, from the shoulder down to his fingertips. He then visually moved the slider, and he could feel his arm changing by the second. First, he put the slider a quarter of the way.

"Whoa, your arm!" Tom shouted in surprise. Seeing it live was completely different from watching a recording. Gary looked down and saw that his fingernails had grown and his arm was a little hairier than usual and slightly larger. It still looked human but didn't quite suit his body.

As he moved the slider to the halfway mark, some skin fell off his hand, and it was just as painful as before. His arm had also grown bigger and now his arm no longer looked completely human. It was covered in a mix of hair and fur, but underneath it was still human tissue.

Finally, Gary turned the slider all the way up, and his entire arm transformed. It was completely covered in brown fur. It hurt, but not as much as Gary remembered.

Both he and Tom were amazed.

"So you can really control it! Does this mean you'll be okay on the full moon?" Tom asked.

Gary shook his head, as he really wasn't sure. He had still received the message this morning, so something was bound to happen. Right now, he didn't want to stop the testing there. Gary continued to test the other parts of his body, and he noticed a few things.

Transforming took up energy; just as Full Transformation used up 20 Energy points, Controlled Transformation also used up Energy, although the amount differed depending on the size of the body part and how much he transformed it. He could also feel his Energy draining away the more parts he transformed, just as the system had stated.

However, what was most impressive was his stats while doing these tests. Changing certain parts of his body also affected his stats. Changing his arms mainly resulted in extra Strength. Transforming his torso and back gave him extra Endurance, whereas transforming his feet and legs translated to extra Dexterity, allowing him to run faster than he could before.

The bigger an area he transformed, the more the slider was on the werewolf side, and the bigger the increase, but also the faster the Energy consumption.

The stats for each area that was partially transformed were even better than when he used Charging Heart. It was clear that this was a big improvement from before. Especially with the Energy.

"Gary, do you understand what this means now?" Tom shouted after watching everything. "You may not have to hide this anymore! If you can partially transform like this, then you can pass yourself off as an Altered!"

Gary could see in his friend's eyes that he was truly happy for him—happy that he no longer had to hide his secret. But Gary felt like he would still have to hide it, at least for now, and he wasn't happy for the same reasons as Tom. Instead, he thought these were the perfect tools to use against Billy.

Outside Bayles High School, Slough's only all-girls school, students were walking out in groups as it was the end of the school day. Two girls walked out arm in arm, just as they did every day.

Stacy and Amy usually walked to the gate before parting ways to head home. They had gone through a traumatic event together, but it had only brought them closer together, and Stacy had solemnly promised that she would never do anything as stupid as that again.

Just as they were about to leave, though, a figure in a black leather jacket and wearing sunglasses stopped in front of the two girls.

"Hey there, I just wanted to ask you a few things," the man said as he pulled his glasses down and recognized one of the girls. "You see, my brother, Hawk, has been missing for a while now, and I was wondering if you two knew anything."

CHAPTER 77

A MISSING BROTHER

Amy and Stacy hadn't quite been the same ever since they went to the Kobo Karaoke Club that evening. They were thankful that theirs was an all-girls school, with only a handful of male teachers. Otherwise, it would have been a lot harder for them to deal with their day-to-day life.

Amy was aware of her condition. Whenever she went to the convenience store, she could feel herself becoming extra nervous, even when she was just paying for her items. This only happened if there was a man or boy behind the counter. The only male person she felt somewhat safe around was her brother.

After experiencing such a traumatic event, the girls went into a shock response when a strange man approached them out of no-where. What's more, he got uncomfortably close to them, making it seem that he was trying to block their path on purpose. Because of this, Amy's first instinct was to place her hand in her pocket, ready to inform Gary of what was happening as soon as possible, just as she had promised him.

"Hawk . . . is your brother?" Stacy asked with a shaky voice.

Amy sighed internally. It might have been for the best if the two of them had pretended not to know who Hawk was. Unfortunately, now that Stacy had repeated his name, it was obvious that her best friend was at least acquainted with the guy.

Seeing the girls' reaction, Raven let out a big sigh and pinched the bridge of his nose. He had been hoping for their help, but this might prove to be a lot harder than he had anticipated.

"It looks like that idiot has mistreated you two girls. I don't know what exactly he has done, but let me apologize on his behalf," Raven said, bowing his head. Surprisingly, he looked quite sincere.

"I don't want to trouble you any more than I have to. I'm honestly just looking for him. As I said, he's been missing for a while, and when I looked through his messages, there was a girl that he had been talking to a lot.

"You two even exchanged photos, so that's how I found you. I'm sorry . . . I actually knew who you were before approaching you, I just wanted to confirm."

Raven was very thankful for the police officer that day; not only had he given him a transcript of his brother's messages, but it had everything. Even information that usually would have been omitted, such as photos and more.

It was obvious that the guy had been a good-natured rookie working at the station. The reason nobody had given Raven any of that information had been primarily so he wouldn't bother the poor girl . . . just as he was doing right now. But it looked like the police hadn't bothered to look this far either.

With all that information, it hadn't taken long for Raven to track Stacy down. The only thing he didn't expect was for her to be . . . as startled as she was.

Amy noticed that Raven was only looking at Stacy when he spoke. Apparently, he didn't know what his brother had tried to do that day. However, her instincts were telling her that this person was bad news. Throughout the whole conversation, he was clenching and unclenching his fist by his side, as if he was angry at something.

Worried that he might lash out, Amy grabbed her friend by her arm tighter and pulled her away. "Come on, we don't even know who this stranger is. What is an adult doing waiting outside a girls' school anyway?" she exclaimed.

Luckily, Stacy didn't seem to object to this and happily went along with her. But Raven grabbed Stacy by the wrist, stopping her.

"Please. I'm just looking for my brother," he pleaded. "Look, I know he can be an asshole, but he's still my brother. Imagine this was your family member who had gone missing. Just tell me what you know, and once I find him, I promise I'll make him apologize for whatever he did to you!

"The last person he texted was you, and he's been missing ever since! If you want, I can compensate you, or make it so he never bothers you again, all right?"

Stacy was trying to get the man to release her arm, but Raven had a hard grip on her, so much that it was starting to hurt. His soft words and hard approach weren't adding up.

"Help!" Amy screamed. *"He's attacking us!"*

Since it was an all-girls school, everyone turned to check out the situation. It looked like danger, as there was a strange man in dark sunglasses holding on to two girls who looked unwilling to leave with him.

The other girls pulled out their phones and started taking videos and photos. Seeing this, Raven scoffed and let go.

Why is it that every time I try to do things the right way, it doesn't turn out? Raven wondered in frustration as he adjusted his jacket. "Fine, if that's how you want it, then you two better watch your back! I promise I'll find out what happened to my brother one way or another!"

The strange man left the school grounds, and a few moments later they heard him driving off on his motorbike. Some students ran over, checking up on the two girls who had been attacked. Stacy fell to her knees.

"Amy . . . what do we do?" Stacy asked as tears ran down her face. She looked up at her friend, shocked and scared.

"Don't worry, Stacy," Amy replied, putting on a brave face. "We really don't know why his brother is missing. A scumbag like that probably got what was coming to him, so don't worry about it. We'll be okay."

Despite her tone, she too was frightened. The man had discovered Stacy's identity from pictures, so what else might he know? If the younger brother was involved in things like that, then maybe the older brother was involved in bigger things.

Thinking about brothers and what the strange man had said, her thoughts went to her own brother. She and Stacy weren't actually the last ones who had seen Hawk. After they left, Gary had stayed behind; at least that was what Stacy had told her. Amy had trouble remembering too much about it after a certain point.

I never asked him what he did that day. I was just so worried about Mom at the time, but Gary didn't look hurt when he came back . . . did he? I can't remember that well. I hope . . . no, that's impossible . . . How would Gary be responsible for this? There were three of them; he probably just slammed the door and ran away. Amy hoped so.

I'll just ask him when I get home today.

CHAPTER 78

THE YOUNG HUNTER

After school, Blake walked home following his usual path, but he was busy with his thoughts. For one, he wondered what was happening to Gary. His body had clearly changed, and the young Altered Hunter had his suspicions as to why.

It looks like his body hasn't finished adjusting to whatever happened to him, so maybe he's more complete now. Only . . . I don't recall any of the books mentioning such transformations . . . Is he some new type of werewolf? Have they evolved since then?

Most importantly, does that mean Billy might also have changed? Will Gary and I really be able to defeat a werewolf that might even be stronger than when he fought my dad?

Blake hoped that Gary was just the exception, and not the rule, but either way, it would be better if they attempted to deal with the situation sooner rather than later. If werewolves were able to naturally get stronger as time went on . . . the young Altered Hunter didn't want to finish his thought.

Although it was true that Altered could also grow stronger, in their case it had to do with the training they underwent, learning how to use their powers and fight with their new bodies. Werewolves, however, were humans who had been born with special genetics . . . at least that was one theory out of many that Blake had learned from his books. In other words, the difficulty could be compared to learning a new language or learning how to walk.

The equipment Blake needed to track down Billy was in the secret room at their house. He was considering many options, such as sneaking in, taking the items he needed, and then later returning them before his father even noticed.

Even if Blake got caught and explained that he was going hunting on his own, he would be cautioned, but his father wouldn't do anything to him. Still, he would rather avoid giving his parents any reason to distrust him. In the past, he had made up many excuses not to go on outings, so if he started to show an interest now . . . He wondered how his father would react.

I could wait until he goes on one of his trips, but who knows when that will be? The longer we wait, the worse it becomes if they really get stronger over time . . .

The heavens seemed to be on the young Altered Hunter's side today. As soon as Blake came home, his father informed him that he had news to share.

"I have been called," Ozacas told his son. "Not just me, but a few of the Hunters. It seems pretty serious this time, so I don't know how many days I'll be gone. I've left enough money on the kitchen table to last you for a week, and you know the code, in case you need more."

Often, when the Hunters felt like they needed help or had a big operation, they would call the senior members with a lot of stars and experience to help. This happened frequently, but Blake had still thought it would be a while until his father was called.

"Off to another Tier 2 city again?" Blake asked.

Ozacas shook his head. "No, this time it's actually a Tier 4 town."

This was an unexpected answer. The lower the tier, the unlikelier it was to run into an Altered. After all, becoming an Altered was only for the privileged, for those who had the money or power to afford it, and those were usually in Tier 2 cities or above.

"I know it's strange, but apparently something has gone rampant down there. More Altered are being spotted than usual, and not even the police force can handle it. Of course, the White Rose agents are doing nothing. If it doesn't affect those who fill their pockets, they don't get involved.

"After subduing the Altered, we might stick around to find out the reason for this change, so this one might take a while. I want you to continue your training while I'm away, so you better not be sloppy! Once I'm back, we will take care of the Altered here."

His father headed for the door, carrying a large bag that Blake knew to be filled with all sorts of equipment. Before he could say anything, Ozacas was already off and heading toward his destination, showing no emotion to his son as he left.

A Tier 4 town? I don't think I've ever even been to one before. I wonder what happened there? I guess after I become a full-fledged Altered Hunter, I will get called to places like that as well, Blake thought; he knew that someday he would have to follow the path of his father.

He was a bit sad seeing his father go, but this was his opportunity. He and Gary had made a deal, and it was the perfect time for them to act. After hearing the car disappear in the distance, Blake went to the training room and tapped the statues to open the secret door; he could see that a lot of the equipment had been taken.

Fortunately, there was a duplicate for nearly everything down there, due to Blake also getting trained as a Hunter. He looked through the items and picked what they needed to track the other werewolf down and subdue it.

After putting everything in a black bag similar to the one that his father had, he checked through it again. And again, and again.

I . . . I can do this, right? It will be my first time going out without my dad . . . and I'll be going with Gary. What if we can't find the other werewolf? What if it's a trap set up by Gary? Maybe they both plan to pinch me and get rid of the problem? He started to second-guess whether it was actually a good idea.

He picked up one of the batons from the back and gripped it tightly, strengthening his resolve.

No, I'm just making up excuses. I didn't realize how much I relied on Dad.

The next day arrived, and it was time for Gary to head to school and do his regular thing. After a stretch he looked toward Amy, checking that she was there, which had become a habit.

She was acting a little strange yesterday like she wanted to ask me something, but she never did . . . Maybe it's girl stuff. I guess I can't replace Mom for everything. Gary sighed at that thought. Thanks to his recent cash infusion, he wouldn't have to worry about the hospital bills, which was a good thing, since their mother had yet to display any signs of recovering.

He checked his phone to see if there were any messages, but naturally the club renovations would take some time. There wasn't any news from any of the others either. However, he noticed a text message waiting for him on his regular phone.

I hope you're ready. Tonight, we'll go hunt down Billy!

CHAPTER 79

WORKING WITH
AN ENEMY

Gary walked to school with a hop in his step. It was a strange feeling, and he didn't even understand it himself right now. Rather than being scared or worried that he would most likely face Billy today, he felt excited.

All this time, everything he had been doing, growing stronger by fighting the color gang members, had been so he could beat Billy, and it was time to see if his hard work had paid off.

Is this really me? Gary thought as he looked at his fist, still not used to its increased size. *I've always enjoyed watching Altered fights . . . but I never fought one before. Well, even if the old me had had the chance to, I would have been done in before I could even blink. Now, though, I feel confident in defeating Billy!*

On one hand, he enjoyed this feeling of great strength, but he reminded himself that there were downsides to it. No, not great responsibility, but more like giant headaches in the form of White Rose and the Altered Hunter. Hopefully, once Billy was taken care of, Blake could claim the credit for it, making both of them disappear from Gary's life.

School seemed to last forever, and while he was in class, he sent a message to the Howlers group chat, informing his fellow gang members that he had plans today. According to Kai, the club was still being fixed, and with it being the middle of the week, nobody needed their leader for anything.

In other words, nothing would get in the way of what was to happen tonight.

Calm down, there's no guarantee that we'll even find him today. It might still be a long time until we do, but it does feel like I'm close to solving one of my biggest problems.

"Say, what's got you so happy? Did you find a secret love letter from Xin or something?" Tom asked teasingly, making him blush a bit.

"Do I require a special reason to be happy? Anyway, tonight, Amy and I planned to watch a film together. With my mum and everything else, it's nice to do something normal for a change." Gary was getting better at lying, which wasn't surprising, considering how frequently he did so.

If it were just him, he might have told Tom that he was going out to hunt Billy, but now Blake was involved. It didn't feel fair to reveal the young Altered Hunter's secrets, seeing as Blake had kept Gary's secret from his own father.

The school day proceeded as normal, and rugby practice was similarly uneventful. Neither Blake nor Gary showed any signs that the two of them had very dangerous plans today. They only interacted as was needed during practice plays.

There was still some time before they headed out. According to Blake, the best time to act would be at night, which Gary was fine with. He believed that Billy wouldn't be out on the hunt until then anyway.

Right now, Gary was out and about in town with an empty bag he had brought from home. With the leftover funds from their recent haul, Gary was in possession of more cash than would be normal for a boy his age, at least in Slough. He went to the convenience store to buy plenty of raw meat, placing it all in his bag, and he also decided to grab some extra clothes this time.

Now that I have a larger Energy pool, I should theoretically be able to go a few days without having to eat anything. It looks like my Energy still goes down at the same speed as it did before, but it also seems to work the other way around. I need to eat three times as much to fill it back up.

With 300 Energy points, he could afford to hunt a few critters occasionally, but he didn't want to be carrying around dead animal carcasses in his bag. Eventually, after he had finished his shopping, the only thing left was to wait for Blake to call him.

He took a bite of meat, just to make sure his Energy was full. One never knew when a couple Energy points might make the difference. Fortunately, his hunting partner didn't make him wait too long. A text on his phone instructed him where they would meet.

It was in a part of Slough he was slightly unfamiliar with, though he recognized it well. This was the area of Slough where the Bruntins' apartment was located, and where the White Rose agents had discovered him the first time.

Enough time had passed without any more news that there were no police or reporters on the scene. They had other work to do, and they couldn't disturb the lives of everyone in the neighborhood for too long. Whatever evidence had been in the apartment, the police had retrieved it long ago.

Just as Gary had suspected, Blake wanted to meet him at Billy's old home.

He doesn't think Billy is still here, does he? Why start here, of all places? Well, I guess it's as good a place as any . . . hold on, could it be that Billy might actually be inside? Surely Blake would have warned me, right? Shit, I haven't prepared myself. Gary felt his heart beat faster.

Blake sent a short text asking him to come to the roof instead, so Gary happily obliged. He was careful to avoid being spotted by any of the residents. Using his nose, he tried to find any strange scents.

Unfortunately, Gary couldn't remember Billy's scent too well, since the last few times they had met, he hadn't had the chance to smell him. On the night of the full moon, when Billy had attacked Innu, Gary had been a werewolf himself, meaning he had no recollection if the other werewolf had a unique scent. However, there was nothing that smelled like himself, at least.

At the top of the stairs, Gary knocked a few times at the door. It swung open, and a plain black mask was staring him dead in the face. It had no gap for the mouth, but only two small square slits for eyes.

"Holy . . . did you really have to scare the crap out of me?" Gary complained.

"Sorry, I needed to make sure that it wasn't one of the residents up here to enjoy a smoke or something," Blake replied after shutting the door behind them and clipping on what looked like a padlock.

Would a resident have a reason to knock, though? Gary argued mentally, but he let the matter rest. Instead, he looked behind Blake. *Whoa, I guess he really is serious about this stuff. Man, I really never thought I would be here working with an Altered Hunter.*

Several weapons were laid out on a piece of cloth, including some items that Gary couldn't even recognize. Now that he was closer, he could tell that the young Altered Hunter was wearing thick armor underneath his outfit, like a knight from the past.

"Is that for protection? From the Altered, I mean?" Gary asked.

"Kinda," Blake replied while he double-checked his equipment. "It's more than that, though. The armor is . . . let's just say it's special."

Although Blake had agreed to work with Gary , he was careful about not divulging too many of their secrets to the werewolf boy just yet.

"So how are we going to track down Blake? Do you have like an Altered scanner or something, if that would even work?" Gary asked.

"I guess you could call it that." Blake scratched his head. "We use a lot of tools for tracking, not just one. In our case, we don't even know what to start looking for because Billy is like you.

"In the case of normal Altered, we can tap into other information networks, like reports from the police, sensors going off at strange hours, and so on. If those are reported, then my father can use that information to help us look in the right area.

"Unfortunately, we don't have that, so I chose the area that would make the most sense to start with. As you said, we don't even know if any of this stuff will work on him because he is not an Altered. So if you don't mind, I would like to test some of these things on you first."

Blake picked up an object and clicked a button on the bottom, shooting out what looked like a bat with spikes from the top of it.

Gary gulped.

CHAPTER 80

OTHERS LIKE YOU

What kind of tests is he going to do on me? Gary felt apprehensive and backed away, placing his hand in front of him. He realized that he didn't really know Blake that well. Perhaps this was his trap; then again, the system hadn't popped up with any type of message saying that he had broken his promise, but he was sure there would be loopholes to his system's bond.

As Blake pressed the button again, the spikes went away, and the batonlike bat collapsed down to something that Blake was able to hold easily in his hand. He then placed it around his belt, which held a number of similar devices.

He touched the side of his mask, and for a second something lit up on the inside, and Gary heard a small mechanical hum as if a computer had been turned on.

"What are you doing?" Gary asked.

"This mask isn't for show; it has a lot of built-in features, such as night vision, heat sensors, and more," Blake explained. "Sorry, but I only have one."

Gary didn't mind; he could actually see quite well in the dark thanks to his enhanced eyesight. Still, the mask sounded very impressive, as expected for people who hunted Altered for a living.

"Altered, even in their human form, give off more heat than normal humans. It's only ever so slight, so it's a rather unreliable way to search for Altered. Otherwise, they would be bringing in every human who has a fever," Blake explained. "Still, it's useful for narrowing down our search, but first, we need to learn if it's the same for . . . your kind."

Gary understood that Blake was referring to him being a werewolf rather than an Altered, yet for some reason he seemed to avoid using that term. The next thing the young Altered Hunter pulled out was a special tube that was encased in something, with a button in the middle of it. The liquid inside it was red but also a little dark, making Gary guess its contents, so he simply asked.

"Altered blood," Blake replied. "Most Altered have a sensitive nose, and they can distinguish between human blood and Altered blood. In their curiosity they may come to this area, but it's not too useful unless we know the general area of a target."

After a few more tests, Blake placed all the items that he needed for quick access around his belt. He then pressed a button on his bag that basically vacuum-shrank the entire thing and swung it over his back. The straps were well placed, and it was hard to even see that he had brought a bag with him.

Of course, the final touch was a large hoodie that almost looked like a robe, but it was clear that it was used to cover his equipment. If people saw him carrying all these items, the police would surely get a few calls.

"What about you, didn't you bring—"

Before Blake could finish his question, Gary cleared his throat, reminding him that he always had everything he might need on him. They walked down together, with Blake taking the lead. Gary was following him carefully, and from just watching his actions, he felt like he was learning a lot.

Blake was careful at every turn, and he even used small devices like mirrors to look down hallways he couldn't see. It was quite amazing, and Gary figured if he had picked up on similar things, then perhaps White Rose would have never found him.

The two reached the outside of the apartment building, and Blake seemed to be looking at the ground for something. Meanwhile, Gary was sniffing the air, hoping to pick up something with his nose.

"The blood is still here, but it's really faint. We could follow it and see where it leads us, but I think the police would have done that already," Blake said.

"We can follow it anyway. Maybe Billy takes all the people he kills to a certain place, and I can sniff him out," Gary suggested.

They followed the trail, and Gary assumed that Blake must be able to see the blood through his strange mask, which certainly seemed handy. In the end, though, the blood trail seemed to stop, and they found themselves heading to another local park near the block of apartments.

Using the mask, Blake searched for anyone in the vicinity with a high temperature reading, but there were only a few. Unfortunately, Gary didn't need a fancy mask to tell that Billy wasn't among them. They continued their search in the forest, and since they couldn't find anything, Gary had some questions for Blake.

"I was wondering . . . do you also hunt beasts?" Gary asked, still thinking about the system message he had received after reaching Level 10.

"Why would you think that? They don't call us *Altered* Hunters for nothing . . . When you say 'beasts,' are you referring to those like yourself . . . or the creatures that Altered are based on?" Blake asked in return.

Gary thought there was a difference between the two, because if there weren't, then he wouldn't have failed the Altered test, but it made him aware of something else. Blake knew about werewolves too, and the words he used when Gary revealed everything to him were certainly strange.

"I guess I'm talking about the beasts that the Altered come from. Are there others around?"

"I have never seen one, nor has my father, but some of our logs talk about hunters in the past having met them. I doubt they were lying, so at one point they certainly must have existed; whether they still do . . . who knows? However, those books also mentioned that meeting your kind was a rarity. In fact, my father claims that they haven't been seen for a few generations now."

Gary suddenly stopped in his tracks, looking at Blake. "You mean there are other werewolves out there?"

"You mean you didn't know?" Now it was the Altered Hunter's turn to be baffled. "If you exist, then isn't that already proof that others exist as well? I mean, you were originally human, right? The changes to you seem to be rather recent. Didn't you become a were-wolf after being bitten? If not, how did that exactly happen? And what about Billy? Even if it was a different way, that has to make you think. Of course, there are others out there."

For some reason, that thought had never crossed Gary's mind. He had turned out of nowhere, and the main culprit seemed to be his Werewolf System, which must have been inside that suitcase.

Even the absurd scenario of a dwarf-size werewolf having been hidden inside wouldn't explain the system's existence. Come to think of it, why did the Underdogs even have that suitcase in the first place? Just who was it meant to be delivered to that day?

Perhaps they had the answers about the werewolves?

"I think I found something!" Blake suddenly exclaimed.

CHAPTER 81

A PAST

After Blake's shout it didn't take long for Gary to zoom to where Blake was digging through the leaves, throwing them everywhere. Now, although Gary couldn't see it, he could smell it.

"There's blood there, right?" Gary asked for confirmation.

"Yeah, but not just here. A lot of the leaves are covering the area, so I wasn't so sure, but there's blood all over in this park and forest," Blake said.

If Gary could smell the blood, and he could do so quite clearly, it couldn't have been shed too long ago. Gary wondered where it had come from. There had been no recent reports of dead people, no bodies or police in this area.

They continued looking; Blake was uncovering piles of blood in certain places and even up particular trees. The problem was they didn't really lead anywhere; it was just blood located in different areas of the forest, and they were unable to find anything else until Gary had a theory.

"I think my earlier hunch was right," Gary said. "We must have uncovered his hunting ground."

"Hunting ground?" Blake repeated, confused. "You mean he killed more people and brought his victims here? But that doesn't add up with the news report."

Gary leapt up onto one of the trees, transforming only his arms, and started to climb it quickly. With his extra Strength and being able to change parts of his body, it was easy enough.

The vibrations of the tree caused a bird to scurry away, but Gary pounced, clawing at the creature. When he landed, his knees bent before he hit the ground and the blood of the lifeless bird was dripping from his hand.

"I can't see the blood like you, but I know one thing. He and I are alike," Gary stated. "I looked at the trees and saw his markings. There are claw marks everywhere at the top. What I just did is an example of what he was probably doing as well.

"Unlike me, Billy is on the run, which means he has no easy way to buy the food he needs. Even if he had the money, it's not like he could walk into a supermarket and just buy it. Werewolves need a high amount of Energy, but the meat doesn't necessarily have to come from humans."

"In other words, he's switched to hunting animals." Blake finished Gary's sentence, realizing what he was saying and now knowing why there were so many blood marks on the ground. It was most likely where Billy had feasted on the animals.

Another thing that Blake noted was how fast Gary's movements had been and how easily he had caught the bird. It was clear that the werewolf he had fought in the park and the one in front of him were quite different. Gary had even slightly transformed in front of him, which the Altered Hunter had been unaware he could even do.

"Does it mean he will eventually return here? If he's using the place as his hunting ground, maybe he's hiding in the vicinity," Blake theorized. "However, if he is, he must be out right now."

Gary turned around for a second. He had killed the bird, and he didn't want to put it to waste, especially since his little show had also used up a bit of Energy. At the same time, he didn't really want Blake to see him eat it, so he had the decency to hide it.

Given how high up the claw markings were, Gary was comparing himself to Billy, trying to gauge how advanced he had become.

"This place might not be his only hunting ground. If he's smart enough to switch to animals, he might also have realized that staying in one place for too long might be too risky. Let's keep an eye out, and if we don't find him, we could always return here another night," Gary suggested.

Blake agreed, and he also started to set up little cameras in the forest, so he could check up on the area while they were away. He placed them in the areas where the largest amount of blood had been visible.

While doing so, Blake had something on his mind he wanted to ask Gary.

"You're different from how you were back then. And I don't just mean that you transformed like an Altered. Last time, you were attacking me like a feral animal.

"If you transform again to fight Billy, will I have to worry about that happening again? I'm not exactly looking forward to having to fight for my life against the two of you," Blake said as he programmed the cameras to send their footage directly to his phone.

"It won't happen again," Gary stated. "I acted that way because of the full moon. Although we're stronger during that time, we also get . . . weirder, more primal. I . . . I couldn't control myself back then, probably because it was my first turning.

"After my recent change, I feel like it might have solved my problem. It's what allowed me to change only part of my body. Anyway, that's also why we need to finish Billy off sooner rather than later. He'll only get stronger the closer we are to the full moon, and I don't know if he can or will transform like me."

After the cameras had been set up, Blake and Gary headed toward the apartment buildings of those that Billy had killed before. They searched the area to see if they could find anything.

When they found trails of blood that were still present, they followed them to see if they could find any clues, but there were none at all.

"Well, it looks like we've been to every place so far where Billy has been, but there's been no luck." Blake sighed, ready to call it a night. If it had been that easy, his father would have surely found the werewolf by now. At least they had some clues to go on now.

"Wait a second." Gary stopped him. "Billy hasn't killed for a while now, but his killing wasn't random. Not counting his parents, he only killed those he lost against in a fight. I was just wondering . . . what if he hasn't given up on going down that list?

"If that's the case, then maybe Billy is just waiting for the right moment . . . maybe he's away, because he's stalking his next target."

"Do you have an idea who Billy is after, then?" Blake asked. He had overheard Gary mentioning something of the sort during his interrogation by White Rose, but the young Altered Hunter didn't want to admit that he had snooped.

Of course, one of those people was Gary himself, but perhaps Blake was also a little worried about Gary because they were both werewolves. He shouldn't know that the green-haired teenager was "older" than the other omega wolf by only a few days. Instead of risking it, there was a far easier target, though.

If Billy came to them, it would be perfect, but it was important to cover all possibilities. There was only one problem . . . he had no idea where Innu actually lived. He tried contacting his friend on the phone, but given how late it was, Innu appeared to have gone to bed already.

So Gary contacted someone who seemed to have the answers to everything, and, unsurprisingly, Kai turned out to still have been awake.

He's not at his apartment, but you can find him at this address. Just remember, if you cause a scene, as leaders of the Howlers it means we're involved as well. Call us if you need us.

"Let's just check this one place out before we call it a day," Gary told Blake.

They finally arrived at the address Kai had given them.

"The other person is Innu . . . but why would he be around here?" Gary said.

"An orphanage?" Blake sounded surprised.

CHAPTER 82

BLACK ROCK

It had been a while since Innu had been able to catch a break. Lately, he had felt as if there was always something to do. His new school was a little farther away than his old one, so it was quite a walk to get to the place he was heading to at the moment.

Hahaha, all those suckers will love these. Innu smiled to himself, carrying two heavy shopping bags that were filled to the top. *It's been a while since I visited them, even before I joined the Howlers. I was always busy trying to make money, but it seems like things are finally looking up these days.*

At school, Innu had asked Kai for a big favor. He wanted an advance payment. Usually, such a request would be put to the leader of a gang, however, the Howlers weren't exactly your typical gang. Currently, Kai was the one looking after all the money that they had gotten from the Gray Elephants raid.

After all, it would be costly to repair the destroyed pool club. Afterward, Kai intended to put whatever was left into other investment avenues. At least that was what he had claimed.

The gang had learned to put their trust in Kai; they had all seen his special and whimsical ways, and none of them thought they could put the cash to better use for the sake of the whole gang.

Everyone still had received a cut from that day, and some even more behind the scenes. The actual cash flow was something only the enigmatic teenager himself was privy to. Of course, as the one in charge of the money, he wouldn't just hand it out willy-nilly, so ultimately Innu had no choice but to explain why he needed the money.

He's a scary guy to talk to, but he also seems to have a soft spot in his heart. That was Innu's assessment of his fellow gang member after he received the cash.

At the moment, Innu was standing in front of a door. It was a wide single-story building on private grounds with a playground in front. Even before entering, he could hear the noise from the other side.

"Ben, will you stop picking on Steward? You know he doesn't like that!" a female voice yelled.

It was Innu's cue to step in as he pushed the door open with his arm.

"Surprise!" he yelled, holding the bags high.

"Huh, is that . . . Big Brother Innu?" a high-pitched voice shouted.

Innu turned the corner and entered a large room. There were countless kids of all ages inside, ranging from as young as three up to thirteen.

"It's Big Brother Innu!" A cute girl with pigtails and a pink dress ran up to Innu and hugged his legs so tightly he was worried he might fall over.

"What's in the bags? What did you get us? Is it food?" a round-cheeked kid asked curiously. The red sauce all over his face indicated that he must have just eaten, but apparently he was still hungry.

"Ah, maybe you would have preferred food, but no, I got you presents," Innu answered as he put the bags down and started to empty them. He had bought all sorts of different things, though most of the items were either toys or something they needed for school, like books and pencils.

"Wow, Big Brother Innu is the best!" they cheered.

Their smiling faces were melting his heart, but he couldn't help but notice the condition of the room.

This place . . . it hasn't changed since I was here, not one single bit, Innu thought, which in reality meant it had gotten worse.

The wooden flooring was peeling up, and panels were missing. Chairs were broken, and pillows and toys had their stuffing falling out. The older kids were left without much to do but just stare out of the window.

They didn't seem as surprised to see Innu as the others were, but an adult wearing large round glasses approached him.

"Innu, you didn't have to spend so much money . . . I mean, how did you even afford all this stuff?" Suzan asked, but she couldn't help but smile as she saw how excited her kids were. Innu thought she had the smile of an angel.

He remembered how many times that smile had warmed his heart, because Suzan was the closest thing he had had to a real mother when he was growing up.

This was the Black Rock Orphanage.

Innu had grown up here before he was adopted only a short while ago, but even then, his current parents weren't exactly the best. For one, this was a Tier 3 town, which meant not many people could truly afford to adopt. But the government tried to support potential adoptive parents, and once in a while, couples applied with different interests in mind.

Innu's adoptive parents were one of those couples. They didn't care about him, only the support money they received for adopting him. He would have tried to leave his adoptive parents and come back here, the place he called home . . . but he knew it would put a strain on Black Rock's already struggling finances.

New kids were being placed in orphanages all the time, and Black Rock didn't receive enough funding to support them. Each year, it seemed like Slough was willing to spend less money on them, and all of that burden fell on Suzan.

Being a bit older, Innu knew this. He knew how hard it was for Suzan. Still, instead of leaving them all, she had decided to stay and support the place. She ran it and put her own money into Black Rock because she herself had once been an orphan. The money she earned for working there often went back to the kids as if they were her own.

I don't want to ever see that smile go away, Innu thought.

CHAPTER 83

SAVE THEM ALL!

Innu wanted to do whatever he could to help Suzan, and he had a plan. Once he got enough money, he would fix up this place and hire someone to help her. But for now, he helped them out when he could.

"You know you didn't have to do this," Suzan said, smiling at him. "Your visit is honestly enough for the kids, and they love just seeing you."

"No, I like presents more!" one of the kids shouted, a boy with red, rosy cheeks. "Every time Innu comes, he should bring a present; otherwise, he's not allowed to come."

The small girl with the pink dress who had hugged Innu hit the boy on top of the head.

"Don't say mean things to our Big Brother."

The group couldn't help but laugh at the cute scene.

Innu got to work, helping where he could. He tried fixing things, but he didn't have much mechanical ability, and he knew it, so he stuck to simple repairs. Still, he could clean and do the dishes.

As he worked, Innu looked around for Suzan, but she was too busy putting some of the kids to bed. He started to unwind the white wraps on his hands, placing them to the side and rolling up his sleeves.

"They look pretty banged up," a voice said.

Turning around, Innu saw a young teenage boy with wild red spiked hair. He looked about thirteen years old. Kevin had been close to Innu when he lived at the orphanage and knew about a lot of what he did.

"Are you still fighting? The bandages and your hands are covered in blood." Kevin pointed to them.

Innu immediately dipped them in the water so the others couldn't see them, and he started to wash up as fast as he could. He was worried that Suzan might come back at any moment.

Kevin gave out a big sigh.

"You know, if Suzan knew, she would never accept any of the money you give her. She would think she was to blame and tell you to stop."

"And that's why you will keep quiet about it. Besides, I don't fight as much as I did," Innu replied.

Kevin couldn't help but laugh at that comment.

"Really, then how did you manage to get the money to pay for all the toys, books, and school supplies you brought today? They couldn't have been cheap. Stop lying. You don't have to lie to me, you know that."

The thing was, Innu wasn't lying. He hadn't been to many of those underground fights. It was how he made the bulk of his income before. Now, although he used his fists, it was different. The fights he had gotten into recently and the money he had gotten were almost extra. He did it because . . . he had wanted to help them.

And now that they had the Wolf's Pool Club, perhaps there would be fewer reasons for him to earn money with his fists.

"Don't worry," Innu said. "I might still be using my fists to make money, but it feels different somehow."

After finishing the dishes, Innu put the bandages back on his hands and said good night to the others, then headed outside with Kevin.

Innu was going to show Kevin a few moves. They had gotten close because of their shared interest: fighting.

As for how Innu knew how to fight, it was a story that no one at the orphanage knew, but when he arrived, it was clear he already knew quite a bit.

One day Kevin had returned from school, beaten and bruised by his classmates, and asked Innu to teach him how to fight.

Innu had taught him how to defend himself. They didn't go to the same school, so Innu couldn't give them a beating himself, but he did the next best thing. After that, the two continued to grow closer until Innu left.

Right now, Innu was showing moves while Kevin was just watching. After nine minutes of nonstop shadow boxing, he was breathing quite heavily.

"Wow, I mean, maybe it's not my place to say, but your kicks and punches have gotten stronger. You've really improved. I guess all that outside fighting has really helped you," Kevin said as he attempted to imitate what Innu had just done.

Innu sat on the floor and watched, giving pointers whenever he saw mistakes. Still, he was a little distracted and hardly said anything because he was thinking about what Kevin had just said.

I've improved . . . I keep thinking back to that day. . . . those twins. We all could have died, but Gary somehow saved us. He went into that container and took care of both of them. No matter how I think about it, no matter how many times I try to envision fighting both of them in my head, I just can't see how I could win in the state they were in. Gary, how did you do it?

This was what had been on his mind. The Gary who had fought the twins at his side would have never been able to accomplish such a thing, so he thought it was impossible for Gary to beat both of them so quickly.

"Hey, I don't know how much I should tell you," Kevin said when he had finished his training. "Lately, some people have been coming to the orphanage to talk to Suzan, and she always seems to be down afterward. I tried asking her, and she won't speak to me about it. Maybe she will speak to you," Kevin said.

"Hey!" a voice shouted from the building.

"Speak of the devil." Kevin started to run back to the building, as he knew it was time for him to go to bed. At the same time, Innu thought that perhaps he should say goodbye to them all before heading back.

He slowly got up. He thought he would do one more round before saying goodbye to Suzan, and he started to shadow box once again, but this time on his own.

He visualized the twins in their strange forms that day and went for a kick to the head. Trying to go faster, stronger, and throwing one more kick, his body spun, and for a second, he thought his eyes caught something.

He turned to look toward the gate, but there was nobody but Suzan there.

Am I imagining things? I could have sworn I saw someone standing there, but there's no one.

Ignoring the images in his head and the shiver in his body, he decided to go inside.

Maybe I'll stay here for the night, Innu thought. *And I'll talk to Suzan about what Kevin said.*

At that moment, outside the gate, a little farther down the street, Gary had tackled a hooded figure to the ground, and standing behind him with two batons in his hand was Blake.

"Looks like we got you this time before you could do anything, Billy!" Gary said with his hands already transformed.

On the ground, from under his hood, the person smiled back.

CHAPTER 84

THE BIGGER WOLF

When Gary and Blake reached the orphanage, they debated whether they should head inside the place and try to find Billy. Although Gary felt like this might cause an awkward situation if Innu was inside, there was also the chance that their arrival would scare Billy away.

However, they thought it unlikely that he would be inside anyway. The place looked quite large, and he was sure there would be multiple people, especially at an orphanage.

I wonder, does Innu visit this place often? Maybe Billy just has never had the chance to attack him. Lately, he's always been around us.

Gary thought about what he would do if he were the one hunting Innu. Billy needed to make sure he wasn't seen by others, and it looked like he was straying from killing others during his task.

But so far, Billy had been doing well not to be caught for his other killings. Perhaps he needed to follow Innu's route a few times before he came up with the perfect plan.

In the end, Gary felt like if they followed Innu every day after school, perhaps they would get their answer. Because of this, Blake looked for a good spot where they could see the orphanage well.

On the street, just outside, was a three-story apartment block, with a ladder on the side that was used as a fire exit. Blake and Gary climbed up it and continued to watch from afar.

Why is Innu visiting an orphanage? Is he an orphan himself? Gary realized that he didn't really know much about Innu.

Honestly, he thought his relationships with many of those around him would be temporary. As time went on, he realized that perhaps that wouldn't be the case at all. All of these people were now members of his gang, and they had risked their lives to save Marie. There was a strong bond between them. It was similar to friendship, but not quite the same.

Eventually, Blake and Gary saw Innu leaving the orphanage.

Should I also leave a Bond Mark on Innu? Gary considered the possibility, wondering what promise would be good to make. Not long after, they saw a large figure walk up to the gate and stare inside for a while.

"His temperature is high, and he's wearing a hoodie," Blake said. "I think we might have found our guy!"

Gary didn't take long to get into action. He jumped off the roof they were on, and before he landed he transformed his legs slightly, allowing them to absorb the impact.

Blake didn't want to risk the jump, so he climbed back down the ladder and chased after Gary, not too far behind.

As he ran, Gary could still see the hooded figure staring at the orphanage. It was almost like the person was obsessed with what they saw. At the same time, a scent had entered Gary's nose.

It was a smell he had smelled before, and memories flooded his head.

It's Billy!

Gary activated his partial transformation, and the muscles in his thigh started to bulge, ripping his trousers slightly. He transformed his arms as well, breaking through his shirt, and his speed drastically increased in seconds. He leapt into the air, his arms aiming for the figure's waist.

Transforming here, Gary? What if someone sees you? Blake thought, but he would continue to follow and support his ally.

After tackling the figure to the ground, Gary was on top of him, looking into the face of the person he had been hunting for all along.

"Hahaha, have you been tracking me down?" Billy couldn't help but laugh. "I never thought you would actually be looking for me. Not sure if I should call you brave or stupid."

Looking at his face, Gary hesitated to attack him.

Why can't I strike him? I struck the twins . . . is it because he looks human?

Gary shook his head and readied his claws, swinging them toward Billy's head, but just before they connected, Billy grabbed his wrists, and a power struggle followed.

He's holding my wrists . . . he has gotten stronger, or maybe he was already this strong to begin with!

Gary seemed to be winning as he pushed forward, his long claws inching closer to Billy's head.

"Why can I hear footsteps?" Billy struggled to say as he saw someone coming toward them. "It looks like you got help."

Then Billy's eyes started to change, and his forearms started to get larger. His whole body was changing on the spot. He lifted his legs and kicked Gary in the stomach, causing him to fall back and crash into Blake.

When they got up, a large black-furred wolf was staring at them. It was bigger than what Gary remembered from the video of himself, and it was clear now that Billy knew how to transform, even though it wasn't a full moon.

However, Billy suddenly turned away in his werewolf form and made a run for it.

"We have to get him!" Gary shouted. "We can't let him get away."

"I agree," Blake said as the two began the chase.

CHAPTER 85

A MONSTER I CREATED

In his full werewolf form, Billy was fast, and for some reason, once again, no matter what Gary tried doing, the marking wouldn't work on him. He wondered if it could even work on others like him in the first place. Still, he could smell Billy's scent and follow that instead.

This time he made sure to remember what it smelled like. Transformed into a werewolf, his smell was different from when he was a human. The werewolf smell was a lot stronger and more distinctive than a human's, allowing Gary to easily distinguish it from others.

Gary turned to look at his partner, who was a bit behind him.

"You go on ahead, I'll find you, don't worry!" Blake said.

"You don't have anything to help you run faster? How do you usually hunt Altered?" Gary couldn't help but ask.

"Usually, we don't go rugby-tackling them in the middle of the street!" Blake shouted back. "I would have waited for a good place to trap him, lure him with the blood, and a lot of Altered are quite arrogant, so they think they can take us in a fight," he added. He was quite annoyed, but he knew they had to deal with the situation, and he flicked his hand outward to signal Gary to go after Billy.

Gary gave chase by just transforming his legs again, so he wouldn't look odd if anyone saw him in the night.

"I'm sorry, Gary," Blake said as he pulled out his phone and saw a marker moving. "I thought something like this might happen, so I needed a backup."

During their little visit on the rooftop, Blake had placed a tracking device on his ally, and he had thrown it into the bag he was currently wearing.

Off in the distance, Gary could still see Billy moving ahead. It seemed like Billy was trying to avoid being noticed by the public as he dodged the more common streets and residential buildings.

Which, honestly, Gary was pleased about. He had worried that Billy might go to a public area like a hospital or downtown and cause chaos, getting all sorts of people involved, and he didn't want White Rose to pop up like last time. Not while he looked like this.

He's too fast! If this goes on, he will get farther and farther away. Does that mean my stats still don't match up to his? Even after selecting that class and reaching Level 10?"

With his legs transformed, Gary's current stats showed that his Dexterity was at 22 compared to his regular 15. His legs were practically fully transformed; that was why he was unsure if he would be any faster if he went into a full transformation.

Yet he couldn't keep up with Billy.

Maybe he's at a higher level, or he's stronger, or maybe it's just because of those he ate. Arghh! I'm just comparing him to the system in the first place. He could just be a regular werewolf! Gary screamed in his head, and continued to run.

Eventually, though, as they entered a quiet neighborhood, especially so late, his sense of smell was much more potent. Finally, Gary stopped, for Billy was now standing in front of him.

They were in an underpass that was used to bypass the traffic above. It was an empty tunnel filled with lights and graffiti on the wall. The tunnel was wide enough to fit a car and a half.

Seeing Billy in the dim light felt like he was looking at a creature straight out of a horror film.

"U-aagh Gahhy . . ." Billy tried to speak, just snarling through his mouth. Gary couldn't understand what the werewolf in front of him was trying to say, but at the same time, he could understand his snarls.

"What are you looking at me like that for? You were the one who turned me into this!" Damn, and he's right about that as well, Gary thought.

"I'm sorry!" Gary shouted. "You're right, I was the one who turned you into this, but me and you, we both share the same thing, but I haven't kil—" Gary's words trailed off as he realized what he was about to say.

Was he better than Billy because he hadn't killed? That wasn't true at all. Gary had killed. He had killed more than once. Perhaps those related to them would be wishing the same thing for him that Gary wished for Billy.

Those he had killed must have had parents, relatives, family, and friends. Everyone had a life. Gary clenched his fists and closed his eyes, trying to toss these thoughts out of his head. He needed to focus on the task that was in front of him.

However, closing his eyes during a fight with such a creature was a big mistake. He heard panting, and when he opened his eyes, Billy's hot breath was coming at him.

His large, powerful jaws were about to snap Gary's head off in one bite. Quickly transforming his hands, Gary shoved them into Billy's mouth and used his strength to pull it apart.

As he tried to get a good hold on the teeth, they pierced right through Gary's hands, causing him great pain, but he didn't care. He needed to make sure Billy couldn't bite down on him.

Still, Billy's hands were free, and he attempted to slash Gary's face. But Gary took the blow on his shoulder and rolled onto the floor.

−12 HP
A deep cut has been made
78/100 HP
Energy points will be used to perform emergency healing
-10 Energy

There was a large wound on Gary's shoulder, but his body was healing it in seconds. Because of the healing, he wouldn't suffer from blood loss, but the more he got hurt, the more Energy would be used to heal his wounds.

Even though the wound itself closed, he wasn't gaining any HP. And Billy did not stop with the attacks, striking at Gary again.

Gary jumped out of the way, and Billy's claw hit the wall and tore it to shreds, leaving a giant claw mark and showering rubble on the floor.

At the same time, Gary appeared next to Billy's legs.

Skill activated: Claw Drain
−15 Energy

His hands were already transformed, so there was no need to go through that again. Still, Gary's attack hit the back of Billy's calf twice. Lifting his leg, Billy didn't flinch from the attack, and he kicked Gary in the stomach, sending him across the floor.

+5 HP
+5 HP
−10 HP

Damn it, the Health I just gained from the Claw Drain just got taken out with the kick. But still, I managed to hurt him, Gary thought, yet Billy's leg began to heal at a visible speed.

"Grrr, grrr!" Billy growled out again.

"Why don't I fully transform? Because I have more control than you!" Gary understood his words and replied, "I have control over my body! You . . . when I look at you, I just see a monster!"

"Rawr!" Billy roared again.

"A monster I created, that's right, which is why I need to deal with you!" Gary yelled, running forward again. For now, he had to use what he had to his advantage: his large Energy pool. Although Billy could heal, it didn't look like the two were the same.

If Billy had a system similar to his, he might have higher base stats than Gary, but Gary was actually at a higher level with more skills. As Gary ran close with both his hands by his side, Billy got ready to attack again.

Just as he was about to attack, his whole body shook, and a blue shock crackled all around him. He wasn't stunned for long, even though the blue shock was still affecting his body. Billy was strong enough to fight through it. Still, it had distracted him just long enough for Gary to stab both his hands right into Billy's stomach, and blood gushed out from it.

"I told you I would find you!" Blake appeared as he changed from his regular baton and dropped a small device he had just used on the floor and instead pulled out two dueling swords. "No matter what, you die today!"

CHAPTER 86

TAG TEAM WEREWOLF

If someone saw him, they might call Gary's fighting reckless, yet he had actually been really careful. He hadn't used his Full Transformation skill yet because he knew it would be better used at a later time.

First he wanted to wear Billy down, then fight him once he could overwhelm him with strength. This was what Gary had planned, as he felt confident that he had more Energy at his disposal than the other omega wolf thanks to his Warrior Class.

However, that wasn't the only thing he was relying on. Gary had something else that Billy lacked, and that was a partner. If Gary had been fighting on his own, he honestly wasn't too confident that he alone might beat Billy, but fortunately he had a strong ally with him today.

Not only that, but Gary had marked Blake, meaning he could use the mist slowly approaching their location. This neat feature told him that his partner was on his way and would be here soon, so he was just waiting for the perfect moment.

Seizing this chance, Gary activated another Claw Drain before stabbing Billy right in the stomach. Billy's head was a little high, and Gary knew he would try to block it from getting hit; there were also those deadly jaws to watch out for. So he had gone for the stomach instead.

Skill activated: Claw Drain
−15 Energy
+20 HP
98/100 HP

Yes! Although I don't know how much I'm damaging Billy because the system is unable to tell me that, I can make a good guess from the Claw Drain. With this healing, I must have dealt a critical hit!

Pulling out his hands, Gary was going to attempt to stab him again, but suddenly Billy grabbed him by the wrists, holding his hands in place. Gary pulled and pulled, but it was clear who was the stronger of the two.

At the same time, Blake charged forward from behind. This time, rather than using the electrified baton, he was holding two short-handled swords. They didn't look like standard medieval swords from ancient times, though. Instead, the hilt had a scale design, and feathers running down it. It almost looked like it had been created from some type of giant animal.

Blake felt most confident fighting with the batons; they were perfect to subdue an enemy, hurting it and slowing it down, but against a werewolf like Billy, the Altered Hunter could take no such risks. He had switched to his swords because Blake planned to kill his target.

Striking as hard as he could, he hit the top of the werewolf's shoulder; the sword sank through but stopped. It was a shallow hit, and he couldn't move it any further.

What is this skin? It's incredibly thick, and even with all my strength I was only able to cut it so deep.

Blake slashed it again, trying to cut Billy deeper. This time, he struck from top to bottom diagonally along the back, but it still ended up being a shallow cut.

Billy pretty much just ignored the attack from the Altered Hunter. Sure, it hurt, but he wanted to deal with what he believed to be the bigger threat first. Still holding on to Gary's wrist, the omega wolf pulled the claws out of his stomach.

The blood was pouring out, but the wound looked as if it was healing quickly. Then he twisted his body and slammed Gary against the tunnel wall.

The blow left an imprint, and blood poured out of Gary's mouth as tiles fell to the floor along with him.

You have been inflicted with a grave injury
–30 HP
68/100 HP
Parts of your rib cage have been damaged
Energy points will be used to perform emergency healing
–20 Energy

It was a big hit, and Gary felt it as he slowly bore the pain. Then he saw Billy focusing on Blake. He took a few swipes, and Gary heard clangs as Blake deflected the claws with his swords.

It was a strange sight to behold; although the omega wolf was faster and stronger, the way the young Altered Hunter was parrying the claws allowed him to redirect most of the strength in the blows. It was almost as if he was predicting where his opponent would attack next.

Blake was backing up close to the side of the wall; Billy struck again, and his failure to hit Blake was starting to make him angry. The Altered Hunter used his strength as he held both swords, skimming them just past the claws and pushing Billy's body behind him, causing the werewolf to crash headfirst into the wall.

His hands were stuck, and Blake didn't waste this opportunity as he relentlessly began attacking his enemy's back, using both of his swords, not letting Billy catch a break. As soon as one sword hit the werewolf, another did, and another.

Doesn't he ever get tired? Gary wondered; even with his stamina, he couldn't imagine how hard it would be to do such a thing. It was almost as if Blake wasn't breathing.

Blood was dripping from Billy's back, and it looked like his wounds were taking longer to heal now. The damage from the two of them was piling up.

I can't believe it; Blake isn't an Altered, he isn't like me or Billy, and yet he can still take on a werewolf? Gary thought in amazement. Still, he had played his part in this all as well, and he stood up, ready to help Blake out.

One thing was clear: Blake's swords were unable to properly strike Billy down and deal the critical damage that was needed, which meant that it was all up to Gary.

However, suddenly Billy's head turned to one side of the tunnel.

"Ahhh!" a woman screamed at the other end.

Gary turned toward the scream, as Billy ignored Blake's strikes and ran past the two teenagers. Although Blake had managed to cut the omega wolf along his chest, their target headed straight for the woman, who had turned around and was running for her life.

It was up to Gary to stop him. He leapt after Billy and reached out to grab the back of his leg, but as he closed his claw he realized that he had missed it by a hair.

Falling onto the ground, Gary lifted his head to see that Billy had already grabbed the woman, digging into her with his powerful jaws.

"Damn it!" Gary cursed.

Skill activated: Full Transformation
−20 Energy
Transformation has begun

CHAPTER 87

FIGHTING LIKE A WOLF

It was clear to both Gary and Blake that the woman was done for. Using his large jaws, Billy took a bite out of her neck, leaving her with barely a few seconds to regret her decision to go out for a walk that day.

While Blake stared at the monster Billy was, a monster who had just snapped a woman's head off, Gary was more concerned about the woman's eyes. Before life left her, a look of absolute, sheer fright had been ingrained in them, and she had helplessly reached a hand out to the two teenagers, begging for help.

I was the one who created Billy, and now he's killed again. Gary felt guiltier than before. *He hadn't killed anyone other than his parents outside his own list! If we hadn't attacked him today, if we hadn't chased him down here and trapped him in this desperate situation . . . then she might have lived today . . .*

He blamed himself for this outcome. Previously, there had been nothing he could've done to stop Billy, simply because he had only heard about the list from Kai. However, this woman had been an innocent bystander, who had just been unlucky enough to be at the wrong place at the wrong time . . .

"Get up!" Blake shouted at Gary. "Get up and let's kill this guy! We have to stop him from killing anyone else!"

Without waiting for his partner, the young Altered Hunter ran toward the feasting werewolf as he grabbed a device from his belt and threw it as far as he could. The strange circular ball flew over Billy's head and landed past him. The next second, the device activated, creating an electric barrier similar to the batons Blake used.

It looked like an electrified wall that was now behind Billy, blocking his path of escape, forcing him to deal with the two of them.

No, he wasn't going to run in the first place . . . Gary was sure of that.

Skill activated: Full Transformation
–20 Energy
Transformation has begun

Gary's body started to change at that moment; his clothing began to rip from his body. He barely had enough time to take off the bag, which he now ripped open, revealing the purchased meat as well as a spare change of clothes that he had brought along.

Fully transformed, Gary immediately grabbed some food as he ran forward on all fours. Although Blake had a head start, he managed to go right past him with his increased speed.

He's transformed fully; he looks the same as he did that day I found him, Blake thought, looking at his partner. *No, that's not right . . . he seems a bit taller and leaner. I was right, his body has definitely improved since then. I just hope he wasn't bluffing when he said he could control it now . . .*

Gary turned his head around as he went past Blake and snarled at the Altered Hunter.

"Rargh!" Gary shouted as he leapt forward.

Consuming the body allowed Billy to heal most of the damage the two teenagers had inflicted on him, and eating fresh meat meant he would be able to stay in his werewolf form longer. In essence, it was as if they would have to fight him from the beginning, while they were now slowly getting exhausted.

Billy threw what was left of the body into the electric wall that Blake's device had made. It shocked the body for a few seconds before it fell to the ground.

The omega wolf then charged to meet Gary's advance. The latter might have grown, yet it was obvious which one was the larger werewolf. The two collided and their claws intertwined. As expected, Billy was heavier and was able to push Gary back, but just as Billy's head moved forward to take a bite, Gary lifted his lower body and kneed Billy right in the jaw, slamming his mouth shut.

Billy's head flung back, and Gary backflipped, and the second he landed on the ground he charged forward again, slashing at the omega wolf's chest while he was still dazed. He got two slashes in before he saw a palm aimed at his head. Gary avoided the attack by ducking down at the right time and grabbing Billy's legs, lifting him off the ground and slamming him down.

While he was in his Full Transformation form, Gray realized that his beastlike fighting urges came out more strongly. He'd noticed it when he fought against the twins, and although that might be helpful in certain situations where Gary didn't wish to be in control, it wasn't ideal when he didn't want to hurt others.

He was nothing but a beast with large tools and a massive body at his disposal. Gary needed to keep a clear head even after being fully transformed, so he could fight just like he had been taught by Innu, to tackle properly like he was taught in rugby, and when it came to it, to let his animal instincts take over.

"I bit you once, so I don't think you'll mind me biting you again!" Gary opened his jaws and bit Billy right on the neck as hard as he could. Blood entered his mouth, and Billy's taste wasn't exactly pleasant compared to others he had eaten before.

Billy stabbed his claws into Gary's side now that he was on top of him, but Gary refused to let go.

−25 HP

"Don't worry, I'm right here!" Blake shouted, as he had gotten right behind Billy. While the two were fighting, he ran around the side, avoiding the conflict. After seeing how Gary fought for the first few seconds, he was convinced that Gary was in his right mind. With Billy on the ground, the Altered Hunter wrapped both hands around the hilt of his sword as he thrust it down as hard as he could, aimed at the werewolf's eye.

It was one of the most sophisticated parts of the body, and it was a way to avoid Billy's strong hide. The sword pierced Billy's eye, causing the werewolf to howl at the top of his lungs.

He quickly pulled his claws out of Gary's side and grabbed the sword with his bare hands, stopping it from going further. With his great strength he snapped the sword in two, and with his large legs he kicked Gary off him and got up once again.

Billy still had part of the sword stuck in his eye, and blood was dripping down his neck. Blake was on one side of the tunnel, and Gary was on the other.

There was nowhere for Billy to run; the two had him trapped, but a wild animal was always the most dangerous when it found itself in a desperate situation.

Aside from the purchased meat and a second set of clothes, Gary had also left his phone in the now-ripped bag. He had been aware that there was a chance he might have to fully transform, and that it would rip his clothes, so he had kept his personal items inside for safekeeping.

Right now, the phone made a sound as a new message appeared on it.

Gary, I'm keeping my promise. I think me and Stacy might be in trouble. There's a strange guy asking for his brother. He forced us to go to a coffee shop with him. Please help.

CHAPTER 88

DOUBLE TROUBLE

When Amy went to school the next day, she couldn't help but replay yesterday's incident. She and Stacy had been stopped by a stranger just outside their school, who had asked them about his brother, the scumbag who had invited them to the Kobe Karaoke Club. However, the two girls weren't completely unrelated to the matter, and they both knew that.

Amy had asked Stacy for a few details, as her memory of that day was hazy. She could remember up until the point where they had taken out the drugs, but Stacy just told her that she didn't know what happened later. Gary had appeared when they had hurt Amy, and then Stacy had just followed his instructions and fled, leaving Gary with Hawk and his friends inside.

No matter how Amy had tried to bring up the topic, though, it just seemed awkward to naturally address that in a conversation. What's more, she was completely baffled about Gary's sudden growth spurt. She knew that boys could have them, and that it would usually occur later than for girls, but for it to happen overnight and add so much muscle mass . . .

Amy wanted to mention it, but then decided against it. What was her brother supposed to say? It wasn't like he could control it. She also didn't want to burden him in any way. He was already doing his best to keep up their household: making her dinner, washing her clothes, and everything nice that he had done for her.

At the end of the day, she just could never imagine her brother doing such a thing, and she decided to ignore the matter.

Alas, the matter wasn't about to ignore her.

"Hey, thanks for what you did the other day," Stacy said as she pulled up a seat next to Amy to enjoy their lunch break with their homemade packed lunches. The truth was, Stacy didn't need to do this, but she didn't want Amy to be the odd one out.

Most of the kids just ordered the canteen food, but while it wasn't overly expensive, it wasn't cheap either. Amy's education was being paid for, but that only included basic necessities like books and her admission fee. She would have to pay for school meals if she wanted them, so it was far cheaper to bring her own food.

"It's all right, and before you ask, no, I didn't get to ask Gary about what happened that day," Amy replied. "I just can't imagine him having anything to do with them. I'm not even sure he could beat up one of them, much less three, even though he seems to have really bulked up recently.

"I don't get why that guy thinks we might know anything about his brother. Didn't they say something about being in some type of gang? They weren't good people in the first place, so maybe they might have gotten hit by another gang? I mean, last we saw them was the day those gangs attacked the Chavley area . . ."

As she talked, Amy saw that her friend was visibly shaking; she seemed to be hiding something. Amy gave her a look, saying she'd better talk about it now.

"The Gray Elephants gang," Stacy whispered after looking left and right. "Hawk . . . he would boast about it often when we were writing."

"You knew that, and you *still* decided to meet up with him?" Amy was furious, and their schoolmates noticed her outburst. Amy knew that her friend could act stupid sometimes, but it was one thing to lie about her age and meet up with her older online boyfriend, and it was an entirely different thing to meet up with a known gangster!

All of this could have easily been avoided!

"I'm sorry, I didn't believe him. I just thought he was trying to impress me, but after we saw his brother yesterday and what happened . . . I'm afraid it's true. I'm scared. What if they come after us again? Should we go to the police?" Stacy asked.

It was the first time Stacy had suggested going to the police, which came as a surprise. Stacy was terrified of her parents and what they might do if they found out what she had done. She felt that cutting off her phone or internet access might be the least of her worries. For all she knew, they might even force her to join a convent.

Stacy knew this about her parents better than anyone, so if that was the case, she must have been really scared.

I guess he's after her ultimately, and not really after me. However, if that guy found out about Stacy, he might have discovered that I was there that night as well. Did Stacy mention me by name in their chats, or did she just call me a friend? Shit, either way, it can't be good. Now that he saw me, I hope he doesn't dig around . . .

Amy let out a big sigh as she remembered something else: a conversation she had with her brother after their mother got hospitalized.

"Amy, from now on it's just going to be me and you for a while, until Mom gets better, all right? Now, I managed to call a friend who helped me out, and he said he would get us a legal guardian, but they can't actually look after us.

"I'm not an adult and neither are you, so if the police find out about us lying, then there is a good chance that social services will come and put us both in orphanages. They might even split us up if they find out that we have no other parent. So don't tell anyone about our situation, okay? I promise I'll look after us both," Gary had told her.

This was why Amy wanted to avoid going to the police. She might come along if Stacy decided to go that route, but Amy couldn't afford to get dragged into the mess.

"Look, I don't think he'll do anything to us, okay? Let's just be careful, and have our phones on us. If you really want to go to the police, it might be better not to tell them about what happened that night or why you're being followed. Just say it's a stalker or something.

"If we tell them about that night, then maybe the real gangsters will come after us." Amy felt a little bad about what she had just said, but she was convinced that it was for their overall safety.

When school ended, Stacy waited for Amy outside of class so they could walk home from school together. Honestly, Amy was wondering if it might be safer to distance herself from Stacy for a while. Yes, they were childhood friends, but that didn't change the fact that because of Stacy's mistake, her life could get ruined at any moment.

Alas, when she saw Stacy's frightened face, she just couldn't be that coldhearted; she grabbed her shaking friend by the elbow and they walked out together.

Amy and Stacy looked outside and saw several parents waiting to pick up their kids from school, while other students just walked home. They were watching for the man who talked to them yesterday but couldn't see him at all.

"We shouldn't wait here too long. We should go while there are a lot of people out; they're less likely to do anything then," Amy said.

Agreeing, Stacy nodded, and they began their walk with hurried steps. It was nerve-racking for both of them. They constantly turned and twisted their heads and at times thought that they were being followed, only for it to be a student or a parent behind them.

There were multiple cars parked not too far from the school. They weren't really allowed to park in front of the school because of the school's regulations. The girls noticed the incoming van far too late, as it drove close to the curb, stopping on the pavement.

What happened next left them with no time to react. A group of masked men rushed out, grabbed them, and pulled them into the van, which instantly drove off again. The entire process lasted only a few seconds.

Inside, Amy and Stacy's mouths were covered by four men. There were also two men up front, but most importantly, a man with sunglasses and a black leather jacket stood in front of both of them.

"I told you I would come back and get what I want from the two of you," Raven said, tilting his glasses as he smiled.

CHAPTER 89

THE MEETING (1)

The vehicle was already on the move, and the girls could tell right away from the rumbling of the ground through the floor and the sound of the old engine. As for where they were going, it was impossible to tell, but right now, both of the girls' minds were racing with fear of what might happen to them.

Amy wanted to reach into her pocket to grab her phone, but she thought that would be too obvious. She was wearing a skirt, and too much movement might cause her to drop it.

I'm surprised they didn't take our phones off us.

But before she could try anything, their hands were forced behind them and fastened together with black zip ties. Their captors also slapped black tape over their mouths so they couldn't scream or call for help.

"Stop resisting. I know it's hard when you're in this type of situation, but trust me, this is also for your sake," Raven said. "We'll refrain from tying up your legs, but you should just cooperate. I'd prefer not having to get rid of two bodies as young as yours. I already have too much on my record and I don't want to be adding this."

Hearing Raven talk and knowing who he was caused both of the girls to gulp. They were suddenly aware how weak they were, how easy it was for a few adult men to restrain them like this. Neither girl thought she had a chance in a fight, and struggling was useless. For now, Amy wanted to hear Raven out, while trying to figure a way out of this situation.

"Great. Now as I tried to tell you yesterday, all I want is some information about my brother. It's obvious that you two know something about it. Just tell me everything that happened the day you met him, because that's the day he went missing. Again, for your own sake, you better not lie to me. I don't want to hear what you might think I want to hear, I just need the truth.

"We could have done it the easy way, but you didn't want to talk, so now we have to do it this way. Relax, I'm not a monster. We won't torture you, since that will most likely just make you tell me what I want to hear.

"No, we're going to head to a coffee shop, and have a nice little chat, all right? A public place where I can't do anything to the two of you, so you both can feel at ease. If you help me, all of this will be over soon. However, if you scream or try to escape . . . well, I don't think I have to tell you the rest," Raven said as he pulled out a blade and slid it up Stacy's thigh.

She couldn't help but pee a little. She wasn't embarrassed, though, as Stacy had far bigger problems than ruining her underwear. She just wanted to make it out alive at the end of all of this. She started to sob, regretting not having told Raven everything yesterday. Maybe then, none of this would have happened.

Eventually, after driving for a while, the car stopped. The men cut off the zip ties and one even wiped Stacy's legs clean. Next, the tape was removed from their mouths, yet Raven made sure to remind them what would happen if they made any noise.

The men took off their masks, and Amy tried to remember all of their faces. Each one left the van, with Raven being the last. They had positioned themselves around the girls, making sure they wouldn't attempt to make a run for it.

Crap, these are real gangsters; they're not even giving us any chances! Amy thought. *And I can't risk calling their bluff. They already resorted to kidnapping, to show us how serious they are.*

The next moment she was surprised that they were actually heading toward a normal-looking coffee shop. School had just ended, so it was still sunny outside, yet there were some customers and a couple of people behind the counter.

When the girls entered, Raven wasn't far behind them, and even more surprisingly, it looked like the men who had kidnapped them would be staying outside.

"Sit, please." Raven smiled and pulled out two chairs for them as if he were being a gentleman. The table was next to a window.

The three of them sat there for a while, Stacy still shaking. Amy wasn't as frightened, but she wasn't saying anything either, and it didn't look like Raven was going to speak. Eventually, three coffees arrived.

Should I write a note, pass something onto the staff? But if we get found out, it could put us both at risk. Amy contemplated her choices.

Raven sipped his drink, looking out the window, and eventually twenty minutes passed with no one saying anything. Stacy seemed to be hanging in there, just barely, but Amy knew it was only a matter of time before she would break and say something.

Why am I so worried about the truth anyway? Amy thought, her heart thumping loud.

In the end, Raven broke the silence.

"You know, I have all the time in the world right now. I can wait here all day if you don't want to cooperate. However, I'm sure your parents are very worried about you by now. I gather a report must have been made by the school already, claiming they saw you two being kidnapped.

"What do you think will happen if your parents are unable to reach you? They'll naturally start to worry about where their daughters are, but you see . . . I don't care! I've had that feeling ever since that day! It's up to the two of you how long your parents will have to suffer that feeling along with me!"

The girls saw a certain look in Raven's eyes; he looked crazy, and it appeared that they had no choice.

CHAPTER 90

THE MEETING (2)

Stacy clasped Amy's hand under the table. It was clear to Amy that her best friend was in no condition to handle the situation, and although this would reveal that Amy was there that night, she eventually spoke up, afraid to test Raven's patience any longer. Although he claimed he had the time, the aggression at the end of his statement made it clear that he was about done playing games.

"That night, we both went to meet up with her internet boyfriend for the first time. I just came along, because Stacy was afraid he might try to do something to her. Seeing as your brother brought two friends along, she wasn't wrong," Amy revealed.

"He took us to a karaoke club, and he and his friends started to offer us . . . stuff. We just wanted to have some fun, but when we refused to take it, he tried to force himself onto my friend. In the end, I screamed, and the receptionist came and saw what was going on. We ran away after that, but we didn't inform the police . . . we were too scared and just wanted to forget what happened, but that's when you showed up."

Amy had decided to partly reveal the truth, only omitting that according to Stacy it had been Gary who appeared. She just hoped that would be enough for Raven to leave them alone, without getting her brother involved in this mess.

Stacy nodded, confirming Amy's story, but Raven just folded his arms and started shaking his head.

"You sure it was the receptionist? Why don't we wait a little longer and see if your story has changed."

Amy got the feeling that Raven had caught on to her lie. Unfortunately, she had no way of knowing that the Gray Elephants leader was aware that the receptionist was a good friend of his brother's. That wasn't the end of it, though. The receptionist had also gone missing without anyone having any clue about his whereabouts. According to the owner of the club, he had suddenly resigned . . .

Since Raven knew Amy was lying, he felt more confident that he was on the right track. They waited another thirtyish minutes in silence. Amy eventually drank her coffee, trying to appear relaxed as if they had nothing to hide, but that didn't seem to be working either.

"May I go to the restroom? I think it might be this whole situation, or the coffee," Amy said.

"Can I go, too?" Stacy immediately asked.

"Of course, but you know what will happen if you try to do something."

They quickly got up and headed toward the restroom, while Raven remained seated. Once inside, Stacy waited for Amy to speak, thinking she had a plan.

"Why don't we just tell them the truth? I mean, I know you don't want to get your brother involved, but if he tells me that he doesn't know where that guy is either, he might let us go, right? Please, can we just tell him the truth?" Stacy begged, her hands still shaking.

"Do you really think a guy who kidnapped us for simply refusing to speak to him is going to let us go, just because we don't have the answer he is searching for? These are gangsters, Stacy!" Amy replied, holding on to her best friend's hands. "You've seen the movies, right? Once they have seen our faces, then it means that they will get rid of us. They're only keeping us alive because we have information that they want. So we have to keep it from them and call for help!"

Amy only half believed the things she was saying. If one ignored the fact that Raven had abducted them, it really seemed like he was an overprotective brother who just wanted to learn the truth. He might even have been honest about letting them go, but right now she needed Stacy to believe that getting Gary involved was dangerous.

When they were finally in the toilet stalls, though, she asked Stacy to try to contact the police and see if they could help. At the same time, Amy decided to send a text to her brother.

However, there was no signal in the restaurant, or at least not in the bathroom stall. It was a little strange, but not impossible. In fact, it might have been a reason why he had picked this place.

The message should be sent once I'm back outside anyway, Amy thought.

The two girls came back, and since they could still see the strange men outside the door, they returned to sit down opposite Raven. He let out a sigh and started shaking his head.

"You know, technology truly is an amazing thing. There are many new inventions that come out every day. I've really tried being nice to you, you know? I told you to not try anything, didn't I?" Raven smiled as he received two text messages on his phone.

Amy wasn't quite sure how, but he must have realized that the two girls had tried something.

Microphones in the restroom? Cameras? Damn, I should have known they didn't just take us to a coffee shop. If that's true then they might have heard everything.

Panicking, Amy did the only thing she felt like they could do now that the situation had escalated.

"Help! We've been kidnapped by this guy! He and those guys outside took us from our school and threatened us! Please help us!" Amy shouted, dragging Stacy along as they rushed toward the worker behind the counter.

It was a last resort and the only thing they could do. She just had to hope that the strangers would help protect them from these gang members.

Why isn't anyone doing anything? Amy thought as she looked around the room. That was when she noticed that many of them were smiling or outright laughing.

"You really are kids. Why do you think I brought you here? This entire coffee shop belongs to the Gray Elephants. Everyone in here is one of our members . . . which naturally includes that worker behind you."

CHAPTER 91

THE PAWN
WEREWOLF

Blood continued to drip, creating a small pool where Billy stood. The wounds on his body were still healing, though slower than initially, especially the area around his neck that Gary had bitten.

The omega wolf was trapped between Gary and Blake, both standing still like statues. They understood that whoever took the first step now would become Billy's next target.

43/100 HP

150/300 Energy

Has it been that long already? No . . . I must have used up more Energy than I realized. Controlled Transformation, Emergency Healing, along with the Claw Drains . . . Yeah, I guess I need to include the natural Energy expenditure while fighting as well. Which means I can't waste any more time! Gary concluded that it would have to be now or never.

Knowing this, he made the first move. Seeing him break their standoff, confirming their assumptions, Billy headed toward Gary, running on all fours like a wild beast. Gary wasn't sure if he was imagining things, but even though his opponent was heavily injured, it appeared that he was still faster.

While Billy charged in recklessly like a bull, Gary leapt onto the side of the tunnel. He extended his claws so they would pierce into the wall, holding him in place, before he pounced on Billy.

His action was similar to what he had done to the twins.

Gary's strong tackle startled Billy, and quickly, not wasting time, he grabbed the back of Billy's head and slammed it into the wall. Blood gushed from Billy's mouth and the side of his head.

The werewolf's skull proved to be quite durable, far more than that of a human or a wolf, which would have been crushed under Gary's current Strength. He also noticed that his fingers felt like they were going through some type of leather armor; they went only so far through the skin until they stopped, and the werewolf's bones were so strong that even with his claws, it seemed impossible to break them.

Werewolves could claw at their enemies, creating big cuts. However, if he punched Billy with an open hand, the muscles in his fingers didn't seem strong enough to pierce the skull, so resorting to punching and grabbing was sometimes more effective than a swipe.

Now, holding Billy's head in place, Gary hoped to be able to pierce Billy's skull and end it once and for all. He threw his fist, with his fingers extending outward, not caring whether he broke them.

Desperate to get out of the situation, Billy tried to push off against the wall, but meanwhile Blake had rolled in between the two werewolves. They were large creatures, so there was plenty of space. He threw a couple of small daggers right into the back of Billy's hands.

They pierced right through, indicating that these small blades were sharper than the big blade that Blake had used earlier, though it still wasn't enough to kill Billy. Next, with his only intact blade left, Blake slashed at the backs of Billy's legs, trying to render him immobile.

Billy had displayed great speed and strength, yet in the Altered Hunter's mind that speed was far more dangerous and needed to be dealt with first. Because of his cooperation, Gary's fingers slammed into the back of Billy's skull. They had initially gone through the hide, piercing it, but then he felt his fingers start to bend . . . and then he got a notification he had been worried about.

You have been inflicted with a grave injury
–8 HP
35/100 HP
Fingers on your right hand are broken
Energy points will be used to perform emergency healing
–10 Energy

"I still have another hand!"

Taking his other hand off while leaving his broken hand to hold Billy's head, Gary made a fist and punched the back of Billy's head. The resulting sound was similar to a stone being dropped onto another stone.

Billy was dazed, and his vision was blurring, but Gary didn't stop there; he pulled back again and punched Billy in the back of the head again . . . and again. Meanwhile, Blake continued to slash at Billy's legs.

With each subsequent blow to Billy's head, his body was shrinking, getting smaller by the second, and the wounds were now becoming clearer. At the same time, Gary heard a message. Because of this, he canceled his Full Transformation, conserving his Energy.

Gary's body started to shrink as well, but he quickly made sure that his Controlled Transformation was active on his hands and legs, just in case there were any surprises.

He had let go of Billy, allowing his body to fall to the floor. Blood covered his whole head. It was hard to recognize him, and the blood pulsed across his eye as well; the other had a gaping hole from the sword.

It looked like Blake was also down on his knees, taking in deep breaths.

He must be exhausted . . . I shouldn't be surprised! He isn't an Altered, or a werewolf like us. He's just human, and he managed to do all of this? Gary's respect for the Altered Hunter grew at that moment.

Then, for a split second, he imagined Blake's father above his friend. Blake wasn't even a one-star Hunter, yet his father was a three-star one. He just couldn't imagine how strong his father might be.

Gary's foot was firmly planted on top of Billy's chest, giving him no chance to escape. Through his feet, he could feel Billy's heart beating. He was still alive, but Gary knew he was down for the count because of the system message he had received not too long ago.

You have defeated an omega wolf (Pawn)
2 Instant Level-Ups gained
Congratulations, you have now reached: Level 12
2 stat points have been granted
Because you have successfully defeated the omega wolf, you may now decide his fate
Please select one of the following options:
1. Kill the stray omega wolf
2. Invite the omega wolf to become a part of your pack

CHAPTER 92

DEFEAT

Gary read the message a few times because he wasn't sure if he had read it right. The system was giving him two options. One was to kill Billy, which was their original plan, but there was also an option to invite him into his pack.

Oh yeah, the system did give me an Optional Quest to accept him into my pack, but it never told me what it was for. Is a werewolf pack the same as a wolf pack, like Tom told me about? A collaboration where they go hunting together?"

For once, as Gary thought about this, the system decided to bless him with an answer.

The defeated werewolf was at the Pawn grade. As a Knight-grade werewolf, you're able to invite lower-ranked werewolves into your pack. By creating a pack, you will automatically become an alpha wolf and receive certain benefits from the system.

An alpha wolf? So it really is like Tom had explained . . . but what kind of extra benefits would that be exactly? Gary wondered. Unfortunately, the system had seemingly exhausted its helpfulness and remained quiet.

Nevertheless, it had left Gary with some valuable information. It had pretty much confirmed that those chess-themed grades were following a hierarchy, and that he was ranked above Billy.

Alas, that thought wasn't exactly calming. He might outrank Billy for now, but the other werewolf's overall strength had nevertheless surpassed his. If he was allowed to continue to grow, it would only be a question of time until Billy surpassed him. Gary felt validated in his choice to fight him now rather than later.

If I remember correctly, at any point in time, any member from the pack can challenge the leader for their position. If that's also true for werewolves, it's pretty much a given that he'll try to betray me at some point. No matter the benefits, I don't want to associate with someone like him. Gary had made up his mind, but just when he was about to select the first option, the system revealed more information.

Accepting the omega into your pack will classify him as a beta wolf. Beta wolves must do the alpha's bidding. A challenge for the alpha seat can only be initiated once a month. Becoming a beta wolf also prevents other alphas from inviting him into their packs, and it prevents omega wolves from forming a pack of their own by subduing him.

Do my bidding? Did the system read my thoughts and concerns and try to explain to me? Well, that's the first time it's ever done that. So as a beta wolf, he'll have to listen to me . . . at least as long as I can outgrow him and best him in a fight once a month.

Why does the Werewolf System seem so keen on me inviting Billy to join my pack? Is it all because of that Optional Quest . . . or is there something special about him? The whole thing sounded too risky, but there was a reason why Gary was contemplating it. He feared that at some point he would have to go against the Underdogs. Gary might not like him, but having Billy's strength on his side would be helpful in such a scenario.

"I didn't want to kill them . . ." Billy spoke up, his mouth dripping with blood, yet the large teenager understood that his life was in Gary's and Blake's hands. "The hunger . . . My mom and dad got into a fight . . . he hit her with an ashtray . . . I just wanted to protect her . . . and everything went wrong. I attacked him, yet she still defended the scumbag, I don't know why . . . before I realized it, I'd killed them both. I didn't do it on purpose. It was as if the hunger and bloodlust took over!"

Hearing Billy tell his sob story, Gary wasn't sure how much of it was true, yet it made him hesitate. It might very well have been the truth. His parents had always been the outliers on his personal vendetta list, and they had been the first reported killing.

Before Gary could make his decision, though, he saw that Blake had recovered and was walking over to the two of them. Gary was about to ask Blake what to do, but the Altered Hunter hadn't come over to join their discussion.

A stream of blood splattered onto his face. When Gary looked at Billy now, he saw that his humanlike head had been sliced off, and his blood was all over Blake's sword.

Without a second thought, Blake lifted Billy's head and checked his mouth. Billy's transformation hadn't completely reversed, as the dead werewolf still had two large fangs in his mouth.

"We came here to do a job, Gary: to kill the werewolf. You saw what he did to that woman. He couldn't control himself. He wasn't like you . . . at least that's what I like to think," Blake said.

The omega has perished
Options are no longer available
Consume werewolf flesh to gain 1 Pawn point

Gary couldn't help but look at Billy's head. He was the one who had turned the large teenager in his first underground fight. Part of him knew that he was responsible for Billy, for all his actions, as well as today's outcome. Nevertheless, Gary was relieved that the omega wolf was dead. It was as if a huge weight had been lifted off his shoulders, something he no longer would have to worry about.

Blake's action was justified; Billy was a murderer. Even if he hadn't been in his right mind when he had killed his parents, what about the next two murders? What about the time he had attacked

Innu in the middle of the day in his own school? What about when he had attacked Gary's friends in the park?

Most importantly, just minutes ago, he had killed an innocent woman just to survive. However, although Gary had yet to kill anyone innocent to survive, he felt like he was walking on a tightrope.

"We should leave this place. I'll take the head with me as proof to show my father that I completed the job. I've left our calling card for the police to find him. This way, they'll believe that the Altered Hunters are behind this, and hopefully you won't get involved any more than that.

"Our collaboration ends here, Gary, and I hope it's the only time you see me like this." With that, Blake placed the gadgets, the broken parts of his sword, and everything else he needed into his strange advanced backpack, and was off—leaving Gary behind to stare at the body.

Gary started to think about the message that had arrived not too long ago.

I consumed bodies before . . . and I need to keep getting stronger, he thought as he lifted part of the arm and took a bite out of it.

He had transformed his head to make it easier, and in case anyone happened to walk down the road again, but no one did, and after a few bites a new message had appeared.

One Pawn point has been granted
Pawn points can upgrade your body to the next grade.
Points can also be used to upgrade skills and for stats.
Warning: Once Pawn points have been assigned, it's impossible to revert the change!

Upgrade to the next grade? Does that mean I'll have to keep hunting werewolves if I want to become something like a King or Queen grade werewolf? But what's the point in that if I can just use it to upgrade my stats? Who cares what grade I am? Gary thought, scratching his head.

The system only elaborated that little bit, leaving Gary to fill in the blanks. With everything over, Gary quickly put on the spare clothes he had brought with him. He was happy that he had been prepared this time.

Grabbing his personal belongings, Gary eventually picked up his phone, ready to put it into his pocket. He glanced at the screen and nearly dropped it as he read Amy's message.

CHAPTER 93

PLEASE REPLY!

For a split second after reading the message, Gary looked at the scene behind him. He had only eaten parts of Billy, but it didn't look like he would gain any more special points or stats from his body.

At the same time, Billy's unique body had allowed him to restore his Energy until it was over 200 points, and he had a feeling with the message he'd read he might just need it.

Is it safe to leave the place just like this? Blake already left, and he said that with their calling card, the police would just assume this was the work of the Altered Hunters.

Gary was hesitating in case anything had been left behind that could be used to identify him. There wasn't much he could do about his blood, saliva, and other DNA evidence that was all over the scene, which had somehow become the norm.

It hadn't mattered before, so he didn't see a reason why it would matter now.

The problem was there might be other items to worry about; he had picked up what was left of his bag and the packages of food he had bought. The question was if there was anything else. Gary couldn't think straight because he was worried about what had happened to his sister. In the end, he decided to just grab his torn bag and his phone—the important things—and run for it.

He wanted to follow Amy's mark, but he appeared to be too far away from her current position to know exactly where she was. Fortunately, she had been smart enough to attach the location from where she had sent the message, which he assumed to be the coffee shop.

What happened? Why is Amy in trouble again? What does it have to do with Stacy? Who is she worried about? Is it the Underdogs? Did they finally find me? But then who is asking about their brother? Should I contact Kai? Too many thoughts were passing through Gary's head, but he continued to run toward the location.

On his way, he sent Amy a few texts, hoping that she could update him on her situation. Text after text, asking her to please answer if she could, yet there was no reply. In the end, Gary tried his luck by calling her phone.

It's ringing . . . if she was captured, wouldn't they have destroyed her phone, so she couldn't call for help?

However, after a few rings, just when it seemed as if she wouldn't pick up, she answered: "Oh no, I'm so sorry, Gary! I just saw all your messages. I'm so sorry, I should have told you earlier." Her voice was audibly panicked.

Stopping in his tracks, Gary wondered what was going on.

"Amy, are you safe? Where are you right now? Tell me, I'll come over straightaway!"

Gary eventually found himself in a very familiar place . . . in front of their own apartment building. He was glad to know that his sister was safe—or at least that was what she had claimed over the phone. Amy had asked him to first come home, so she could tell him everything about what had happened today, in person. Apparently, it would have been too much to explain just over a phone call.

If that had been her attempt to calm him down, it had only worried him more. Still, learning that she was supposedly back at their apartment, he took that as a good sign. Nevertheless, Gary couldn't help but feel like it might be a trap.

He sniffed the door a few times, in case there might be any for-eign scents. Unable to find any, he climbed up the side of the apart-ment building and looked through the windows to check inside, but there were no signs of anyone being home.

I checked the whole area, so it should be safe, right? But what if it's not? Should I call Kai? Do I get him involved in this?

Gary wasn't sure how to deal with this situation. He had his phone by his side, ready to make the call. He unlocked the door with his key and slowly pushed it open. Taking a few more sniffs, all he picked up was Amy's scent, as well as the smell of roses and coconut.

"Shampoo?" Gary realized in surprise.

"Amy!" he shouted as he entered the apartment, carefully look-ing around every corner. He hid one hand behind his back and used Controlled Transformation on it. It would allow him to deal with any intruder, while at the same time hiding it from his sister, in case she was actually alone.

"I'm in the kitchen!" she shouted back.

Gary's heart was beating fast, worried that perhaps his nose might be lying to him, but when he turned the corner, he saw his sister. She was sitting at the table with a towel wrapped around her head.

"Amy, you're really okay." Gary heaved out a heavy sigh of relief, canceling the transformation. Seeing that his sister was safe, he im-mediately started to inspect her for any markings or bruises. There was nothing on her at all . . . She looked fine.

"I'm so sorry for worrying you. I was in the shower when you called," Amy said, her head buried in her hands, unable to believe how stupid she had acted. "I'm really sorry . . . After everything, I really needed that shower. My mind was at a loss. I couldn't think properly; I should have explained first."

When Amy said these words, Gary could hear her heart beating louder. She was clearly scared and worked up about worrying him, and Gary wanted to know what on earth had happened to make her this flustered.

"What about you? You look a mess," Amy said, noticing that his clothes were in terrible shape; one of his sleeves had ripped after his earlier instance of Controlled Transformation. To top it off, he had a torn bag on his back.

"Don't worry about that." Gary shook his head, pulling up a seat opposite her. "I'm fine, so please tell me what exactly happened to you. I know you wouldn't jokingly send me such a message.

"Who asked you about their brother? Why did they force you to come along? What did you mean when you said you needed my help? I need you to tell me everything."

Amy looked to the side, and tears started falling down her face.

"I-I'm sorry, Gary, I-I tried not to g-get you involved. I r-really did! . . . But they kn-know about you now a-and . . . I-I'm worried that they might come after you next!"

CHAPTER 94

IS SHE REALLY SAFE?

Amy started over from the beginning, telling Gary how the strange man had come to their school the other day, looking for his brother, Hawk. Amy also revealed what Stacy had told her the day after, about how she had known that they were meeting up with a gang member, one claiming to be part of the Gray Elephants.

Amy was talking a lot, explaining every little detail, even adding her own opinion as to how Raven might have gotten this information. She felt incredibly guilty and wanted Gary to know that, every step of the way. She had never wanted to reveal anything to the gangsters about who he was, or the fact that he had been there that day.

When she was talking about the kidnapping, she noticed that Gary was gritting his teeth and clenching his fists. Of course, Amy had expected this kind of reaction; her brother had been very protective of her ever since the day their mother had been hospitalized. However, Gary stayed quiet and waited for Amy to finish her story.

Eventually, she reached the point where she had cried for help in the coffee shop, only for Raven to reveal that everyone inside was a member of the Gray Elephants gang.

"I didn't see a way out. I really, really didn't want to tell them anything, hoping to be able to stall for more time so that you might come to save us. I don't even know what you could've done, but I didn't want to break my promise to you . . . but Stacy spilled the beans.

"She told them that we weren't the last people with Hawk . . . that it was you, Gary. Stacy told them how you barged in, told her to get the two of us out, and that that was the last time we had seen that guy's brother."

Amy's hands were shaking more than ever, and Gary instinctively grabbed them, trying to comfort his sister.

"It's all right, Amy. There's nothing for you to worry about. I'm honestly just happy that you made it out safe. You should have just told me everything after he came to your school. I would have told you to just tell him the truth and let me deal with it." Gary gave Amy a weak smile.

"I knew you would say that, Gary, but you can't just take on everything yourself," Amy said, wiping her tears away. "I've seen you trying to replace Mom while she's in the hospital, so I didn't want to burden you any more than that. It's all Stacy's fault anyway.

"I . . . I haven't spoken to her since . . . I didn't text her, write to her, or anything . . . Not only that, but I'm not even sure I'll ever want to see her again. After she told them everything . . . Hawk's brother told her that she was free to go . . .

"And you know what happened next? . . . She left . . . She didn't even try to ask them to let me go with her . . . She didn't try to convince him to let me go too . . . She just gave me a brief look before she practically ran out of the shop . . ."

Gary didn't know what to say. He could tell that Amy felt betrayed by her best friend, but during his time with the Underdogs, he had seen this situation happen time and time again.

Fear was a strong tool, and everything that Raven had done so far had been to instill fear into the girls. Making them feel safe, and then realizing that even the place they thought was safe was not. He had broken Stacy down; Gary was honestly surprised she had stayed quiet for as long as she had.

Of course, Stacy's actions were abhorrent . . . but they were also the norm. Knowing this didn't stop Gary from inwardly cursing her for leaving his sister, especially since it was Stacy's fault in the first place that the Dem family had been dragged into the entire mess. Just when Gary was about to ask his sister how she had escaped, Amy continued:

"I thought I was done for at that point. That guy told me that they had some type of jammer in the coffee shop. I couldn't call anyone and my message wasn't sending . . . but then he just looked at me and laughed. He seemed to be greatly enjoying seeing me so hopeless and desperate . . .

"Nobody did anything to me, so I sat back down, afraid of what would happen next . . . I was prepared for him to ask me about you, about what happened that day again, but . . . for some reason he just sat down opposite me and continued to drink his coffee.

"Occasionally, he seemed to give his men some orders, but otherwise he only looked at me with a smirk on his face. I must have sat there for at least a few hours . . . I don't know how long exactly, but eventually he just stood up and left."

"I was shocked, afraid that this might be another sort of trap. I continued waiting there for a while, but nobody seemed to care about me . . . eventually, I gathered my courage and slowly headed toward the door . . . Seeing that nobody stopped me, I ran out as fast as I could.

"I was so stunned by everything that happened, I couldn't even process it all," Amy finished, putting her legs on the chair and wrapping her arms around herself. Gary immediately came up and gave her a hug. His sister didn't push him away; she just started to sob into his chest.

They stayed in that position for a while, until Amy stopped crying.

It looks like that guy I got rid of was really important to someone in the Gray Elephants gang. Not just anyone could use an entire place like that and use so many people . . . so now the two biggest gangs in Slough are after me, huh?

This might mean I need to act. I might have to act against the Gray Elephants as well. They know me, and they did all this to my fucking sister!

While Gary was lost in his thoughts, Amy patted her brother's arm, indicating that she was okay. He let go of her and went back to in his seat. Amy's eyes looked swollen and puffy. It reminded Gary of the day they found out what had happened to their mother.

Amy had been through a lot that day, and Gary never wanted her to have to experience something like that again, but because of him . . .

Why didn't I just threaten them . . . hurt them a little . . . no, there's no guarantee it would have ended with that. That Hawk guy threatened me with consequences, and based on the way his brother acts, he would have definitely come back for revenge.

"Gary." Amy called out to her brother in the midst of his thoughts. "Can you tell me what happened after Stacy and I left the room? I wanted to ask you the other day . . . but that guy did tell me a bit more. He said that not only his brother had gone missing, but everyone who had been there in that room, except for me and Stacy."

This was a question Gary had been dreading, but of course he had prepared an answer for it. He just hadn't had to use his excuse.

"What do you think I did?" Gary sighed as he looked at his sister, trying his best to look innocent. "Honestly, I was in a panic. I mean, I came in and saw what they did to you. So . . . I shouted at them like a madman, threatening to kill them if they ever touched my little sister again.

"I've heard that acting crazy is the best way to scare people away, since they can't predict what you might do next. It seems like some of that was true, or perhaps they were just too confused about my sudden appearance.

"I just wanted to buy you two enough time to get away, and when it seemed like they were about to attack me, I decided to run away. Believe it or not, I'm quite a fast runner now," Gary explained, pointing to his now strong body.

His sister made a strange face at his explanation. Gary's suddenly changed body was actually another mystery that Amy was unable to comprehend.

"Those guys must be gangsters like the one who kidnapped you, right? I bet they're involved in all sorts of stuff. I wouldn't be surprised if they were on the run from the police or something, but you don't have to worry about any of that, okay?"

With that, the conversation seemed to have come to an end, and Amy stood up. It looked like she was ready to go back to her room, but before she did, she turned around.

"Gary, you've changed a bit these days," Amy said, and she saw the worried look on her brother's face, so she quickly smiled. "I don't know if it's a good thing or bad thing yet, but whatever happens, you'll always be my big brother!"

Back in her room, Amy lay down on her bed. She was exhausted in more ways than one, not even caring that she had barely eaten anything this entire day. However, she was sure she would have a hard time getting to sleep tonight, especially since she couldn't stop thinking about one thing.

She sat up in her bed and looked toward the wardrobe—but it wasn't her own wardrobe she was looking at, it was Gary's.

Why are those in there? Amy wondered.

CHAPTER 95

CALLING CARD

It didn't take long for the police to be called to a particular devastating crime scene. Anton Millstun, Slough's chief of police, was called because a certain person was involved in the matter. Currently, both sides of the tunnel were sealed off with yellow police tape.

The area close by was blocked off just in case any evidence might have been left behind, and finally there were only a few police officers at the scene taking photos. A higher-tier town might have used more, but for the likes of Slough this could already be considered a large force.

The detective had been inspecting the body for a while, and evidence had already been collected. Standing up, Anton took off his white gloves, passing them to one of the other officers, and began to rub his eyes.

"You should be careful; what if some blood got on your hands?" the young officer Roo cautioned his superior. He held a clear evidence bag, revealing the card inside.

"We got a report back from the lab. You know who that is, don't you?" Anton asked the young rookie.

"Isn't it another victim of the Altered murderer? Although this is the first time that they appear to have sliced the head off like that," Roo answered as he quickly turned to look at the scene and away again. This body was in a worse state than the others, and it appeared that a large part of the arm had been eaten.

"Wow, you really are a rookie; do they let anyone pass these days? Or is it just that the force is desperate for more people?" Anton shook his head. "Even before the results came back, it's obvious that our Altered murderer has been here. The surprising part, however, is the male victim.

"We've been looking all over for him. This is Billy Bruntin, who we had initially suspected to be our Altered murderer. According to the guy in the lab, he's not an Altered, yet for some reason the Altered Hunters have left their calling card. Still, his blood does match up with the blood found at the other scenes, so he is our murderer all right. Have Hunters started becoming judges of death now as well?"

Lifting the bag, Roo spun it around, trying to get a better look at the card. He thought it was strange for a card to be left at the scene, and he had initially mistaken it for a business card.

"Why would they use a red dragon on their calling card? I thought they hated all types of Altered . . . although I've never heard about a dragon type of Altered," Roo said in confusion.

"That's actually classified information that is prohibited to be revealed to the public, since the government doesn't want copycats appearing. You can also tell fakes from clears, using a special method, but you will learn that as you go on. By the looks of it, they got here way before we did." Anton let out a big sigh.

"But then what about the arm? It looks like it's been eaten by a beast!" Roo complained.

This was the strangest thing, because they had found DNA that they had on file. In fact, it had appeared in multiple areas, but they had yet to find out more about this mystery Altered.

Could it be two Altered fought each other? . . . I've heard of Altered getting in fights with each other over the territory they claim, but to actually hunt each other? Or maybe Billy was working with an Altered when he was doing his killings and one got away?

Another option: do we have an Altered Hunter who is an Altered himself? . . . That or a hunter was working together with our mysterious Altered. Anton chuckled at this ridiculous thought. *Like that would ever happen. The day I see that, pigs might fly.*

Inside the empty underground dojo, a young teenage boy was sitting cross-legged, his back straight. Blake was currently in the secret base that his father had created, one that only Altered Hunters knew how to locate and open.

On the table, inside a glasslike container, was the severed head of Billy Bruntin. His sharp teeth were still showing—more so on one side than the other—and there were also some other nonhuman details on the head, such as colored fur and slightly pointed ears.

It's a good thing that I cut the head off when I did. It seems like it was in the middle of reverting, Blake thought. *We only assumed Billy was the Altered who had been killing those people, but we never confirmed it . . . Well, technically he's not an Altered but a werewolf. I wonder if Dad will recognize the difference.*

Thinking about his father, Blake wondered a few more things. When his father came back, would he be proud that his son had managed to hunt an Altered on his own? Would it count toward his first star? Or would he be upset with Blake that he had risked his life during his absence?

Looking to his right, the young Altered Hunter also saw the broken sword and all the gadgets he had used up. Some of them Blake could reset or repair so they could be used again, but the same couldn't be said for the sword.

Altered Hunters crafted most of their tools themselves. This was true for the small gadgets, but the swords and armor weren't things one could easily create.

Each hunter has access to certain items from the Hunters' Association based on their rank. Once I get my first star, I will be eligible to get better equipment for myself. A better sword would be nice.

I wonder what kind of items those five-star top hunters have access to . . .

For a second, Blake caught himself daydreaming about his future as one of them. It came as a bit of a shock that he had actually enjoyed what he had done today. The thrill of fighting, risking his life, besting a superior enemy.

In the past, he had hated that his father had forced him into the Altered Hunters' lifestyle. Ozacas Hunt often claimed that it was in their blood . . . and for the first time, Blake understood what his father had meant.

So far, he had tried to avoid it; Blake had typically made excuses when his father offered to take him out hunting, but killing Billy had felt . . . satisfying. He felt as if he had actually achieved something.

When you come back, Dad, maybe . . . maybe I'll start to take this hunting thing seriously, Blake thought as he stood up, and for a second Gary flashed in his mind. The two of them working together to take down Billy.

If only you hadn't become a werewolf . . . You would have surely made a great Altered Hunter . . .

CHAPTER 96

TO THE GRAVE
WITH ME

Surprisingly, Gary had enjoyed the best night's sleep he'd had in a long time. One might think that the knowledge that both of Slough's major gangs were after him would make him sleepless . . .

However, compared to Billy, a large werewolf that had been going around killing people, the Gray Elephants gang seemed like less of a big deal. In a way, it was almost as if he had traded one problem for another. The only unfortunate thing about this entire situation was that it had involved Amy.

I wonder why they let her go, though? Gary thought as he stretched his body. His sister was still sleeping peacefully. She must have only recently fallen asleep, because Gary had been watching her constantly, and she had still been wide awake before he had shut his eyes.

He knew how she felt; when one's mind was full of worry it was almost impossible to sleep, but eventually the tiredness would overwhelm you. He had told Amy it was best if she took the day off school today, and she had agreed.

She would have still gone, but honestly, the main reason why she had agreed was that she didn't have the energy to deal with Stacy.

However, she couldn't take too many days off. Her attendance was already dropping and if it did any more, parents would be called in, which might open up another can of worms.

Name: Gary Dem
Class: Warrior
State: Human (Omega)
Grade: Knight
Level 12
Exp: 340/1890
Health: 100/100
Energy: 300/300
Strength 15
Dexterity 15
Endurance 15
3 stat points unassigned
1 Pawn point available

Looking at his status, Gary was contemplating how he should distribute his accumulated stat points. In the past, he would have increased his Energy, but that didn't seem to be a problem any more. Despite using a lot of his skills, he still had plenty of them left, not to mention he had found out that he could replenish them naturally during a fight as well.

No, the area he was lacking in were his three natural stats. Choosing the Warrior Class had increased all of his stats until they became balanced. Nevertheless, he had been unable to beat Billy with that alone. There was no way to tell if the deceased omega wolf had had higher base stats, or if he had gained more from eating meat.

Should I keep them balanced . . . or should I specialize in one direction? . . . I guess I can leave the stat points for now. It's easy enough to apply them during a fight anyway, but this Pawn point is another story.

According to the system, I can use it to upgrade my body's grade, upgrade my skills, and for stats. The first option seems useless, unless I plan to create my own pack. I don't even know if there really are other werewolves out there, and after Billy, I don't actually want to convert anyone.

This whole alpha wolf thing isn't too different from being a gang leader, so are there any other benefits? Gary thought. He was half expecting the system to answer his queries, but he was disappointed.

Claw Drain seems to be the only skill that's upgradable right now. However, I can just use Controlled Transformation to get the claws, so its only benefit is its life-stealing effect. It would also be bad if it turns out that I can increase it naturally through usage.

Gary was seriously worried about wasting his Pawn point, and unlike stat points, which he could gain by leveling up, it wasn't like he came across a werewolf every day. So he decided to let it be for now.

It was time for Gary to head to school, and to his surprise Amy stood by the bedroom door, sleepily rubbing her eyes.

"Hey, what are you doing up so early? Didn't we agree that you would stay home today? You must have gotten, what, like two hours of sleep." Gary spoke to his sister in a loving tone.

"I know . . . I just smelled the food, and it woke me up. I think my body is just used to waking up at this time and eating," Amy explained, getting hungry as her stomach demanded its fill. "I'll just eat some food and go back to sleep."

"All right." Gary held his hand up to his mouth to avoid snickering. "Remember, if anything happens, if you see anyone out—"

"I'll call you immediately. Trust me, I have you on speed dial, and I only need one click to send you a prepared message." Amy cut him off and shooed her brother out with a big smile . . . which disappeared the second he was out the door.

She walked into their room and headed toward Gary's wardrobe. She stood there for a few seconds.

Surely, it must have just been a dream . . . she tried to convince herself. *Please tell me it was a dream.*

Pulling the wardrobe open, Amy saw a lot of Gary's clothes, but stuffed in the corner, under a large pile that seemed to not have been washed in ages, was something else. She knew this because she had seen it yesterday.

Once again, she reached under the pile, pulling out a shopping bag, and in the bag itself were clothes. Not just any clothes, either.

She pulled out a red tracksuit set that was covered in blood and ripped in certain places. The blood was mainly on the back, but there was more. Amy gripped onto the clothes tightly. She quickly stuffed them back in the bag and placed it back underneath all the other clothes.

After fleeing from the coffee shop, Amy had been worried about Gary. She had no idea what Raven might do to him. Rather than thinking about herself, she had opened Gary's wardrobe and started to pack his clothes, so that he might run away and hide.

In the midst of doing all that, she had spotted the shopping bag. She was completely startled, and she didn't know if any blood had gotten on her clothes. It was dry, but she wasn't thinking straight, and it felt . . . dirty. As if she had never wanted to see it in the first place, Amy had placed all the clothes back the way they had been and had decided to take a shower, hoping to clear her head.

It hadn't been long, but it had served as the much-needed escape for the girl to come to terms with what had happened to her, and what was likely going to happen next.

It wasn't a dream . . . *that means Gary really must have been the one to make them disappear* . . . *He killed those guys* . . . *all of that for me? You did it to protect me, right?* . . . *Even now* . . . *you must be still hiding the truth from me to protect me.*

Everything you have done is for me and Mom, and yet I can't do anything for you. Amy slumped down, holding her knees as tears ran down her face, cursing herself for being weak and useless.

The only thing I can do for you . . . You obviously don't want me to know about this . . . So I'll pretend I never saw this. I will never say a word about this to anyone, and I will take this secret to the grave with me, because you are my brother, Amy solemnly swore to herself, as she wiped the tears from her eyes.

ABOUT THE AUTHOR

JKSManga is the pen name of UK-based, New York Times–bestselling LitRPG author Kawin Jack Sherwin, whose series include My Vampire System, My Dragon System, and My Werewolf System. His works have sold fifteen million copies worldwide, and several have been adapted into comic books.

Visit JKSManga online for updates and exclusive content:
Instagram.com/JKSManga
Facebook.com/JKSManga
Patreon.com/JKSManga

DISCOVER
STORIES UNBOUND

PodiumAudio.com

A REAL LEADER

BOOK 2 · A REAL LEADER

JKSMANGA

Podium

To my wife, Wandong Chen.

After we met, my writing journey began. None of this would have been possible without you buying me a new laptop when we had just met.

Cover design by Husa

ISBN: 978-1-0394-2130-1

Published in 2023 by Podium Publishing, ULC
www.podiumaudio.com

Podium

A REAL LEADER